‖‖‖‖‖‖‖‖‖‖‖‖‖‖‖‖‖‖‖‖‖‖‖‖‖‖‖‖‖‖

TWO MEN

T0326985

Legacies of Nineteenth-Century
American Women Writers

SERIES EDITORS

Sharon Harris
*University of
Connecticut*

Karen Dandurand
*Indiana University of
Pennsylvania*

TWO

MEN

Elizabeth Stoddard

EDITED AND WITH AN
INTRODUCTION BY
Jennifer Putzi

University of Nebraska Press
Lincoln & London

Part of the introduction originally appeared
in "The 'American Sphinx' and the
Riddle of National Identity
in Elizabeth Stoddard's *Two Men*"
in *American Culture, Canons,
and the Case of Elizabeth Stoddard*
(Tuscaloosa: U of Alabama P, 2003).

© 2008 by the Board of
Regents of the University of Nebraska.
All rights reserved.
Manufactured in the United States
of America ⊗

Library of Congress
Cataloging-in-Publication Data
Stoddard, Elizabeth, 1823–1902.
Two men / Elizabeth Stoddard; edited and
with an introduction by Jennifer Putzi.
p. cm. — (Legacies of nineteenth-century
American women writers)
Includes bibliographical references.
ISBN-13: 978-0-8032-9347-2
(pbk.: alk. paper)
1. Domestic fiction. I. Putzi, Jennifer.
II. Title.
PS2934.S3T86 2008
813'.4—dc22
2007048254

Set in Fournier.
Designed by A. Shahan

For Simon and Sam

CONTENTS

||||||||||||||||||||||||||||||||||||||||||||||||

ACKNOWLEDGMENTS

Many people read drafts of my introduction to *Two Men*, and I am grateful to them for their feedback and support: Sherry Harris, Karen Dandurand, Simon Joyce, Liz Barnes, Melanie Dawson, and Elizabeth Stockton. Elizabeth's passion for Stoddard and her work is absolutely infectious; without a doubt, our stimulating conversations about *Two Men* contributed to my thinking about the novel. Two former William and Mary students, Heather Debby and Mary Teeter, also gave their time and energy to this project, and I thank them for their assistance. Thanks also to Rob Nelson for his technical expertise and his infinite patience.

In addition, I am grateful to all of the libraries and librarians who helped me gather Stoddard's letters together: Rare Books Department, Boston Public Library; Rare Book and Manuscript Library at Columbia University; Colby College Special Collections; Division of Rare and Manuscript Collections, Cornell University; Houghton Library, Harvard University; Manuscript Division, Library of Congress; Special Collections, Middlebury College Library; Manuscripts and Archive Division, The New York Public Library; Rare Books and Manuscripts, Pennsylvania State University Libraries.

Finally, my love and thanks to Simon Joyce and Sam Putzi, the "two men" in my life. This book is dedicated to you both.

INTRODUCTION

‖‖‖

As she began work on her first novel in May 1860, Elizabeth
Stoddard presented James Russell Lowell, editor of the *Atlantic
Monthly*, with a starkly honest assessment of herself as an artist.
After having been warned by Lowell that she had a dangerous
tendency to go too "near the edge" in her writing, she asked him,
"Do I disturb your artistic sense by my want of refinement?"
and insisted, "I must own that I am coarse by nature. At times
I have an overwhelming perception of the back side of truth."
She claimed she was incapable of "do[ing] that [which] will not
show up in my constitution." Despite her protests, Stoddard was
indeed eager to be published, and she sought Lowell's advice and
that of other editors on how to balance her originality with the
demands of the literary marketplace. She was unsure, however,
as to the merits of actually acting on such advice: "Tell me," she
asked Lowell, "whether in writing, one should aim at entering
a circle already established — or making one?"[1] The idea that
she *could* do one or the other, join a circle or make her own,
depending on what Lowell thought one *should* do, is distinctly
Stoddard — arrogant, perhaps, but also refreshingly self-assured
at a time when American women writers were rarely and reluctantly recognized as serious literary artists.[2] Ultimately, Stoddard
did both: she took what she needed from established literary
circles while making her own unique contribution to nineteenth-
century American literature, a contribution that has only begun
to attract the attention it deserves.

Stoddard's artistic "constitution" was certainly distinct from that of any other writer of the nineteenth century, male or female, and, as several scholars have noted, it is impossible (and indeed unproductive) to reduce her body of work to any single literary movement or style. She was neither a strictly romantic nor a strictly realistic writer, a sentimentalist nor a regionalist; rather, she took advantage of shifting American literary tastes to craft a different kind of narrative fiction. She was committed, as she tells Lowell, to the unflinching truth, no matter how uncomfortable it made her or her reader. She objected especially to the idealized representation of women in the fiction of her contemporaries and insisted that her "mission" was "a crusade against Duty—not the duty that is revealed to every man and woman of us by the circumstances of daily life, but that which is cut and fashioned for us by minds totally ignorant of our idiosyncrasies and necessities" ("Lady Correspondent," Aug. 3, 1856). Stoddard was also an innovative stylist, particularly in her use of dialogue. Influenced by the theater, she often relied upon dialogue to do the work of her fiction, consequently frustrating readers who wanted more authorial direction. "It is Mrs. Stoddard's practice," a disapproving young Henry James wrote in an unpublished review of her second novel, *Two Men*, "to shift all her responsibilities as story-teller upon the reader's shoulders, and to give herself up at the critical moment to the delight of manufacturing incoherent dialogue or of uttering grim impertinences about her characters. This is doubtless very good fun for Mrs. Stoddard; but it is poor fun for us." He concluded the review by insisting that "Mrs. Stoddard's notion is to get all the work done by the reader while she amuses herself in talking what we feel bound to call nonsense" (qtd. in Kraft 272, 273). Quite simply, Stoddard had a reputation for being difficult.

Stoddard's seemingly deliberate perversity discomfited friends and critics alike. While one family friend labeled her "the Pythoness," another suggested (in a letter to Stoddard herself, no less) that she was an "incorrigible bundle of contradictions and constancies, of whims, philosophies, absurdities, truth, and grandness."[3] A female friend more generously insisted on Stoddard's social brilliance, but still described her as an overwhelming personality. Looking back at her acquaintance with Stoddard, Lillian Aldrich called her a "singular woman, who possessed so strongly the ability to sway all men who came within her influence. Brilliant and fascinating, she needed neither beauty nor youth, her power was so much beyond such aids. On every variety of subject she talked with originality and ready wit; with impassioned speech expressing an individuality and insight most unusual and rare" (*Crowding Memories* 14). Throughout her marriage, Stoddard's passion and "individuality" were at the heart of constant disagreements between the Stoddards and their friends, who, one after another, dropped out of her life after a brief period of intimacy. For better or worse, she understood her own character and the problems it caused, telling a new friend, "There is not one particle of 'nonsense' about me. I cannot stand blarney, roundaboutedness. As I have not many good qualities of disposition I feel sure of this, which as many a member of my family have told me, makes me often hateful. My father said once he never saw any human being with such a talent for the disagreeable."[4]

Combined with Stoddard's stylistic innovations, critics feared this "talent" rendered Stoddard's fiction unreadable, even immoral, in a literary marketplace that frequently valued the didactic, the virtuous, the inoffensive. A reviewer for *Godey's Ladies' Book*, for example, admired many technical aspects of Stoddard's first novel, *The Morgesons*, but balanced these compliments with a caveat: "It is not such a book as we would place in the hands of the young, whose taste for reading is forming. . . . There is a morbid tone about it, which is apt to have an unhealthy effect upon the mind, to say nothing of the morals of the reader" (301). Another reviewer acknowledged that "critics are undoubtedly right in crediting Mrs. Stoddard with powerful and unique talent," but added that "the public is also right in tacitly pronouncing her books unacceptable for its entertainment" (*Literary World* 324).[5] All three of Stoddard's novels— *The Morgesons* (1860), *Two Men* (1865), and *Temple House* (1867)— elicited a similar combination of reluctantly good reviews from critics coupled with limited popular acclaim or sales. Most critics agree that the disappointing response to her three novels caused her to forgo novel-writing for periodical publication, which was both more lucrative and less painful. Despite a reissuing of her novels later in the century, she never achieved the kind of literary success of which she dreamed.

For more than eighty years after her death in 1902, Stoddard remained a footnote in American literary history—that is, when she was remembered at all. Many critics of American literature knew her only because her fiction was quite famously held up as a point of comparison when Thomas Wentworth Higginson first visited the Dickinson family in Amherst: "I shan't sit up to write you all about E. D. dearest," he wrote to his wife, "but if you had read Mrs. Stoddard's novels you could understand a house where each member runs his or her own selves."[6] It wasn't until 1984 that Stoddard's work was reprinted and given serious scholarly consideration. Lawrence Buell and Sandra A. Zagarell's edition of *The Morgesons* (which also included two short stories, early journalism, a handful of letters, and Stoddard's only journal) introduced students and scholars to the author's work and made a thoroughly convincing argument for her recovery.[7] They placed special emphasis on her three novels, claiming that "Stoddard was, next to Melville and Hawthorne, the most strikingly original voice in the mid-nineteenth-century American novel" (xi). Attention to Stoddard's work has since grown over the past twenty years, with professors teaching *The Morgesons* (as well as Stoddard's only anthologized short story, "Lemorne *Versus* Huell" [1863]), publishing articles about the novel and her short fiction, and increasingly exploring more of her oeuvre. In 2003 Stoddard's work became even more accessible with the publication of *Stories*, collected and edited by Susanne Opfermann and Yvonne Roth. An edition of critical essays on Stoddard's work—the first of its kind—was also published in 2003, edited by Robert McClure Smith and Ellen Weinauer. Notably, the collection includes essays on a broad range of Stoddard's work, including her biweekly column for the *Daily Alta California* (published from 1854 to 1858), her poetry, her short fiction, and all three of her novels. While very few of these primary texts have actually been reprinted, the essays demonstrate the need to extend our understanding of Stoddard's work beyond *The Morgesons*.

The project of recovering Elizabeth Stoddard continues in this edition of her second novel, *Two Men*. As in much of her fiction, in *Two Men* Stoddard transgresses the boundaries of what was considered acceptable (especially for women writers) in nineteenth-century American fiction: her second novel features unhappy marriages, complex female characters, semi-incestuous relationships, and miscegenation. For its daring and unconventional plot alone *Two Men* deserves recognition. The novel is also an exemplary specimen of Stoddard's experimentation with narrative structure and style, as well as her blending of romanticism and realism. Finally, it is the most political of Stoddard's three novels, a reflection of the time in which it was written: a Civil War novel that ignores the war itself, *Two Men* is an exploration of the politics of race and citizenship that concerned the North throughout the war, but especially at its close.

The Life of Elizabeth Stoddard

Elizabeth Drew Barstow Stoddard was born in 1823 to a prominent family in Mattapoisett, Massachusetts. She was one of nine children, only five of whom lived to maturity. Her father, Wilson Barstow, owned a shipbuilding yard with her grandfather Gideon Barstow and is best known for having constructed the *Acushnet*, the ship that carried Herman Melville to the Marquesas on the voyage that would inspire his first and most commercially successful book, *Typee: A Peep at Polynesian Life* (1846). The *Acushnet* would go on to greater fame as the ship that served as the model for the *Pequod* in *Moby-Dick* (1851). Despite the superior quality of his vessels, Wilson Barstow's business failed a number of times throughout Stoddard's lifetime. This would often place the family in a precarious position within the Mattapoisett community, rendering her forever sensitive to social slights. Perhaps because of their financial instability and perhaps because she was a girl, Elizabeth's education was sporadic. The most important educational experience for the budding author was surely her access to the extensive library of Mattapoisett's minister, Thomas Robbins. Her husband would later claim that Robbins's library represented "the only education she ever had" (*Recollections* 110). Like many other New England shipping yards, the Barstow's business was ultimately closed due to the Panic of 1857, the Civil War, and the decline of whaling internationally. While Stoddard's mother, Betsy S. Drew Barstow, died in 1849, her father lived until 1891, when he was more than ninety years old. Two of Elizabeth's siblings were especially important to her: her sister, Jane, who died of consumption in 1848, and her brother Wilson Barstow Jr., who remained a constant friend and companion until his death in 1869.[8]

It was Elizabeth's relationship with Wilson that first took her to New York City to live in 1849. While she had visited before, this more permanent relocation established a lifelong pattern of movement between the city and Mattapoisett—the former a source of stimulation and excitement for Stoddard, and the latter one of inspiration and comfort. Most of her fiction would be set in small New England communities like Mattapoisett, but New York was also essential to her development as an artist. Here she attended the literary salon of Anne Lynch (Botta), where she became acquainted with prominent literary figures; one of these new acquaintances was Richard Henry Stoddard, a poet whom she married in December 1852. Although she occasionally complained of his inability to understand her work, Richard did, for the most part, support Elizabeth's writing career financially and emotionally. His career was at times more successful than hers, but he was never able to provide for his family entirely by writing, no matter how many unpleasant editorial positions he accepted. To help supplement his income he also worked for the U.S. Custom House in New York City—a position he held for seventeen years and which he originally obtained with the assistance of Nathaniel Hawthorne—and for the Department of Docks, also in New York City. The marriage between Elizabeth and Richard was marked by the painful loss of their three sons (their youngest, Lorimer, was the only one to survive childhood, and even he died before his parents, in his late thirties), poverty, and disagreements with friends—usually thought to have been caused by the ill-tempered Elizabeth. Throughout, however, the two loved and supported one another in their constant battles with friends, critics, and, in Richard's words, "that ASS the public."[9]

In 1853 Stoddard began her literary career with the publication of sketches and poems, and the following year with a regular column for the *Daily Alta California*. While it isn't known exactly why she wrote for this particular newspaper, scholars speculate that she may have wished to use the venue to keep in touch with Wilson, who had moved to California in February 1853.[10] Whatever the reason, Stoddard published biweekly columns in the *Alta* between 1854 and 1858, writing about everything from literature and the theater to politics and women's rights and roles in American society. The *Alta* columns allowed Stoddard to develop a distinctive personal voice, one that is evident in all of her writing, both private and public.

Her first novel, *The Morgesons*, was published in 1862. This female bildungsroman, based loosely on Stoddard's own early life, features a young woman named Cassandra Morgeson whose passionate nature and fierce sense of independence were a rarity in nineteenth-century American fiction. While this unconventional portrait probably had much to do with the novel's lack of success, Stoddard would also later claim that the timing of the novel's publication was poor: "*The Morgesons* was published ten days before Bull Run," she wrote. "It was selling but from that day stopped. *The Morgesons* was my Bull Run, but it had a success of esteem. A very great deal was said about it."[11] The novel's commercial failure did not stop Stoddard from commencing work upon *Two Men*, but it quite possibly delayed its publication; insecure and self-conscious, she wrote slowly and without confidence. In July 1863 she confessed to her close friend, Edmund Clarence Stedman, "I *am* writing a novel. . . . It is an awful task and I write it by the square inch — I do not seem to gain any facility in composition with practice."[12] A year later, she was still struggling with the book, thinking consciously about its marketability; in July 1864, she wrote to Stedman again, lamenting the fact that she could not join he and his wife on a tour through the White Mountains: "For refreshment and solace I am going to attack the 'style' of my Ms novel, and clock and drug it for the market."[13] To Stoddard's great disappointment, however, responses to her subsequent novels were almost exactly the same as those to her first: critical acclaim, but limited popular sales. Stoddard's only long work of fiction published after 1867 was a children's book, *Lolly Dinks' Doings* (1874).

Stoddard continued to be a prolific writer, however, and to focus on the novels that she *could* have written, had she received more positive recognition for her work, is to ignore the importance of periodical publication in her career. Like many writers of the period, Stoddard relied on periodical publication both artistically and financially; ultimately, she placed more than one hundred stories, sketches, and poems in publications like the *Atlantic Monthly*, *Harper's Weekly*, *Putnam's*, *Appleton's Journal*, and *Lippincott's*. The quality of this work varies considerably, but the best of it exemplifies her strengths as a creative writer — vivid, unconventional characters and intense, often elliptical, dialogue — and exhibits a tightness and control of plot and structure that was sometimes missing in her longer fiction.[14]

In the early 1880s, the combined efforts of literary friends and admirers — Stedman, Julian Hawthorne, and Junius Browne, most notably — convinced Stoddard that new editions of her novels would prompt a much-needed critical reassessment of her work. With Stedman's promise to write a preface for *Two Men*, the novel he thought most worth reprinting, Stoddard made minor revisions and signed a contract with Cassell and Company, a British publishing firm, who released the novels in 1888 and 1889. The novels did indeed effect a reconsideration of Stoddard's oeuvre, with at least one critic telling her, "I have lately read *Two Men*, the power of which has made a very great impression on my mind. Why, what has the world been about, all these years—where have I been?—not to know more about this book and you?"[15] Stoddard herself was both relieved and grateful for the reappearance of the novels and the attention from literary friends, but she continued to be dissatisfied with the response to her work. In an 1888 letter to a friend, for example, she lamented, "I would laugh bitterly when I think how I have been ignored, how often in the presence of those who have been lionized whom I *knew* were *not* my superiors I have been passed over and unnoticed. I have almost been crushed" (Oct. 5, [1888]).[16] The republication of her novels, then, was a bittersweet triumph.

The success of the 1888–1889 editions of her three novels probably contributed to the publication of Stoddard's collected *Poems* in 1895 by Houghton Mifflin, and a reissuing of the novels by Henry T. Coates and Company of Philadelphia in 1901.[17] This was not enough, however, to maintain Stoddard's health or spirits. On August 1, 1902, almost a year after the death of her only surviving son, Elizabeth Stoddard died at the age of seventy-nine. Her husband followed her less than a year later.

Links in the Chain: Stoddard's Literary Contexts

Critical responses to Stoddard's novels often highlighted what they saw as the author's originality; whatever her shortcomings, they claimed, she was unique among her contemporaries. In his review of *Two Men*, for example, William Dean Howells approvingly noted that "the author's faults . . ., like her merits, are almost wholly her own" (537). Much later, in his book *Literary Friends and Acquaintances* (1900), published just before Stoddard's death, he asserted more strongly that "whatever [Stoddard] did, she left the stamp of a talent like no other, and of a personality disdainful of literary environment. In a time when most of us had to write like Tennyson, or Longfellow, or Browning, she never would write like anyone but herself" (87). In a review of *Temple House*, George Ripley emphasized the novelist's originality in similar terms: "She may sometimes suggest the style of a great author, but she takes no one for a model, and has abundant power to give form to her fancies. . . . She accepts no authority, treads in the footsteps of no other, follows only her own nature, and is always herself" (6).

Stoddard undoubtedly took such comments as the compliments that they were intended to be; she strongly believed in the notion of romantic genius, and lamented frequently the inability of others to recognize it in her and her work. Yet while efforts to distinguish Stoddard from other writers were often intended as complimentary, they also served her poorly in the long term. The paucity of scholarship on Stoddard's work can, at least in part, be attributed to the critical inability (or reluctance) to position her in American (or transatlantic) literary history. (It is worth noting, however, that many an "original" male writer—Herman Melville comes to mind—has not suffered a similar fate.) We may actually owe much of Stoddard's current obscurity to well-meaning critics like Howells, Ripley, and Mary Moss, all of whom seem to have had great respect for Stoddard and her work. Published just after Stoddard's death, Moss's "The Novels of Elizabeth

Stoddard" illustrates this dilemma most clearly. The culmination of decades of reviews emphasizing Stoddard's originality, Moss's piece begins with her insistence that "to their few ardent admirers the writings of Mrs. Stoddard are an unexplained eddy in the current of literature, a dark and turbid backwater leading nowhere, connecting no two points, neither illustrating a tendency nor exercising an influence" (260). Similarly, she later claims Stoddard's "books form no link in the chain of literature, since she exerted no influence; nor are they to be studied to see how she got her effects, for these effects are quite spontaneous, almost accidental" (263). Thus Moss effectively privileges the notion of romantic genius over Stoddard's skill and professionalism as a writer, and, just as damaging, denies her a place in literary history. Moss's refusal to consider Stoddard's ties to the literary movements of her day—romanticism, sentimentalism, realism, regionalism—sets in motion a self-fulfilling prophecy: having been influenced by no one, and influenced no one herself, Stoddard becomes an "eddy," an enigma who is easily lost or dismissed.

The disappearance of Stoddard has also been facilitated by critical paradigms of the late twentieth and early twenty-first centuries that mark the Civil War as the point at which romanticism gave way to realism, thus creating a sharp distinction between antebellum and postbellum writing. When examined through the careers of individual writers like Stoddard, however, this distinction is complicated. Like the fiction of Rebecca Harding Davis and the poetry of Walt Whitman and Sarah Morgan Bryan Piatt, Stoddard's work—the bulk of which was published during the Civil War and the years immediately following—provides scholars and students of American literature with an object lesson in how authors of this period adjusted to changing literary tastes, using a toolbox of literary techniques rather than adhering to a strictly romantic or strictly realistic approach to their work. The practice of drawing hard distinctions between these two movements—of positing the Civil War as the site of an easy and immediate philosophical and stylistic shift from romanticism to realism—has obscured the reputations of writers like Stoddard for far too long, while the silencing of Stoddard for other reasons (her gender, her temperament, her subject matter and writing style) has simultaneously prevented critics from exploring this period in American literature in sufficient depth.[18] The increasing availability and popularity of Stoddard's work should change these circumstances and prompt further research, both on her and the period in which she was writing. *Two Men* holds an important place in this reconsideration. Many of the ideas Stoddard explores here are romantic, yet they are positioned within a very real social context, one shaped by the politics of the war going on around Stoddard as she wrote. The novel as a whole is indicative of a nascent realism that has been obscured by the focus on male realists of the late nineteenth century. Stoddard was, by no means, the only writer of the period to incorporate realist techniques and sensibilities into her artistic practice, but she is central to the reconfiguration of this movement from romanticism to realism.

Although Stoddard sometimes resisted being called a realist, she showed affinities with both romanticism and realism, finding both useful for her creative purposes. Late in life, after being told that she had "started the realist school," she insisted that she was "*not* realistic." "I am *romantic*," she claimed "the very bareness and simplicity of my work is a trap for its romance."[19] Yet even this stark denial betrays an awareness of her use of realistic techniques to create bare and simplistic settings and characters, no matter how romantic her overall vision as a writer. Her commitment to "the back side of truth" prompted her to describe life as she saw it, despite the reservations of critics like Lowell. In a letter thanking Howells for his positive review of *Two Men*, for example, she delighted in his recognition and approbation of her creative technique: "I write things as *I* see and feel things and the things are like surgical specimens preserved in bottles! Isn't that good?"[20] In fact Stoddard often described her work in visual terms, foreshadowing the realist emphasis on perspective. Writing to Stedman after the publication of *The Morgesons*, she insisted, "I endeavored to make a plain transcript of human life—a portion as it were of the great panorama without taking on a moral here or an explanation there."[21] Stoddard's "surgical specimens" and her "portion of the great panorama" appear to be early manifestations of Howells's grasshopper and James's "house of fiction" with a million windows; all highlight the visual aspect of realist practices, as well as the limitations on such vision. Yet Stoddard was not completely comfortable with the notion of art as the mimetic reflection of reality. Her words on photography, from an 1857 *Daily Alta California* column, are revealing: "Photographs are the ugliest invention of the day. . . . There are no fine shades. . . . This is what I complain of—the truth of the pictures. Beauty is ideal; we want an artist to render its expression, not to give us an ugly fact" ("Lady Correspondent," May 3, 1857). This comment seems curious coming from a woman who would three years later proclaim herself to be "coarse by nature" and would soon after claim to look at life as a "surgical specimen." Yet, to some degree, Stoddard's entire career was a negotiation between the romantic sensibility she so admired in writers like Charlotte and Emily Brontë and Nathaniel Hawthorne, and the realist technique that she found most appropriate to her "plain transcript[s] of human life."

Like many romantic writers, Stoddard focused on the development of the individual soul; marked by family and societal relationships, her characters remain solitary, romantic figures, responsible only to themselves for their own intellectual and emotional self-fulfillment. In *Two Men* Philippa Luce's school friend Theresa Bond comes to visit her and her family, and Stoddard explains, "The individual independence of the family first struck her. Apparently no member of it involved another in any pursuit, opinion, or interest" (64). (This may be one of the passages that led Higginson to compare Emily Dickinson's family to those in "Mrs. Stoddard's novels.") The development of Jason Auster, perhaps the most romantic figure in the novel, is of primary importance. Throughout the course of *Two Men*, Jason grows from a youth whose "soul" has never been "awaken[ed]" to a man who must pursue his own passions if he is to achieve independence and personal satisfaction (4). At the beginning of the novel Jason mistakenly believes that social causes such as "Socialism, Abolitionism, and Teetotalism" can fulfill him, yet the speed with which he relinquishes these causes after his marriage to the aristocratic Sarah Parke demonstrates how little they actually mean to him (2). His passionate nature is left to smolder throughout his loveless marriage to Sarah, who soon neglects her husband for a suffocating relationship with their son, whom she names Parke Auster. Jason's role as steward of the Parke family fortune also functions to stifle the expression of his passions. For Jason, as well as for the rest of the family, the Parke family legacy is "like a beast, [which] has welked and waved its horns before all the family . . . and held [them] in thrall" (253). More than any other character in the novel, however, Jason is ultimately able to find a way to balance the passionate and the practical, the romantic and the realistic.

Stoddard's discourse on passion played an important part in her work throughout her long career. She recognized and articulated the difference in this regard between her and other women, telling a friend, "I have stronger passionate powers than most women, therefore I run riot in these matters"—presumably both in life and writing.[22] In fact much of *Two Men* focuses on the implications of individuals expressing their own passions—Osmond's escape to South America, Parke's sexual relationship with the mixed-race Charlotte Lang, Jason's love for Philippa. Notably it is men (with the possible exception of Jason) who are allowed to express passion freely, regardless of its effect on others; women—Sarah, Philippa, Charlotte—must pay dearly for the indulgence of their passions, and they are thus impelled to control themselves and their circumstances if they wish to survive. Philippa, for example, recognizes her own attraction to "the phantoms of Liberty and Pleasure," yet chooses to remain in Crest despite her father's invitation to join him in South America. "How can I tell," she asks him, "whether I could bear the license of your life? I succumb to tradition and custom because I love them. But if these barriers should be removed, I feel I have that within which could rise and overtop excess" (200). Clearly, as the example of Charlotte Lang proves, it is neither appropriate nor safe for women to experience passion that "overtop[s] excess," so Philippa opts instead to be "contain[ed]" by Crest (169).

This insistence on depicting the realities of women's constricted lives seems to have driven Stoddard to experiment with a nascent form of realism. While the movement is usually identified with male writers of the late nineteenth century—most notably Howells, Henry James, and Mark Twain—many women writers had been employing realist techniques in their fiction since at least the 1850s. For example, sentimental novels like Susan Warner's *The Wide, Wide World* (1850), Maria Susanna Cummins's *The Lamplighter* (1854), and Fanny Fern's *Ruth Hall* (1855) explored the gendered politics of family, education, work, courtship, and marriage in the mid-nineteenth century. Although such novels are often didactic in nature, their focus on the realities of women's lives renders them important precursors to the realists of the late nineteenth century. Yet Stoddard's critique of many of these women writers reveals that they did not go far enough for her. Above all she chastises women writers for being too spiritual, for turning a blind eye to the material aspects of everyday life: "Why will writers, especially female writers, make their heroines so indifferent to good eating, so careless about taking cold, and so impervious to all the creature comforts? The absence of these treats compose their women, with an eternal preachment about self-denial, moral self-denial. Is goodness, then, incompatible with the enjoyment of the senses?" ("Lady Correspondent," Aug. 3, 1856). Sentimental women writers, Stoddard argues, were often guilty of idealizing their female characters, limiting them out of some imagined religious or moral responsibility to their readership. She rejected the notion that writers owed their readers "an eternal preachment" and attempted instead to depict heroines who reflected the realities of women's lives in the mid-nineteenth century.

Stoddard's own female characters feel passion and hunger, anger and frustration, and often consider the duty that a woman owes to herself in addition to the one she owes to her family. Stoddard refused to sentimentalize her female characters, preferring her readers to be unsettled by their unattractive humanity. Sarah Auster, for example, is one of the most unsentimental mother figures in all of nineteenth-century American fiction:

fiercely, almost obsessively, protective of her son, Parke, she feels nothing at all for her ward, Philippa, and goes out of her way to thwart and embarrass her. Philippa's capacity for empathy is similarly limited; while she initially responds warmly to Charlotte Lang, the young mixed-race woman who arrives in Crest with her mother and younger sister, she is quick to call Charlotte a "slave" and a "beastly African" when Charlotte threatens Philippa's own plans to marry Parke and consolidate the family fortune (156, 161). Stoddard once told a close woman friend, "I hate the everlasting introduction of morals where they have no business," and she thought they had no business in a novel that purported to tell the truth of a woman's life. She also would not hesitate to borrow from real life—no matter how ugly or unpleasant it might be—in order to make her characters more believable: "I am full of venality," she admitted. "I'll sell my grandmother's high temper, my uncle's drunkenness in articles. I think of taking Stoddard for a hero, but he say[s] *don't*, your hero[e]s are so disagreeable."[23]

As early as 1865 critics like Howells recognized Stoddard's refusal to moralize as a sign of things to come in American literature, a productive step away from romanticism and sentimentalism. In his review of *Two Men* Howells noted the fact that Stoddard "seldom vouchsafes a word of comment or explanation on anything that her people do or say; and yet, from their brief speeches and dramatic action, you have the same knowledge of motive which you acquire from the philosophization of some such subjective romance as 'The Scarlet Letter.' We think this admirable" (537). For the most part Stoddard avoided pointing out morals or lessons in *Two Men*; instead, as Howells noted, she allowed "brief speeches and dramatic action" to stand alone, and thus her unorthodox treatment of taboo subjects is mirrored in a formal nonconformity that critics often found objectionable. Like many of the realists of the late nineteenth-century, Stoddard reveled in understatement and resisted the luxury of narrative omniscience, in which the narrator tells the reader what to think or to feel.

Compare, for example, an uncharacteristically didactic moment in *Two Men* with Stoddard's usual method of addressing moral issues. In the first example Charlotte Lang returns home after having had her first sexual encounter with Parke.

> Charlotte did not light a lamp, but put away her bonnet, folded her shawl, and crept to bed in the dark. Did the angels of Pity and Patience guard that bed? Or waited a demon there, to behold the spectacle of dead chastity in a lovely shrine? Who will summon either to pass judgment upon a drama in which they were neither actors nor spectators!
>
> Ignorant, confiding, weak, poisoned with ancestral blood, none shall judge thee, Charlotte — but God! (141–42)

Here Stoddard's sympathies are clear — she directs her reader not to judge Charlotte, but to leave such judgment to God (who will, presumably, find the seduced woman innocent). Such didacticism is reminiscent of the sentimental novels that Stoddard found so frustrating. Of one such author she wrote, "I object to the position she takes in regard to the reader — that of a teacher. The morality is not agreeable, and [is] quite impossible" ("Lady Correspondent," Aug. 3, 1856). More problematically, Stoddard attributes Charlotte's weakness to her "ancestral blood," or the blackness she has inherited from her mother. In this she distinguishes herself from African American writers such as Frances

Ellen Watkins Harper who, in *Iola Leroy* (1892), would create characters who find strength in their African American ancestry. She is not, however, so different from her white contemporaries, Lydia Maria Child and Rebecca Harding Davis, both of whom published 1865 novels featuring mixed-race figures as well; all three relied on essentialist notions of race and character that modern readers quite justifiably find troubling.

Stoddard's discussion of Charlotte's behavior and subsequent judgment by God is very different from the more complicated moment in which Parke returns home from Charlotte's funeral to his father, Philippa, and Osmond Luce. Here elliptical dialogue takes the place of authorial intervention, making it difficult to know who, if anyone, Stoddard wants her readers to sympathize with.

> Parke instantly rose and faced his father, thus paying his first tribute of respect to him. Jason turned his head to the window, to the doors, towards Parke, and nodded with a nod which contained the old permission of full liberty.
>
> "Upon my soul," Osmond silently commented, "that man is a genius, and an honor to human nature. If he develops, I should like to make a raree show of him."
>
> Philippa rolled up her work, and made some stir over her work-basket, wondering why they did not speak—this was the occasion! Presently, as the silence continued unbroken, with a mixture of courage and simplicity she said, "Silence is sometimes a want of truth."
>
> "Always," said Jason; "but what are you going to do about it?"
>
> "Philippa is simply an idiot," thought Osmond.

"Is it not enough that I have returned?" said Parke; "or will you have a sermon preached?"

"Oh, that has been preached," Jason answered.

"I thought so," said Parke. (189–90)

Throughout this scene Stoddard refuses to privilege any single point of view, therefore avoiding the didacticism of the earlier passage. The scene shifts from one character to another, with little authorial direction other than perhaps the mention of Philippa's "courage and simplicity." The characters' dialogue is sparse but suggestive, leaving the reader to determine the overall significance of the exchange. Is Philippa an "idiot" for wanting to talk about what has happened, for being unwilling to perpetuate the silence surrounding Parke's transgression (and what she sees as her own betrayal)? Or is it impossible for Osmond to comprehend what she means, because he doesn't understand the extent of her emotions for Parke? What is the "sermon" that has been preached and who, if anyone, has it pronounced at fault? A similar avoidance of didactic or invasive narration, and an attendant emphasis on the use of dialogue, would become a hallmark of realist fiction in the later nineteenth century.

While it apparently frustrated critics like James at the time *Two Men* was published, Stoddard's unconventional stylistic and philosophical approach to moral questions seems particularly appropriate in the cultural moment in which she was writing. Long after the publication of *Two Men* and the conclusion of the war, Stoddard connected the confrontational realities of her fiction to the violence of the Civil War: "There is *truth* in me and *my* truth should, if it hasn't, make my characters find *their* truth[.] [P]eople go to their graves blind & dumb as to their capacities, passions, traits, appetites, etc. just as countries and nations do—Did any body ever believe 25 years before that the North and the South would spring at each other['s] throats—and drink deeply of each other['s] blood?"[24] In the "grand panorama" of the Civil War period, Stoddard skillfully utilized her toolbox of literary modes and techniques to create a "plain transcript of human life" absent from the work of her literary peers.

Eli*z*abeth Stoddard's Civil War

Critics of nineteenth-century American literature have long struggled with the question of what happened to American literary production during the Civil War. Daniel Aaron, for example, has famously argued that the Civil War went largely "unwritten," while Edmund Wilson, in his *Patriotic Gore*, was forced to look outside the realms of poetry and fiction in order to find contemporary writers' experiences of and reflections on the war. Yet as Elizabeth Young points out, "When we begin Civil War literary history with women's texts at the center, the traditional account of that history seems not only partial but preemptive" (6–7). Women wrote about the war during the war years in letters and diaries, as well as magazine fiction, and responded to its aftermath in longer fictions such as Rebecca Harding Davis's *Waiting for the Verdict* (1867), Lydia Maria Child's *A Romance of the Republic* (1867), and Elizabeth Stuart Phelps's *The Gates Ajar* (1868).[25] Much of this work was erased from the American literary canon, however, in part due to critics' expectations about what *should* constitute Civil War fiction. Detailing critics' privileging of texts like Stephen Crane's *The Red Badge of Courage* (1895) rather than Civil War texts by women writers, Young explains, "Critics have not only masculinized but remasculinized the Civil War, constructing it as the apotheosis of literary masculinity from a perceived state of emasculation. Rather than simply ignoring women, this remasculinizing account displaces the female author and reader from their foundational positions within the making of Civil War fiction. Reconceived as a central presence in the literary history of the war, women's Civil War fiction constitutes a rich field for cultural analysis" (10). *Two Men* is one such text that may allow scholars to rethink that field.

Despite its 1865 publication date, very few critics have attempted to read *Two Men* as a response to the Civil War or related issues. Stoddard's biographer, James Matlack, has gone so far as to claim that her interests in the war were more personal than political: "Once the war began, her major concern lay with relatives and friends who were in the armed forces, not with the moral or political principles at stake" (372). It is certainly true that Stoddard, like many Americans, worried more about the safety of her loved ones than she did about the causes or outcomes of the war. Stoddard and her brother Wilson were very close, and she spent much of the war concerned about his military career and health. In later years she would somewhat disingenuously (given the amount of writing she clearly accomplished in the war years) claim that "When the Civil War broke out every other interest was swept away" ("My Record of the Stage" 355). Stoddard no doubt had opinions on the "moral or political principles at stake" in the war, but they are difficult to determine exactly. Her concern for the troops seems to have been sincere, yet her support for the war itself, and President Abraham Lincoln, was lukewarm at best. While Elizabeth was opposed to slavery and was by no means a Southern sympathizer, both she and her husband had reservations about Lincoln, and Richard was a Democrat who wrote for the antiadministration *New York World.*[26]

There can be no doubt, however, that Stoddard found creative inspiration in the war years. In an 1888 letter to a friend, written in response to the republication of *Two Men*, she insisted that she maintained a "special interest" in the novel for several reasons. First, she was writing it when she found she was pregnant with her third child: "I began it, wrote about half and discovered that Master Lorimer was also being edited—I stopped till he was well under way in the arms of his wet nurse and finished it." But there was far more going on in Stoddard's world than just the birth of her baby, no matter how important that was to her after the deaths of her first two children, prior to Lorry's birth. The letter continues: "That period of my life was the most dramatic—My brother Colonel Barstow was an officer on Gen. Dix's staff—and Edwin Booth & his young wife almost lived with us—Daily contact with war matters, our first connection with the stage[,] made life scintillate, as if a sword was drawn from its scabbard."[27] The war years, made "dramatic" both by the events of war and by Stoddard's intimacy with the Booths and her love for the theater, were also some of Stoddard's most productive: she published all three of her novels between 1860 and 1867, as well as more than twenty short stories and poems.[28] Her extreme productivity in these eight years should prompt critics to reassess her relationship to the war and its political and cultural context.

Stoddard uses the war as a backdrop and features soldiers as characters in several of her short stories, which are important for what they tell us about Stoddard's attitude toward the war and for the ways in which she makes the seemingly conventional wartime narrative her own. Her first Civil War publication, "What Fort Sumter Did For Me," appeared in *Vanity Fair* on May 25, 1861, a little more than a month after the surrender of Fort Sumter to the Confederates marked the beginning of the war. The short

story features a young woman whose initial sympathy for the
South turns into fierce allegiance to the Union's cause—and,
quite predictably for magazine fiction of the period, a Union soldier—after the bombardment of Fort Sumter. "Oh Charles!" she
asks her lover, "won't you bring me home a Secessionist?" (242).
The story satirizes the young woman's romantic notions about
Southern life—particularly the relationship between slave and
master: "I had heard, too," the heroine naively reports, "of Aunt
Charlotte, who had great dinners every day, which were mostly
eaten by her negroes, who rule her, and to whom she intended
to give her plantation, when she found time to make her will"
(241). However, "What Fort Sumter Did For Me" is not simply a jingoistic tale meant to inspire support for the Union and
the war itself; rather, Stoddard demonstrates that the heroine's
Southern sympathies are no more romantic or misguided than
her sudden loyalty to the North. Her "politics," such as they are,
are based on a misunderstanding of the realities of war. Indeed
most of Stoddard's Civil War fiction—stories such as "Gone To
The War," "Tuberoses," and "Sally's Choice"—feature characters who, as in Matlack's assessment of the author herself, care
about the war primarily because they have loved ones fighting
or, worse yet, because it is the fashion to be patriotic.[29] Few characters demonstrate any clear understanding of or concern for
the causes and politics of the war; this does not mean, however,
that Stoddard herself was not aware of or concerned with such
issues. In fact stories such as "What Fort Sumter Did For Me"
call attention to the danger of willful political ignorance.

In a tantalizing letter to Stedman, Stoddard half-jokingly
expressed a desire to write about the war in a nonfiction format:
"If only some newspaper would engage me to write a few femi-
nine *seat-of-war* letters! I could do them well I know. But there

seems to be no luck for me."[30] Given the success of Stoddard's early work for the *Daily Alta California* and the strength of her editorial voice, the proposed letters would have undoubtedly been a fascinating addition to the field of Civil War correspondence, and would have told us much more about Stoddard's feelings about the war and American politics. Unfortunately Stoddard seems never to have followed up on such a plan, and we are forced to cull her political opinions from her private letters and, to a lesser extent, from her fiction. It is in *Two Men*, a novel that is not overtly about the Civil War, that Stoddard develops her most clearly articulated perspective on Civil War politics.[31]

It is unclear when Stoddard actually began writing *Two Men*, although she was certainly immersed in the manuscript by May of 1863, when she told a friend, "I am now writing on my book — Till that is completed I shall not be much of anybody."[32] In July, just after the Battle of Gettysburg, she confided in Stedman that she was "writing a novel — trying to write the history of a man this time."[33] What she ended up with was more than just the history of one man. Instead, by focusing on one small family and one claustrophobic New England town, she explored the impact of the rapid social changes brought about by the Civil War — most importantly, changes in racial relations, but also changes in gender roles and class status in communities throughout the United States. Published just two months after the surrender of the Confederate Army at Appomattox Court House, *Two Men* addresses issues of national identity that were brought to the forefront of American politics during the war.[34] What did citizenship mean? And what place did race, gender, class, and region have in these negotiations? As the war ended it seemed essential that Americans decide collectively who was, in fact, American, and upon what that identity depended. As James H. Kettner writes, the Reconstruction period comprised "a major effort to resolve problems of allegiance that had long plagued the nation, to bring consistency of principle at last to the concept of American citizenship" (341). The Civil War, some propose, ultimately "mark[ed] the inauguration of a single American identity" (Norton 7). The question of race is central to the effort to define this identity; as Anne Norton explains, "The recognition of the role—and the meaning—of those groups which are peripheral and 'other' to any given polity is essential to the demarcation of that polity's boundaries and to the comprehension of the contents of the identity those boundaries define" (7). Throughout *Two Men* Stoddard explores the dissolution and reconstitution of citizenship, particularly as it is challenged by society's "others." The most important figures for her in this regard are the Langs, a mother and her two mixed-race daughters who have presumably been freed from slavery and have moved north to begin new lives.

Prior to the war abolitionist authors had used the mixed-race figure strategically, in order to garner support and sympathy for their cause, while their adversaries wielded the specter of interracial sex to work against abolition and the subsequent integration of African Americans into American political, cultural, and social life. The mulatto figure appears to have been useful for abolitionists in various ways. First, as early critics explained, the mulatto stereotype allowed white readers to identify with a slave character who was physically similar to them. Sterling Brown, for example, claimed that "the audience was readier to sympathize with heroes and heroines nearer to themselves in appearance. The superiority wished upon the octoroons was easily attributed to the white blood coursing in their veins, and the white audience was thereby flattered. On the other hand, the unfailingly tragic outcomes supported the belief that mixture of the races was a curse" (113). Thus, according to Brown, the mulatto figure in texts like Harriet Beecher Stowe's *Uncle Tom's Cabin* (1852) was a carefully negotiated political tool, wielded by white abolitionists more concerned with the reaction of their white audience than the truthful depiction of mixed-race individuals.

Other critics have since complicated this reading of the mixed-race figure, pointing out that the mulatto stereotype was popular in texts written by both whites and African Americans, and insisting that while audience identification may have been important, the mulatto also allowed for more complex discussions of race. The mulatto, Hazel Carby argues, is a "mediating device" in two ways: "it enable[s] an exploration of the social relations between the races" and serves as "an expression of the sexual relations between the races, since the mulatto was a product not only of proscribed consensual relations but of white sexual domination" (xxi–xxii). In other words, the mulatto, the visible representation of sexual intercourse between blacks and whites, functioned to highlight the power dynamics of racial relations throughout the nineteenth century. The mulatto figure was not limited, then, to texts that argued for or against the abolition of slavery, but appeared more broadly in fictions that critiqued Northern racism, such as Frank J. Webb's *The Garies and Their Friends* (1857) and Harriet Wilson's *Our Nig* (1859); and post-war racial relations, such as Child's *A Romance of the Republic*, Davis's *Waiting for the Verdict*, and Harper's *Iola Leroy*.

Given Stoddard's Democratic sympathies, however, *Two Men* must also be positioned within the larger panic over miscegenation that followed Lincoln's Emancipation Proclamation in 1863. Lincoln's proclamation freed slaves in eight of the eleven

slaveholding states and committed U.S. armed forces to protecting their freedom. His political enemies exploited this move in
an effort to embarrass him and threaten his chances for reelection. As Elise Lemire explains, "Lincoln's opponents reasoned
that, if blacks were now free to earn wages and to thereby rise
to the highest economic and social positions, whites might want
to marry them. Political pamphlets in New York City aimed to
convince readers that inter-racial marriage would begin to happen not just in the South but across the nation if Lincoln was
reelected" (2).[35] Thus mulatto figures—the potential product
of interracial sex and marriage—were key to Democratic scare
tactics at the very moment in which *Two Men* was written and
published.

    While the miscegenation episode in *Two Men* clearly bor-
rows from a tradition of mulatto figures and miscegenation plots,
Stoddard differs from most of her predecessors in her realisti-
cally stark treatment of the young lovers and the larger community's response to them. Unlike the anti-Lincoln pamphleteers,
she does not condemn the interracial relationship. Yet Stoddard
also refuses to romanticize these figures or their actions, and
therefore their relationship does not become symbolic of a new
social order, as such relationships often do in post-war texts like
A Romance of the Republic. Rather, as James Kinney observes,
the relationship functions as a "catalyst" by which all other characters in the novel are "tested and judged" (87). The novel as a
whole hinges upon this episode of miscegenation, as well as the
presence of Charlotte Lang and her family in the northern coastal
town in which *Two Men* is set. Indeed, the Langs illustrate Toni
Morrison's assertion that "black people ignite critical moments
of discovery or change or emphasis in literature not written by
them" (viii). Thus in *Two Men* the Langs prompt the fracture

and eventual reconstruction of the Parke-Auster household, destroying Sarah's hold on her son and allowing eventually for the installation of Jason and Philippa, the outsiders, in the family home. Yet none of this works to the advantage of the Langs; as Morrison also points out, functioning as catalysts or igniting change does not ensure success or even survival for African American figures in nineteenth-century American literature.

In many ways the Langs are stereotypical figures, borrowed from types used by both abolitionists and anti-abolitionists throughout the first half of the nineteenth century. At times Stoddard's own racism is evident, particularly in her depiction of Mrs. Lang: "She had been a lithe, sinewy, gay savage," Stoddard writes, "but her day was over; a double expression was dominant in her face now—of weariness, from some long-continued strain, and of repose, because of safety attained. Her manners reflected the hut, the boudoir, and the Methodist gatherings of plantation slaves" (96–97). Both Charlotte and her sister, Clarice, are beautiful and more sophisticated than their mother, but they too are stereotypes to some extent, "tragic mulatta" figures whose mixed blood prevents them from full participation in either the white or the black community. The product of a liaison between a slave woman and a white man, both girls are physical embodiments of such sexual exploitation and are therefore vulnerable to it themselves. Although Charlotte, with her "light-blue eyes" and "straight, silky chestnut hair" could clearly pass for white, she makes no effort to do so; she seems destined to share the fate of her mother and sister, both of whom are also of mixed-race but appear "yellow" and "swarthy," respectively (96–97). As a "black" woman who appears to be "white," Charlotte, like many other mixed-race figures in nineteenth-century American literature, symbolizes the fluidity and ambiguity of identity. Yet for all of her expansiveness, Charlotte is also reduced to a sexual object. In this she is reminiscent of characters like Rosa of Lydia Maria Child's "Slavery's Pleasant Homes: A Faithful Sketch" (1843), a mixed-race figure whose beauty subjects her to sexual attention from black and white men alike; her own desires are irrelevant because she can have no control over her sexuality as long as she remains enslaved.

While Charlotte is not legally a slave, slavery clearly informs Stoddard's reading of her appearance and her sexual relationship with Parke. Charlotte claims to believe that Parke's love for her proves the insignificance of difference, yet she is unable to explain their relationship in any way other than the rhetoric of bondage. "He came after me," she tells Philippa. "I never asked anything of him. I never shall." She continues, "I act according to his wishes. He governs me" (161). Parke frames their sexual relationship in a similar way, reflecting on "a new and terrible joy in his possession" after their first sexual encounter (140). Indeed, the encounter is haunted by "the baying of dogs along the woody road, the rustling of footsteps among the leaves" (142). Parke later tells Philippa that the dogs "sounded like bloodhounds" (139). Thus Charlotte's sexuality, which she fancies she gives freely to Parke, only reduces her to a figurative slave for whom capture and punishment are imminent. Parke is her sexual partner, but their relationship does not endanger him; in fact, it establishes his power over her, making him, in effect, her master. The presence of the bloodhounds highlights Parke's successful pursuit of his "slave," and Charlotte's inability to escape either the history of black servitude or her identity as a black woman.

Charlotte's inevitable pregnancy certainly does not facilitate liberation of any sort, despite Parke's determination to marry her. Like many "tragic mulatta" figures who share a similar fate in abolitionist fiction, she is not allowed to survive the exploitation of her sexuality; not only she and her child, but also Mrs. Lang and Clarice disappear from the novel. It isn't clear what happens to Charlotte's mother and sister, but they do not appear to have escaped Crest or their fate as mixed-race figures. When, after Charlotte's death, Clarice asks her mother if they can leave Crest, Mrs. Lang refuses, insisting, "we should have to take what we are with us, wherever we went" (186). Thus Charlotte's achievement—her relationship with Parke and his subsequent commitment to marry her—is hardly worth the price she has paid, as it has not materially assisted her or her family in any way. It has not provided them with any sort of moral victory either, at least as far as the people of Crest are concerned; Sam Rogers speaks for his entire community when he tells Parke that "nature is against" interracial relationships—indeed, against "the whole race" (150). Charlotte's death, as well as Stoddard's refusal to express overt sympathy for any one character or point of view in her fiction, forces us to try to position *Two Men* and her depiction of an interracial relationship within the context of her conservative political stance on slavery and the Lincoln administration. Parke's decision to marry Charlotte, however reluctantly, may be a reflection on the dangers of interracial sex and marriage—not for the vulnerable African American, but for the white partner, white society, and nature itself. Scientific treatises published in the mid-nineteenth century insisted that mulattoes were produced in "violation of nature's laws" and that the "mingling" of white and black blood would result in "social decay and national suicide" (qtd. in Lemire 127). Charlotte's death and that of her child may simply be read as the natural result of such an unnatural "violation."

Stoddard herself, however, is careful to provide her readers with enough evidence to exonerate Charlotte from blame in her own seduction and death. Even as she succumbs to a sexual relationship with Parke, Charlotte is decidedly *not* representative of black women's uncontrollable sexuality. Rather, the relationship highlights the way in which her race renders her vulnerable to men, like Parke, who would never consider pressing a white woman into sexual activity. (Parke and Theresa Bond, for instance, are attracted to one another, yet there is never any indication that he would approach her sexually in the way he does Charlotte.) Charlotte is also far more complicated than the "tragic mulatta" figure whose only option is to die after being seduced. When Philippa insists that Charlotte should wish to be dead, Charlotte refuses to succumb to the stereotype. "I won't," she tells her, "you needn't think it. I am strong enough to bear every thing" (162). While Charlotte's death may indicate a failure on Stoddard's part to think beyond the seduction plot, she does endow this black woman with the strength to face her accusers and at least express a desire to survive.

It is also important to understand the ways in which Charlotte's ambiguous racial identity highlights that of another female figure in *Two Men*—Philippa Luce—and to position such ambiguity within the context of Stoddard's larger destabilization of status relationships at the end of the novel. While there are obvious differences between Charlotte Lang and Philippa Luce, Philippa also strives to leave her past behind her in order to achieve social and familial acceptance. Her right to belong to the Parke family is constantly called into question, and Stoddard frames this question in terms of citizenship and national identity. When, for example, Theresa references the Bible and quips that Philippa is a prophet in her own country, Sarah asserts that "Philippa does not happen to be in her own country." Then, "For once Parke caught and understood an expression of pain in Philippa's face. 'Philippa,' he said, affectionately, 'my country is your country, isn't it? You are as much of a Parke as I am'" (84). Parke's defense of Philippa reveals the ways in which national identity and familial identity are intertwined in *Two Men*. To belong to the family is to be "in [your] own country," whereas to be an outsider is to be a "foreigner." Because Philippa's origins are something of a mystery, she risks being labeled a foreigner. And while this alienation forms the basis for a bond with Jason, it also threatens her relationship with Parke and her right to the Parke family legacy.

Although Philippa's childhood is referred to several times in the course of the novel, much about her past remains a mystery because of the almost complete textual absence of her mother. Her father, Osmond, explains that the girl's mother is dead, and Philippa reveals only that she has spent at least part of her childhood in the American South. Yet Philippa's physical appearance raises doubts about her "Americanness" that are confirmed in a conversation with her father in which he calls her "half foreign" and insists, "in your native town I have seen dozens of girls like you—with a difference" (201). While Philippa's exact origins are never made clear, Stoddard clearly suggests that her heroine is linked in one way or another to not only the southern United States, but also South America. Given Osmond Luce's adventures in Venezuela, it seems possible that Philippa was born there, the daughter of a Venezuelan woman.

Less distinct but even more interesting, perhaps, is the possibility that Philippa may not only have been born in Venezuela but may, in fact, be of mixed race. As Winthrop R. Wright explains, "Since the late eighteenth century, travelers to Venezuela repeatedly identified racial mixing as the most striking feature of

Venezuelan society" (13). At the end of the colonial era in 1910,
60 percent of Venezuelans "had African origins, with a substan-
tial Indian influence. Indians made up another 15 percent of the
inhabitants. So-called whites comprising *peninsulares*, creoles,
and Canary Islanders, formed the remaining 25 percent of the
population. Of these, some 90 percent were creoles, of somewhat dubious racial origin, many of whom probably had African
ancestors" (14). "By all accounts," Wright insists, "racial and
cultural mixing affected the inhabitants of Venezuela more than
almost any other American society" (21). Such "mixing" may
go far toward explaining the ambiguity surrounding Philippa
and her past.

Thus Philippa, like Charlotte, is an outsider and may, in fact,
be a true "foreigner" and a mixed-race figure. The primary
difference between them, however, is that Philippa's identity
is determined through the paternal, rather than the maternal,
line. Sarah calls Philippa a "cockatrice," and this image of the
cockatrice—a mythical serpent that is hatched by a reptile from
a cock's egg—serves to highlight the importance of Philippa's
father to her sense of identity (46). Charlotte and Clarice do not
have the luxury of this sort of identification. When Clarice insists
that Mrs. Lang "had a white husband," her mother claims that
their father's identity is insignificant: "*I* brought you into the
world, you are my chil'n—bone of my bone, flesh of my flesh,
with all your beauty" (130). As the children of a black woman,
Charlotte and Clarice are legally and socially black in the United
States and are thus unable to escape their maternal legacy. While
Philippa's relationship with her father helps establish her right
to inherit property, the status of the Lang daughters establishes
them as potential property themselves. Rather than fostering
sympathy between them, however, the ambiguity of Philippa's

bloodline pushes Philippa into a defensive position; her own vulnerability, combined with her love for Parke, prompts her to reject Charlotte's plea for understanding, for acceptance, for citizenship.

Philippa is saved, of course, because no one questions her racial identity; although she is desperate to prove her claim to the Parke family name and fortune, she does not have to prove that she is white. Unlike Charlotte, she is also allowed to relinquish Parke because he is not necessary to her very survival. Once Parke has rejected her and left Crest, she learns to love her guardian, Jason Auster, with whom she develops a more egalitarian relationship. With Jason, Philippa learns about interdependence; he is both her "burden" and her "protection" (258). The allusion to Brontë's *Jane Eyre* (1847) is unmistakable: their partnership is an egalitarian one, facilitated by the sacrifice of Jason's hand. The relationship has incestuous overtones, however, in that Jason names Philippa his "daughter" at one point (165). Philippa herself is not sure how she regards Jason. She tells him that she sees herself "as a young woman, refusing to marry a man much older than herself, with whom she has lived as a relative," but admits to herself that "she could not name the character of the relation; he never had appeared like a father, and she had never thought of him as a brother" (236). As was the case with Charlotte and Parke, Stoddard refuses to condemn either Jason or Philippa for their attraction to one another. Thus Jason and Philippa, both initially outsiders whose right to the Parke family legacy was constantly questioned, end up citizens in their own country while the true Parkes are either dead or in South America.

This is not to say that the conclusion to *Two Men* is without its problems. After Parke leaves for South America, Jason and

Philippa entertain Mrs. Rogers, who encourages both to leave the house more often. It is damp, she insists, and "its beams and foundation must be rotting." "It may fall on us some day," Philippa remarks, and then agrees with Jason when he says, "I hope nobody will take the trouble to unroof us if it happens." "Be sure to let us alone," Philippa instructs her neighbor (226–27). The image of Philippa and Jason left alone in the wreckage of the Parke family home is troubling; it is as if Mr. Rochester and Jane Eyre had continued to live in the burnt-out ruins of Thornfield, with all of its disturbing memories. The containment of Philippa in Crest and in the Parke family home is reminiscent, to some degree, of the imprisonment of the Langs. Neither she nor the Langs share Parke's mobility, nor even that of Jason, whose journeys provide a frame of sorts for the novel. Yet Jason, too, is trapped by the Parke family home and legacy, even though his relationship with Philippa, coupled with Sarah's death, delivered him from apathy. He is certainly a different man than he was when he married Sarah Parke—older, more assertive, more passionate—but his relationship to the family is the same: he is the steward of the family fortune. Is it not possible that living in Sarah's house and married to Sarah's husband (as it is safely assumed she will be), Philippa will simply become another Sarah? What are the implications of Philippa's rejection of one semi-incestuous relationship (with Parke, her foster-brother and cousin) for another (with Jason, her guardian and foster-father)? This ambiguity is typical of Stoddard's work, but it also reflects the national tenor at the time *Two Men* was published. What would the nation look like as it made its way toward reunion and reconstruction? Would it be recognizable as the same country it once was? And perhaps most importantly, who and what would be sacrificed in the process?

Ultimately *Two Men* is much more than a Civil War novel, although repositioning the text within its cultural and political moment is a necessary step on the road to its full recovery. Like Stoddard herself, *Two Men* is delightfully complex and sometimes frustrating. The simplest questions—for example, who are the two men in *Two Men?* —are more complicated than they initially seem. It is this complexity that has brought readers back to Stoddard more than a hundred years after her death, and it will continue to fuel the recovery of her work.

Notes

1. Elizabeth Stoddard, letter to James Russell Lowell, May 5, 1860, James Russell Lowell Papers, call number bMS Am 765 (727), by permission of the Houghton Library, Harvard University. In a similar but more tongue-in-cheek comment, Stoddard opened the first of a series of columns for the *Daily Alta California* by emphasizing her own originality and the conventionality of other women writers: "This being my first essay to establish myself in the columns of your paper as one of 'our own,' I debate in my mind how to appear most effectively, whether to present myself as a genuine original, or adopt some great example in style; such as the pugilism of Fanny Fern, the pathetics of Minnie Myrtle, or the abandon of Cassie Cauliflower" (October 8, 1854).

2. See Boyd, *Writing for Immortality*.

3. George Boker, letter to Bayard Taylor, July 30, 1894; and Bayard Taylor, letter to Elizabeth Stoddard, September 28, 1861. Both in Bayard Taylor Papers #14–18–1169, courtesy of the Division of Rare and Manuscript Collections, Cornell University Library.

4. Elizabeth Stoddard, letter to Elizabeth Akers Allen, [Dec.] 17, year unknown, Colby College Special Collections, Waterville, Maine.

5. This review was of the 1889 edition of *The Morgesons*. In July 1888 the *Literary World* published a review of *Two Men* that expressed the same sentiments in language more complimentary to Stoddard and her talent as a writer. According to the anonymous reviewer,

A very wide appreciation, in the sense of popularity, Mrs. Stoddard's novels will never have. Their quality is too rare and fine, their trend too philosophical, their presentation of character too abrupt and fragmentary, their deficiency of plot too great, to permit hope of attracting the mass of readers, who care only for the sensation of the moment. But whoever looks for the personal note in fiction, whoever values men and women for what they are, whoever is superior to conventional standards, whoever is willing to look through the veil of custom and see the naked souls underneath, whoever looks to humanity for possibilities and motives and not for superficial goodness, will relish the story of *Two Men*. (15)

6. Thomas Wentworth Higginson, "To Mary Channing Higginson," n.d., letter 342a of *The Letters of Emily Dickinson* vol. 2, ed. Thomas H. Johnson (Cambridge: Harvard University Press, 1958), 473–76.

7. See Buell and Zagarell, *The Morgesons and Other Writings*. The novel was republished, along with Buell and Zagarell's introduction, in the Penguin Classics series in 1997.

8. Lisa Radinovsky argues that the relationship between Elizabeth and her brother Wilson was "unusually intense, even romantic" (208). She goes so far as to suggest that Wilson may have fathered Stoddard's third son, Lorry (208–9), and that the relationship between Philippa and Parke in *Two Men* is influenced by the "incestuous attraction" between Stoddard and her brother (208).

9. Richard Henry Stoddard, letter to Manton Marble, June 10, 1862, Manton Marble Papers, Manuscript Division, Library of Congress, Washington DC.

10. Margaret A. Amstutz sees the *Alta* columns as "something other than private correspondence between the two" siblings. "Indeed," she writes, "rather than merely holding a private dialogue with Wilson, Stoddard uses the forum of the columns to identify more generally with her Californian audience and to insert herself, in a thoroughly performative way, as a chronicler of the widening canvas of individuals who exist in relationship to others in a transcontinental frame" (74).

11. Elizabeth Stoddard, letter to Edmund Clarence Stedman, November

18, [1887], Edmund Clarence Stedman Papers, Rare Book and Manuscript Library, Columbia University.

12. Elizabeth Stoddard, letter to Edmund Clarence Stedman, July 12, 1863, Edmund Clarence Stedman Papers, Rare Book and Manuscript Library, Columbia University.

13. Elizabeth Stoddard, letter to Edmund Clarence Stedman, July 22, 1864, Edmund Clarence Stedman Papers, Rare Book and Manuscript Library, Columbia University.

14. In a letter written to William Dean Howells while she was writing *Temple House*, Stoddard showed a preference for the shorter form, lamenting, "Do you not think there must be a good deal that is trivial in a novel? Poetry does not own that necessity. If I could push the course of my lives in a hundred pages, I could make them cut like a scythe, but a novel mustn't consist of a hundred pages." August 31, [1866], Howells Family Papers, call number MS Am 1784 (460), by permission of the Houghton Library, Harvard University.

15. George Parsons Lathrop, letter to Elizabeth Stoddard, August 8, 1888, Richard H. and Elizabeth B. Stoddard Papers, Manuscripts and Archives Division, The New York Public Library, Astor, Lenox, and Tilden Foundations.

16. Elizabeth Stoddard, letter to Julia Dorr, October 5, [1888], Abernethy Library Manuscripts, Special Collections, Middlebury College, Middlebury, Vermont.

17. The Coates reprint used the plates of the 1888–1889 editions. Katherine Hooker, an admirer of Stoddard's, bought the plates at an auction and gave them to Stoddard; the reprints are accordingly dedicated to her "in grateful remembrance of a kind deed."

18. Boyd sees the neglect of this period as particularly damaging to women writers. In her study of Stoddard, Louisa May Alcott, Constance Fenimore Woolson, and Elizabeth Stuart Phelps, Boyd concludes that these and other postbellum women writers must be examined in order to complicate our notion of "American women's literary history as advancing from sentimentalism to domestic literature to local color to modernism" thus "obscur[ing] the value of many women writers who do not fit neatly

into any of these categories" (249). Julia Stern suggests that Stoddard's work, especially, "allows us to reimagine a postsentimental genealogy for American women's fiction of the Civil War and post–Civil War eras" (123).

19. Elizabeth Stoddard, letter to Edmund Clarence Stedman, April 21, [1888], Edmund Clarence Stedman Papers, Rare Book and Manuscript Library, Columbia University.

20. Elizabeth Stoddard, letter to William Dean Howells, n.d., Howells Family Papers, call number MS Am 1784 (460), by permission of the Houghton Library, Harvard University.

21. Elizabeth Stoddard, letter to Edmund Clarence Stedman, June 22, 1862, Edmund Clarence Stedman Papers, Rare Book and Manuscript Library, Columbia University.

22. Elizabeth Stoddard, letter to Margaret Sweat, June 4, [1852], by permission of the Allison-Shelley Collection, Rare Books and Manuscripts, The Pennsylvania State University Libraries.

23. Elizabeth Stoddard, letter to Elizabeth Akers Allen, March 28, year unknown, Colby College Special Collections, Waterville, Maine.

24. Elizabeth Stoddard, letter to Lilian Whiting, June 25, [1888], Ms. A.9.2.9.107, Boston Public Library, Department of Rare Books and Manuscripts. Courtesy of the Trustees.

25. Many Civil War–era diaries by women have been published; these include C. Vann Woodward, ed., *Mary Chesnut's Civil War* (New Haven: Yale University Press, 1981); Charles East, ed., *Sarah Morgan: The Civil War Diary of a Southern Woman* (Athens: University of Georgia Press, 1991); and John Q. Anderson, ed., *Brokenburn: The Journal of Kate Stone, 1861–1868* (Baton Rouge: Louisiana State University Press, 1975). For magazine fiction about the Civil War, see Kathleen Diffley, ed., *To Live and Die: Collected Stories of the Civil War, 1861–1876* (Durham: Duke University Press, 2002).

26. In an 1856 *Daily Alta California* article, Stoddard commented acerbically on a southern clergyman who insisted that the restoration of the slave trade was the only way to ensure the Christianization of Africa: "I call that man an intellectual Juggernaut. The slave trade become a missionary of

Christ! The hold of a slave ship a temple of the Lord; the scourge and the Iron chain the pleasant medium of conversion!" ("Lady Correspondent," November 18, 1855).

27. Elizabeth Stoddard, letter to Lilian Whiting, June 25, [1888], Ms. A.9.2.9.107, Boston Public Library, Department of Rare Books and Manuscripts. Courtesy of the Trustees. Gen. John Adams Dix (1798–1879) was sixty-two when the Civil War broke out; prior to the war he had served in a variety of governmental posts, including as U.S. senator from 1845 to 1849. Because others were concerned that he was too old for strenuous service during the war, he was given appointments that kept him from the field of battle. He ended the war in command of the Department of the East in New York. As Larry C. Skogen notes, "His Civil War military service was steady but unremarkable" (607). Edwin Booth (1833–1893) and his wife Mary Devlin Booth (1840–1863) were intimate friends of the Stoddards throughout the war years. In his time Booth was best known for legitimizing American acting abroad, but he is now remembered as the brother of John Wilkes Booth, the man who assassinated Lincoln. The friendship ended early in 1864, about a year after the death of Mary, because Edwin blamed Elizabeth for having told his wife about his drinking problems while he was touring. The Stoddards were fitfully reconciled with Booth much later in life.

28. Stoddard clearly saw her first two novels as casualties of the Civil War. In the same letter in which she refers to *The Morgesons* as her Bull Run, she complained that her publisher's poor treatment of *Two Men* caused the novel to meet "with a violent death." Elizabeth Stoddard, letter to Edmund Clarence Stedman, November 18, [1887], Edmund Clarence Stedman Papers, Rare Book and Manuscript Library, Columbia University.

29. In "Gone to the War," a humorous piece published in *Vanity Fair* on December 21, 1861, Stoddard ignores the causes of the war entirely, focusing on a young woman's search for her brother, Job, who has enlisted because "Mary Bowen told me she wouldn't have me unless I went" (276). Turning soldier has not refined Job, however; on the contrary it reveals him to be an uncouth, unmannered rustic whose acquaintance with sol-

diers will only introduce him to more bad habits. In "Tuberoses" (*Harper's Monthly*, January 1863), one of the best of Stoddard's stories to be published during the war, few of the characters seem to care much about the circumstances or consequences of war. Rather, the war functions primarily as a plot device to separate the lovers; the hero seems to enlist out of pique because he assumes that his lover wants to marry his friend instead of him. "Sally's Choice" (*Harper's Weekly*, May 30, 1863) similarly refutes romantic notions of military service and allegiance to one's cause. For example, one character in the story laments the fact that a young soldier has been "demoralized" by "[h]is thirteen dollars a month, and his being taught that he is a machine." Stoddard also mocks the ambiguity of war when she explains that in the course of her story, "[o]ne of those vague Western battles . . . occurred, in which a great many men are killed, and which are called victories on both sides, and for which victories both the commanding generals are removed." The war is no less morally ambiguous for Stoddard's female characters. Sally, the title character of the story, succumbs to the romanticization of war (and the machinations of her mother) and marries the upper-class Major Brewer rather than John Cutter, the lower-class man she truly loves. When Brewer dies and Cutter returns home to tell her the details of his death, Sally refuses to sacrifice her happiness yet again to the allure of wartime romance: "As he handed the watch to Sally, and told her that the Major had kissed it for her, his eyes filled with tears, from self-pity as much, perhaps, as from a remembrance of the sad scene. Sally took it and laid it on the table, and looked at him to go on with his story, as if it was time that he should come to himself" (342).

30. Elizabeth Stoddard, letter to Edmund Clarence Stedman, March 20, 1862, Edmund Clarence Stedman Papers, Rare Book and Manuscript Library, Columbia University.

31. It is unclear exactly when *Two Men* is set. One clue might lie in the fact that a marriage between Parke and Charlotte is apparently legal, albeit not desirable. Massachusetts made interracial marriages legal in 1843, so the novel is likely set after that date. It also seems fairly certain that the novel takes place prior to the 1850 Fugitive Slave Act, in which runaway slaves would be at risk of recapture in both the North and the South. It

is important that Mrs. Lang could expect her daughters to be reasonably safe in a northern community like Crest. Finally, José Antonio Páez, upon whose "pampas" Osmond proposes to be a "cattle-hunter," was exiled to the Caribbean and the United States in 1848; in order for Osmond to consider such an adventure, Páez would still have to be living in Venezuela, where he served as president and unofficial "supreme caudillo" from 1830 to 1848 (Lombardi 181–82). Based on these considerations, I believe we can safely assume that the novel is set between 1843 and 1848.

32. Elizabeth Stoddard, letter to Louise Chandler Moulton, May 6, 1863, Louise Chandler Moulton Papers, Manuscript Division, Library of Congress, Washington DC.

33. Elizabeth Stoddard, letter to Edmund Clarence Stedman, July 12, 1863, Edmund Clarence Stedman Papers, Rare Book and Manuscript Library, Columbia University.

34. Much of the argument in this section revises or reprints Putzi.

35. The term "miscegenation," from the Latin for *miscere* (to mix) and *genus* (race), was coined at this historical moment by the authors of a seventy-two-page pamphlet entitled *Miscegenation: The Theory of the Blending of the Races, Applied to the White Man and the Negro* (1864). Posing as supporters of Lincoln's bid for reelection, the authors insisted that the Republican party shared the views of abolitionists, some of whom argued that the mixing of races was the only way to eliminate slavery as well as racism (Lemire 116).

Works Cited

Aaron, Daniel. *The Unwritten War: American Writers and the Civil War.* New York: Alfred A. Knopf, 1973.

Abernethy Manuscripts. Julian W. Abernethy Collection of American Literature. Abernethy Library, Middlebury College.

Aldrich, Lillian Woodman. *Crowding Memories.* Boston: Houghton Mifflin, 1920.

Allison-Shelley Collection. Rare Books and Manuscripts, The Pennsylvania State University Libraries.

Works Cited

Amstutz, Margaret A. "Elizabeth Stoddard as Returned Californian: A Reading of the *Daily Alta California* Columns." *American Culture, Canons, and the Case of Elizabeth Stoddard*. Ed. Robert McClure Smith and Ellen Weinauer. Tuscaloosa: University of Alabama Press, 2003. 65–82.

Brown, Sterling. "The Negro in Drama." *Negro Poetry and Drama*. Washington DC: Associates in Negro Folk Education, 1937. 103–42.

Boyd, Anne E. *Writing for Immortality: Women Writers and the Emergence of High Literary Culture in America*. Baltimore: Johns Hopkins University Press, 2004.

Buell, Lawrence, and Sandra A. Zagarell. Introduction. *The Morgesons and Other Writings, Published and Unpublished*. By Elizabeth Stoddard. Philadelphia: University of Pennsylvania Press, 1984. xi–xxv.

Carby, Hazel. Introduction. *Iola Leroy; or, Shadows Uplifted*. By Frances Ellen Watkins Harper. Boston: Beacon, 1987. ix–xxvi.

Dickinson, Emily. *The Letters of Emily Dickinson*. Ed. Thomas H. Johnson. Vol. 2. Cambridge: Harvard University Press, 1958.

Howells, William Dean. *Literary Friends and Acquaintances*. Ed. David F. Hiatt and Edwin H. Cady. Bloomington: Indiana University Press, 1968.

———. Rev. of *Two Men*, by Elizabeth Stoddard. *Nation* 1 (1865): 537–38.

Howells Family Papers, Houghton Library, Harvard University.

Kettner, James H. *The Development of American Citizenship, 1608–1870*. Chapel Hill: University of North Carolina Press, 1978.

Kinney, James. *Amalgamation! Race, Sex and Rhetoric in the Nineteenth-Century American Novel*. Westport: Greenwood, 1985.

Kraft, James. "An Unpublished Review by Henry James." *Studies in Bibliography* 20 (1967): 267–73.

Lemire, Elise. *"Miscegenation": Making Race in America*. Philadelphia: University of Pennsylvania Press, 2002.

Lombardi, John V. *Venezuela: The Search for Order, the Dream of Progress*. New York: Oxford University Press, 1982.

Lowell, James Russell. Papers. Houghton Library, Harvard University.

Marble, Manton. Papers. Manuscript Division, Library of Congress, Washington DC.

Matlack, James Hendrickson. *The Literary Career of Elizabeth Barstow Stoddard*. Diss. Yale University, 1968. Ann Arbor: UMI, 1968.

Rev. of *The Morgesons* by Elizabeth Stoddard. *Godey's Lady's Book*. September 1862, 301.

Rev. of *The Morgesons* by Elizabeth Stoddard. *Literary World*. September 28, 1889, 324.

Morrison, Toni. *Playing in the Dark: Whiteness and the Literary Imagination*. Cambridge: Harvard University Press, 1992.

Moss, Mary. "The Novels of Elizabeth Stoddard." *Bookman* September 1902. 260–63.

Moulton, Louise Chandler. Papers. Manuscript Division, Library of Congress, Washington DC.

Norton, Anne. *Alternative Americas: A Reading of Antebellum Political Culture*. Chicago: University of Chicago Press, 1986.

Opfermann, Susanne, and Yvonne Roth. Introduction. *Stories*. By Elizabeth Stoddard. Boston: Northeastern University Press, 2003. ix–xxxi.

Putzi, Jennifer. "The 'American Sphinx' and the Riddle of National Identity in Elizabeth Stoddard's *Two Men*." Smith and Weinauer. 183–201.

Radinovsky, Lisa. "(Un)Natural Attractions? Incest and Miscegenation in *Two Men*." Smith and Weinauer. 202–31.

Ripley, George. Rev. of *Temple House*, by Elizabeth Stoddard. *New York Tribune*. January 27, 1868, 6.

Skogan, Larry C. "Dix, John Adams." *Encyclopedia of the American Civil War: A Political, Social, and Military History*. Ed. David S. Heidler and Jeanne T. Heidler. New York: Norton, 2000. 605–7.

Smith, Robert McClure, and Ellen Weinauer, eds. *American Culture, Canons, and the Case of Elizabeth Stoddard*. Tuscaloosa: University of Alabama Press, 2003.

Sollors, Werner. *Neither White Nor Black Nor Both: Thematic Explorations of Interracial Literature*. New York: Oxford University Press, 1997.

Stedman, Edmund Clarence. Papers. Rare Book and Manuscript Library, Columbia University.

Stern, Julia. "'I Am Cruel Hungry': Dramas of Twisted Appetite and Rejected Identification in Elizabeth Stoddard's *The Morgesons*." Smith and Weinauer. 107–27.

Stoddard, Elizabeth. "From a Lady Correspondent." *Daily Alta California*. October 8, 1854: 2; November 18, 1855: 1; August 3, 1856: 1; May 3, 1857: 1.

———. "Gone to the War." *Vanity Fair* December 21, 1861. 275–76.

———. Letter to Elizabeth Akers Allen. [Dec.] 17, n.y. Colby College Special Collections. Waterville, Maine.

———. Letter to Elizabeth Akers Allen. March 28, n.y. Colby College Special Collections. Waterville, Maine.

———. Letter to Lilian Whiting. June 25, [1888]. MS A.9.2.9.107. Boston Public Library, Department of Rare Books and Manuscripts.

———. "My Record of the Stage." *Saturday Evening Post*, November 4, 1899. 354–55.

———. "Sally's Choice." *Harper's Weekly*, May 30, 1863. 342.

———. *Two Men: A Novel*. New York, 1865.

———. "What Fort Sumter Did For Me." *Vanity Fair*, May 25, 1861. 241–42.

Stoddard, Richard Henry. *Recollections, Personal and Literary*. Ed. Ripley Hitchcock. New York: Barnes, 1903.

Stoddard, Richard H., and Elizabeth B. Stoddard. Papers. Manuscripts and Archives Division, The New York Public Library.

Taylor, Bayard. Papers. Division of Rare and Manuscript Collections, Cornell University Library.

Rev. of *Two Men*, by Elizabeth Stoddard. *Literary World*. July 21, 1888: 227.

Wright, Winthrop. *Café con Leche: Race, Class, and National Image in Venezuela*. Austin: University of Texas Press, 1990.

Young, Elizabeth. *Disarming the Nation: Women's Writing and the American Civil War*. Chicago: University of Chicago Press, 1999.

A NOTE ON THE TEXT

The present text of Elizabeth Stoddard's *Two Men* is based on the first edition of the novel, published in October 1865 by Bunce and Huntington. Silent changes in punctuation were made in a handful of places throughout the text, but only in those places when there is a sense that some sort of printer's error had been made. The flavor of Stoddard's style is retained wherever possible. A second edition of *Two Men* was published in 1888, and these plates were used for a 1901 reprint as well. Most of the revisions that Stoddard made for the second edition are insignificant—often matters of punctuation or word choice. Those revisions deemed significant are addressed in the notes appended to the novel.

TWO

MEN

To Wilson

Who will so well remember what I knew
As you, whenever comes the day to part?
We have ascended one wide scale,
With all emotion in its pale;
Girl, boy, woman and man, untrue and true,
Together or apart—with the same heart.

E. D. B. S.
New York, 1864[1]

"Let us treat the men and women well: treat them as if they were real: perhaps they are."

"Nature, as we know her, is no saint. The lights of the Church, the Ascetics, Gentoos, and corn-eaters, she does not distinguish by any favor. She comes eating and drinking and sinning. Her darlings—the great, the strong, the beautiful—are not children of our law; do not come out of the Sunday-School, nor weigh their food, nor punctually keep the Commandments."

EMERSON[2]

CHAPTER I

‖‖

WHEN JASON AUSTER MARRIED Sarah Parke he was twenty
years old, and a house-carpenter. As he was not of age, he made
some agreement with a hard father by which liberty was gained,
and a year's wages lost. He left his native village filled with no
adventurous spirit, but with a simple confidence that he should
find the place where he could earn a living by his trade, and
put in practice certain theories concerning the rights of men and
property which had already made him a pest at home. The stage-
coach which conveyed him thence, traversed a line of towns that
made no impression from his point of view—the coach window;
but when it stopped to change horses at Crest, a lively maritime
town, and he alighted to stretch his cramped legs, he saluted
Destiny. Its aspect, that spring day, pleased him; he heard the
rain of blows from broad-axes in the ship-yards by the water's
edge, and saw new roofs and chimneys rising along the irregular
streets among the rows of ancient houses, and concluded to stay.
He unstrapped a small trunk from the stage-rack, carried it into
the tavern entry, and looked about him for some one to address.
A man who had been eying the trunk advanced towards him with
a resolutely closed mouth, and hands concealed in his pockets.

"Do you keep this tavern?" Jason asked; "and do you want
a boarder?"

"Yes siree," the man replied, in a loud cheerful voice.

"What is board now?"

"Three dollars per week."

"I think I will stop here. My name is Auster."

"I agree; but maybe you had rather go to the other tavern where they sell liquor, with flies in it. *I* keep a temperance house."

"Good," answered Jason, pulling off his overcoat. "I have got a temperance lecture in my trunk; I wrote it last winter. I'll lend it to you to read."

"I ain't much of a hand at reading handwriting," the tavern-keeper replied with a dubious look; but catching sight of Jason's carpenter's rule, his face brightened. "Guess you are a carpenter," he exclaimed; "just the place for you. We are growing like the mischief since whale-oil is so high."

The arrangement for board was concluded, and Jason began life in Crest with ten dollars, two suits of clothes, and a few articles, which consisted of several shirts, two books whose titles were "Man's Social Destiny,"[3] and "Humanity in Limbo," a pin-cushion with *Forget Me Not* embroidered upon it, and the temperance lecture.

Before night he had taken the bearings of Crest, and was satisfied that he had made a good choice. The week following he sent to a boss-carpenter a novel design for mantle-pieces, which proved the means of an engagement to work with a gang on the inside of a Congregational church about to be built. With the whistling of his plane he began to air his theories of Socialism, Abolitionism, and Teetotalism, and amused his fellow-workmen, who never mistrusted that he intended to be believed, or that he was in earnest, for his manners belied his words. He appeared shy, cold, and indifferent, self-forgetful, and forgetful of others.[4]

As the church progressed it became a place of resort, especially in the fine summer afternoons, when groups of young women perambulated the aisles, sat in the doorless pews, or hung over the unfinished gallery. One day two ladies went up the pulpit stairs, while Jason was at work on its moulding below; looking up to caution them against stepping on certain loose boards in the flooring, he saw that he was too late, for the lady in advance was already half in the cavity under the floor, and only kept herself up by a clutch on the desk. Jason bounded up the stairs and extricated her; as he did this he heard a shrill laugh from her companion, which made him laugh too.

"I wish it had been you, Sarah Parke," she exclaimed. "Thank you, sir," she said stiffly to Jason, without looking at him.

"You are welcome to my help," he answered quietly. "Of course, I owed it to you." And he returned to his work.

"Who was the black-eyed girl that didn't fall in?" he asked of one of the workmen, named John Davis.

"Squire Parke's grand-daughter," he answered. "It would be worth your while to walk into her affections; but she don't look at carpenters, I tell you."

"She looked at me," Jason said grandly.

"How could she help it?" replied John satirically; "you have got such eyes!"

"Why shouldn't she look at carpenters?" Jason persisted.

"The Parke family are next to the Lord, in this county, though it is not what it was once. One of 'em knocked off his heel-tap on Plymouth Rock the day the Pilgrims came ashore; one of 'em was a governor; one of 'em settled here—cheated the Indians, I guess, out of the pine woods that belong still to the old Squire, and died universally unlamented. I never heard any good of the name, nor any thing so very bad. There's a streak in the family; one or two in every generation are all streak—which means that they go to the devil. I must say though, that most people have a good word for the old Squire; he ain't meddlesome. I wonder what has come over this Sarah lately? I see her about with folks, as if she was tired of being by herself."

"The Parkes, I take it, have not understood the correct balance between Man and Wealth."

"Oh yes, they have, and have got all the wealth from every man they ever had any dealings with!"

"Such men delay the progress of social harmony."

"Speaking of harmony, will you go to the sing to-night, with all hands? Miss Jane Moss, the girl you pulled up from the pulpit just now, is the head-singer in our choir. I sit behind her in the gallery, and pass cloves and cardamom seeds over to her every Sunday."

"What are you going to sing?"

"We are getting ready for the Dedication."

"If you will come round to the tavern for me, I'll go."

John consented, and, at seven o'clock, made his appearance dressed in his best, and found Jason in his best also. But notwithstanding the change of clothes, there was a strong piney odor about them; also a dryness of complexion, a roughness of hair and whiskers, and a cracked condition of the hands, which suggested beams, boards, and shavings. Jason had been nicknamed "The Lath."[5] The physiognomy of "The Lath" promised to be interesting, if the soul should ever awaken; eyes of light blue, fringed with thick black lashes, now somewhat vague and wandering, would then flash with conquering power, or diffuse, tender, appealing rays. At present, Jason was not handsome; neither was there any fascination in his bearing, attitudes, gestures, or speech.

He did not confess on his way to the singing-meeting that he knew nothing of music, but when he arrived took a seat among the singers, and turned the leaves of his music-book at the proper instant. Opposite him, in the place of honor, sat Jane Moss and Sarah Parke; he soon discovered that Sarah was no more of a singer than himself, though her lips moved, and her eyes followed the notes. She looked at him in the middle of a prolonged "Amen," and perceived that he understood the sham; she turned her head away to conceal a smile, turned back again, and learned, as the choir burst out again, that he was an accomplice in her fraud.

John Davis informed him, when the meeting broke up, that he had about made up his mind to ask Jane Moss if he might escort her home, though he didn't know but that it would make her mad.

"Go in," said Jason; "I'll support you."

John, with a stiff "Good-evening," thrust his elbow out before Jane, and she condescendingly placed her hand inside it. A moment after, Jason was introduced to Sarah, and shook hands with her modestly, and walked beside her without attempting conversation; he waited for her to address him. His deportment was so unexceptionable, that when he left her at her door, she expressed a hope of meeting him again.

It was known in Crest soon after that Jason had called at Squire Parke's. Then it was rumored that he spent whole evenings there, playing backgammon with Sarah, or whist with the Squire. And finally the town was surprised to hear that Jason and Sarah were to be married. It charitably said that she must be bewitched to marry a poor carpenter, and that he knew which side his bread was buttered on, but that he might not find it so pleasant to go up in the world after all. But it was not allowed to be present at the marriage ceremony, which was performed one evening in the Squire's west parlor. Two persons besides the minister were present; the Squire and Elsa Bowen, the housekeeper. The next morning Jason took his place at the breakfast-table, as an inmate of the family. The household consisted now of six persons; the Squire, Sarah, his grand-daughter, Elsa Bowen, a middle-aged woman who had lived with the second wife of the Squire for years, as housekeeper, friend, and fourth cousin, a hired man, "Cuth," who had been in the Squire's employ from a boy, a youth named Gilbert, and Jason himself.

CHAPTER II

||||||||||||||||||||||||||||||||||||||||||||||

SQUIRE PARKE HAD HAD two wives and two children. They were dead. His first wife gave birth to a son in the second year of his marriage, and died shortly afterwards. In a year from the time of her death he married another wife, who bore him a daughter, and lived till three years before Jason's arrival in Crest. The son and daughter by the different wives grew up, married, and died, each leaving a child, a boy and a girl, to the care of their grandfather, the Squire. The girl had just become Sarah Auster, and the boy, Osmond Luce, was in parts unknown. As soon as his grandmother was buried he announced his determination to leave home, and although the Squire cried and reproached him for being like his uncle, Sarah's father, who had deserted home years ago, Osmond persisted in his resolution. He must have freedom, he said; he had paid his respects to the family myths long enough, and he would transfer the duty to Sarah, who believed in them, and whose authority with them would more than compensate for the loss of himself.

"You think so?" queried Elsa Bowen, who was present when he opened the subject.

Osmond gave a look which silenced her, till the Squire rose, struck his cane on the floor, and with an emphatic "Go," left the room; then she burst out with, "You'd better try your luck with Sarah; she won't take it so easy."

"I am glad you are on hand to do up the croaking, Elsa."

"Yes, you will find me here, and at it, after many a long year

7

of your devil's wanderings. What do you suppose became of your Uncle Osmond?"

"'His bones are whitening the caverns of the deep.' — *Washington Irving*."[6]

"Maybe."

Osmond rumpled his long, thin curls into a light mass, and said, "I shall present myself as the fretful porcupine who mustn't be opposed. Where is she?"

"It will be more like if you go as a weasel. I shan't tell you where she is."

He knew better than Elsa how Sarah would take the news of his departure, but he carried them to her with a reckless audacity that would have silenced any ordinary opposition. But Sarah was not an ordinary person; a conflict took place which left both torn, bleeding, breathless; in one sense, however, he was the conqueror, for he went away in spite of it. The Squire sent him out in a vessel loaded with merchandise for some Southern port; the cargo was sold, and Osmond, taking the proceeds, left the port to go further South. Nothing had been heard of him since the vessel returned. For a time the Squire spoke of him as one not far away; then Elsa noticed that he began to relate the anecdotes she had heard him repeat in connection with his own son, Osmond Parke, confounding them with the childhood of Osmond Luce; in her mind it was a sign that the old man had given him up, and that he was as good as buried. In Sarah's mind his image was not confused. As a banner floats in the wind, he was ever floating before her mental vision, with his hundred flitting expressions of wrath, mirth, and recklessness; but she never spoke of him. Once Elsa went to a chest where some of his clothes were packed, to see if they were damp; dampness, according to a superstition in Crest, being the proof of a seafaring man's death by drowning.

When she told Sarah they were as dry as a bone, she looked agitated, and begged her never to speak of them again.

After Sarah's child was born she spoke of Osmond for the first time to Jason, as a half-cousin, who bore no resemblance in character or looks to herself. He was the only one, she said, who had any claim on her grandfather's property, that might ever trouble them. She doubted whether he would ever come back, for the Parkes who had deserted Crest never returned. There was a hectic flush on her high cheek-bones after this conversation, but Jason did not observe it.

She named her boy "Parke." He was a Parke, every inch of him, she remarked to Jason, and asked him to notice how much his hands were shaped like her grandfather's. She might have added that they were like Osmond's, too. Jason looked at his own hands instead, and shrugged his shoulders.

"Do you consider yourself a Parke?" he asked.

"I am like my mother," she answered sharply.

Jason examined her face as if he intended to make a study of race, and then looked at the baby experimentally.

"What does the Squire think of him?" he asked.

"What you do, I suppose."

The thump of a cane was heard, and Sarah said, "Here he comes, you can ask him."

But he only smiled when the Squire entered and stood by the cradle, and before he spoke Jason was gone.

If Sarah had been imaginative she might have mused on the picture before her—baby Parke, aged three weeks, and the Squire, eighty-four years. As she was not, she inquired which bin in the cellar Cuth had put the potatoes in.

"Yah, yah, Sally; whatever bin Cuth has put the potatoes in is the right one."

9

"Grandpa, Cuth does what he likes with you."

"So, give me a coal, Sally."

She held one in the tongs for him to light his pipe, and then moved her chair near him. His face was never so pleasant as when he was smoking, and she loved to look at it. He scattered ashes over his double-breasted waistcoat, and sparks dropped on his pantaloons, but she did not venture to brush them off, because it would have annoyed him. The serenity of his mien, the result of a wonderful selfishness, was always her envy and admiration. She thought him one of the best men in the world, because he generally allowed people their own way,—provided their way did not cross his. He was an amiable host to all the virtues, but he never sought their society.

"When are you going to comb my hair again?" he asked.

"Why, Grandpa, hasn't Elsa combed it?"

"Elsa has been like a gale of wind in the house since you have been shut up."

"Why didn't you check her?"

"I should, if I had been too much in the draft."

She combed his long silvery locks till she was ready to faint with fatigue, and till Parke woke up with a cry. When he was hushed the old man fell asleep in his chair, and his slumber was quiet, dreamless, and deep as the child's beside him.

CHAPTER III

IIIIIIIIIIIIIIIIIIIIIIIIIIIIIIIIIIIIIIIIIIIIIIII

WHEN JASON SAW SARAH'S executive ability as the mistress
and manager of her grandfather's establishment, in doors and
out, and comprehended the absolute position of the Squire, he
felt the impotence of his crude ideas, and his individual isolation.
Nothing practical could be done in the way of equal rights with
the Squire's garden, orchard, woodland, mills, houses, and ships,
presided over and governed by the arbitrary wills of such a man
and such a woman. The prestige of possession dazzled his view
of the tenth point of the law, and he fell down among the "nine-
holes" of the game, which is an inscrutable one to those who do
not hold a hand in it.[7] He did therefore what most men do, when
suddenly ushered from one sphere to another, — ruled his actions
according to the circumstances he was placed in. Now and then
he made use of the phrases which belonged to his smouldered
theories. When Sarah requested him to give up his trade, he
replied that it was better to be a carpenter than to live by the
extortions of commerce, or an undue proportion of land; whereat
she laughed so loud he discovered that some of her teeth were as
sharp-pointed as needles, and that they gave her a tigerish look.
His connection simply with the Squire permitted him to make
up his own hand in the game he thought he despised. Contracts
were obtained on the strength of it which brought him money,
and at the end of three years he was the owner of several stores
and houses, planned by himself, which paid a better rent than
any of the Squire's buildings. In the beginning of his enterprises

he seemed the same to his acquaintances. They joked with him, and laughed at him; but the jokes grew few, and the laughs faint. Finally no one ventured to be familiar with him, except John Davis, who was now married to Jane Moss.

From the day that Jason entered the family he suffered from an intangible something in the Squire's bearing which deprived him of his natural demeanor, and made him feel, by contrast, unfinished, awkward, incapable. Whatever the influence was, he succumbed to it, and its effect lasted long; in fact, the Squire was the first potter that kneaded Jason's clay.[8]

The fourth year of his marriage came, and the Squire still lived; he went his daily rounds over his possessions in his chaise, accompanied by Cuth, smoked, dozed, played with little Parke, and listened affably to all Sarah had to say. It was the calmest, most satisfying period of her life; Jason was no trouble to her, no inconvenience to the Squire, and not an object of interest to his boy, beyond the knowledge that he was to be called "father."

The thread of the Squire's life, strong as it seemed, snapped suddenly at last. In the early morning of an autumn day, Sarah, always up betimes, heard a strange babbling noise as she passed his door. She opened it, and went to his bedside, and saw that the "Shadow feared of man" had come.[9]

"Grandpa," she whispered, terror-struck.

He knew her, and with one trembling hand,—the other was paralyzed,—drew her face against his, and vainly tried to speak. His tongue was paralyzed also; tears burst from his dim eyes,—the only speech that was left him,—and they wrung her to the soul. She released herself and ran to the kitchen—Elsa was not yet down stairs—then to the barnyard for Cuth.

"My soul," said Cuth, rising from his milking-pail, when he saw her flying towards him, "what is it?"

"He is going, Cuth; run for the doctor."

"Mr. Auster?" stammered Cuth.

"Grandpa," she shrieked.

"It can't be; I've known him forty year. But I'll go. What do you think it is?"

"It is death."

Cuth shook his head, as he started on a swinging trot, and said to himself, "Numb palsy — I give him up." He stopped every person he met, without stopping himself, to say that the Squire had had a shock, and before Jason heard of it, it was spread through the town.

When Sarah went back, Elsa was busy making a fire.

"What upon earth ails you, Sarah Auster?" she exclaimed.

Sarah took her by the hand, and led her into the Squire's bedroom, and Elsa understood all.

"He'll last over to-day," she said presently; "see how well he breathes."

Sarah dropped on the floor beside him, and buried her face in the bedclothes. He began to babble again. Elsa slipped out and went up to Jason's room.

"Mr. Auster," she said, putting her head in at the door, "the Squire is struck with death."

"Death," he muttered, starting from a sound sleep.

"Easy though, almost as easy as your nap. The neighbors will be flocking in now. Can you dress Parke? I've got to go right down again, and Sarah won't think of anything, except her grandfather."

"What are the neighbors coming in for?"

"Don't be droll," she said, closing the door.

Jason dressed, and sat down by Parke's crib. He softly touched his beautiful hair, and put his finger inside his little hand, which closed upon it with a clinging grasp. He counted the network of delicate veins in his fair temples, and watched the tranquil motion of his white bosom. Then carefully covering him, he went down to the kitchen. The outside doors were already open, and people were lingering about and talking to each other in subdued voices.

"The doctor has come," said Elsa, motioning him toward the bedroom.

"Gilbert," said Jason, giving his first order, "go up stairs and watch Parke."

"Nothing can be done," he heard the doctor say as he entered the bedroom. Sarah's eyes were fixed on the Squire's face, and she made no reply to him.

"Why, Mrs. Auster," he continued, testily, "would you never be willing to part with him?"

"Sarah," said Jason, in a firm voice, that compelled her attention, "your grandfather is leaving life without suffering."

"He is going out like a candle," added the doctor, pinching his fingers together as if they were snuffers.

"No link now," she muttered; "and where is the other end of the chain, grandpa?"

The doctor rasped his chin, and looked at Jason, who wore a stolid expression.

"Come, Sarah," called Elsa, "come to breakfast, do. There's no use in putting off meals; they will come round, and they must be eaten. Come, now; the neighbors are here, longing to do something for you."

"Come," said Jason, raising her from her knees.

As she turned he met her eyes; there was a wild look in them, which stirred his pity. He made a motion as if to put his arm round her, but she glided by him, and went over to the table

alone. When she returned, Jason went up stairs to release Gilbert.
Parke was awake, and in high glee.

"Go away, father Jason," he screamed, "and let me dress
myself."

"Be good, for grandpa is sick."

"Then I am sick," he replied, getting into his crib again, and
shutting his eyes.

"Do you know that there are lots of people down stairs?"

"No," Parke answered, hopping out on one foot. "Tell me
about it, and you may dress me. But you can't wash my face; if
lots of people are here, I won't stop to have my face washed."

After he was dressed, he insisted on being taken down stairs
on Jason's shoulder, and having his breakfast handed up to him
on his perch, and tried to balance his plate on Jason's head.

"Where's my mother?" he asked; "there hasn't anybody kissed
me yet."

"Go to her," said his father; "she is in the bedroom."

Sarah heard the patter of his feet, and rose to lead him to the
bed. "Poor grandpa," she said.

"He isn't poor," said Parke. "Why don't he get up?"

The chintz bed-curtains, on which was printed a fox-chase,
in red and white, attracted him, as they had done a hundred
times. He put his hand to his mouth, and tooted in imitation of
the huntsmen, and cried "gee-up" to the galloping horses. The
Squire began to babble at the sound of his voice, which made him
turn away frightened, and beg his mother to let him go.

"Will you kiss grandpa once more?"

"No, not now, but to-morrow."

She put him down outside the door, and he ran back to Jason,
who amused him all day by whittling boats, animals, and uncouth
toys, with which they played together.

"Dear me," said Elsa, who was by no means melancholy, "how little that child realizes what is going on."

Jason smiled. "Would you have him howl?"

"Hadn't he ought to have a realizing sense of death?"

"Never, if possible."

At dusk the doctor pronounced the Squire's life to be ebbing fast; he would go before morning. Elsa immediately went all over the house and changed the order of the furniture. The chairs were placed in rows, and all small articles were moved into the closets. It was the third time, she soliloquized, that she had shoved things about for a funeral since she had been in the house; the first happened ten years ago, and was that of Sarah's mother, the wife of Osmond Parke, and if ever there was a creature ready to go, she was. "I ain't so mad," concluded Elsa, "as I was then. It did me good to hustle the furniture round, and wish it was that villain Osmond Parke, who was alive somewhere, we thought; though we hadn't seen him for years." Having finished her work, she closed the shutters on the front of the house, and opened wide all the doors. "If his old spirit," — she muttered, meaning the Squire's, — "wants to take a turn, to see if things are according to his ideas, he is welcome to do so." She then retired in a peaceful frame of mind, after having read some passages in the Bible, which reminded her of the vanity of the world, and contained the text, "What profit hath a man of all his labor which he taketh under the sun?"[10]

Cuth remained in the kitchen as a watcher; Jason took care of Parke, up stairs, and Sarah stayed alone with the Squire. She was tormented by irrelevant thoughts, which she constantly checked by a strained attention to his breath, which grew more and more difficult.

About four o'clock, he spoke clearly, but hurriedly, and without a motion, these words:

"It all comes to this, Sarah."

She bent over him, and he was dead.

For an instant, while she looked upon the calm face, from which Life had fled, and Death assumed its mask, she felt as if her soul was poised on the wings of the spirit going heavenward. It was the first and the last sublime moment of her life.

Suddenly she recollected that there were no more Parkes, and she felt a pang because she was a woman, and had been obliged to change her name.

"It comes to this," she repeated, "either way." She called softly to Cuth, and told him that it was over.

"I know it, marm, I know it," he answered. "Give me your hand." He shook it, patted her shoulder, and continued: "Go to your bed, marm; I've known him forty year, and I've a right to get him ready, and stay by him; and I am a-going to."

She yielded the wish.

The funeral took place in three days, in the forenoon. People came from far and near to see the burial of the last of his name. Cuth took a solemn pleasure in the occasion; he crammed the horses that brought the funeral guests with oats, and cursed Gilbert's mischief in exceeding the order he gave him to mark the carriages and harness, with their owners' names upon them in chalk. The spectators of the long funeral procession had the gratification of knowing that "Capt. Smith, A 1," rode in one of the carriages, and "Mr. Brown, B 2," in another, and so on through the line. Elsa in a lustrous black silk and blonde cap poured numberless cups of tea and coffee that day, and cut many slices of ham and loaf-cake. It was late in the afternoon before the house was emptied of visitors, and then a dreadful blank was felt which neither Jason nor Sarah could endure. She wrapped Parke in a shawl, and took him into the garden. Behind it, and beyond the orchard, a hill rose, whose side towards the town was shaded by a few tawny crooked cedars, and whose top was covered by a small grove of oaks and a brushy heap of rocks. Parke begged to go up there, and she carried him in her arms.

"Oh, the red water!" he cried, as she placed him on a rock, "and the red sky, mother. God is burning up, I am afraid."

"It is only the sunset, Parke," and she began to cry as she had not cried since the Squire died. She was unmindful of the beautiful bay, whose wide limits could be seen from the hill-top, — of the splendid western sky, of the red harvest moon rising in the gray east, of the swallows circling round the hill, of the faint columns of smoke ascending from the chimneys of the town, — unmindful even of Parke, who, regardless of her weeping, slipped down from the rock, and played among the fallen leaves. A cool wind came moaning round them, and the sky darkened; he began to count the stars, and there were not so many of them as there were tears on his mother's handkerchief. She wiped her eyes, caught him up, and said they must go back to supper. Elsa had it ready. Extra lamps were lighted and set on the table. There should be, she said, no gloomy corners that night for Sarah's eyes to wander in. She wished, though, that she had made Mrs. Rogers stay; she might have occupied that empty chair, and once occupied, its being set against the wall afterwards would not be noticed. Jason had not yet come in, but she insisted on serving tea; he could have his at any hour; he wouldn't remark whether it was cold or hot. She seemed to be over and in every dish, with a comfortable bustle which exhilarated Parke and soothed Sarah.

Jason was plodding the beach which skirted the south part of the town. As he watched the heaving waters creeping towards him in the moonlight, a thought of the Eternity which was eternally creeping towards men came to him.

"By my soul," he said, "it is beautiful, though."

He threw a pebble into the sea.

"As easy as that, a man sinks there. But if there is light, motion, color as there is here, I shall like Eternity."

CHAPTER IV

IIIIIIIIIIIIIIIIIIIIIIIIIIIIIIIIIIIIIIIIIIIIIIIIII

THE SQUIRE LEFT NO WILL. Sarah informed Jason of the fact when she felt obliged to call upon him for aid; until she did he asked no question concerning the property,—then he assumed the whole control of it. He was months in mastering its details. There were no debts, but it was widely scattered, and existed in a variety of forms; that part of it situated in Crest was the least productive, and therefore he sold it. This was considered as a thorough break-up in the town of the family interest, and Sarah winced more than once at his innovations; but believing in his plain sense, and that he was probably considering Parke's future, she compelled herself not to interfere. When he laid the schedule of what he had retained before her, and the amount of her income, derived principally from the iron-works at Copford, ten miles below Crest, and the tanyard at Millville, six miles above, she was astonished. It amounted to nine thousand a year.

"A hundred and fifty thousand dollars!" she exclaimed. "Just enough."

"The Squire did not know how much he was worth. I have sold all the shipping interest in Crest,—all the houses. You only own certain tracts of land here, which will be worth more by-and-by. You have fifty thousand dollars in money."

"I don't recollect of any Parkes having so much before. Of course, it will go to my Parke?"

She looked anxiously at him.

"Certainly, as it appears now, it is *all* yours, and his. How much shall I pay you for my board?"

"Nonsense."

"I have a few hundreds, what shall I do with them?"

She blushed, because she wished Parke and herself to owe him nothing.

"You will accept my labor, but not my money?"

"You are my husband."

"Because I have given you an heir?"

"If you wish to be odd, Jason, I cannot prevent it."

"Your heir, not mine."

"By the name of Auster."

The expression with which she uttered the name made him turn white. From that time he was proud enough never to interpose his paternal feelings between her and his child. Instead, therefore, of his being a bond of unity, he was the means of an anomalous condition, which is not supposed to exist between man and wife, where there are children.

To all appearance the family flourished and were happy. But one day, the day that Parke was nine years old, Sarah beheld, "sitting at the king's gate,"[11] her cousin and co-heir, Osmond Luce, who had been absent twelve years. He was not alone; a strange-looking little girl came with him—named Philippa.

Day to be remembered in the annals of Sarah's experiences—as well remembered as the day he left his grandfather's house!

"Of course," were his first words, "I am foolish in expecting to see my grandfather."

She withdrew her hand from his grasp, and mechanically resumed her seat; her mouth moved as if she was in a spasm.

"He is dead," he continued.

"Five years ago," she made out to say.

"And I have been as good as dead twelve years."

"No, not as good," she said, the lustre of her black eyes returning.

"Ha, I recognize my native air."

"He died without a thought of you; he had forgotten you, I believe, and forgotten all your claims."

"So much the better for him. Sarah, Sarah, I have come thousands of miles with this girl,—she is mine,—to leave her on ancestral ground. Her mother is dead. Will you keep her?"

"Papa," interposed Philippa, "will you allow me to go about this funny house?"

"Go anywhere," he said, and opened the door for her.

Philippa immediately mounted the wide stairs, and tried to open the door of the great clock, which stood on the landing in the middle of the flight.

"Take care," cried a voice above her, "the pigeon may fly out."

"What boy are you?" she asked, stretching her slender neck to get a glimpse of him.

"Don't you know me? I am Parke; this house is mine."

"I have come to live in it."

He descended slowly, looking intently at her.

When he stood beside her, she said, "Tell me about the pigeon."

"I will; but I don't think you are handsome."

"You are, indeed, you are."

They sat down on the stair in front of the clock, and after taking in his hands her braids of hair, and saying how yellow they were, he told her that one day, when the clock was open, and Elsa was going to wind it, a pigeon flew in from the window into the clock, and that it still lived there.

"That is all nonsense," she commented.

"It makes a noise before the clock strikes, and I say it is there."

"What does it get to eat?"

"Nothing."

"Then it starved to death long ago," she said triumphantly. "Why don't you have it stuffed? I've got a stuffed macaw."

"You'd better go home," Parke said.

"I can't."

"Must you stay?"

"We came with an awful trunk; the coachman said 'By vum,' when he put it by the gate."

"Let us go and see it."

They hopped out amicably, and Jason found them on the top of the trunk deep in conversation when he came home to supper.

"What little girl is this?" he asked kindly.

"I didn't ask," Parke answered, "but she has come to stay."

"You had better go in; it is growing chilly."

"If I choose to go in, I shall," replied Parke in the mildest, most indifferent of voices. Philippa looked at them both in astonishment.

"I will go with you, sir," she said, offering her hand.

Parke followed them at once to the parlor. It was dark there, and perhaps Jason did not see Sarah's compressed lips, nor the red spot on her cheeks; but he divined who the stranger was before she introduced him.

"I am the prodigal son, Mr. Auster," he said; "but you won't trouble yourself about the fatted calf."[12]

"No trouble," replied Jason, "it is the time of year for veal."

He said this so seriously, that Osmond looked at him attentively.

"Mother," said Parke, "this little girl flew in as the pigeon did, but we must feed her."

"Yes, or she will starve," she said, with a harsh attempt at pleasantry which made Jason feel as if a grater had passed over his nerves. "And I must attend to the supper, as Elsa will go into a tantrum now."

She went to her room first, however, and looked at herself in the glass.

"Oh, I see how changed I am," she said with a touch of womanly regret; "how unbecoming light dresses are to me. I should be dressed in mourning; yes, yes, in black from head to foot. What has he got a child for? How can I bear it? And it has not come into Jason's head, how much poorer we are than we were this morning!"

"What a handsome boy!" exclaimed Osmond, as soon as the door had closed on her. "Come here, you rascal."

"I do not think that I am a rascal," answered Parke; "but here I am."

He climbed up on Osmond's knee, and looked him frankly in the face. They were of the same race. Osmond, though sunburnt, hardened, coarse, stamped with lines that spoke a wasting history, bore a wonderful resemblance to the boy.

"And his name," said Jason, "is Parke."

Osmond looked at him again closely.

"Where could Sarah have picked up that man?" he thought.

"I like you," Parke declared, satisfied with his inspection.

Osmond kissed him twice, and smiled for the first time since he entered the house.

Jason was looking at Philippa. When her father kissed Parke, she moved her eyes as if seeking to escape something painful. Jason went to her quietly, removed her bonnet, unpinned her brightly-flowered shawl whose deep fringe had trailed in the dirt, and placed her upon the sofa.

"I came here to stay once too," he whispered.

"Cuth and Elsa," said Osmond, starting up — "I must see them, the old souls. I know where they are."

He banged the door behind him, and passed through the rooms whistling a lively air.

"That whistle," said Jason to himself, "is a wind of doctrine."[13]

"The Everlasting!" screamed Elsa, when Osmond found her, "I knew you would come back. Now we are in a mux. What will folks say?"

"Never mind, I am going again."

"What did Sarah say, Osmond? You have seen her."

"Guess."

She shook her head.

"Blood may be thicker than water, and it may not; *I* ain't any judge." And then she sobbed.

"What has happened in the last dozen years? Tell me, old girl," he demanded, carefully wiping her eyes.

"Haven't had any news since Mr. Auster came to town, and the Squire died, till this very minute."

"I did not expect his death — he was so hale — and the Parkes live long, you know."

"You did not expect to find Sarah married, either."

He laughed.

"I am glad she is married, though," she continued, with a wrathful look. "You are as much like Satan as ever."

"You are not glad, and as for Satan —"

"If here ain't Osmond Luce!" she cried, for Sarah came in with a jar of preserves. "I thought I should have fainted when I saw him."

"Elsa is the same, Osmond," said Sarah.

"Not a day older. She is a system of wires made of steel, and won't rust. Where is Cuth? Shall I find him in the yard?" Elsa caught him, to pick some threads from his coat, and then she brushed it.

"Where's your baggage?" she asked.

"In the parlor, talking with Cousin Jason."

"Oh Lord! You haven't come with a wife?"

"Ask Sarah," and he rushed out.

"He has brought his daughter to live with us."

"Oh Lord, what an imbezzlement! But she has a right here —no mistake in it, and I'll see to her."

"Thank you."

"How he favors the Parkes! He wants the Parke money, I suppose."

Sarah's eyes flashed, and her shining black ringlets set up a dance round her forehead.

"Nothing like family affection. Oh pest and the deuce take this teapot nose, it is choked with tea-grounds," continued Elsa, not appearing to notice Sarah, who said, after a moment's silence, putting the jar on the table with a hand which Elsa saw was trembling, "These grapes are for tea."

"The fathers haven't eaten the grapes this time," said Elsa, turning the jar round in her hands, after Sarah had gone, "to set the children's teeth on edge.[14] Sarah has got fangs, fangs, I tell you," tapping the jar sharply; "and yet she remembers that Osmond liked grape preserves!"

Cuth was at the wood-pile. Osmond went up behind him, and said, "Old Cuth, how are you?"

For a moment Cuth did not stir, then he turned, and said, "Curse you, if you would go, why didn't you stay? What are you here for?"

"Your blessing, Cuth."

"You had that, you dog, along with the Squire's."

Osmond offered him some plug tobacco, which he seized, threw into his mouth, and seated himself on a log.

"You've come for something," he said, spitting furiously.

"For half of this wood-pile, and half of you, Cuth."

Cuth growled, spit high in the air, and swore a deep oath.

"What has Auster done?" Osmond asked abruptly.

"What you would never have done, if you had stayed here a hundred years. How have you passed your time?"

"In riotous living, Cuth."

"Well, Auster has passed his in no living at all. Tell me some of your adventures," and Cuth's shaggy eyebrows lifted themselves above a savage sparkle in his eyes.

"Have you been in the Spanish main?"[15]

Osmond laughed so loud, that Cuth, disconcerted, turned to the wood-pile, and began to lay the sticks upon it with careful precision.

"I always thought you were mad, Cuth, and now I know it. How have your passions stood this sort of thing so long?"

"The Squire pared my heels, and pared my toes, and cut out my tongue, and I loved him."

"Ah, I never could do as he did."

"In a measure, you are stormy though, raging and raving, as you always were, I take it; by my own mind just now, I take it so."

"Cuth," said Osmond absently, "I have brought my daughter here. Do you think that the paring-the-heels-and-toes system died with my grandfather?"

"Why, have ye now, Osmond? well, I like that. The child is here, hey? Sarah Parke is sharp, but she don't bind folks to her; and she is too likely a woman to be afraid of,—or—to be, to be—"

"Loved," added Osmond.

Before he was called to supper, Cuth had given him so much information concerning Jason and the life of the family, that there was little left for him to learn.

The taste of the grapes to Osmond, was the link between what seemed to be two dreams; that of having been in Crest, a boy, and the one of being there now, a man. A wild feeling of loss and home-sickness swept over him, and then, like a ship in a rough sea, whose prow rises to meet the breakers, he overrode the feeling with a determined will. Sarah watched him with a restless, furtive eye, which betrayed to him her unquiet soul.

"Not one of you have asked how long I intend to stay!" he exclaimed.

The bread on the way to Philippa's mouth was arrested. A loaf of cake was near Jason's hand; he cut it in two with one blow and offered the plate to Osmond.

"Elsa," he said, with a smile, and taking a bit, "I never thought you would have allegorical cake. Will you share in it, Sarah?"

She understood it, and, with a bitter look at Jason, answered, "Not just now."

"None of your foreign lingo here," cried Elsa; "I'll warrant you haven't tasted such cake since you left."

"None like this, so sweet, so good," said Osmond in a deep voice, and, with a gesture towards Jason, "has been offered me."

"Perhaps Philippa would like some," said Sarah; "she has your taste, Osmond, undoubtedly."

"Perhaps she would," he cried, a light coming into his face, "perhaps she would; 'I thank thee, Jew.'"[16]

But Philippa declined the cake, and patiently resumed her bread. She was accustomed to her father's vagaries; Elsa seemed to recall them too, and asked him if he was as fond of his "reading books" as he used to be.

Jason proposed cigars after supper, and he, with Osmond, started on a walk.

"Philippa is an outlandish name," said Sarah, still at the table. "How old are you?"

"Ten years."

"Do you expect to be contented here?"

Philippa shrugged her shoulders, and fixed her brown eyes upon Sarah, who could not repress a thrill of irritation.

"Philippa, Ippa, Ippa, Philippa," Parke sang.

"Parke," ordered Sarah, "go to bed."

"Not yet," continuing his song, "Ippa, Ippa, I must nip her."

"Ippa" smiled, and pushing from her ear her yellow curls, offered it to him. "You may nip it if you like."

"I am going to play with you for a while," he said, accepting her offer; "but you must play as I say."

"Go into the kitchen, then," Sarah begged.

"Along with you," said Elsa.

The evening wore on, and Jason and Osmond did not return. Sarah was curious enough to muffle herself in a shawl, and dash out to Jason's office down the street to see if there was a light there. The rays of a lamp streamed from a hole in the paper window-curtain; she hesitated a moment, then went forward and looked through it. Jason was smoking a short clay pipe. His hat was pushed back from his forehead, and he was tilting on two legs of his chair; now and then with a ruler he struck at and turned over the pages of a ledger, which was on the desk before him. His appearance fascinated her, so much depended with him, if he but willed so! While she devoured his face, attitude, motions, she was gauging the depth of his moral nature. "We never know what we are till we are tried," she reasoned for him, in her mad hope that his conscience was solving a problem which could not trouble hers. "We can't make nice distinctions always. What is duty in such a case? Haven't we every right to what we have so long cared for, and he neglected? *I* would punish him." Osmond, who was beyond her vision, spoke; she could not hear what he said, but she saw a frank smile spread over Jason's countenance.

"I might have known," she thought, "that Osmond would strike at the heart of the business at once; and I am a fool to have dreamed that he would not turn Jason round his little finger."

She would not let her anger admit that his honesty was proof against any temptation, or rather, that temptation could never approach him. She turned away with a step that stirred the gravel on the walk, and made Osmond listen.

"Somebody going by," remarked Jason, observing his attention.

The front door was ajar, as she had left it, and she believed that she had not been missed. Parke had gone to bed, probably, under Elsa's supervision; the house was too still for him to be awake. But the girl!—no arrangement had been made for her. It struck her, then, that she would rather have Philippa under her eye, as a hostage. Osmond might not cut and thrust so liberally, with his plans and wishes, so long as she should remain in Crest.

"Well," said Elsa, "I have waited to hear where Philippa is to be put, till her eyes are glued together with sleep."

"Keep her with you to-night."

"She has a kind of way of saying prayers. I suppose she

thought she wasn't going to bed, and that she had better mum 'em in her chair, and sleep there. She ain't one bit like her father. I believe she is a Roman Catholic myself."

"Don't notice it, Elsa, if she is; she won't be one long with me."

"Where are they?" asked Elsa, abruptly. "At it, I conclude."

"No matter where they are," Sarah replied, with a stamp of her foot.

Elsa slammed the door for a retort, and vanished.

Jason lit the lamp in his office, exchanged a little commonplace talk with Osmond, and then became silent.

Osmond lit another cigar, which he took from a Manilla case, and asked, "How much was the old man worth?"

"His estate is now worth a hundred and fifty thousand dollars."

"I had no idea of so much."

"I have bettered it, since I took it in my hands."

"You might have cheated me like the devil."

Jason tapped a row of books in his desk.

"Sarah has supposed you would not return; I thought you might. Look at these."

"Do you mean to say that my half is ready?"

"Why not?"

"I might have been a magnate here, if my grandfather had not treated me as a boy," said Osmond irrelevantly, for Jason had so astonished him that he hardly knew what to say.

"You were a boy when you left him," said Jason, gently. "*I* was a man when I entered the family, and yet he never trusted any thing to me."

"I vow to God, if it were not for Philippa, I would give you every dollar that may be mine; then"—he stopped, for something in Jason's face struck him. "Sarah would not have it so," he resumed. "She must have Nemesis, though."[17]

"Who is that?"

"A relation of the owner of that sword which was suspended by a hair over the head of one of the ancients."[18]

"Cut it," said Jason, looking up as if he saw the sword in the air.

"I decided to-night to renounce my claim here, and give Philippa all my rights; having done this, I shall cut my stick; did you mean that? Will you be her guardian?"

"Yes. Why did you bring her here?"

"From mixed motives. I will confide to you, however, that she is an obstacle in my way of life, and that I have never felt a strong interest in her. I have studied out the means of happiness for her notwithstanding. She will be happy here; hers is no Southern nature; she belongs to the North."

"Well," said Jason, thoughtfully, "she is one of the family."

"And will hold her own sooner or later. I shall plant a few ideas in her brain which will take root, and in time bear fruit."

"There will be nothing for me to do."

"Who knows how much? I should have made a different arrangement, had I found you a different man. Excuse me, I shall not find a man I dare be so frank with again;—how came you and Sarah to marry?"

Jason turned white, and looked up into the air again.

"I'll think about it, and let you know," he answered, presently.

"Cousin Jason, you are a trump. Now about your fees, or your salary, or salvage, or commission, whatever you may please to call the emolument of guardianship."

The preliminaries were settled in a moment, and Osmond proposed a walk round the town. His memory was still green, he said, as they passed through the silent streets, and he recounted boyish episodes, which let Jason into the secret of his character. The story of his later life was also told, and his listener heard an experience, so different from his own, related as a matter of course in the history of men's lives, that he felt his past had been but a sleep-walking. Osmond's tongue was like a wedge, hard, insinuating, forcible; in spite of Jason's impassibility it made its cleaving way into undisturbed recesses, which being once invaded might prove him a man like other men.

Osmond remained a few days only. He made what he called the hereditary tour, — that of the old burying-ground, and a few visits to his grandfather's friends, but renewed none of his own early associations. He could not escape, however, the spirit of the past which Sarah evoked for him. The fire burned on the same altar which he refused to sacrifice upon years ago, where he might have flung himself and been consumed. Hatred and love were equally probable passions between such temperaments, and equally fatal. Her manner was so stinging, so bitter and excited towards him, his so cool, daring, watchful, and resolute towards her, that they were obliged to be only mindful of each other; even Philippa, who might have been tossed from one to the other, like a bone between hungry dogs, was neglected. Jason had given her an account of his business interview with Osmond, but she made no comments upon it, either to him or to Osmond. There was a squareness in Jason's way of setting forth facts which made her distrust her influence with him. Osmond was satisfied that she had at once acquiesced in Jason's guardianship, and so Philippa was ignored. The day he left he was closeted with her for a long time; she shed no tears when he departed, but Parke cried in his arms, and begged him, with kisses, to come again. Osmond promised, with a significant look at Sarah, to be with them in ten years, for by that time there would be questions to ask which he would be old enough to answer. He demanded of Cuth and Elsa that they should live till then, and rode away with a careless ease which made Sarah grind her teeth and Jason smile.

"He sows to the wind," said Elsa, "and always will."

"And we reap the whirlwind,"[19] said Sarah, looking at Philippa.

"The wind don't blow," cried Parke, looking out of the window.

"I wish it did," said Philippa, whistling, as she had heard the sailors whistle at sea; "I wish a hurricane would come this way."

If the faculty to detect the principle which directs the march of circumstances had been given to Jason, it is probable that his history would be impossible; he would have rendered it nugatory from the moment that Osmond Luce returned to Crest.

CHAPTER V

JUST BEFORE OSMOND'S VISIT, Jason, at Sarah's request, drew a plan for the alteration and improvement of the old house; she approved it, and he made a contract with John Davis to do the work. But after Osmond's departure she informed Jason that she had changed her mind, and thought the house was well enough as it was. He insisted that the contract must be fulfilled, and for the first time there was a positive disagreement between them; but he carried the point, and the workmen commenced operations.

The old ceilings, the old partitions, and the old windows were removed, and the foundation raised, in order to make a terrace in front for shrubs and flowers, and a flight of granite steps. The house was so changed that nothing reminded the family of its previous shape, except the wainscoting in the west parlor, and the broad brick hearth in the kitchen.

"Thankful to the Lord for these remnants," Elsa exclaimed, who partook of Sarah's ill-humor without knowing why. Jason tried to console her by promising that the yard below the terrace should not be touched.

"As if any thing could be done there with hammer and chisel," she said, scornfully. "I'd like to see John Parke's row of balsam-firs cut down."

"Why did he plant one row to the east, and none elsewhere?"

"To make it lonesome, and shut out the houses down the street, I imagine. I have heard he was half crazy; but he was the only one of the family who ever planted trees. When I used to say to the Squire that he'd better plant some, he'd answer that he should not live to enjoy their shade, and would not do it."

While the confusion and disorder of rebuilding lasted Jason and the children were companions. He resumed chisel and plane with an avidity which attracted Parke, and sent him to his mother to ask if his father were a real carpenter. Philippa learned the fact through John Davis; she overheard him say that he thought it a pity so good a workman as Jason should be spoiled, all for the sake of the very institutions he had once gone against; he could see, though, that a man in the downs had better try the ups of life, before he decided that high and low were only empty names. Philippa silently wondered at what she had heard, and was so watchful of Jason at his work, that he could not help, at last, being watchful of her in return. One day, when Parke, tired of the shavings, the blocks, and the racket, had gone to ride with Sarah, Jason broke the silence which had been maintained between Philippa and himself. He was planing a long board, and she was walking behind him, picking up the best curled shavings. He looked back and said, "You are my ward; if you want any thing you must ask me for it."

She dropped her apronful of shavings and answered, "My father told me that I was your ward; but he said I was not to ask for any thing till I grew up. Do you think I am growing?"

He turned entirely round, looked at her, took a measuring-rule, and kneeling before her, measured her length.

"Not a mite," he answered, seriously; "but we will keep account hereafter of your inches. At present you are a very small girl indeed."

"And ugly, too."

"Who said so?"

"Parke. Can you make him ashamed for saying so?"

The question made him reflect on the influence his non-interference with Parke might have, and how much it might affect his guardianship, and he instantly determined to exercise no authority with her beyond the management of her money; there should be no difference shown by him in his treatment of the children. The price of existence with the Parkes must be an eternal silence.

He threw down the rule with a slight laugh, took up his plane, and while feeling its edge said, "Little boys of nine forget politeness now and then; he won't say it again."

"But it was true."

"Why should he be ashamed of speaking the truth, then?"

"I thought you might know he said so, and not let him hurt me."

"I only know how to drive the plane, the hammer, and the saw,—my brothers."

"Then you are not spoiled," she said, remembering John Davis's remarks.

"I don't know about that," he answered, wondering what she meant, but not choosing to ask, for he thought he had said enough.

The summer was ended before the house was done. Jason made over the premises to Sarah, but from some unaccountable whim she refused to buy any thing new. The old furniture was put in the new rooms, and the old aspect was renewed as much as possible. Then she took Philippa in hand to train: all the indulgences that she lacked, at Philippa's age, Philippa was to lack; she should be taught to be useful, not to enjoy herself after any fashion of her own. What had been right for herself, Sarah said, must be right for Philippa, whether it suited or not.

37

"The times," remonstrated Elsa, with whom she discussed the subject, "are different from what they were when you were a child; besides, you must call to mind that she has got an independent fortune; you hadn't, you know."

She was not to be spoiled on that account, Sarah replied, and money or no money, she must be taught a sense of duty, and the practice of it. So Philippa went through a course of dish-towel hemming, patchwork, fine stitching, knitting, muslin work, counting spoons and linen, setting the table, and clearing it, keeping chairs at the right angles, airing rooms, closets, clothes, and furniture, and taking care of her own room, all of which was intensely disagreeable to her. She was sent to school regularly, and made to give Saturday afternoon entertainments to her schoolmates, and return their visits, which was never a source of enjoyment. In short, she was confined to a system as rigid as that of the penitentiary, with one exception—liberty to associate with Parke, and share his pleasures as he saw fit. To give Sarah her due, she was just towards Philippa in all that pertained to her material welfare; her health was guarded, she was not subjected to fatigue and exposure—her associations were limited to the orthodox standard, and she was as one of the family. But Philippa never exposed to her the tumults of childhood, its fears, its doubts, hopes and wishes. Except for a demeanor which indicated a persistent will, and the display of a peculiar frankness when pushed too hard, she appeared to be a docile child; not particularly pleasing or interesting, but quiet and self-contained. The most noticeable fact in her biography for several years was a fever, which attacked her every summer, and left her gaunt and sallow for months after. And although Sarah watched and tended her in these illnesses, and fretted over them, she never remembered being kissed or smiled upon, or having her hand pressed with an affectionate grasp. Sarah hated her. Was it because of her hate that she allowed herself no escape from the performance of every external duty? Or did she believe that it was the spirit, not the letter, which killed? Could she have washed her hands of Philippa's life and rights, would she have done so? Or would she, from some strange necessity in her nature, still prefer to keep her as her familiar demon?

The reflection of Parke's serene, joyous life spread over Philippa's, and prevented her from being miserable. At once he had engaged her affection, and her devotion to him was as unqualified as his mother's. He was beautiful; his temper was perfect, and his manners were winning. As he grew older, the mould of his childish character enlarged, but did not change. His good-humor, his facility to discover means of enjoyment, his perpetual, pleasant, gentle activity, were delightful. His atmosphere kindled all who entered it into brightness, and created a desire to shine as he would shine. He loved truth, was devoid of suspicion, and took it for granted that men and women were what they appeared to be. Fact held the place in his nature which depth occupied in Jason's, and a becoming way of self-gratification contrasted with Sarah's abnegation of pleasure. He had a cool head, a cooler heart, but a tender disposition, and with all these traits lay hidden in his soul the capacity for a terrible abandonment to the passions.

In the course of time it began to be observed by Jason's business acquaintances that he entered into no speculations, and made no contracts. They said among themselves that he must be intending to retire, and live upon his income, which was rated as very large. They could not guess, of course, the truth. He decided that for himself the little he had made since his marriage was enough, and that he would not risk again either Parke's or Philippa's money. He was determined that when they came of age their incomes should be equal. There never should be an issue regarding the Squire's property, as far as he was concerned; if it depreciated naturally, the heirs must bear the loss equally. Whether he had a troubled, mist-like vision in his mind respecting Sarah, if any question of loss should come up between them; or whether he had as dim a remembrance of his socialistic principles; whatever the cause, he carried out his plan with the tenacity of a man who has but one idea at a time, and so tied up the property beyond his control, that, morally speaking, he was able to consider himself as outside of the family. From this time of mental independence the habits of his life changed. In order to continue his out-of-door life he took up gunning and fishing, and spent days in the woods, and days on the sea, but he rarely brought home any game or fish. With his dogs he beat the dense oak and pine woods which bordered Crest, and acquired an occult love for every tree he passed under. In his two-masted, sharp-hulled boat, he coasted the shores of the bay, or pushed out beyond the islands across its mouth, and followed the trackless paths of ships that went down the great deep, and the sea became one of his deities.

The onus of bringing up the children, of sustaining their position, and the claims of society, he left to Sarah, who bore the burden becomingly. She was a friend to the poor and the aged, because it was the custom of the family, and she continued the time-honored gifts of salves, cordials, and food for the sick. She was a good member of the upper class, for she dressed handsomely, entertained handsomely, and was never inconveniently intimate with it. Without a profound comprehension of the spiritual, devoid of pious aspirations, she was a believer in the tenets of the Congregational Church, and had joined it a year before

her marriage. She was full of the business of religion, and ministers were under her especial patronage. With all her prestige, all
her influence, she was not loved abroad, nor envied; her want of
softness, her shrill laugh, her cold words, the restless expression
in her black eyes and thin lips, and her repellant manner, made
people afraid of her.

The years advanced through Parke and Philippa's childhood,
and brought Sarah and Jason to the borders of middle age with
a monotony which concealed the swiftness of their flight, and
kept in check that prescience of change and loss which generally
hovers over the mind.

CHAPTER VI

||||||||||||||||||||||||||||||||||||||||||||||||

"THE SNOW-FLOWERS SHAKE with the cold," said Elsa, "and the apple-blossoms are all of a didder this afternoon. It's more like fall than spring, and here we are on the edge of summer."

"Have you been out?" inquired Sarah, looking at her watch.

"I've taken the round of the fences for the first time this year. I tell you that Cuth is failing; he don't attend to the garden as he used to."

"Don't you perceive that we are all growing old?" Sarah asked maliciously, but Elsa turned the subject.

"Philippa will be in by six, won't she?" she inquired.

"I suppose so."

"And walk down from the dépôt?"

"Why not?"

"Oh, nothing; only it seemed to me, as she has been gone two years, somebody might have waited upon her for once."

"We might have had an oration, and banners, beer and gingerbread, if you had spoken in time. At all events, you could have asked Cuth to put the horse in the chaise, and drive up for her. Gilbert must be sent up with the wagon for her baggage."

"I should have thought that Mr. Auster would have staid at home to-day."

"He forgot that she was coming, I dare say, though her bills only came in yesterday—heavy ones, too; but I trust that the boarding-school business is over now."

"She would go, you remember, as soon as Parke left for college; of all the grit I ever saw, she was the grittiest. When you told her that it was folly for her to think of going, she surprised me even. Are Parke's bills heavy, too?"

Sarah looked at Elsa with a dark face, for it seemed as if she were trying to exasperate her; but the old woman's countenance was imperturbable; her round cheeks, rosy as winter apples, glistened provokingly. Sarah could have snapped her fingers against them with pleasure, or scratched the smooth, glassy enamel of her shining eyes, that were made to penetrate, not to be penetrated.

"A man's bills are different," Sarah answered calmly, for after all she loved Elsa.

"A man! what business has he to play the man? I could trot him on my knee this minute."

"You have done so often enough when he was a troublesome child."

"I have; I never begrudged my time, when I took care of him. Well, he has grown up worth looking at. Would you like some toast, Sarah? You are not very well?"

"Oh yes, I am; but I do not object to toast."

Elsa proposed attending to it immediately, but instead of going to the kitchen, she went to the back stairs where she had deposited a branch of apple-blossoms, carried it to Philippa's chamber, and put it in a mug of old transparent china decorated with a theatrical shepherdess in a curled wig that had belonged to the Squire's first wife. Stepping back to observe its effect, she mentally remarked, that it was nine years ago this very month since Philippa came to Crest, and that time had not changed Sarah for the better. Time, she supposed, brought healing on his wings; it was not so always, for something dropped from them like corrosive sublimate in its effect, when he passed over certain heads. Crossing the room on tiptoe, as if she saw and avoided those venomous fallen drops, she opened the blind of a western window, and looked out. No sunbeam streamed past her; but the light of a purple sky broke along the dark walls. The woods, which circled half the west, were still piebald with the hues of a late spring—pale green, brown, and dingy red, and vast purple clouds, furrowed like the sea before the town, hung over the house.

"If I should die the death of the righteous," she muttered, "I could not say that I thought this weather was what the Lord ought to send. It gives me the creeps."

She turned from the window without observing Philippa, who was walking towards the house, in a green shawl which brought her in strong relief against the slaty sky. Her own window was scanned first, and then she looked at the front door, but it was closed; no one was awaiting her. As she entered the hall, leisurely untying her bonnet, Sarah, who heard her footsteps, dropped her work and rose to meet her with an extended hand. Philippa took it, and an automatic movement passed between them, which was, in meaning, a chapter in the biography of their relationship.

"Why, Philippa!" said Sarah, with a smile which did not unclose her lips, "you have grown a head taller. Your dresses must be all too short."

Philippa tossed her foot out from the edge of her skirt, and said: "I crouch when it is necessary. Are you well, Cousin Sarah Auster? Where is Jason? When did you hear from Parke? How is Elsa?"

Elsa rushed in, crying: "Good for nothing girl, you might have come home before. *I* wanted you. You are a little better looking; hope you have got over being yellow; guess you have at last. How are you? I am not fit for much this spring. I'll take

44

your things. Gilbert has gone for your trunks. Gilbert's wife has got a baby. She asked me if she might name it Philippa; I told her she had better name it Gilippa—you could make it a present any way—and she was mad with me. You've got on your old black silk, haven't you? it is tattered and torn. Did you know that we had a new minister, all shaven and shorn? You are eighteen now. Your father will be thirty-eight next month, won't he, Sarah?"

"What is the matter with your tongue, Elsa?" she asked; "I am too confused with it to answer your questions."

"Elsa, you are the only handsome old woman I have seen since I left you," said Philippa. "I am glad to be where you are."

"Questions and all, hey? But here is Mr. Auster."

"So you came, Philippa," said Jason, "before I could beat up the harbor. I expected to be at the dépôt for you."

She advanced to shake hands with him, but he looked so awkward when she reached him, that she was sorry she had made the attempt. Still, she felt that his manner was not unfriendly. He made an effort to converse with her, but it was an evident relief to him when Elsa summoned them to tea.

When Philippa's trunks arrived, she went to her chamber and commenced unpacking. An hour after she was interrupted by Sarah, who came to say that there was company at Mrs. Rogers's that evening, and to inquire whether she would go for a while.

"It is too late to dress, and I am shabby any way," she answered.

"Our new minister will be there. Everbody will be asking about you, and Mrs. Rogers will feel hurt if you refuse to go to her house."

"Very well, I will go then to her."

"Shake out those dresses, and let me see the condition they are in."

Philippa complied, and Sarah gave them a close examination, and accused her of carelessness and extravagance, and begged to know if it was impossible for her to be a credit to the family.

"Credit!" echoed Philippa, "I don't like that word, and do not mean that it shall be used, as far as relates to me. As for carelessness, to please you, I'll amend; as for extravagance, I have absolute faith in my own money."

"Did you learn that at school?"

"From one of the family preceptors — my father, Osmond Luce. I only mention my faith in self-defence."

Sarah threw down the dress she had in her hand, and left the chamber. Meeting Jason in the hall, she said, excitedly, "We have hatched a cockatrice."[20]

"We! Who?"

"Philippa."

Jason changed his mind about going out, and returned to the parlor, where he took a chair and ruminated. When Philippa came in, ready for the party, he raised his eyes and scrutinized her sharply, and found himself wondering whether all cockatrices had pale yellow hair that looked as if about to float into the air like the down of flowers. There was something strange in those speckled eyes, though!

She wondered what he was so abstractedly staring at.

"Are you a cockatrice?" he asked, suddenly.

Sarah opened the door, ready also, and Philippa turned a grave look towards her, with an expression which conveyed to him that she knew the source he had derived his question from.

"What now?" asked Sarah, contemptuously. "What makes you theatrical?"

"Are you a cockatrice?" Jason repeated.

"Yes," said Philippa, "I am."

The cold sea-wind blew round them as they walked down the street, leaving Jason still in the parlor. The monotonous fall of the waves on the rocky beach in the distance sounded in Philippa's ears like the old march to which she had stepped through life beside Sarah. When they reached the row of weeping-willows before Mrs. Rogers's door, she said:

"Why put ideas in Jason's head that belong to you, Sarah?"

Sarah made no reply.

"Tell me, upon your honor," and Philippa stopped here, "whether my father was guilty of any fraud or act which should deprive him or myself of our rights?"

"Let go my shawl, Philippa Luce; your father must answer for himself, and so shall you."

"Once for all, Cousin Sarah, give me the information I ask for, or I shall compel Jason to give it to me."

"Have you got a pistol about you," sneered Sarah, "to enforce your demand?"

Philippa gently shook the shawl in her grasp, but Sarah felt as if she was in a vice of steel. She thought of a diversion—a piece of cunning—which was effectual.

"If Parke saw you, your hand would fall paralyzed. Philippa, let go the shawl."

"You are right," she replied. "But I know what you only could say because you refuse to speak. I am satisfied concerning my father."

Sarah gave a loud knock on the door, which brought Mrs. Rogers immediately.

"Why didn't you come right in? I am no hand at ceremony, you know. Is this Philippa? How do you do, my dear? Welcome home. Take off your things, and walk in the parlor. The company are all here."

She untied Philippa's bonnet and smoothed her hair. "Pretty enough," she said, "but you don't favor your father a bit."

"How is Sam?" Philippa asked, smiling brightly, for her heart was warmed by Mrs. Rogers's cordial welcome.

"Sam's to sea; I guess he'll be gladder than ever to get home. You are his favorite, you know."

"I shall visit you often till he comes."

"So do; I am a lonesome old thing. Parke used to come, especially when Sam was here, and I miss him too."

She led the way, and at the parlor door introduced, in a loud voice, "Mrs. Auster and Philippa Luce, just come home." There was a general movement, as if a new and unexpected element was admitted, which subsiding, the conversation began again, but with a forced tone, as if the talkers felt a critic had arrived. But Mrs. Rogers, to whom "kings and potentates," to use her own expression, "were no more than just so many worms," broke the chill, with her loud, cheerful voice and comfortable manner, by saying, "We were just talking, Mrs. Auster, about having the pulpit new covered—the old red velvet is in rags, for it has not been changed since the meeting-house was built—and what color we should have. I am in favor of green, on account of its being a good color for weak eyes, you know."

Sarah looked towards a young man of composed mien, who was twisting his watch-key, and smiled when she met his eye. When an opportunity occurred, he took a seat beside her, and asked if she believed that "a minister had the rights of a man." "Mr. Ritchings must remember," she answered, "that Mrs. Rogers was something of a fool, though a good-natured one, and that she had endeavored to adapt her conversation to the taste of the company, which consisted of the members of the church." He sighed, and with an eye wandering in Philippa's direction, said, "They make me tired of it sometimes. Is that your ward, Miss Luce?"

"It is."

"She has a remarkable face."

"I never thought so," and Sarah glanced towards her. "But perhaps she has a peculiar expression. What did you think of Deacon Blair's party?"

"It was just like this. Introduce me to Miss Luce, will you—if I may ask the favor?"

She beckoned to Philippa, who was obliged to betray the shortness of her dress, for there was a great space in the middle of the room to cross, but betrayed no confusion. She bowed coolly, and took the chair which he offered her. He blushed as he asked her some trivial question about coming home, and Sarah felt annoyed.

"Plum, pound, and sponge," interrupted Mrs. Rogers, presenting a piled-up plate of cake. "Philippa, you know what my cake is. I'll warrant you did not get better at boarding-school."

"I did not, indeed," she answered, taking a large piece.

"Ministers," Mrs. Rogers continued, "are fondest of plum-cake."

"How much should a young one eat?" Mr. Ritchings asked.

"You can eat as much of *my* cake as you please, for it is made wholesome."

Sarah joined another group, while Mr. Ritchings and Philippa were deciding on the merits of the cake, but she could not help looking in that direction occasionally. A thought that Philippa might be considered attractive, presented itself to her unwilling mind, and she passed an involuntary criticism on her. It was beyond her power to analyze the character of Philippa's face, but she made a disparaging inventory of its features. Her wide forehead, eyebrows so arched and far apart, her pale brown eyes, her curved solid chin, her thin lips, could not be called beautiful, certainly; but Mr. Ritchings at the same time came to a different conclusion. In his opinion, those vermilion lips were like the delicate, flaming leaves of some tropical flower, and her beautiful yellow hair reminded him of the plumage of a tropical bird; but her clear, cold eyes were like the tinted iceberg, which rides towards its fall in the summer sea. He was amazed that so slight a creature, half-grown, apparently, could appear so dignified, so unimpressed; yet there was a carelessness in her manner that amounted to audacity. She was unconscious of his scrutiny, and not only ate her own cake, but part of his, taking it from his plate in pinches.

Somebody said that it rained, and everybody started up to go. Jason arrived with umbrellas and overshoes, and staid in the entry till Sarah came out of the parlor. He had a moment's affable sparring with Mrs. Rogers, however, on the matter of his never coming before folks, his not doing the good his position required of him, and his being poor company for his wife.

He waved her off with a laugh, and beckoned Philippa to hurry, but still he was obliged to wait on the shell-paved walk while Sarah exchanged a few words with Mr. Ritchings.

"Are you going to be fond of ministers, Philippa?" he asked. "They take up a great deal of time."

"Not if they are over pious."

CHAPTER VII

||||||||||||||||||||||||||||||||||||||||||||||||||

EITHER THE RAIN chilled Philippa, or her reception at home, for she began to feel ill in a few days after her return. Shading her eyes from the light, she crept listlessly from room to room, disinclined to speak, eat, or sleep. Elsa declaring that she was as yellow as saffron, thought her suffering from one of her old attacks, but the doctor pronounced her case one of fever, and on the ninth day she was delirious.

Elsa denied her delirium—said that she was lightheaded for the want of sleep, and confused with the doctor's nasty drugs; but one night, while sitting by her bed, she changed her mind.

Philippa raised her little hand with an appealing look and said, "Don't bring apple-blossoms; pull me some magnolias, mammy."

"I'll bring 'em in this minute, Philly, if you will be quiet," Elsa answered, her heart in her mouth.

"Where's my rosary, Philip? I have not had it since yesterday."

She slipped out of bed, shook the pillows, threw the contents of her work-box on the floor, while Elsa stood aghast and unprepared.

"Don't you remember, Philly dear," she said, desperately, "that you are not a Roman Catholic now, and that you don't need your rosary?"

"My rosary," cried Philippa in a rage, "find it, or I'll flog you till the blood runs. Gloria Patria[21]—that ends it."

And she began to strike on the door with her clinched hand, crying louder and louder, "My rosary."

Sarah heard the noise and ran up stairs; Philippa's countenance changed when she saw her.

"You have hid it," she said doggedly, "and unless you produce it I will kill myself."

"For the Lord's sake, Sarah, get her the beads, if they are in the land of the living."

"The rosary, Mrs. Auster, if you please," said Philippa; "look in the depths of your conscience for it."

"I'll go for it," Sarah replied mildly, and whispered to Elsa that she had no idea where the thing was; but it was found, and Philippa consented to go back to bed.

The delirium ended in a stupor. The doctor said that her hair must be shorn, and Jason was called to assist in the operation; he caught the tresses as they fell, and looked upon them as one might look upon a friend for the last time; tears dropped from his eyes which he was not aware of, till Sarah told him that if he was going to be overcome by a handful of hair, he would not be of much use in the sick-room.

While she lay in stupor, Cuth was seized with a mortal illness, which compelled Jason to watch over him. His time had come, Cuth said; he knew it, because tobacco did not taste good any longer. He begged Jason to bury him without having any palavering, and to have his coffin carried out at the back door; in consideration of having these requests fulfilled, he made a will in Jason's favor, for he had a thousand dollars in money, and a thousand dollars in land. If it was all the same to Mrs. Auster, he would like to be buried in the Parke lot. Sarah promised him that he should be laid in the desired spot, and he died, silently and firmly, like a wolf. The day of his funeral was the day, also, of the funeral of Gilbert's child; when it was over, Mary, his wife, came to assist Elsa, and remained in the family from that time. The day she came Philippa's doom was pronounced; a few hours more would close the scene, the doctor informed Jason and Sarah. Jason wrote to Parke to come home, and then disappeared. Sarah, exhausted, went to bed, leaving with Philippa Elsa, whose last office seemed to be to moisten her poor lips. Jason returned by sundown, and wandered through all the chambers but the one Philippa was in. The doctor came again, and went without a word. Towards morning Philippa's breath was so far gone, that Elsa bent over her to learn if it had not stopped forever; but she opened her eyes wide, and said, "Jason!"

Elsa called him. He came in and kneeled by the bed.

"Good-by, Jason. Thank you. Kiss Parke," said Philippa, in a hoarse voice, and again closed her eyes. He thought her dead; but Elsa sent for the doctor, who said she had fallen into a natural sleep; that it was possible she would not die after all; though it would be curious if she did not, for the consulting physician, Potter, had said there was no hope, and his death-warrants had never failed.

"Sarah Auster," exclaimed Elsa, breaking into her room an hour or two after, "that poor creature is going to live after all. Now I can turn the world upside down with some heart. Come, the table has been spread three days, and not cleared; nobody has eaten any thing."

Sarah rose up in bed, with a clear perception of not being rejoiced at Elsa's tidings. She must go on with her task! Yawning, she asked if coffee was made.

"Coffin, did you say?" Elsa retorted, purposely misunderstanding her.

"Elsa, are you a fool? I said coffee."

"What do you suppose I have made, motherwort tea? That is bitter, you know—as bitter as gall and wormwood."

"Herb-tea and medicine will run in your head for weeks. I am glad there will be an end to drugs. Jason has been up all night, I suppose. I'll go up and attend to Philippa; she must have something to nourish her immediately."

Jason left the sick-room to her, sauntered into the yard, and sat down on the steps of a shed. His dogs, Ike and Jake, came and laid their noses on his knee.

"Good-by," he repeated, pulling their ears. "Thank you. Kiss Parke."

The dogs whimpered and beat the ground with their tails, while he gazed abstractedly into their eyes, which were limpid with love and hunger. Elsa called him to breakfast, and they followed him into the dining-room.

"'Tis no matter for once," she said, more amicably eying them, as they squatted beside him, than was her wont. Sarah came in, and Jason involuntarily looked at her for sympathy. She saw his agitation.

"Well," she remarked, "the siege is raised. You have been anxious, Jason. Philippa rivals your dogs—doesn't she? and they are jealous."

Elsa wished in her heart that they had Sarah between their teeth, and shaking the devil out of her. Jason tossed a mouthful to them and answered: "Hardly, but I wished her to live."

"If the pains we have taken can prolong life, she will outlive us all."

"You have done your best, Sarah, that I know, and so has Elsa. As for me, my mission as usual has been—uselessness."

"I couldn't help doing my best," said Elsa.

Parke arrived the next day, with a pair of horses that he had hired in the town where he found he must wait for a train to Crest.

"How is she?" he asked; "where is she?"

"In her room," his mother answered, without deranging herself. But Elsa took him by the hand, and led him thither. He was so shocked at the change in Philippa, that he could not speak. Her languid eyes rested on his fresh, fair face, and rivers of tears flowed from them; he was touched, and wept with her, but he felt a painful physical repugnance at the sight of her.

"There," said Elsa, with a slight sniff, "if you are going to act so, you must go right away, Parke; the time for crying has gone by!"

"I am so glad to see you, Parke," said Philippa.

"I am so sorry to find you sick. How you must have suffered! But it is over now."

"Look at my hair."

"I don't see any."

"Your hair will grow out handsomer than ever in no time," interrupted Elsa.

"Yes, indeed," said Parke. "I hope you will be well immediately, for I do not mean to go next term. I shall stay here."

"Oh, Parke, you must go through."

He shook his head.

"There, there," Elsa broke in, "colleges or no colleges, you must go down stairs, Parke."

"Come up early to-morrow," Philippa begged, "and tell me what you mean to do."

He promised, kissing his hand to her, and smiling himself outside the door; but as soon as it was shut, he shuddered.

"So Cuth is dead, Elsa? I thought he was good for years yet."

"He was tough; but it is all the same to death — tough and

rough, tender and delicate, when he appears with his broom, we are brushed off like so much dust into a dust-pan."

"Poor Cuth! he belonged to us heart and soul."

"For good wages. Whether he belongs to the Parkes in heaven, depends on what they can pay there. Gilbert can take his place here very well, and we must hire an additional man."

"We must, for I mean to have additional horses. Where's mother? I want her."

"Now, Parke, don't pray keep us in hot water about this college business; go back. Are you going to turn out shiftless, like some of your relatives?"

"Shut your mouth, Elsa; do you suppose that I am not aware of my intentions, clearly and plainly? I have stayed from home three years because I liked it, not because I wanted to be fitted for college, or to go through college. Old woman, I know when I want a thing, and how I want it, better than anybody else."

He spoke so pleasantly, and with such a lively air of interest in the "thing" he wanted, that she began to feel personally concerned in his obtaining it. She said no more. His mother vehemently opposed his remaining at home; it was not worthy of him to leave a task unfinished; he would be accused of a distaste for scholarship. She consulted Jason even, but obtained no satisfaction. He replied, that he did not believe in education; he was not surprised at Parke's being weary of playing at knowledge; he imagined that of the two sorts of men—those who were taught by systems, and those who made them—Parke would prefer the latter; and that he would create one himself and bring it to perfection—the art of amusement. And why not?

In vain she urged Parke to return. He had made up his mind, he said, to stay at home, and he hoped that she would not find him disagreeable.

In his absence, he declared, the dust of antiquity had gathered over the house; but it was blown away before he had been there many days. A piano came with his baggage, cases of books, pictures, and numberless trifles. All outside of college life, Jason observed to Sarah, and better established at Crest than elsewhere. Parke was so occupied that he only found time to visit Philippa a few moments each day, but he said so much of his plans that he left food for thought.

Until she was able to leave her room—and her recovery was slow—Jason was assiduously attentive. Her ugly, helpless convalescence, removed his coldness and shyness; but from the day she came down stairs he subsided so completely into his old self, that the remembrance of his care and anxiety merged into the dream her illness grew to be. Her life was absorbed in Parke's.

CHAPTER VIII

||||||||||||||||||||||||||||||||||||||||||||||||||||

THE NAME OF THERESA BOND appeared often in the reminiscences of Philippa's school life with which she sometimes entertained Parke. When she showed him the daguerreotype of her friend—a splendidly handsome girl—he suggested that she should be invited to Crest. Philippa wrote her accordingly, and the invitation was accepted. She arrived at the appointed day, and when Parke saw her he was satisfied with the prospect her coming offered; so was she. That day a summer rain fell from morning till evening; it sheeted the windows with mist, hummed against the doors, and smote the roof with steady blows. Jason found sufficient excuse in it for once to remain at home, for even he felt a curiosity regarding the visitor; his way of gratifying it entirely concealed his object. He lounged in the distance, or, if he followed Parke, Philippa, and Theresa, from room to room, he appeared to do so from an interest he took in the books, engravings, and knick-knacks, which were strewed everywhere.

It was a day to discuss character, Parke said, and to make confessions; the afternoon was before them where to choose. It was a wonderful spectacle to Jason, when he beheld the ease and adaptability of Parke's manner, while seated between the girls on a sofa. Theresa chattered like a magpie of her passionate likings, her venomous dislikings, while Philippa's office was that of listener to both. Occasionally Parke took her hand, carelessly patting it, and dropping it forgetfully, as he appealed to her to ratify his opinions. The effect he produced reacted upon himself, and increased his amiable vivacity. They were happy. That summer day might have extended over a week, a month, a year, perhaps, and his sense of enjoyment in this happiness have lasted. But when the prince hovering over the lips of the Sleeping Beauty touched them, the palace was disenchanted.

Theresa played a brilliant fantasia on the piano, which made Jason's ears ring; he went to a window remote from the piano, and through the streaming pane saw a pair of robins, ruffled with the rain, flying into the branches of a fir below the terrace, and piping a song in its shelter which soothed him. He looked towards Philippa, who had quietly gone to the centre-table, intent upon restoring it to order. Parke stood beside Theresa, following her music with the delight of an artist.

"You play and sing by ear, Philippa says; do try something," she begged.

He complied, and sang a Polish melody, so vivacious, yet so passionate and melancholy, that she was electrified; even Philippa felt that he sang with a new spirit. Sarah looked in at the door, a linen apron in her hand, and passed on, with a pleasant picture in her mind. When Parke began to sing, Jason moved from his place, near Philippa, and asked her, in a low voice, if she understood that outlandish music.

"No," she answered; "but I like it."

"There's a couple of robins outside doing quite as well, in my way of thinking."

He then betook himself with his book to the panelled parlor on the opposite side of the hall, but it was not long before his solitude was invaded. Theresa having revealed that one of her passions was old annuals,[22] they came in to look over the contents of an ancient mahogany bookcase, whose doors, covered with green silk, had not been opened for a long time. "Gems" were disinterred from the top shelves—"Friendship's Offerings" and "Keepsakes," the New Year's gifts of Parke and Philippa's childish days.

"These make me feel a boy again," said Parke, "when life wasn't 'full of sunny years.'"

Why not? thought Philippa. But she, too, had chronicles for those times.

"Some of the pictures are deliciously funny," said Theresa. "'Contemplation,' for instance. How came you by such a lot?"

"New Year's presents," Parke replied. "How many belong to you, Philippa?"

"Seven."

"Do you remember that Saturday night, when mother came home from some journey, and brought 'Tales of the Revolution,' which we both began to read Sunday morning, and that she took it from you, and made you go to church? I stayed at home, and finished it."

"Why did she do that?" Theresa asked. "Why did she not make you go?"

"Why didn't she make me go, Philippa?" Parke echoed.

Jason smiled faintly, and raised his eyes to Theresa's face; he listened for Philippa's reply, but she made none.

"Why didn't she?" Parke repeated, nipping her ear. As Philippa continued dumb, Theresa concluded to change the subject, and make Parke forget his question. She plunged into the annuals again, but Jason pondered over Philippa's silence. As he thought of it he became conscious of feeling worried, mystified, unsettled. What could it be? He would not be housed up another day; he believed one such day was as a thousand years. What did that young lady remind him of? The tiger-lily in the back garden, which Ike had barked at the day before! Books, music, fine talk, did not suit him; they were for Parke, who became them so well. Then his thoughts wandered to the day when he thought Philippa was dying, and to the words which he supposed her last. He rose involuntarily, and stretched himself to his full height; he was towering. Theresa's glance fell upon him and rested there. Their eyes met, and Jason, returning her glance with an honest, unabashed gaze, stalked out of the room. She suddenly found a style of coiffure in the portraits of "Beauty," and dragged Philippa away to experiment upon it.

At tea-time they reappeared. Parke snapped his fingers at Theresa, and whistled the Bolero. Her glossy black hair, dressed in Spanish fashion, fastened by a high-topped shell-comb, one of Sarah's treasures—with a red rose on one side of her head, and a black lace scarf on the other, brought out the warmest tints of her dusky beauty. Philippa looked strangely unlike herself; her short hair clung round her head in a mass of ringlets—vivid golden rings. A wide scarlet ribbon hung down each side of her face, on the ends of which Theresa had pinned bunches of delicate green leaves. A large, loose cape of spotted white lace was adjusted on her shoulders, like a robe, and her bare, slender arms were decorated with bands of black velvet. The impassive character of her chin and forehead was brought out by this dress, and its violent contrast of colors revealed the imperfection of her complexion, and the curious specks in the brown irises of her eyes.[23]

"She is hideous," said Parke.

"She is not," affirmed Theresa; "she is the American Sphinx."[24]

Sarah gave a shrill laugh; not that she comprehended the allusion, but there seemed a fitness in it which gratified her. Jason, in his place at the tea-table, removed his eyes from the cold joint he was carving, and said: "She is the Genius of the Republic."

Philippa was profoundly indifferent to her appearance. Never was creature more free from vanity. She composedly ate her cold meat and drank her tea, forgetting that she was *en costume*, except when the ends of her wide head-dress flapped across her mouth.

With the tea night came—a harder rain and thicker mist. Theresa threw up a window, and from habit, Sarah and Philippa, and even Parke, drew back from the wind and mist which rushed in, but she delighted in the atmosphere, and expressed a desire for a walk. Jason instantly felt a sentiment of respect for her, and in its blush suggested "India-rubber boots."

The suggestion was exclaimed against, and Sarah observed to him, that he need not suppose, because he passed so much of his life in India rubbers, that anybody besides would fancy doing so.

"What do you do in them, Mr. Auster?" asked Theresa.

Sarah hastened to reply for him: "He lives in the woods—going through the ceremony of carrying a gun—or, on the water, manoeuvring with a boat."

"Pleasing and harmless pursuits," added Jason, with a peculiar smile.

"He has stayed at home one day, though," Parke remarked, "because something new has happened."

"I am sure we have company enough for him to remain with us, but he never does," said Sarah.

"None half so delightful as the present," said Parke.

Theresa blushed beautifully.

The voice of the sea grew loud. Its short yelp came up to the house, to fall back baffled, and wail despairingly along the shore.

"The people don't appear to mind that mad music outside," thought Theresa.

"Do shut that window, Miss Bond," entreated Sarah. "The water is terrible to-night."

"You will take cold," said Philippa.

Theresa closed it, but remained with her face close to the pane. A moment afterwards Parke stood beside her.

"You think us insensible to the influences of the spot," he said; "but you do not understand what a perpetual struggle is going on between us and the climate. The wind, fog, damp, and rain, frost and ice, are the causes which compel us to combat for a time for business, pleasure, and repose—to say nothing of health. For my part, I like to forget 'Nature,' as I have to-day."

CHAPTER IX

‖‖‖

IT WAS A MERRY, restless life which prevailed now. Something new was taking place—a different development—and all because Theresa Bond was paying a visit of a few weeks to several people who interested her. They were alive with life, and did not know it—that was her opinion. A new brand is sometimes wanted to kindle up the embers of a smouldering fire, and this was the office she performed; and then "all the winds of the world blew up the flames."[25]

The individual independence of the family first struck her. Apparently no member of it involved another in any pursuit, opinion, or interest, except Parke, who involved Philippa. Elsa was the only one able to spin the threads together on the family distaff. It could not have been so always. There was an air of transmitted habit grafted on the ways of the house, which proved its age and pride. This accounted for various incongruities in their style of living, which, at first, surprised the city-bred, aristocratic Theresa. Sarah and Philippa were engaged much of the time in house-work and sewing. Philippa did what she had been accustomed to do from a child, and Sarah assisted Elsa everywhere. There was an utter absence of ceremony and display at the table, and over the house. Parke smoked and read the newspapers in the kitchen, and Elsa shelled beans in the parlor. The errands came in at the front door, and visitors at the back door, whenever it suited the convenience of the respective parties, and were entertained wherever they were met. Yet the prestige which money gives was not lacking.

64

In spite of their different idiosyncrasies, they were much together, and all the rooms were occupied in common. Jason was rarely at home, it is true, but if there, he lounged about in his odd way, brooding in a corner of the kitchen hearth, musing in the parlor windows, sitting on the door-steps, or lying among the bushes on the terrace.

Theresa had no key to the family history, except the fact of Philippa's being a pupil at Madame Mara's. That was a proof of means and respectability, for Madame never admitted anybody without these antecedents. Philippa was not communicative: she was a mystery, and mystery piqued Theresa. She made advances towards Philippa, who responded, but in a provoking, reticent way. A theory started itself in Theresa's mind, which she imparted to her—that from the negation of her character, and the utter absence of the dramatic in her nature, a tragedy would one day come, fall on her, and devour her, as the wolf devoured Red Riding Hood. Philippa not only returned Theresa's regard, but was grateful to her for aid extended in various ways. Theresa was a fine scholar—an adept in the art of dress, full of finesse. Philippa was dull at her books, devoid of taste, and devoid of tact. Theresa smoothed away her difficulties, attempted to polish her, with a slight degree of success, and learned to love her still more.

The friendly relations immediately established between Theresa and her family so thawed Philippa's silence, that when Theresa one day said, "Your Cousin Jason is eccentric," she did not parry the remark, but replied, "Because he is quiet?"

"Did you never notice him?"

"I have not speculated on this point of eccentricity. Why do you ask? You say I never study those about me."

"It seems to me that he has not found his vocation."

"He changed it. When he married Cousin Sarah he was a carpenter."

"Dear me," said Theresa, eying Philippa with a one-sided glance, like that of a cunning bird, "you are refreshing."

"He is my guardian."

"Are you rich enough for that?"

"Parke and I, both. We inherit our great-grandfather's property."

"That is when Jason has done with his share."

"Jason! he has nothing."

"Why not? Your Cousin Sarah comes into the property before Parke, and what is hers is her husband's."

"Oh no," said Philippa, seriously, "it was not fixed so. Parke and I have it all — or will soon."

"Jason's position, then, is inferior to his wife's, his son's, and yours?"

"I never thought of it. What a way you have of representing things!"

"I like him," exclaimed Theresa, after a pause; "he is dignified and single-minded; but whether he has much heart I have not yet learned."

It was evident to Philippa that Theresa was upon one of her "clues."

"He is honest," she declared, after another pause. "What will you do with money? When are you going to begin to spend it?"

"What would you do with it?"

"I would not be stingy."

"I dare say you will call *me* so; I rarely have generous impulses. Parke is always giving. I think I shall keep my money."

"You will save it for some spendthrift; then hey for my tragedy. Property is always dispersed in the course of a generation or two."

"My idea is consolidation."

"Jason would help you in that—nobody else."

"How do you know that?" Philippa cried, irritably.

"Would Parke? Would your relative Sarah?"

"I won't be dragged into one of your analytical abysses, Theresa; so let me alone."

"For the present, then; but I shall not give you up, since I have seen oysters in an aquarium."

Parke planned admirably for Theresa's amusement. A saddle-horse arrived one day. She improvised a habit and rode with him constantly; they scoured the country, inspired with the hope of picturesque discovery, leaving Philippa at home—with her idea of consolidation, probably. They described their tours with animation, and Jason, if present, never failed to say that he and his dogs had been on the same rounds; but to Philippa the descriptions were novel, for she knew nothing of the country.

"Why don't you take walks?" asked Sarah, when she heard her say so.

"Why not try boating?" Jason asked, before she could reply.

"Boating," exclaimed Theresa; "oh, yes, why hasn't it been thought of before?"

"I cannot manage a boat," said Parke.

"Jason will go with you," said Sarah, graciously.

"Yes, once," he answered, roughly.

"Let us have a party, then," said Parke. "Mother, will you go?"

"I am afraid of the water."

"Well, then, Philippa, Miss Bond, myself, and father."

Jason remarked that Philippa was afraid of the water, too, and he thought it likely Parke was; but if he could rely on Miss Bond, sufficient courage could be mustered for a short sail.

Sarah thought of Mr. Ritchings, and, without consulting any one, sent him an invitation to join the party. The next morning he made his appearance without an overcoat, and in a suit of summer clothes.

"The merciful man!" exclaimed Elsa, when she saw him coming in at the gate. "Who asked him?"

"I did," Sarah said, in a serene voice.

"Let him go, Elsa," Jason laughed.

There was a land breeze, the waves ran from the shore, and the bay looked almost smooth.

Philippa brought out cloaks and thick shawls, and recommended a lashing down of hats and bonnets.

"How comes she to know that it is blowing outside?" Jason asked Elsa. "She never went sailing."

"Why, yes, you forget she made a voyage more than eight years ago."

"True; why she is a woman, isn't she?"

"If she isn't she never will be; the time will come, before you know it, when she will be of age."

"All hands, ahoy," called Sarah, moving down the walk beside Mr. Ritchings, and accompanied by Gilbert, who carried a basket of provisions. She was so lively that the rest of the party were silenced. Theresa heard her bandying jokes with Mr. Ritchings with surprise, and concluded she was a moral mine, and that it would not do to walk over her. As the boat left the wharf she turned and walked slowly home, drawing a full breath when she entered the door, and experiencing an unwonted sense of relief. Through the empty rooms she passed as if she was seeking a spirit she had no hope of finding—the "something beautiful" which had vanished from her life. Perhaps its airy nothingness came the nearest to a habitation in Parke's room. She lingered

there and inspected his belongings; they were scattered everywhere, letters, boots, gloves, hats, daguerreotypes, crumpled
handkerchiefs. Ends of cigars and opened books were lying on
his bed, the table, and window-seat; his watch was run down, and
all the stoppers were out of his perfume-bottles. From this confusion there was a subtle, delicate emanation, which could only
belong to him. Idly opening several of the picture-cases, which
contained the likenesses of his college-chums, she came upon
that of Theresa, which he had borrowed of Philippa. Suppose he
should marry Theresa! She wondered if it would be agreeable to
Philippa. There was a belief in Sarah's mind, like a fatality, that
she was so devoted to Parke she would not marry herself, but
that his marriage would be the most important event of her life.
All that she had done from a child went to prove that she was to
be a sort of human providence in his career. Sarah was also fixed
in a belief that she was not a girl to be sought or loved, or desired
to be. The idea of his marriage was painful even to herself; she
questioned whether mothers were ever glad of a son's marriage.
A bitter lonely feeling came over her, and hot tears welled into
her eyes, which Elsa interrupted:

"What time may we expect them?" she asked, pretending not
to see Sarah's tears.

"About nine, I think."

"And we must have a hot supper. Of course the parson will
stay to it?"

"Certainly—why not?"

"Nothing; only he is after our Philippa. You needn't contra-
dict, Sarah. He looks at her when he is preaching even. He hasn't
had his eyes off her this day, unless he has been sea-sick."

"Why hasn't Mary put Parke's room to rights?"

"What is the use of putting *his* room in order? I pity the woman *he* marries."

"Matrimory runs in your head, Elsa?"

"Wouldn't it be wise in you to think of the possibility of somebody's being married? Or do you expect to cut and carve everybody into an eternal single blessedness?"

"Mr. Ritchings is friendly and polite—nothing more."

"Oh, that is all, is it? Mary says that Gilbert says the whole town declares that Mr. Ritchings is in love with Philippa. We'll shut the town up."

"Never mind, Elsa, don't speak of it; gossip irritates me; but I shall forget presently."

"Ministers are such a mark, you know," said Elsa, her anger all gone; "but any how he shall have a good supper."

"If you please, Elsa."

"What ails her now?" queried Elsa, on the way down stairs. "Something or other discourages me. I wish I could find out who is doing it. Ministers *are* a mark, and I don't know that I blame her for getting mad, but that man is in love with Philippa—and—her money."

Sarah, still restless, went up garret, towards sunset, to look over the bay. The wind had died away, and the tide was out; the sea lay within its rim of yellow rocks, that looked alive with stirring snaky weeds, like a blue, wrinkled banner. Not a sail dotted its wide surface. Jason and his companions were not within its limits.

CHAPTER X

||||||||||||||||||||||||||||||||||||||||||||||||||

"WHERE DOES THE WIND come from?" Theresa asked. "It makes no flurry, yet its force keeps the water flat."

"When it blows from the north at this time of year," said Jason, "it blows strong; but we shall have no flaws with it."

Philippa looked up at him reassured.

"You are scared, Philippa," he said.

"Let me sit on the other side," she begged; "there is very little boat between me and the water here."

"Stay where you are. I shall cross the bay presently; with the wind behind us, the boat will right."

"This is fine," Parke remarked; "we glide over glass."

"Splendid," replied Mr. Ritchings. "Your father is an excellent boatman, isn't he?"

"His attitude betokens security, at least."

He was half lying, half sitting; his right hand was on the tiller, his left under his head, his legs were crossed in the air, and his face was half hid by an old felt hat, which was very much crushed.

"Isn't he an original?" Theresa said, in a low voice, to Mr. Ritchings.

"Hush," he whispered, with a laugh, "they are a tribe of originals; don't you find them so?"

"All but Philippa," she answered mischievously, looking into his face. He turned very red, and asked Parke where they were going.

"Pitt's Island," suggested Philippa.

"That's a good place," said Jason, pushing up his hat.

"What is on the island?" Theresa asked.

"Huckleberries and wood-ticks, at present," Jason replied.

"We shall have to wade ashore," Philippa cried.

"Philippa is so sensible," Theresa exclaimed. "For my part, I want to wade."

Jason put up the helm for Pitt's Island. It would take half an hour to round Hawk's Point, behind which the island lay, and a few minutes more to reach shoal water, he said, reclining at the tiller again.

Parke and Theresa crept forward, and sat down on the other side of the sail; his boot-soles against the ballast stones, and the edge of her skirts, were all that could be seen of them at the other end of the boat. The sun shone in their happy, handsome faces, and the breeze blew: sufficient was the day for their pleasure thereof.

"We shall return with red noses," he said.

She dabbled her hands in the water, and filliped some in his face.

"If you do that again, while I am so helplessly lying at your feet, supporting the weight of a cloak for your sake, I'll—throw it off."

She looked at him lazily, and said, "What changeable eyes you have!"

He raised himself on his elbow, and brought his face close to hers.

"How handsome you are, Theresa!"

"So are you."

A pause, during which both looked into the deep, green sea.

His hand fell softly upon hers; their fingers locked, and palm was pressed to palm.

72

The voices of the syrens rose from the depths of the sea, and a wild, sweet, delicious melody floated round the pair.

"We hear nothing at the other end," she said, at last, releasing her hand.

"Do you wish to hear?" he asked, dropping back in the folds of the cloak.

"I am not anxious about it. Mr. Ritchings is happy, I suppose?"

"Why Mr. Ritchings?"

"With Philippa, you know."

"Nonsense," he exclaimed with energy: "he is nothing to her."

"I dare say; but he is smitten to the core with her."

"*He!*"

"Now you are going to hate him. How selfish you are! I wish Philippa would flirt, and worry you to death."

"Can't you teach her the art?"

"Do I possess it?"

He whistled "Lively Polly," and then closed his eyes as if he was sleeping.

Mr. Ritchings engaged Philippa in conversation, and Jason was left to his thoughts, and steering.

"I have seen very little of you of late, Miss Philippa."

"We have missed you from our house; that is the reason, is it not?"

"You have been so much occupied!"

"A little more than usual."

"But you are always a good deal occupied since your cousin came home. Do you read together?"

"Oh no."

"Is he not fond of reading?"

"Novels."

"You do not like novels?"

"No; nor fairy stories, nor poetry."

"Not a literal novel, like 'Jane Eyre'?"[26]

"Literal! Charlotte Bronte cheated her readers in a new way. She threw a glamour over the burnt porridge even, at the Lowood school, and the seed-cake which Jane shared with Helen Burns. Did red and white furniture ever look anywhere else as it did at 'Thornfield'? Haven't we all red and white articles which have never stirred us beyond the commonplace?"

"The glamour of genius."

"Genius describes ordinary life for us, and then we suffer in reality the discrepancy of its words."[27]

"But life must be illustrated."

"It cannot be; the text ruins the attempt."

"Does not passion illustrate it?"

"I do not know."

"Somebody says: 'Nothing is so practical as the ideal, which is ever at hand to uphold and better the real,' and I believe it."

"Shoal water," cried Parke from the bow.

"We are among the rocks, Jason," said Philippa, bending over the side.

"We are on the ledge," he answered. "I am going to put you ashore from it. You can step from rock to rock along the point; Miss Bond shall wade ashore, if she prefers to."

"'Oh pilot, 'tis a fearful thing' [28] to have to scramble up that bank in front of us,"Parke remarked.

"There's a path somewhere," said Jason.

"I see a little flag-staff on the summit!" Theresa exclaimed.

> "Down with the red flag,
>   Up with the black,"

sang Parke, assisting Theresa out of the boat.

Jason tied the sails and threw the anchor into the sand, while the rest climbed the bank, and disappeared in a thicket which bordered it. Theresa pulled the wild shining smilax, and wreathed it round Parke's hat and her own. They crossed a ravine filled with half-sunken rocks and dense bushes, and came on the face of a hill, their destination, whose top was covered with magnificent pines. Philippa discovered that the provision-basket had been forgotten, and slipped into the ravine to meet Jason and remind him of it. He had not seen it, and both of them went back to the boat.

"You pushed through the swamp, did you?" he said. "I know a better course."

She followed him into a dark, slippery path, black with vegetable mould, and choked with rocks which were beautifully stained with red-eyed moss, green velvet moss, and a ruffled, fringed, scaly fungus-growth of wonderful microscopic plants, which she carefully avoided, with the idea that they must be poisonous.

"Don't you call this a handsome carpet?" he asked.

He was answered with a scream; looking round and taking the direction of her eyes, he saw a lazy snake coiled upon a rock she was about to step on; he seized and flung it far into the bushes. Rubbing his hands with grape-leaves, he said: "You are afraid of every thing."

"Yes, I am," she answered meekly. "How could you take it up?"

"Because it frightened you, and the sooner out of the way the better. I do not believe you can climb this hill."

"Oh yes."

He caught her up, and with a few strides was at its top, where he deposited her beside Theresa, and told her the frightful adventure with a snake.

"Are you not well, Philippa?" asked Parke.

"Certainly."

"Are you in good spirits?"

"Yes, as I always am."

"I am awfully hungry."

She started up to unpack the basket, and Parke threw himself beside Theresa, who declared she was in raptures with life. The dazzling, tremulous blue sea was round her; over her stirred the green, scented, feathery sea of the pines.

"'Ringed with the azure world,'" said she, "we sit upon this smooth, elastic, red mat, commonly called pine needles."

"And 'like a thunderbolt we'll fall'[29]—on the repast which awaits us in the shadow of yon towering tree. Come, sylvan goddess, the minister has spread the cloth, and put a stone on each corner of it to keep it from fluttering."

"Roast chicken, Miss Bond, buttered bread, tart, cake—which, or all?" asked Mr. Ritchings.

"All."

"We have no plates, but napkins."

"I eat with my fingers," said Theresa.

Jason asked to be excused from coming to the table, on account of the lowness of the seats and his inability to dispose of his legs. Parke suggested the fork of a tree, near by, not more than fifty feet from the ground.

"There is no plum-cake here, Mr. Ritchings," said Philippa, with a smile that warmed his spirits.

"I am out of office to-day."

"Oh, how happy I am," sighed Theresa, with her mouth full of chicken.

"I am too," said Parke, taking a bit of tart.

"Are the others as happy, think?" she asked.

"If they are as hungry."

"Animal!"

Philippa came towards them with a glass of coffee, and Mr. Ritchings followed with a paper of sugar and a bottle of cream.

"There is one spoon only."

"How delightful!"

"There," said Parke, flinging a cone at Philippa, "the inhabited world may dine now."

A merry chat followed. Jason offered cigars; Philippa, a little tired, reclined against a tree, and contemplated the white clouds which floated in the aerial deep, and curled their edges in relief against the pines. Theresa subsided into silence.

Suddenly Jason unlocked his tongue. "There is some thing in this scene, Mr. Ritchings, beyond ethics; it confounds and annihilates them."

A shade of annoyance passed over Parke's serene face. He moved his cigar to the other side of his mouth. Mr. Ritchings looked on the ground and picked up a twig, but Theresa's subtle instinct understood Jason's meaning.

"You are right," she said.

"A man does not value the Creator so much here; he thinks of the created. Here falls the crown of humanity upon his head in its circle of beauty, suffering, and uncertainty. The speechless air, the deaf earth, the blindness of substance — what do they but render us back vagueness for vagueness? Why was Christ tempted on a mount? Not because he could see therefrom the kingdoms of the earth. I read these lines in one of your books, Parke:

> 'To her fair works did Nature link
> The human soul that through me ran.'[30]

I think Christ was tempted with the loss of faith in his heroic mission."

"The old gent is breaking out with a vengeance," murmured Parke, in Theresa's ear.

"You must read the Gospel with a good deal of imagination," cried Mr. Ritchings. "In what do you believe?"

"In what I feel."

He lighted a fresh cigar. His mood changed. He made quaint remarks that forced even Philippa to laugh, and Theresa thought him a genius. Six o'clock came, and it was time to go. Sweeping the napkins into the basket, he strode out of sight down the hill. Philippa and Mr. Ritchings picked up the shawls and followed. Parke moved in a roundabout way from tree to tree, for Theresa was not inclined to leave.

"The picnic opened a mine in my governor," he said.

"I have been struck with him from the first. He is a genius."

"A what, Miss Bond?"

"And geniuses never have children like themselves."

"He must be one, then."

"Why do you call me Miss Bond?"

"I call him a prime old fellow, any way, and you — *Theresa*."

"Shall I ever again have so beautiful an hour as this, Parke? Let us never go into the world of human beings!"

She clasped the trunk of a pine, and signed to him to go on.

"I'll stay here forever, if you say so."

"You would not."

He was busy breaking off scales of bark, but he raised his eyes. There was a tide of beautiful, dangerous darkness in them.

"They will be waiting for us," she added, drawing towards him.

"Let them wait," he said, with his lips on hers.

"Kiss me, Theresa—again."

The voyage home was a silent one. It was past eight when they reached the house, and when they sat down, by blazing lamps, to supper, they felt dazed—like those who come from a distant, different land, into a forgotten home.

CHAPTER XI

PHILLIPA'S LIFE, THOUGH apparently so pale and cold, in contrast with the blooming richness of Theresa's, increased its silent forces. Theresa's regnancy, instead of subduing Philippa's expectations and intentions, developed them. She waited for a favorable moment to reveal them.

Theresa determined to make a collection of grasses, and for a number of days went to the fields. After the grass came a passion for sea-weeds, which also lasted a number of days. Parke's enthusiasm lasted through both phases, as did also Philippa's patience. By brook, thicket, and hedge-row, in the shallows of the tide, among the rocks, along the length of the rough beach of Crest, she pondered many things.

At last the opportunity came, as she believed, when the star of her empire should take its way. It was introduced by Mrs. Rogers, who accosted her at the church door, one Sunday.

"My Sam," she said, "was spoken off the River Plate, in April, with eight hundred barrels of sperm oil. He'll be in this fall, sure, and he hasn't a white shirt to his name. I must make a set, and want to borrow a pattern of the collar Parke had on. My mind would wander from the sermon to-day. I do wish Mr. Ritchings would be rather more doctrinal; he would get a more lively attention from *me* then."

"Of course you shall have a pattern. We shall all be delighted to have Sam at home."

"When is your Miss Bond going? Parke and she are a handsome couple. Are they going to make a match?"

"No," said Philippa, sternly.

"Beauty goes a great ways, Philippa, if it is only skin deep. Though it is none of my business, for all our families have been connected, as it were, for many years, my second husband being one of the Squire's best captains, I have thought it would be worth your while, and Parke's, to keep the property together. You are not much akin. Sarah would die in peace then."

The Yankees rush in where angels fear to tread;[31] but Philippa could not help giving her motherly friend a tight grasp of the hand. She made a careless reply, however, and referred to Sam again; but Mrs. Rogers understood her whole heart.

That evening Philippa mentally arranged a conversation with Theresa, and the next morning, while she was puttering with gum-arabic and sea-weed, took some sewing and went to her room.

"Theresa, you have quite educated Parke."

"Will he be grateful, think?"

"I hope not."

Theresa burst into a gay laugh.

"Theresa, I am going to speak to you about Parke."

"Speak away, then," said Theresa, with a haughty motion.

"Mrs. Rogers asked me if he and you were going to make a match. I said, 'No.'"

"You did!" Theresa carefully affixed the filaments of a delicate spray on a sheet of paper, and continued: "And why?"

"You must not marry him. I speak my mind, because I am willing for you to understand my devotion to him; it will allow nothing to stand in its way."

"Not even *his* way, I suppose."

Philippa clinched her hands.

"What right, Philippa, have you to expect me to be more generous than yourself? You are a fool."

"I know that I must appear so to you; but neither he nor you know that I can do more for him than any person in the world. I do not mean in episodes of grass, and sea-weed, parlor talks, and music, and the fine appearance of life. I mean something which your capacity does not include—the care and watchfulness of slow years, without reward—the patience to endure all weakness, indulgence, selfishness—the bond which begins with a white veil, and ends in a shroud! There are states and circumstances which justify us in the attempt we make to take into keeping the lives of men like Parke Auster. I would not," and Philippa rose and paced the room as if she was measuring every inch of him, soul and body, "give in to his own resistance against me. I will compel him finally to *me*."

"And for this," said Theresa, "you would deprive him of the passion, which is the glory, the exaltation of life. Dear me, you are fit for human nature's daily food—that's all. You dream that it lies with us women to govern the destinies of men. We may indulge them with episodes, though, while they treat us to *our* destiny. I told you a tragedy would come to you; you are making it for yourself. It is possible that you may succeed in your plans,—the tragedy will be no less; I do not think that you will. No assimilation with Parke's tendencies, no dovetailing with his habits, no devotion, ever so absolute, will avail a moment when the inclination seizes him for something different. Now, Philippa, there is one thing I will do—not another which may in any way refer to him—if you say so, I will go home to-morrow."

"No," answered Philippa gently, and kissing her cheek, "I wish you to stay."

CHAPTER XII

IIIIIIIIIIIIIIIIIIIIIIIIIIIIIIIIIIIIIIIIIIIIIII

IT WAS THE SUMMER OF A Presidential campaign, and
stump orators were going over the country. The celebrated
Pisgah Spring, Member of Congress from the Fourth District,
was invited to make a speech at Millville, the central village in
the county, but so much scattered itself that it consisted merely of
four corners, on one of which stood a large, dilapidated meeting-
house, and in which Pisgah Spring was to hold forth. Jason was
chosen as delegate from Crest, and Sarah proposed, as it was
moonlight, that they should all go to the meeting.

"Ritchings is going," said Jason, "with the Hall family."

"Suppose you and I go on horseback, Theresa?" asked Parke.

"I'll suppose so, with pleasure."

"Philippa will go in the carriage with us, Sarah, then," said
Jason. "We must start at half-past six. Who will make me a blue
rosette? I am one of the fools to sit on the platform."

"All of us," cried Theresa. "Come, Philippa, to a shop; I want
a piece of ribbon."

It was bought, and Theresa decorated the whole party, including the horses, with the rosettes. Philippa wore that night a white
muslin dress and a white shawl. Theresa called Parke's attention to the effect of the rosettes in her hair. He remarked, that
she always looked well, except when arranged as the American
Sphinx.

"She is a sphinx, however. Why don't you try to guess the
riddle she propounds?"

"Is she more mysterious than any other woman?"

"Don't be a goose, Parke," said his mother.

"Nothing erratic in Philippa—is there, mother?"

"I haven't discovered it."

"Prophets in their own country,[32] Mrs. Auster," Theresa observed carelessly.

"Philippa does not happen to be in her own country," Sarah replied, with a laugh.

For once Parke caught and understood an expression of pain in Philippa's face.

"Philippa," he said, affectionately, "my country is your country, isn't it? You are as much of a Parke as I am. Mother, why did you marry a foreigner?"

Jason entered and prevented her reply. He had been putting in the horses himself, he said, as Gilbert was obliged to take one of the saddle-horses to the blacksmith's to have a shoe fastened.

"That was my business," said Parke.

"Why didn't you attend to it, then?" his father asked.

"Because it is so much easier for me to trouble others than it is to trouble myself. I suppose I am very selfish."

He looked so remorseful that two-thirds of the party felt eager to deny this supposition.

"How blue you all are," said Jason, cheerfully. "Theresa, where is my badge?"

She pinned it to his coat, smiling so pleasantly upon him, that he could not help patting her pretty hand.

"You do not need a badge," she said. "Your eyes would answer for one; they are bluer than this ribbon, and are so much handsomer."

Jason comically poked his fingers into his eyes, and said he never knew till then that he had eyes.

"You are a deuced coquette, Theresa," said Parke, when he adjusted her foot in the stirrup.

The atmosphere had been a strange one all day. The sky was dun-color, and the sun rolled through it—a ball of orange fire. A beautiful blue haze ringed the horizon and hovered over the bay, which had faded and fainted in the heat, and lay white and motionless, not stirring under the pencilled shadows which rayed its edge. For a short distance the road stretched round the shore. The deep silence of the sea made Theresa feel silent also. When Jason struck into a road which turned abruptly from it, she drew a long breath. They entered dense woods, already gray with dusk, and alive with the mysterious stir of invisible creatures who do not love the day, which called out some instinct of enjoyment in her. The cool odors of the ferny swamps, and of flowers yielding to the night, penetrated her with a wild sense of luxury. But Parke was silent and absorbed; he pushed along at a rapid pace, keeping near the carriage which preceded him. At a bend in the road Theresa stopped her horse, while the carriage, and Parke with it, wound out of sight.

"Oh night and heat, sound and odor, why can't I burst into apostrophe! There is something exquisite between you and me: and why not teach me what it is, and why it is—senseless Powers, that overpower me!"

Parke turned back as soon as he missed her.

"What is the matter, Theresa?"

"Nothing; I stopped to get the effect of those splendid white moths on Poll's mane."

"They hover round *you*, after the fashion of moths out of the woods."

"Ah!"

"I have been thinking of Philippa."

"Philippa! ah, yes."

She whipped the leaves from the bushes near, with her riding-whip.

"What do you think of her sometimes?"

"I think of her always, as a peculiar girl, of noble traits."

"She frets me. What does she really enjoy? Any thing?"

"Living for you."

"I do not deserve so much from her. Why should she be so wonderfully single-minded?"

"There is where she is peculiar."

"What will make her attend to her own happiness, I wonder, instead of mine?"

"I am sure I cannot tell."

"Look this way, Theresa."

"One way is as good as another, for it is dark."

"Give me your hand, won't you?"

"How thick the glow-worms are."

"And the moths are thicker, too. Give me your hand."

She surrendered it, and he pulled off her glove.

"Tell me that I am not quite worthless, Theresa."

"I do not know," she answered, dreamily, "whether you can be worth much to *me*. You tempt me, as I tempt you. Suppose I tell you—this is just the moment to confess it—that my senses are all on your side. Confessing this, compare me with Philippa, whose soul shines in a lambent light, which you could go through life by—clear, pure, calm life. Would you like it?"

"The comparison does not interest me much," he said, quietly, holding up her hand, and trying to slip on her glove.

"Don't put on my glove," she said, petulantly.

He offered it to her, and she snatched it from him.

"Shall we go on, Theresa?"

"Are you angry?"

"Confess more."

"Can you—on your soul?"

"Let us go on." And he laughed strangely.

"Just so," she answered, giving her horse a sharp cut.

They overtook the carriage as it entered the town, or rather as it reached the meeting-house, about which a crowd was gathered. It was decorated with pine boughs, mottoes in ground-pine and tissue-paper, and dimly lighted with candles, lamps, and torches. An active committee had knocked out the windows and a part of the end wall, where a platform was raised for the accommodation of Pisgah Spring and the delegates. The body of the house was nearly filled with ladies. A polite usher, however, found a front seat for Sarah. Theresa and Philippa went to a pew under the gallery, near one end of the platform, and Parke stood among the men by the doors.

When Pisgah Spring came forward he was immensely cheered, especially by the galleries. Theresa happened to be looking at Jason, who was on the platform near them, and remarked that he was scrutinizing the supports of the gallery in their vicinity. She forgot him in a moment, however, and was attracted by the change in the evening sky and the rising of the moon, which she saw through the opening in the wall.

At a burst of applause for a display of eloquence an ominous creak was heard. A pillar gave way. The beams above Philippa and Theresa snapped, and a rush was made to get out of the gallery; the house was filled with cries—the audience struggled with each other to get out. The girls clasped hands; they could not move, the pressure was so strong against them, by those who were endeavoring to get out through the opening in the wall behind the platform.

Jason leaped from it with an oath, and fought his way to the corner where they were. With a blow he demolished a sash, and thrust them through it. They had scarcely touched the ground before Parke and his mother were there. Theresa trembled and wept, and Philippa, who had dropped on the ground, quietly fainted. Jason took her up in his arms and pushed out of the crowd, telling Parke to be quick with some water. Theresa saw him put his hand on her forehead, and then clasp her close to him, throwing back his head, as if he were making a mad appeal for help.

"She won't die with the fright, will she?" she asked Sarah.

"She will come to presently," Sarah answered, taking from Parke the cup of water he had found and dashing it in her face. "Put her on her feet, Jason."

"What did you say, Sarah? Who is hurt?" she asked, struggling to stand.

"There is more dust than wounds," Parke replied; "two or three are hurt, however. The meeting is over, of course. I'll bring up the horses."

"How are you?" called Mr. Ritchings, passing in his carriage. "My coat is torn. Are you frightened? Did Miss Philippa faint? Did she, indeed? But she has recovered, I see. I shall come over in the morning to your house."

"All right, Mr. Ritchings," Parke bawled. "Come, Theresa, are you recovered enough to ride home on horseback, or shall I put you in the carriage?"

"We will go as we came, if you please."

They started in advance, for Jason was detained a few moments. Meantime the crowd dispersed; the lights were put out in the church, and the four corners deserted. Night reigned with her ancient silence; the dew fell afresh, the crickets came afield, the silver spears of moonlight gleamed everywhere, and the stars marched against the dawn.

"Sit on the front seat, Philippa," said Sarah, when Jason came up. "I want all the back seat to take a nap on."

He rolled up his coat for a pillow and put it against her head; yawning a few times, and complaining of being chilly, she soon appeared to be sound asleep. The silence was only broken by Jason speaking to his horses, which were restive. Philippa could not shake from her mind the picture of Theresa's crying on Parke's shoulder; she was very weary, however, and when the horses subsided into a monotonous trot, her head drooped as if she was falling asleep also. Jason loosened his hold on the reins and turned to look at her; the shawl had fallen from her shoulders; he drew it up, and, to his surprise, she laid her head against his breast, remaining there so motionless that he thought her sleeping. Better for him to think so then, if one may dare say that there are moments when a man's soul is rightfully his own, in its supreme and sublime selfishness. In truth, Philippa's feelings in regard to Parke were so plain to herself, that she believed Jason—her fellow-alien, the only unobtrusive, kindly being she had ever known—sympathized with her, and understood them. As for him, his heart stopped beating, then bounded forward, and dragged every nerve into the terrible development which made him a *man*. One by one his savage instincts were revealed to him; he knew that he was a natural, free, powerful creature.[33] What then compelled this monarch to still drive his horses carefully, which were conveying his wife and ward home? Will any one man or woman, who has noticed his or her own autobiography, answer? May the saints forgive Jason for ever afterwards retaining the sweet ability which this night brought him! Ever afterwards the summer sky and summer earth, "moving eastward," shared with him the secret—a right between them, which no power could annihilate, for it was not a guilty fact, but an undying truth.

At last he gave utterance to some peculiar note which the horses understood, and they flew home at a thundering speed.

Jason hung about the stables till Gilbert locked the doors and went away. He then made the circuit of the house, and saw only a light in his own room. He pictured Sarah winding her watch, putting her numerous ornaments in their boxes, and pinning her curls. A sudden desire seized him to go to her, and give her a chance to understand him. In a moment he was in the chamber, and seated near her—to surprise her by seeming interested in her toilet. She felt so constrained by his observation that she turned from the glass, and asked him what ailed him. His eyes wore so eager, thirsting, searching an expression, that had she been any thing but the plain, honest woman she was, she would have felt disturbed.

"You have taken cold, Jason; you look feverish."

"Let us talk," he said.

"Do you know that it is past one?"

"Let the clock go. Did you notice Theresa in the alarm to-night?"—removing from the subject he intended to introduce.

"No. What do you mean?" She tied her cap with more resignation to the "talk," and sat down on the side of the bed.

"She flew to Parke, and cried, with her head on his shoulder"—Jason shivered—"as if it was *the* place for her."

"No doubt she thinks so. Most girls would."

"Being his mother, you flatter him."

"Fiddle-stick! He is rich and handsome, and Theresa is a sharp, worldly-minded girl."

"Why did we marry, Sarah? I was neither handsome nor

rich—only a stupid, green boy, just as I *have been*—a stupid, ignorant man."

"It proves, don't it, that I was not sharp, nor worldly-minded?" And she gave one of her abrupt, shrill laughs.

"Did you notice *me* with Philippa to-night?"

"Philippa! I have had enough of Philippa! She didn't fall on anybody's breast, did she? She fell on the ground—a better place for her—and you picked her up. Why didn't you let her lie there? But you pride yourself on your justice."

Jason was astonished. He saw that Sarah hated Philippa. If he should confess to his wife that through Philippa he had become a different man, what would be the result? A more cruel hatred. He was dismayed at the danger he had been ready to thrust her into, for it would be impossible for Sarah to make fine distinctions; so if there was any thing now existing in him which was damaging to his conjugal honor, he could not make expiation by its revelation to Sarah.

"She must needs faint," added Sarah, passing her hand over her face, as if to smooth out the evil expression there. "She has a Southern constitution. Those Southern women are incapable, helpless babies."

"Sarah," and Jason stood up resolutely, "have I ever loved you?"

"I really do not know, Jason," she answered, as resolutely; "and, if you will force me to say it, I do not suffer to know."

"Thank you." And the conversation was ended.

As thankful as Jason was, he could not sleep. He was busy cutting down the Tree of Knowledge which had suddenly grown up before him.[34] Practically he demolished its leaves, blossoms, and fruit. This was his expiation.

CHAPTER XIII

⸽⸽

AS THE TIME FOR Theresa's departure drew near, she felt impatient to be gone. Separation was the test she thought best to apply to the relation between herself and Parke. Had she been sure of his feelings, she could have explained her own; but there was such a mixture of impetuosity and coolness, so much *abandon* at one moment, so much hard reserve at another, in his manner towards her—such moods of clinging, appealing tenderness, and of trying, imperious demands, that her self-possession was completely overthrown. Away from the magnetism of his presence, she expected to be able to analyze the influence which each had over the other. She deliberated whether she would renew the subject of Philippa's former discourse regarding him, and so make common cause with her; but an undefinable belief that, after all, Philippa had not proved herself the fool which Theresa had called her, in her estimation of the position she would claim and assume with him, prevented. It was possible that his temperament could be run down by the slow, concealed, indefatigable pursuit of a temperament like Philippa's.

"Well, Philippa, I shall soon be gone," she said. "What shall you do without me?"

"Subside."

"You are a fatalist, Philippa."

"Human life goes on with and without precept and example, failure or success. We have some sustaining principle which is independent of circumstances. Is that fatality?"

"The industrious apprentice does not always come to be Lord Mayor, nor does the idle apprentice always come to the gallows."

"I shall miss you, Theresa. The whole of Crest, outside and in, is not so lively and brilliant as you are."

"Thanks; I am pyrotechnical, I know. Look about you, after I am gone, for rocket-sticks, exploded crackers, and black wadding."

"I owe you something."

"Pay me."

"You have taught me the value of patience, and you have helped me to understand how useless it is for me to attempt to imitate you, in having any positive pursuits. I am not like other girls, and I shall not try to be. If you had not been here, I should have been for some time to come tormented with a feeling that I ought to study, to read, to feel passions, have tastes. By what you are, I have seen what I am *not*."

"By patience—what do you mean?"

"That I have had an awful trial with you, and that I have borne it."

"Do write your biography: 'Philippa, A Late Christian Martyr.'"

"Not a martyr."

"Your conceit surpasses any thing I ever saw."

When Theresa's bonnet was tied, and she was on the point of leaving the house, Sarah said: "You are coming again?"

"Of course she is," Parke interposed.

"Will you invite me, Mrs. Auster?" Theresa asked.

"If any thing depended on my invitation," she answered, "it would be worth while to ask me for one."

"Oh, mother, you are too modest; ask her to come and live with us."

Theresa's color rose. Sarah tossed the row of curls along her forehead as if they had been little bells, but her face kept a neutral expression; but the invitation was cordially given.

"Good-by, Miss Theresa," said Jason, with the feeling that he was shaking hands with an episode. He walked beside her to the gate. She broke a spray of flowers from a bush which bordered the walk.

"These betoken autumn," she said; "are you superstitious, Mr. Auster?"

"Not in the least."

"There is not a flower here whose emblem is *Remembrance*."

"Glad of it."

"Why, how ungallant you are at the last moment! Come, I am treasuring the last words of you all. Can you give me no better?"

Philippa was depositing Theresa's shawl and basket on the seat of the carriage; his eyes rested upon her.

"As if we needed emblems," he said.

"They are foolish," she answered, following the direction of his glance; "but then there are fools. Keep this flower, will you? *not* for remembrance."

The tone of her voice startled him; he looked at her so sharply that she turned crimson.

"Give it to me, then," he said. "Is there any thing else you could give me?"

"Nothing."

When the carriage went on, he stuffed the flower in his vest pocket, and passed out at the gate.

Elsa thought that the house was like a funeral the whole day, and recommended a course of company year in and year out. She reckoned the family improved by being distracted from itself. As for Mr. Auster, she had seen him something like folks for several times since Miss Bond came.

Philippa rearranged Theresa's chamber, and made a retrospect of her visit. Her looks and ways were so vividly remembered, that Philippa felt able to assume her identity; but these recollections did not cause any change in a resolve to act without reference to her relation with Parke.

When Parke returned from the station, he carried out a purpose, long postponed, of breaking a filly in harness. When he was tired of the effort, he sought Philippa, and kept her with him the whole afternoon, looking over his stock of music, and singing the familiar songs. The old life had begun again.

CHAPTER XIV

‖‖

SOME CAPRICE DETERMINING Sarah to refurnish the house, she asked Parke to accompany her on a journey. She desired him to recollect how many years the furniture had lasted, and hoped that what she intended to buy would last as long. They were absent a week. Before their return, there were two arrivals in Crest, which excited some interest—that of the bark *Unicorn*, whaler, of which Sam Rogers was mate, and the schooner *Emily*, which brought as passengers a family from the South, consisting of a mother and two daughters, named Lang. The captain's story concerning them was meagre in its details, but the gossips of Crest were obliged to content themselves with it, as nothing more could be obtained. He said that Mrs. Lang's passage was engaged, when he was in port at Savannah, by an elderly planter from the interior, who made inquiries respecting the eligibility of the small towns on the coast of New England as a place of residence, and decided upon Crest. What relation he was to his passengers, the captain did not discover; but he guessed he was a wise old cove to send them to the North.

The glitter of negro blood was in Mrs. Lang's eyes, and the negro modulation in her voice; her complexion was a deep yellow, and she wore a wig of dark, straight hair. Though past middle age, her carriage was still splendid. She had been a lithe, sinewy, gay savage, but her day was over; a double expression was dominant in her face now—of weariness, from some long-continued strain, and of repose, because of safety attained. Her

96

manners reflected the hut, the boudoir, and the Methodist gatherings of plantation slaves.

Her daughters, Clarice and Charlotte, sixteen and eighteen years of age, were handsome. Clarice had a brilliant swarthy complexion, shining, curly, black hair, large black eyes, with a vindictive sparkle, and manners which were a mixture of the sulky and the vivacious. Charlotte reminded one of the Calla Ethiopia,[35] she was so tall, slender, bending, and graceful, her complexion so smooth and opaque, and the curves of her face so beautiful. Her lips were always parted, her wistful light-blue eyes widely opened, and her straight, silky, chestnut hair disordered. She impressed those who saw her with a pitying admiration, a wondering regret, and a mysterious doubt. Mrs. Lang hired a cottage on the outskirts of Crest, in a little by-street, which Jason had cut and graded, intending to build a row, but never had, and set up housekeeping, without hiring assistance, or introducing herself to her remote neighbors. Some, calling her "nigger," wondered if she expected that anybody would associate with her and her daughters, if she did, she would find herself mistaken, and kept in a repellant attitude, in case she should make an advance; then relaxed that indignant pride, and began to suffer from a lively curiosity regarding the habits of the family, and, finally, made an attempt at acquaintance, which was met with the coldest response. Others heard of the arrival of the Langs with the same indifference that they heard of the arrival of a circus, or a lecturer on the lost arts or poetry; among these was Sarah, who, when Elsa told her the news, on the night of her return, was too much engrossed in her new purchases to pay much attention to it.

"I walked up that way, while you were gone," said Elsa, "and

I saw Mrs. Lang; she wears a wig, because she is ashamed of her woolly hair."

"Oh, Elsa," said Philippa, "do you wonder that a woman with white blood in her veins should try to hide the black?"

"A nigger is a nigger, and the Lord means to keep him so. I have no patience with the race; and it seems as if He hadn't, sometimes, by the way things go on here and in Africa."

"Mother," asked Parke, "didn't you buy something for Elsa?"

"Yes, a new front; what the shopkeepers called a 'ventilated front.'[36] You needed one badly, Elsa."

"Goodness!" she exclaimed, putting up her hand to a rusty false band of hair that wouldn't stay on her forehead, "did you think of me, Sarah?"

"Poor Mrs. Lang!" said Parke, comically.

"Now, Parke, you need not twit me; but I must say that youngest daughter of Mrs. Lang, who came here to see Mr. Auster about the house they have hired of him, is the most lovely creature I ever laid my eyes on. She beats Theresa Bond out and out."

"Does she?" Parke asked, with an air of interest. "She is to be pitied, then."

"Look at the shells Sam Rogers brought me." And Philippa brought out a box for Parke to inspect. He regretted that he had not known of the gift, so that he might have brought a little cabinet to place them in, and said he must visit Sam that night.

"I'll make you one," said Jason, who had not said a word of the Langs, though he knew more of them than Elsa did, for he had seen them several times in reference to rent and repairs.

"Jason, I believe you have a longing to follow your old trade," said Sarah.

"It amuses me to play with edged tools," he answered.

"The kings somewhere," said Parke, "learn trades, so that if their kingdoms upset, or they are compelled to abdicate, they can earn their living. Who was it made baskets?"

"That is the case with me," remarked Jason, "all but the kingdom."

"This is the first time, Parke," Elsa observed, "that I have had a specimen of your college learning. I conclude you got that story there."

"Put on your false front, Elsa, and don't be troublesome."

"Theresa Bond should have stayed longer, to see our new things," she continued.

"She will have the chance any time to enjoy my choice," Sarah answered. "I do not wish to have the house renovated for fifty years. Whoever will disturb it, disturbs me, dead, or alive."

Elsa reflected upon this remark afterwards, and did not wonder at Jason's saying "all but the kingdom." Nobody had ever succeeded in standing against Sarah, except Osmond Luce. Jason, Philippa, and Parke were under her sway. If a struggle should ever come between her and Parke, he would either give up and die, or she would harry him to death.

Parke made himself quite irritable during the renovation; that is, he contradicted her once or twice, and looked annoyed because Philippa showed so much indifference about any change in her own room. One day he brought a letter from Theresa for her to read, which contained some suggestions he had asked for, concerning her taste.

"I do not want to read it," she said.

"Why not?"

"Theresa writes me, you know,"

"So I supposed; but she does not answer *my* questions in *your* letters, does she?"

"She might as well, though."

"To save postage?"

Something wild flew into her eyes, which he saw. All the sallow tints in her face disappeared like magic, and a line of fire ran into her lips.

"What is it?" he asked. "You mean to convince me that she cannot manage me alone? Why must I have so *much* done for me, Philippa?"

If she had possessed the least subtlety of feeling at that moment, she would have given up the contest she waged; but she only thought of what she was herself, and how he should know it.

"Theresa has talked with you, of course, about me?" he asked again.

"I talked with her."

"Where is the distinction?"

"Parke, you do not understand yourself."

"Nor you. I thought you liked Theresa. Do you want me to break with her? I have only not to answer her letter."

"I do like her."

"Come, let us go and ride. The afternoon is fine."

"Shall you answer the letter?"

"I'll take the ride first."

The horses were at the gate in a few minutes, and Parke turned them in the direction of one of the necks of the bay. Philippa was foolish enough to feel happy again. There could not come a time, she believed, when her life with Parke would cease. It would not be in the nature of any circumstance that could happen to him that she would not, in some way, be involved in it, and influential with it. As for him, there was something in the atmosphere that made his spirits rise—something more with every mile that made them equable, fair, and full. The vast white clouds that moved in the blue sky, and let fall darting shadows over the still and solitary landscape—the mild sea-wind, rustling the faded corn-leaves on their dry stalks—the grasshoppers, singing their last songs in the warm turf—the purple and yellow flowers and red grass in the ditch—the low, level fields, dipping to the shore, beyond which he caught glimpses of the sea—the tranquil twilight of an old pine woods, whose needles filled up the sandy ruts, whose tops of vital green covered a gray skeleton army of trunks—the maples, whose leaves are the couriers of the frost—the flickering birches, dropping pale-yellow leaves—the tri-edged, shining grass of the salt-marshes—the whir of the brown birds—the umber-colored brooks, with their borders of cool sand—one and all belonged to the pleasant condition of his mind.

CHAPTER XV

PARKE WAS, AND ALWAYS had been, intimate with Sam Rogers, and until the house was in order Sam stayed at home and received visits from him, and saw but little of Philippa.

The Squire's mahogany sideboard, his spider-legged tables, looking-glasses in carved frames, chests of drawers, and high-post bedsteads, were removed to the garret, and left to cob-webs. The dingy carpets, and straw-bottomed chairs, and sofas invented by Torquemada, or some other inquisitor, were removed, and gay French furniture took their places. Crimson and green—drab and blue prevailed. The sombre, quaint char-acter of the old *régime* vanished; its irregular air of comfort faded in the new splendor. Some fine old curtains of damask and Indian chintz were pulled down, and a wretched combination of bro-catelle and embroidered lace was put in their place. The house, in short, was more changed in Sarah's hands than it had been in Jason's. Philippa successfully combated the assault upon her apartment—one of the largest in the house. There was but one alteration: the old-fashioned white dimity coverings and curtains were taken away, and pale-green chintz dotted with rose-buds substituted. She regretted the ancient white fringes—the danc-ing dolls of her childish imagination. The chintz, however, gave the room a cheerful look, which it had never worn before. She covered the elephantine sofa and the immense tester over her bed with it, and the oak chairs with high backs. There were no pictures on the walls, and no books, except a little pile of volumes bound in leather, and marked "Osmond Luce." Nothing, in her estimation, could be more pleasant than this room; its plainness and freedom from small rubbish were excellences. She pictured Theresa in her own room at home—as she had described it—a museum of grasses, "immortelles," weeds, plants, engravings, coins, and china, and wondered how she should enjoy herself in the Bond family, for Theresa had urged her to spend the winter with her.

One day, when she was perched on the large sofa, she heard Jason calling her; he opened the door as she answered, with the shell cabinet in his hand. Seeing her on the chintz sofa, he thought of a humming-bird.

"Here, missy, is the thing for your shells."

She sprang up with thanks, the warmer for having forgotten all about it, and asked him where she should put it. He made a tour of the walls, setting the cabinet in different places to try its effect, and finally concluded to fasten it over the mantel. Before he had finished nailing it, Sarah put her head in at the door, and looked round with a critical eye.

"I heard a pounding," she said. "What! have you only finished that thing just now?"

"Yes; is this the place for it?"

"I think so. How you have puckered the top of the sofa-cover, Philippa!"

"It suits me very well," Philippa answered; "as well as any thing can in the place of the fringed dimity."

"I can remember when grandmother sewed the fringe on. She worked hard always, but I believe she was never as tired as I am."

"Are you tired?" asked Jason.

"Yes; should you not suppose so?"

"I wish you to do nothing."

"Things would come to a pretty pass, wouldn't they—especially with Philippa perched on her great-grandfather's sofa?"

"It is mine now, and I am glad my great-grandfather is dead."

"Speaking of your grandfather, Sarah," broke in Jason, "when do you expect to be done with your furnishing?"

"Soon; and when it is once done, it is done forever with me."

"Well, I wish we could have some apple-fritters for supper."

She laughed, and vanished.

"Forever," repeated Philippa, running her finger along a line of calico rose-buds. "Forever is a long word."

"But," said Jason, raising his hammer as if about to strike the word, "there are such words, even in this world—the same as in Eternity."

She looked at him with surprise, for there was something pathetic in his voice.

"Yet," he continued, with a laugh, "there was an end to grandmother's fringe."

"How well that cabinet looks, Jason," she said, with a desire to give him some sort of encouragement.

He snapped his white teeth together, and stifled a sigh of self-pity, threw up his hammer in the air, caught it, turned on his heel, and left the room.

When they met at supper, Sarah beamed behind a heaped-up dish of apple-fritters, for which Jason expressed becoming gratitude.

"Is the struggle about over, mother, with carpets and things?" Parke asked.

"About."

"We are forehanded with the fall, this year," said Elsa.

"Let's have a party for benighted natives, and show them our furniture," suggested Parke.

"Don't be foolish," said Sarah; "but we must have company on Mr. Ritchings's account, and Sam Rogers's."

"It is almost a month," said Jason, "since any thing was done for Ritchings by the female parishioners."

"Anyhow," cried Parke, "we'll give Sam Rogers an entertainment."

Philippa laughed at the idea of Sam's enjoying company, but Parke was in earnest. He had a chivalrous feeling for Sam, which did him honor, especially as he was aware that his friendship was gratuitous; indeed, it was the only friendship he had ever sought. There was no similarity between them; they never liked the same people, nor held the same opinions. Sam never took any trouble to please Parke, but he was not insensible to his attachment. At first Sam flatly refused to attend Mrs. Auster's party, but he was the earliest guest who appeared. He came early, he said, that he might stow himself away somewhere. He laughed more shyly, and spoke with more vehemence, than was his wont; but he did not change color, or lose his tongue. Parke took a survey of him, and admired his manliness. Philippa directed him to sit beside her, if he did not wish to receive any attention. She could not help contrasting him with Parke, and taking him for just what he was worth, as she in her thoughts expressed; how much higher in the scale Parke stood! Sam was all over brown, face, hands, and hair, which last was so thick, short, and curly, it would not part. His nose was large, and his mouth wide; his eyebrows were close together, and his eyes were small, but they were keen and penetrating. Parke's serene, marble-like brow, the faint bloom coming and going in his cheeks, his large, sensitive eyes, his firm, beautifully-cut mouth, the indescribable, unconscious grace of his attitudes, the movement of his head, and his air of repose and self-possession, proved him worthy of Philippa's ideal.

"What did you let mother have the pattern of this choking collar for, Philippa?" Sam growled. "I am strangled and miserable."

"Ha, old fellow," said Parke, "you have come to wearing something like what I wear. Thanks, Philippa."

"I could not thwart your mother's ambitious views for you," Philippa replied.

"Mother is losing her wits."

"You are an only child, remember."

"Say, Philippa" (Parke had turned away), "is Mrs. Auster as soft on Parke as she used to be? He has grown up to be just what I thought he would be."

"What is that?"

"He has never checked one of his tendencies, nor had them checked."[37]

"We differ about him," she said, gently.

"You are soft yourself about him, as you always were, hey?"

He was embarrassed, looked down on his hands, and opened and shut them as if they were his safety-valves. She looked at them, too, and for the hundredth time noticed the blue stars and crescent moon pricked in India-ink on his right hand.

"He is enthusiastic about you," she said.

"He is a fine fellow, and ought to go whaling," he answered, with an expression which denoted that he should say no more to her about Parke.

She was called away, and he amused himself by shuffling a pack of cards, which he took from a table near him, and studying Philippa. He feared that she, too, had grown up to be what he suspected four years ago; he knew her too well to hope that her feelings would be changed by any ordinary grief or disappointment. All that could be done for her, in case Parke should break her heart, would amount to very little, for she would accept no consolation. He had dubbed himself her knight when she was a small girl, however, and he would, in his own fashion, stand between her and harm. She would never perceive it, so he might as well make the effort. Who would, if not he? She never had a real friend in her life. "Damned shame," he almost said aloud, and struck his knee so that the cards fell in a shower at his feet. Looking up, he saw Parke contemplating him.

"Avast," said Parke, when he met his eye.

"Avast it is. Look here."

"I am."

"What about that gal mother told me of, who has been visiting here?"

"I'll show you her picture, if you will step out."

"How many have you collected since I went off?"

"My collection is small, but choice."

"And important, if true."

Parke led the way into his room, and was obliged to look in several places before he could find Theresa's picture, which fact Sam noted.

"There," said he, producing it; "isn't that stunning to your harpooning mind? Did you ever see a handsomer face?"

"I have seen a better one."

"Of course, you must detract. Have you a suspicion that I am in love with the owner of that face?"

"You may have more than a suspicion that you are; but you are not."

He tossed the picture on a pile of books, and stared at Parke.

"It is no go," he said.

Parke returned the stare, and answered: "It all depends on your decision, my brave tar, of course. I have only waited for you to come from your ancient and fish-like calling, to be settled in life."

They reappeared in the parlor, arm in arm, and Sarah remarked complacently to Mrs. Rogers, that it was pleasant to see Sam's delight in the society of Parke.

"I don't know," Mrs. Rogers replied, "which he makes the most of, Philippa or Parke; but I reckon he'd do any thing to please Philippa."

Sarah sneered; but the sneer was lost on the good-natured Mrs. Rogers.

"Jason sticks to his rule still," she added, "of not making his appearance when there is any company round."

"He is a poor hand at entertaining people."

"Now I don't agree with you; *I* find him an excellent companion."

"He does seem to be at home with you," Philippa remarked. "I wonder why?"

"Trot right off, Philippa, and attend to Mr. Ritchings; he don't take his eyes off of you."

Sarah bit her lips, and looked round at him angrily.

CHAPTER XVI

||||||||||||||||||||||||||||||||||||||||||||||||||||||

THE HOUSE IN THE ORDER she destined it to be, Parke settled at home, looking forward to no change — what remained for Sarah but repose? A thorn grew in her spirit, which rendered nugatory her well-earned content. She could no longer disguise the fact that Mr. Ritchings loved Philippa. It angered her to see that his love was not received as a favor, with gratitude and agitation; and it angered her to know that a man whom she respected and admired should think of selecting Philippa for his wife. It irritated her also to understand that he might place Philippa in a position where she could, by her money and name, aid him in his career more than she herself loved to aid him. She determined to caution him. The caution was well conveyed; it influenced him, but did not bring him to the point of ending his hopes.

Philippa was, so Sarah said, peculiarly unfitted for the place a minister's wife should occupy. Under the most favorable circumstances, it was disadvantageous for him to select a wife in his own parish; it was sure to create dissension in all its families, except the one he married into. It was a familiarity on his part that bred him contempt—falling in love, courtship, engagement, marriage, should be performed afar off. Under unfavorable circumstances, as in Philippa's case it would be, the state of things would be far worse. She was not admired; she was cold; had no friendships in Crest—no interest.

"Her property is an interest, is it not?" he asked.

"What do you know about that?" she asked sharply. "Has Jason—"

"Jason has said nothing," he answered haughtily. "I have asked him nothing. But if ever a girl understood what the 'sentiment of the soil' is, it is Philippa." It is incredible, but she continued, without actually lying, to give him an impression that it was by no means certain that Philippa would inherit much of the "soil;" her father was still alive—a man of reckless character and extravagant habits, who would prove a curse to him, should any relation be established between them.

"In all the years," taking up the topic of her character again, "I have never heard one expression of gratitude or affection from her. I have watched over her when ill, day and night." A real tear shone in Sarah's eyes, which he credited, for he knew that she had most carefully watched over Philippa, of whose regard and devotion to Parke he tried to speak.

"He makes devotion easy, you know; he has the power and means of gratification far more than you have. Besides, she has grown up with him, and affection between them is a habit. She is a creature of habit."

"Is she entirely devoid of passion?" he asked, with a flushed face.

"There," she replied, with a contemptuous sparkle in her sharp eyes, "you step on ground I know nothing about. *I* do not look into such questions."

"Why don't you?" he said roughly; "society hinges on questions like these. You, a wife and mother, ignore them."

She tossed her curls. "I presume we differ in our ideas."

"In describing Philippa," he said, in an exasperating voice, "I fancy you have described your model in spite of yourself; she is one not to be moved by a man's love, nor his hate."

"Experiment for yourself, then; I have spoken for your good alone, against one whose father is my nearest relation. You must know that I am in earnest."

From the time of this discourse, his conduct towards Philippa was a curious mixture of neglect and watchfulness, the satirical and the dignified, the perplexed and the determined.

To watch him, and distrust his strength, to lay up a store of irritation against Philippa's insouciant behavior towards him, became the task which prevented any folding of the hands, and drove Sarah at the old speed.

Mr. Ritchings haunted the house and the whole family. If he met Jason in the street, he turned and walked with him; if he saw Parke riding, he beckoned to be taken up and conveyed to some place he had no previous intention of going to. He appeared to have discovered that Elsa was an "original," and made frequent raids into her territory; but he never talked of Philippa—not even to Sarah did he again mention her.

Elsa met his advances with an air of simplicity which made Jason laugh, and speak to her of the condition he knew Mr. Ritchings to be in. He was working, he said, against wind and tide.

"My opinion is," she replied, "that beaux won't interfere much with her; but if she should ever set her heart on anybody, she will hold on like grim death to him. She is like her father there; he had but few ideas but they were strong ones. I hope she never will fancy she loves some man."

"Why not?"

"Because she will be disappointed, most likely."

"No she won't; she shall not be."

"We are all disappointed, for that matter—don't you think so? If we reach up to a round above us in the ladder, we have to let go the one we stand on; then we look back on it, and are sorry we moved. If we don't reach up, we are looking up. Mr. Ritchings is in just such a fix."

"We are all disappointed, are we?"

"I don't know that you are. Neither death, disgrace, nor poverty, have knocked at your door yet."

"Disgrace has."

"Why, Mr. Auster, you scare me; you are joking."

"Disgrace has knocked at my door with a lantern in her hand."

He was forgetting himself, but her disturbed face recalled his thoughts.

"She comes to most people in the dark, I guess," she said, hastily. "I only knew you when you were first married; if you had any by-gones before that, hadn't they better be by-gones? How well I remember your wedding-coat!"

"Blue, with brass buttons;—where is it?"

"Why, Sarah cut it up the other day; I guess it was moth-eaten."

"Did she?" A look of pain passed over his face.

"Do you expect Osmond Luce to come back ever?" she asked, suddenly.

"I think he will come; why do you ask?"

"In case Philippa should change her mind about Mr. Ritchings, what a nice father-in-law he would make a minister!"

"He is not so bad, Elsa; he gave up his rights to Philippa, you know."

"That was because he didn't want them, you may depend; if he had, heaven and earth would not have kept him out of them. Dilly-dallying here won't make my pie-crust, though."

She vanished from the kitchen, where she had held her confab, into the adjoining buttery.

Jason was moody; he seemed to himself to have been but a dull clod. He had droned in Crest and had his wedding-coat cut up, while Osmond Luce, breaking every shackle, like the bold, generous spirit that he was, had made himself free, and had followed out his true impulses. He—Jason—too, had been troubled with some ideas about improving Humanity! He should be glad now to have it proved that he had made himself a little wiser and better than he was when he started on the tour of life; the sunshine, the fair tideless river, had tempted him, and he had laid on its banks, like a hulking beast, gaping for flies. His face grew dark, and the muscles hardened round his mouth like iron cords; he rose and stretched his hands above his head, striking with his palms the ceiling. At that moment Philippa entered by the porch door, with a branch of maple in her hand crimsoned by the October frost. She had been taunted by Sarah that day; to escape her, and her own feelings, she had gone into the distant fields, and skirted the borders of the woods, till she was utterly fatigued. She paused when she saw Jason; the electrical atmosphere of a perturbed spirit passed from one to the other; it produced in her a vague wish to be understood by him, and in him an emotion which made him curious.

"Look at this, Jason. I brought it from the Bartlett fields; there is a line of maples blazing up there."

She approached him.

"Have you been so far?"

"Yes; Gilbert is up there, with the dogs."

"The dogs have run away."

He kept his eyes fixed upon her face, but with an expression of self-assertion and self-mastery that made him look kingly. The branch was extended to him; he took it and twirled it to and fro;—a heavenly smile broke over his sorrowful eyes.

"Thank you, Philippa."

"Oh, I am not going to give it to you; I promised Theresa to gather her some autumn leaves."

He was thanking her—not for the crimson branch, but for appearing before him then, to make him remember that at least he could suffer nobly. He handed it back to her.

"Theresa must have all she wants," he said.

"No, not every thing."

"Don't you think so?"

"Why, no; do you?"

Surprised at the tone of her voice, he was silent, while she stripped every leaf from the branch so slowly that he counted each one as it fell; with the last she looked up. Her eyes made him wonder what the matter was with her.

"Do you mean any thing concerning Parke?" he asked.

"Yes."

"There is nothing wrong, I hope; he still likes her, does he not? They like each other;—a very happy match, I should say."

"I thought you might know, Jason," she almost whispered. The truth burst in upon him.

"What—what, *what?*"

"That I have believed—that I myself should marry—"

It was beyond his power not to put his hand over her mouth; he stifled the name between her lips. She saw he knew it, but could not understand the check. Elsa made a providential clatter close by them, and she attributed it to that. A wave of anguish dashed over him, followed by a host of roaring, crawling, cruel emotions, that rent him asunder; he felt as if soul and body were parting.

"Come in the dining-room," he said, calmly; "Elsa is noisy."

Half leading, half carrying her, he placed her on a sofa and himself beside her, and then, as the room was darkened by blinds and shades, he allowed his pain, amazement, and perplexity to fight as best they might. In her profound egotism she thought that he was considering how her wishes could be brought about.

At last he said, "Can Parke make you happy?"

"I was happy with him."

"Could Theresa be happy with him?"

"*He* would not be with her."

"Ah!"

"I think there is no engagement between them."

"None?" he asked, bitterly; "what were they doing together here?"

"Trifling."

"It was that, was it? Trifles do not disturb you?"

She was abashed at his accent, but said in a firm voice, presently, "Jason, if our lot is cast with another's, we must bear all the crosses, as well as our own hopes. My *judgment* sanctions all that I would do. Do not believe that I am mistaken."

One of the parlor doors opened, and Sarah entered with her hands full of some sort of sewing-work.

"You are posted here, are you?" she said, when she perceived them; "but it is not necessary to keep in the dark, is it?"

Jason rolled up the shade, and threw open the blind.

"Will you sit down?" he asked.

"Are you talking over business?"

"Oh no!"

Philippa felt towards her a repulsion which acted like a charm; she wished—in a lethargic way, however—that the charm would vanish, so that in some shape she could hurt her.[38]

"Philippa has talked a great deal to-day," Sarah said.

"We were speaking now," Philippa replied, "of Theresa."

"You don't approve of her, I suppose."

"Nonsense, Sarah," said Jason; "why should she approve of her? because she flirted with Parke?"

Sarah looked very angrily at Jason; his manner was unusual.

"Are you putting your finger in the pie?"

"If you mean a match between Theresa and Parke, yes,—I oppose it."

He left the room before she could reply to him.

"Are *you* influencing him?"

"What makes me dislike you so utterly?" asked Philippa; "I cannot account for it."

"Answer me—what does he mean?"

"I'll answer you nothing just now."

"I advise you not to meddle in anybody's love affairs, if that was the subject of your discourse."

"Love!" cried Philippa; "yes, that was the word. Do you know it?"

She rose from the sofa, with glittering eyes fixed upon a distant something, and clasped her hands together with an inspired gesture, which reminded Sarah of the episode of the rosary.

"You are crazy," she said.

"I have been mad for years; do you think that I should have lived with you if I hadn't been?"

Light flashed in upon Sarah's mind also. "Had Philippa been idiot enough to expect to gain Parke?" she thought. If it was so, she would never allow Philippa to dream that such a thing was possible. It was not possible, as far as Parke was concerned, and yet—there was the property, which might be all his again. But no, the idea of that girl being his wife was not to be thought of. She started up with an energetic movement, and said, "Don't show that you are cracked to more people than you can help. If

Jason has nothing better to do, he can listen to you. I wish you to attend to those pillow-cases I spoke to you of."

"Yes," said Philippa, with the habit of obedience, "I will."

"Here, here," called Elsa, from the passage, "whose litter of leaves is this? Sarah, I want you in the buttery."

Mr. Ritchings, the unconscious agent of this development, came that very evening to the panelled parlor, where Philippa sat stitching the pillow-cases, and Sarah knitting. It would seem as if that day's turbulent life included him in its outward circling waves. With Philippa's scissors, and on her side of the table, he snipped paper, and talked philosophy which was full of calm bitterness. Sarah sympathized with him and Philippa coldly combated. Parke had gone to pay a visit somewhere; Jason and Elsa were absent, but Sarah maintained the field, which he wished was clear. She grew jocose, and compelled him to listen to her.

"It is too cold to open the window, I suppose," he said, at last. "You should see the moon to-night."

Philippa rose, threw up the sash, and stepped out on the terrace.

Sarah looked up at him with a restraining eye.

"Why do you sit in this room so much?" he asked, impatiently. "These dark panels oppress me; haven't the walls the power of contracting?"

"You would breathe more freely outside."

"To tell you the truth—yes."

"Go, and have done with it," she said, suddenly, and somewhat sadly. "Philippa has been a whirlpool before to-day."

"Whirlpools have one advantage—they don't leave a wreck behind."

"I thought differently—that all sorts of things would come tossing ashore with every storm, from their depths. I feel it is so." And she shivered. "The house seems full to me of spoils that have been destroyed by their ungovernable rage."

He had followed Philippa. Sarah laid down her knitting, crossed the room several times, and then stopped before a portrait of the Squire, painted at the age of forty.

"She is contemplating her ancestor," he thought, casting a look backward. "Why don't she give up her vanity and vexation of spirit before that representation of sublime selfishness?"

Philippa was pacing to and fro between a row of shrubs and the windows. The moon, midway in the sky, sailed up from a bank of clouds, and dispersed them in a pearly shower of vapor which sped its way before her. Under the horizon the sea, struck by its waves, ran hither and thither—a world of billows without a margin. Crest lay half in shadow, half in light, wrapped in the mysterious silence which is inseparable from moonlight. Never does the soul feel so far from human life as when a man finds himself alone in the vistas of the moon, either in the streets of a sleeping city, the avenues of the woods, or by the border of the sea. Earth, swayed perhaps by her powerful satellite, withdraws her sympathy from him, and he wanders in a white void, wondering if he was born to be thus annulled.

"Does this beauty make you feel that you

'Would be something that you know not of,
In winds or waters?'"[39]

Mr. Ritchings asked, pacing beside her.

"No; I think of lunatics in moonlight nights. There is no wind, but the atmosphere is full of chilly moisture."

"Let me get you a shawl. Don't go in; walk down the path with me."

She declined the shawl, but assented to the walk. They went down the terrace. He endeavored to take her hand, but she quietly folded one over the other, and prevented him.

"I read a horrid thing the other day," she said, "'Christabel.'[40] I am reminded of it to-night."

They stopped before the gate. Surveying the road below it a moment, he said, in a matter-of-fact way, "I wish you would walk down the path of life with me."

"You really wish it?" she asked, confronting him.

"If you were not the coldest, most insensible girl in the world, you would have known my wish long ago."

She shook her head slightly. Cold as she was, the sight of her at that moment of soft, subdued light, standing under the rolling sky, the dark trees round her, alone with him, sent his blood warmly through his heart. She wore a dark dress, which, with the shadows, concealed her form, but her head and face looked angelic. Her fair, flowing hair, her firm brow, her sweet mouth, her little hands, which moved restlessly, made a picture that hung in his memory long after.

"Believe me," she said, in a broken voice, "I could never satisfy you."

"That I know. But I love you."

"I beg you," she said, in a gentle voice, "to give up all hope."

"Why should I?"

"Because I can only be your poor friend."

"You are very young, Philippa. You may be more yet to me."

"My character is not formed,—you would say?" she asked quickly.

"Precisely."

He would have it a drawn game.[41]

"Well, let us walk back," she said, and to compel him to do so, she placed her arm in his.

Sarah had resumed her knitting. She did not raise her eyes, but began to chat as soon as they entered. Philippa was silent. She judged that Mr. Ritchings might be as persistent in his feelings as she was in hers, and she did not know how to manage him. He soon bade Sarah good-night, but instead of going home, walked beyond the town, till he heard the baying of Jason's dogs in the woods. He wished, for a moment, to change places with that "free, indifferent, rough man, the delicacy of whose feelings would never stand in the way of his happiness." At that moment Jason was lying in the depths of the woods, half buried in the falling autumn leaves, so still that the "wingless airs"[42] crept about him undisturbed, so sad that the leaves were moistened with his tears.

CHAPTER XVII

||||||||||||||||||||||||||||||||||||||||||||||||||

SAM ROGERS WAS AWARE of the state of Mr. Ritchings. They met often at Jason's, and he was the only one of the coterie whom Mr. Ritchings neglected — the one who alone could have given him an insight into the real life of the family. He called him "the whaler," and "your awkward friend," and "the nautical man," and asked Sarah what the attraction was about Sam, and why Parke and Philippa were never bored with his society. Sarah replied with some asperity, that his courage, honesty, and perseverance had won him everybody's respect, and that he was a *protégé* of her grandfather's. Mr. Ritchings said no more. Sam had a fondness for chess. He induced Philippa to learn the game, and evening after evening they pored over it. He also professed to have more ear for music than formerly, and often engaged Parke at the piano. Some kind of a nucleus was needed, he argued with himself, in that house, for Philippa's sake — something to knit them together and bring out their good qualities. He wished that he could play the family as he played chess. The winter must be passed pleasantly; therefore when Parke suggested that there should be a series of cotillon parties, he cheerfully consented to be manager with him, although he was only in the jig line himself. The visit to Theresa Bond was put off till the latter part of winter, and Philippa, since Parke's heart was in the cotillons, made up some evening dresses and practiced waltzing with him in the parlors. Elsa called waltzing the devil's ring-round, but she must say that she thought Philippa was an adept in it. Sarah made no opposition to the scheme, because it was Parke's, and said nothing in its favor, because she was a member of the church, which disapproved of frivolities. Her tacit consent was borne out by the fact that most of the dancers were children of church-members, like herself, who said "the young will be young," and "nature will out," in spite of the tenet that dancing was one way of going to perdition.

After the first cotillon party, however, Mr. Ritchings preached a Calvinist sermon, which made his hearers nod and wink at each other, with a grim sense of humor at their deserved punishment. This was the only way he noticed Philippa's evident pleasure in the cotillons. It made him heart-sick as well as polemical; it was a matter in which the line of separation was an iron chain. Why should a man's profession compel him to take part against himself? Why should a man's calling be so much better than himself, that to keep up with its demands he must play the hypocrite? Not that he wished to dance—far from it—but he did not wish to be excluded from Philippa, who was all that could make him good.

A universal excitement prevailed, when the cotillons opened at the Crest Hall, among those who went, and those who stayed at home; a new sensation was felt, because they were under Parke Auster's auspices, who had never been prominent in any public enterprise before. Even the staid Gilbert went to the hall entrance to see the guests enter; when he returned, he asked Mary who she supposed was there? Elsa, startled from her doze by the fire, said, irritably, "Your master, the devil."

"I shouldn't wonder, Elsa; but, besides him, Mrs. Lang's girls are there."

"Oh, gracious!" exclaimed Mary, "well, I never; did you, Elsa?"

"Who invited them?" asked Elsa.

"The managers, I suppose," he answered, lighting his barn-lantern; "Parke Auster, Esq., and Sam Rogers, Esq."

"You'd better confine your observations to the barn," suggested Elsa.

"Think so? Well, I will." And he disappeared.

"It's that Sam Rogers's work," says Mary; "he don't know who to invite, and who not to. How should he? been whaling all his life."

"No, it isn't," Elsa replied, rubbing her glasses thoughtfully.

"Those girls haven't been about any to my knowledge. I never saw either of them."

"I have."

"I wonder what they have got on to-night."

"Pshaw, Mary; do you know who you are talking about?"

"I believe I do—fugitive slaves."

"Niggers: let them alone."

Mary was silenced, and Elsa took a lamp and went to bed.

The Lang girls were the latest at the dance. Parke was dancing with Philippa when they entered; as soon as it was over, Sam Rogers went to him to inquire how they got in.

"They came with Tim Jones."

"Did he bring them here without consulting you as to the propriety of so doing?"

"He spoke of bringing them when he took his ticket."

"You consented?"

Parke gave him a rigid stare.

"I did more."

"Have you seen them before?"

"Since you are getting up a catechism—yes. I saw Charlotte Lang once with her mother; they came to the office. I think her extraordinarily beautiful, and that is why I did it."

Sam looked at his calm face with a keenness which was mixed with admiration. He knew he could not make him lie, yet there was something inscrutable in his countenance which he could not read. It wore a mask of marble.

"They won't get any partners."

"Tim Jones must look out for that. There are different sets of people here, you observe; the *sang azure* would not cover the floor."[43]

"Damn your French," said Sam, turning on his heel.

Clarice Lang, in a short time, defined her position.

"If the managers ask us to dance," she said to Charlotte, "we shall not have made a mistake in coming; otherwise, I shall understand Mr. Parke Auster's invitation."

"How, Clarice?"

"He is pleased to make an experiment, perhaps."

Charlotte sighed.

"You always say such things."

"You are a fool. Don't you see that we are a card for once? I have no doubt but that Mr. Auster is daring enough; he shows people that what he chooses to do, he will do."

"Then Mr. Jones is daring, too," said Charlotte, logically.

Clarice shrugged her shoulders.

Several young men were introduced, and begged the pleasure of dancing with them. Clarice refused coldly, and Charlotte declined with a gentle grace.

Philippa was amazed at Charlotte's beauty. She thought of a time, in the twilight region of early childhood, when she had heard the sound of the lash on shoulders as lovely as Charlotte's, perhaps; at any rate, it cut the flesh of her race. Suppose she were tied up to a whipping-post at this instant, what would be the tide of feeling? would it change from the contemptuous coldness now shown to pity and protection? She asked Parke what he thought of her.

"I think she is too beautiful to be lost in this Sahara; I pity her from my heart. It is of no use to fight with imbecility, though; you can see how those girls are received among the coarse boobies here. I only asked to have them treated like human beings."

"Shall I speak to them?"

"No, it is not best," he said quickly; "I would rather not have you. Ask Sam what he thinks of them," he added, with a laugh.

He danced with no one that evening except Philippa. Several times he addressed a few words to the Langs. While he spoke, Charlotte continually looked at him, and continually averted her eyes from him, and he scarcely appeared to see her, but he felt that a sure, irresistible, slow current was setting towards her. There was one fatal dower between them! Each time that he left them, Clarice instinctively turned to Charlotte and eyed her sternly. All the world might have heard what he said; but Sam Rogers watched his mouth as the words fell from it, as if they had been reptiles he would have strangled. When he next came across Parke, he said, in a voice whose accent of ire and derision it would be impossible to describe, "I wish the yellow cook of the *Unicorn* was here; I'd introduce him to those wenches."

"Would you?" Parke answered, flipping his glove; "how good of you!"

Sam went to Philippa.

"I am almost sorry," he said, "that we have undertaken these parties; there is such a mess here—cabin and forecastle mixed."[44]

"I am sure it is a success; I never saw such universal smiling before. What is the matter with you, Sam? You look worried."

"I feel like a fish out of water. How I hate these gloves. If you are pleased, it is all right; I was afraid you would not like it. Parke is as headstrong as the devil; look at him."

He was speaking again with the Langs, who had never moved from the seats they had first taken.

"Oh, what do you mean, Sam?" and she looked vexed; "don't you approve of his noticing those poor girls?"

"*Noticing*—bah! you speak of him as if he were a lord, going round among his vassals. I tell you candidly, Philippa, if he does go to hell it won't be all his fault."

She bit her lips with furious anger.

"You are a pretty friend," she said. "Why not let him alone, and give up the pretence of being his Mentor?"

"Philippa, I am nobody's friend but yours; I do not consider all Crest as being worth the snap of my finger in comparison with you."

"Then you are Parke's friend, if you are mine."

"Bother Parke!"

He looked deeply hurt.

"Forgive me, Sam, but you are so foolish."

"Never mind about my forgiveness, give me yours; I think I am rather foolish." And he looked at her fondly and pitifully, cursing himself inwardly for expecting her to understand him, or anybody else, and promising himself to immolate his opinions and acts, in just the way she would have him. Her hand crept under his, and if they had been alone she would probably have pulled his hair, or pinched him. And so the quarrel ended.

When Sarah heard that the Langs were at the party she gave her shrillest laugh, and begged Jason to learn to dance. Such things were in accordance with his ideas. She never dreamed that Parke was the means of their being invited. Not the slightest uneasiness crossed her mind as to the place they might attain;

she knew the pride and prejudice of the most humbly born of Crest too well for that. Had she known, even, that Parke had been good-natured enough to invite them, she would have felt no concern beyond ridicule; the spirit of society was too strong even for his wilfulness to go beyond a certain point.

The next evening Parke took a walk in the direction of Mrs. Lang's house. His splendid dog "Bruno" went with him, and when they came opposite her windows, Parke said to him, "Speak, Bruno!" A deep yelp brought Charlotte to the window of an unlighted room. Man and dog passed slowly along and repassed, Bruno slouching with his black head close to the ground, and Parke firmly, with his fair face upturned to the window. He saw a curtain move, that was all; but it made his heart knock against his breast, and he felt his will rising imperiously.[45]

CHAPTER XVIII

THE LANGS MADE no second appearance at the cotillon parties. At the next Parke zealously danced with the prettiest girls in the room till ten o'clock, when he disappeared, and returned in the space of an hour, remarking, to those standing near the entrance, that he had been taking the air and a cigar. In connection with these were facts which he did not mention. He went to the tavern stable, where he knew there were saddled horses which belonged to some of the party, and applied to an ostler for one, telling him there was a mistake about a card of invitation which must be rectified at once. He gave the man a handful of cigars as he made the request, and in a moment a horse was led out, and he was on his way to Mrs. Lang's. Arrived there, he fastened the horse to the palings of the little yard, ran up the path, and knocked at the door. It was opened by Mrs. Lang, holding a lamp, and shading it with her hand.

"Good-evening to you," said Parke.

"Good-evening," she answered, intent on keeping the lamp alight.

"Are your daughters at home?"

"Yes, sir. Here, Clarice, Charlotte." And she retreated, placing the lamp on the window-shelf of the sitting-room, so that its rays fell across Parke on the steps, glanced down the path, revealing the black stalks of the hollyhocks, and the dark shape of the horse tied to the paling. Clarice came out, followed by Charlotte.

"I called," said Parke, in a polite voice, "to inquire whether there was any mistake in your card of invitation to-night."

"None at all," replied Clarice; "we decline going."

She turned away abruptly, and vanished, but Charlotte lingered.

"You left the party to come so far to inquire?" she said, regretfully.

"It was my business, as manager, to do so."

"You are very kind, sir."

"You could not enjoy yourself much the other evening, of course."

"Oh, no!" she answered, plaintively, moving forward, and bringing her face into the lamplight, which revealed its pure, fragile, delicious outlines.

He shivered at the sudden sight so palpably, that, to hide it, he exclaimed it was a cold evening.

"Excuse me for keeping you." But, instead of making a move to return, she took another step forward. "I feel the cold, too, sir; the change in the climate is great; there is nothing warm here."

"Oh yes! something." And he advanced a step. His silky mustache almost touched the band of hair that fell low down her face.

"No," she repeated, "there is nothing of the South here."

The thought of Philippa flashed into his mind.

"I have a cousin from the South."

"I saw her," she said, disdainfully.

"I must go; I shall be missed. Good-by."

"Did you ride up here?" she asked, discovering the horse.

"Yes. Do you like to ride?"

"Very much."

"Some time will you ride with me?"

"Oh yes!" And she clapped her hands with delight.

"You will see me soon, then; good-night."

"Why did you stand and palaver with that young man?" asked Clarice.

"Why Clarice!"

"He would not come by daylight."

"Yet you called him daring."

Mrs. Lang closed the hymn-book she had been reading, and looked first at Clarice and then at Charlotte.

"It is of no use," she said, "for you to fret each other; give it up so. What one wants, the other wouldn't have. I tell you to make the best of every thing."

"The best!" said Clarice, with contempt.

"Alive or dead, you will stay in this place. Make a way if you can. God Almighty knows I am content."

"Mother," asked Clarice, "you had a white husband."

"Who tole you so?" she answered, with an indescribable grimace.

"I asked you," screamed Clarice.

"*I* brought you into the world, you are my chil'n—bone of my bone, flesh of my flesh, with all your beauty."[46]

"That's the curse of it."

"Devil's brat," cried her mother, "your father will find his chile, sooner or later."

Charlotte, who, had not uttered a word during the scene, now rose and put out the light.

"What's that for?" her mother asked.

"We are all of a color now."

Mrs. Lang shrieked with laughter. "She beat you, Clarice; she do always."

Charlotte unbraided her long hair, which, in the fire-light, even, looked silky and elastic, cautioned Clarice about the fire, and glided from the room; but Clarice immediately followed her, and Mrs. Lang was left alone.

She carefully set up the firebrands against the jambs, squatted on the hearth, thrust her feet in the hot ashes, and talked to herself, breaking into a laugh occasionally, and checking it with a "Bless de Lord." Her head dropped on her knees, and she slept, till a loud dash of rain startled her.

> "Hi, hi, the trade-wind blows,
> Ha, ha, the good ship goes!"

she sang, feeling about the floor for the shoes she had kicked off, to put on, and go to bed properly before "dose girls."

CHAPTER XIX

‖‖‖

TO KEEP UP WITH THE improvements in Crest made in his absence, Sam Rogers, with an ivory cane, made occasional excursions about the town and suburbs. Crossing a field, one gray December afternoon, to shorten the distance to an unfrequented road which he wished to gain, he saw a pair of horses which he knew, toiling up the hill, and stopped behind the stone wall till they reached the place where he stood, and passed. He saw Parke in his light curricle, and Charlotte Lang beside him. He noticed that the whip was in its rest, and that only one of Parke's hands was employed in driving; the reins hung loosely, and the horses went to one side of the hill and then to the other, as they chose. Sam looked after the carriage till it rolled out of sight; then he sat down on the wall, wiped his face with his handkerchief, and said: "Damned strumpet—cursed fool—coward—knave!" He sat there a long time, staring at the hill, before he could make up his mind what plan to follow.

That evening he made the tour of the stores where men gathered to gossip over the events of the day, and listened to them with jealous attention, but heard nothing that he feared and half-expected to hear concerning that chain of circumstances—a link of which he had seen that afternoon. The next morning he haunted the bar-room of the tavern, the stable, the ship-yards, and wharves, and made several calls among his female acquaintances, but heard no mention of the fact, which was nearly breaking his heart. On all sides he was accosted with raillery for his rare and unexpected appearance. "You are getting tired of your aristocratic friends," said one; and, "Have you had too much of the Austers?" said another; and, "We were afraid you were going to give up us and whaling," said a third. To all of which he growled expletives more forcible than elegant. On his way home he met Jason, and, suddenly wheeling about, walked with him. Thrusting his hands into his pockets, he fell into a deep study. Jason was reminded of Mr. Ritchings's vagaries, and wondered whether Sam, too, had not fallen a victim to the same trouble. He made no effort to break Sam's revery, but walked beyond his own house, and would have walked still farther, if Sam had not suddenly looked up and struck him on the shoulder.

"How are you, Jason?"

"I think, Sam, I am better than you are."

"I vow to God, I hope you'll keep so."

He wheeled round suddenly, left Jason without another word, and went home to his dinner, which he attacked with an absent-mindedness that amazed and distressed his mother.

"You eat," she said, "but you do not set any value on your food. I thought that apple-pie would go to the right place. I put cinnamon in it on purpose."

He immediately bit a large piece, but with an expression which by no means satisfied her.

"I do believe you wish you were off to sea again, and I am no better than the pelican in the wilderness."

He laughed wildly.

"Any neighbors been in lately, mother?"

"Mrs. Jones, Tim's mother, was here yesterday, after some carpet-rags."

"What did she say?"

"She was so bound up in rags she couldn't think of much else."

"A she Lazarus."[47]

"She *is* afflicted with a bad humor," Mrs. Rogers said, solemnly.

He laughed wildly again, and she declared that she shouldn't wonder if he was coming down with the canker-rash—it was about.

"The Jones family live near those Langs, don't they?"

"Yes, the Jones's house is the nearest; about half a mile from it."

"She did not mention them, I suppose?"

"Well, she did say that they kept themselves to themselves, as they ought to; and she said, too, that Mrs. Lang always washed on odd days of the week, instead of Monday. She must have queer ways, but I believe she is regular at the Baptist meeting."

"I thought you were going to have a tea-party for me?"

"Law, Sam, I will any day."

"Some day this week?"

"Let me see, to-day is Tuesday—well, Friday, say."

"Who shall we have—the Austers."

"And Mr. Ritchings."

"Of course. Did you ever ask Elsa Bowen to tea, mother?"

"Many's the cup of hyson she and me have had together in years gone by. What a hand with sick folks she was! We used to go watching together; I always thought she was all the more lively in times of distress. She never goes out now, and I don't see much of her."

"She never will forsake the Austers."

"Not on account of any trouble they may be in, for she is so odd; she may go from some whim. She is proud of her connection with them; you know she was second cousin to Mrs. Maria Parke, the Squire's second wife."

"You believe one person is as good as another, don't you?"

"Pretty much, unless they are Universalists."

"I am a Universalist."[48]

"Don't let anybody know it in Crest. Take your notions of salvation to the natives, if you want to. Dear me, how can you believe that the wicked ought to be saved?"

It seemed as if her discourse soothed him. He smoked several pipes while she ran on, and his countenance assumed its wonted expression of tranquillity. For a moment he could not believe in the reality of calamity. His mother's placid face, the tones of her voice, so free from anxiety, denied it for him. He remembered that she had passed through trouble, but not a vestige remained. The material atmosphere about was alone marked with permanence; the most trivial objects outlasted the heaviest affliction the heart could bear. There were the brass candlesticks on the shelf, which had been kept bright year in and year out, in the face of disaster and death; and the eight-day clock, with its dull, enamelled face and gilt top; and the chair-cushions of broadcloth patch-work were kept in their old place, while millions of men had gone mad with trouble, and out of life. The smell of the old wood-work, the light from the green knots in the old window-glass, the nameless sounds which come and go where people live, which were associated in his mind with events of the past, and had survived them, assured him that in such things alone existed perpetuity. The creaking of his mother's old chair, in which she sat rocking, and had rocked so many years, he listened to, and compared it without emotion to the creaking of the cordage of the ship which went down,[49] carrying with her his shipmates, and leaving him with a solitary boat, on just such a day as this, when there was a long, unbroken swell in the sea, with silvery reflections from the pale, cold, angry sun. What did the sea know of that event to-day! The gulls dipped into the swell with their gay scream, and chased each other, with wildly-flashing wings, over its gray surface. That was all he remembered.[50]

Early in the evening he went to Jason's, and sat down to chess with Philippa. There was an unusual bustle in the house, owing to some kitchen anniversary. Elsa made frequent inroads into the parlor, where they were, and Sarah frequent exits from it. Great fires were burning, and lamps were alight in all the rooms. The atmosphere was exhilarating, fixed, secure, and Sam could not help feeling comforted. As the evening advanced quiet settled over the house. Sarah, fatigued, rested silently in her chair by the fire. Jason sat by himself over the dining-room fire, with his feet on the fender, and his arms folded. Parke came in, and with a nod to Sam, and "How are you, shipmate?" seated himself by the piano, and played, at first, a loud, triumphant march, full of reiter-ated notes, and then a waltz, which opened with a silvery trickle, deepened into a wild, rushing flow — a chaos of tumultuous, bro-ken, whirling foam, and ended in a vague, solemn, unvarying swell. Sam's sensibilities, excited again, traced the spirit of the waltz, its wild cry for possession, its unappeased longings, its wail of satiety, its necessity for the eternal, and its despair.

Jason's pale face passed the door, and repassed.

It was Philippa's turn to move, but the game had stood still. Sam gave the board a shake, which toppled the chess-men over, with noise enough to rouse Parke from his musical dream. He left the piano. Sam furtively searched his face. He saw only the same tranquil, winning beauty. But Parke's lids drooped over his eyes. Behind lay a world, concerning which Milton invoked the heavenly muse to sing, —

"Of man's first disobedience."[51]

Parke drew a chair beside his mother's. He smoothed her glossy, waving hair, turned the curls over his fingers, asked her about the brooch that fastened her collar, took her hand, and feared it was hardened with too much work; she must not do so much for them all. She met his eyes with a smile, and he looked into hers, with an expression which she could not read, because for her "the handwriting on the wall" was never visible.[52] The kind mood expanded and included Philippa, who yielded to his irresistible sway. Could she have understood his face and manner, there was that in them which would have made her soul quell with pain. An apprehensive chill struck Sam. He felt that *danger* emanated from Parke's behavior. It betokened the wakefulness of a faculty which had roused all the other faculties into play. It betokened a farewell to the relations between him and his mother—Philippa—all! A cowardly fear assailed him lest Parke should envelop him too, and then, with his infernal candor, show him the sword oscillating over their heads.

"What has become of Jason?" he exclaimed, starting up. "By-the-way, I am going to have a tea-party. Will you all come, on Friday?"

"Of course," said Sarah.

"Of course," Parke echoed, dreamily.

Sam passed quickly into the room where Jason was, instead of leaving the house by the front door, and spoke to him, listening for some movement from Parke. He had gone to the piano again. Relieved from his fear, Sam went into the kitchen, hoping to get out unobserved, but Elsa and Mary were still busy there.

He walked round the table and asked Elsa to give him something to take home to eat—he was starved.

"Gracious, Sam, if you don't like your mother's cooking, I can't suit you."

"What's the news?" he asked, peering into her acute face.

"I don't go about collecting the article. Haven't you brought some? You look wise."

"Yes, the devil isn't dead."

"Is that news? Here, take this mince-pie, and clear out with your devil. Bury him if you can."

He took the pie, with a laugh, and disappeared.

"He is bright," said Elsa to herself, "and good. People don't know him as well as they think they do. And his father was a stupid man, and his mother is a stupid woman."

CHAPTER XX

||||||||||||||||||||||||||||||||||||||||||||||||||||

THOUGH MRS. ROGERS delayed tea on Friday evening on Parke's account, he did not arrive till the feast was in *débris*, and the company withdrawn from the tea-table to the parlor. He had been out with his horses, he said, too late, though the weather was excuse enough for driving that afternoon, so mild and soft for a winter's day. Had anybody noticed the sunset, and the silver mist that wrapped every thing in its vail, he asked. At Mrs. Rogers's request, Philippa came back to the table to keep him company while she was gone in the kitchen preparing a hot short-cake for him, and drawing fresh tea.

"How pale you are, Parke!" said Philippa.

"Am I?" he said, without looking at her.

"Where did you go to-day?"

"Up by Millville; do you know whether father was in the woods to-day?"

"I believe so."

"I heard his dogs, I was sure."

He folded his arms on the table and hid his face in them, but raised it instantly and stared into the corner of the room.

"I thought," he continued, absently, "that they sounded like bloodhounds."

"But you never heard bloodhounds."

"Have you?"

"Once."

"Have you?" he repeated, without having heard her, and

instantly taking a knife from the table, with which he struck an empty glass near him, he endeavored to modulate the tinkling sound into a familiar air with an appearance of profound attention; but his mind was dwelling with rapt fidelity on a new and terrible joy in his possession. The secret was no burden now, but the source of a strange pride, which made him consider himself apart from the rest of the world by the right it had given him.

Philippa was moved by his paleness, lassitude, and mysterious excitement; a protective, pitying feeling impelled her to go to him, put her arm about his neck, and kiss his cheek. As a city falls to ruin, with its pulse in full play, in the embrace of an earthquake—so fell his sin into the depths of his soul. He met her clear, strong, upholding gaze, because he *would* meet it; because, come what might to him, he never could fail to meet the eye of any human being with an unflinching daring for the truth. But a shadow of something prophetic fell on him; the loss of a beautiful hope, which he might have felt. To her it seemed as if her touch had made him a statue, he was so motionless; every feature was set in calmness, only his eyes were wildly dark. Her arm fell from his neck, and she turned away, repenting of the first caress she had ever given him.

Happily, Mrs. Rogers bustled in with the fresh tea. She begged Philippa to attend to his wants, for she only just wanted to take out the tea-cups—she shouldn't wash them—and, with a pile in her hands, she disappeared again. Philippa poured the tea, which he took silently and drank slowly; but he ate nothing. When had he heard from Theresa, she asked, to break the silence. That very day he had received a letter, which he sorted out of some papers, and gave her, with "There's nothing in it."

"When shall I visit her?" she asked.

"Before long; any time."

"How long do you intend this meal shall last?" asked Sam, thrusting his head in at the door. "I must smoke a pipe."

"Come in, old fellow," said Parke; "I'll smoke with you."

Sam filled his pipe from a box on the mantel-shelf, and was soon absorbed; and Parke, taking a cigar from his case, lighted it, and fell to talking on the subject of Sam's next voyage. So pertinent were his questions and remarks relating to it, that Sam was drawn out completely, and gave descriptions of sea-life, to which Parke added information so entertaining that Philippa was oblivious of the parlor, till recalled by an ill-humored reproof from Sarah. He had made himself so pleasant, that Sam, in a generous moment, accepted the excuse he offered for going home without appearing before the visitors. A plunge into the long, black night was what he most desired—"a sleep, and a forgetting."[53]

It was hours, however, before he slept. His sagacity stood in the way of repose. His relation with the world—meaning Crest—must be changed, sooner or later. He had lost Theresa. A barrier was raised between him and Philippa which she would never cross. Of his mother he did not think; he had been so trained that the consequences of his wishes and will never struck him as involving any thing of her but her compliance. *But*—he had gained Charlotte.

That evening Charlotte Lang found the house deserted on her return from her ride with Parke; her mother and sister had gone to the evening meeting of the Baptist society which Mrs. Lang had joined, and which was in the progress of a revival. Charlotte did not light a lamp, but put away her bonnet, folded her shawl, and crept to bed in the dark. Did the angels of Pity and Patience guard that bed? Or waited a demon there, to behold the spectacle of dead chastity in a lovely shrine? Who will summon either to pass judgment upon a drama in which they were neither actors nor spectators!

Ignorant, confiding, weak, poisoned with ancestral blood, none shall judge thee, Charlotte—but God!

Her thoughts were intent upon Parke alone. To-day he had been hers; to-morrow he would be hers. Mother, and Clarice, and the people in Crest—he could keep them all away. Half stifled in her exquisite hair, what dreams came to her! She heard again the baying of dogs along the woody road, the rustling of footsteps among the leaves, the murmur of a sweet, muffled voice. The gray dusk crept round her, and the silver mist, and the breath of love: not a false, selfish, cruel love, but the love for life, till death; sweet, kind, tender love; forgetting all, meaning all,—but distrust, disgust, satiety.

CHAPTER XXI

||||||||||||||||||||||||||||||||||||||||||||||||||

THE WINTER PASSED. No shock or jar deranged the machinery which society keeps in running order, and which sometimes runs over society, crushing, tearing, mutilating it. Even Sam Rogers nodded in the vicinity of its wheels, and Parke trifled with its cogs and springs, playing a desperate game, to test it. Early in the spring, the owners of the ship *Hesper* offered a captain's berth to Sam Rogers, for an Arctic voyage, which he accepted, and prepared to sail. The cotillon parties ended in February, but a grand ball was projected by Parke, which included Sam in his managerial capacity. It was postponed several weeks, on account of the severity of the weather. Spring arrived, with snow, gales, and rain. As soon as the sun softened the roads into decent travelling, the night for the ball was appointed. Everybody had been dull before, but now Crest was astir. A thin blueness stole up the sky, and tinged the bay, whose waters, released from the bondage of ice, danced upon the shore in chopping billows and hissing foam. The pools, which had stood in the fields and ditches, sank through the mats of dead grass, and the frogs began to croak in a circle round the town. Garden paths grew smooth, and garden patches mellow, in anticipation of the burst of leaf and bud. Elsa said the weather had been so bad, that she wondered why the Lord hadn't started a grove of Ingy-rubber trees, so that people might have the stuff for shoes at hand, to paddle in the water with. It was the way things went in this world; she supposed that the trees grew where it never rained nor snowed.

Jason remarked that he was sorry to have Nature lay down her arms; he liked the music of her bands better than the fiddles and horns at the hall. It was a pity, she said, that he had not been born a wild Mohammedan, so that he might have trained as he pleased, and nobody been the wiser for it.

"After the ball, Philippa," said Parke, "we will visit Theresa."

"After the ball," Sam commented, "I shall be off, thank God, in the *Hesper*."

"After the ball," hoped Mr. Ritchings, "something of the old time may come back."

"The ball is nothing to us, Charlotte," said Clarice Lang. "Our privileges are the same."

"The same," Charlotte replied, with a conscious smile; "it makes no difference whatever to him."

"*Him*," said Clarice angrily; "I wish he would not come this way so often. Have you but one thought?"

"When was he here?" Charlotte asked, too willing to talk on the dangerous subject.

"I believe he comes when we are away; I know it, you poor, silly fool; he amuses himself by showing you attention."

"Mind your own business, Clarice," said Mrs. Lang, looking inquisitively at Charlotte. "It is for you to attend to the concerns of your soul."

"Pooh, I go to meeting to kill time. What is the use of my soul to me? No more than my body is. Both are worthless."

Charlotte looked at Clarice with such an expression of denial and doubt, intelligence and superiority, that her mother, who was still observing her, shook her head so violently that she attracted a wondering attention from Clarice, who asked her if she wasn't flared.

"Stay at home, then, you abominable," Mrs. Lang cried.

"No," said Clarice firmly, "I wish to keep out of the way."

"Dear me," exclaimed Charlotte peevishly, "what way?"

"For all me, he shall have full swing; when some other whim takes his idle brains, I'll give up religion, as you have, and bear your whining and pining till you get over it. A little of you will suffice his vanity."

"We get over every thing, we do," said Mrs. Lang, giving to the winds whatever secret thought might have disturbed her. Kicking off her shoes, as she always did in moments of excitement, she broke out with a souvenir of the plantation: —

> "Pull up de yam two feet long;
> Eat up de yam two feet long;
> For de massa wants us strong;
> What he wants is nebber wrong."

Clarice cursed her, and Charlotte cried bitterly.

The ball made a difference to them all. It opened the door of discovery. Two of its guests, from a town below Crest, named Clark and Cook, made themselves obnoxious to Sam Rogers in the early part of the evening, by telling him they were on the look-out for a handsome girl with a streak of black, named Lang. "She may be coming," said Mr. Clark, "as she keeps company with the manager, young Auster; we have seen them in our village several times. I can't say as I blame him; she is as pretty as a pink. Ain't they talked about here?"

"What will you take to drink?" Sam asked abruptly, longing to knock him down; "there's something below."

"What will you take, Cook?" asked Clark, dubiously.

"Oh, any thing that's round; beer, cider, lemonade, or switchel."[54]

"Switchel be damned!" cried Sam; "come down stairs."

If those fellows were only on board his ship, he thought, he'd truss them by the throat with a clew-line.

They were ushered by him into a small room at the back of the hall, where, on a table, stood a candle, a few tumblers, a sugar-bowl, and a bottle that was empty.

"Somebody has availed himself of all the opportunity," Sam said. "Excuse me a few minutes, I'll bring up a supply."

Clark and Cook begged him to take his time Miss Lucy[55]—they liked a chance to cool off, and he started on a run for Jason's.

"There's no watered liquor there," he muttered; "I must chisel some brandy out of Elsa, and drink those blackguards drunk."

He reached a back door breathless, and entering on tiptoe, listened at the kitchen door—there was no sound within; of course Elsa had gone to bed! He must have the brandy, however; so he crept up the kitchen stairs, opened the doors of several dark rooms, and at last opened the door of her room. She had on her night-cap, and was reading aloud in the Bible when he entered, "Or the golden bowl be—"

"Broken,"[56] he said.

"What are you conjuring about here for?" she asked, surveying him with composure; "to read my Bible, and repent of your sins, sir?"

"Elsa, I want a bottle of that old Cognac; quick, they sell poison at the tavern, you know."

"What do you want of it?"

"I've got a case at the hall—a brace of strangers, who will have liquor."

"You needn't come here with your braces; however, I'll ask Sarah."

"No, no—don't torment me; I am in earnest."

She was out of the room with her candle, and pretended to be uncertain where to find it.

"It is up garret, in a demijohn."

"I'll go for it."

"No—it is down cellar, in a jug."

"Give me the candle; you are enough to make the parson swear."

"There's a bottle in the buttery; now, I recollect Sarah opened it yesterday, to give old Mr. Weaver a gill. Now, old Mr. Weaver"—and she stopped short.

"Mr. Weaver wove a yarn as long as yours, which will be cut short, mam." He put his arm round her waist, lifted her feet from the floor, and carried her down into the buttery, where, after some exploration, the bottle was found.

"Much obliged, Elsa, we'll drink your health," he said, hurrying out.

"I shouldn't wonder," she soliloquized, on her way back, "if he should look upon the wine that is red. His father drank more than any man of his age in Crest; he was full from morning till night."

"Shall I mix your grog, gentlemen?" he asked, reentering the room where Clark and Cook sat drumming on the table, keeping time with the band overhead. Looking at each other, they said they didn't think they needed it strong—they were not used to it—but that they might be as well hanged for a sheep as a lamb, and he might. He poured brandy enough in each glass to make a green hand madly drunk, mixed much sugar in it, and handed it to them. It was taken with "my respects," and winking eyes, together with a declaration that it was "first-rate swipes."

"Now for a jig," exclaimed Sam, with an air of high satisfaction.

"Jig it is, and with the beauties, *if* you please."

Partners were found for them, and places in the dance. Sam stood in the vicinity, to watch for the first symptoms of intoxication, for drunkenness in the ballroom should be put down with a high hand. The heat of the room, the noise and the motion, he calculated could not be borne many minutes. But to his surprise, when the quadrille was over, they came to him, and asked how the bottle stood.

"Where we left it; come, try luck again."

"If it is all the same to you."

The dose was increased and repeated; its effect was sudden. Sam immediately proposed going over the way to the tavern, to have a smoke. An assent with a hooray was given, and without hat or overcoat the party rushed over, and Sam piloted the way into an empty room.

"Norr cigars," said Mr. Clark, who felt poorly in his head; "something strong—fetch on pipes and some niggerhead."[57]

"Exactly," said Sam, locking them in as he went out, and returning in a moment.

"Speaking of niggerhead," remarked Mr. Cook, who had seated himself on two chairs, and was poising his head on the sharp slat of a third, "Where *is* that Lang girl? I didn't see young Auster round, either—taking a walk in the suburbs, maybe."

"Let it all out, you white-livered son of a gun," said Sam, furiously, "What do you mean?"

"'Mong frens, you know," said Mr. Clark, placably.

"By George," answered Mr. Cook, "you had better be milder, it would be good for you. Your town will have news soon that will run like wild fire, and your sprig, Auster, with his dam airs, will have a hyst."

"Dam," Mr. Clark uttered.

Mr. Cook bent forward and whispered in Sam's ear, lost his balance, and fell on the floor, where he went to sleep. Sam looked at Mr. Clark, who was trying to smoke a pipe with the bowl downward, and vainly igniting Lucifer matches on his boot-soles, his cuffs, his knees, and the carpet.

"You'll do," said Sam.

"We'll do," replied Mr. Clark. "An gor, thank you—you'll *do* to-morrow."

Before noon the next day, despite Sam's precaution, an intangible rumor spread over town. It was not traced to any particular source, no one dared to meddle with it at first, but Rumor is an "insane root"[58]—once partaken of, its madness grows. From "Have you heard?" the step was taken which confirmed the truth of the connection between Parke and Charlotte. In common with every soul in Crest, with the exception of the Auster family, Sam heard all the gossip. Parke Auster's good name bit the dust. The most grovelling details accompanied the descriptions of Charlotte Lang's beauty and gentle manners. If the blow had fallen—as the feeling and the tongue of the public would, in the first flush of detection, have had it fall—on the family, it would have crushed Sarah and Philippa, but tongue and feeling were soon exhausted, and the family were still in ignorance. Sam went to Jason's every day with the heart of a culprit. He looked into the faces of each one for some inspiration to direct him what course to pursue—how to temper the awful fact. None came. The *Hesper* demanded his time, was the excuse he gave for making his visits so short, and for avoiding Parke. But one evening, when Philippa had begged him for a farewell game of chess, they met.

"Your last games?" asked Parke.

"Yes," Sam answered.

149

"I have half a mind to go on the voyage with you."

"Better stay here."

The tone of his voice was so significant, that Parke went round to the back of Philippa's chair and mutely interrogated him. He returned the look with one eloquent with contempt.

Parke quietly took a chair near him, and waited till the game was finished, and he had risen to go. When the outside door was reached, Parke laid his hand on the latch, stood before him, and said, "You have heard something."

"Let me pass," demanded Sam, with a husky voice; "let me pass, or—"

"No, it won't be worse with me if you stay. Sam, you know it all."

"I do."

"I imagine the town knows it."

"Everybody."

"Do they know," he spoke with an accent that made Sam's blood run cold, "that I shall marry Charlotte Lang?"

"Now by God, Parke, you shall not do it! You must not, cannot do it! Nature is against it—the whole race!"

"I am a little old fashioned, Sam; she is the mother of my child, Parke Auster's child! Has the town mentioned that fact yet?"

His tone of self-disgust, resolution, dogged daring, and his air of painful *ennui*, *blasé*, suffering, are not to be described.

"I—I'll see you to-morrow; there's a man waiting for me now, about a chronometer. Good-by. How could you? If she hadn't been—damme, give me your hand!"

Parke was crying now like a baby in Sam's arms. He wiped his own eyes, moved from one foot to the other, swore at the world, and every thing in it, and finally led Parke into his room, and sat up the whole night with him.

CHAPTER XXII

ɪɪɪɪɪɪɪɪɪɪɪɪɪɪɪɪɪɪɪɪɪɪɪɪɪɪɪɪɪɪɪɪɪɪɪɪɪɪɪ

ELSA WAS LOOKING FOR clothes-pins that had strayed in the greensward at the upper end of the orchard, the next morning, when she saw Mrs. Rogers nodding to her to come up to the fence, the boundary between the road where she was walking and the orchard.

"I am just passing along," said Mrs. Rogers. "How be you these days, Elsa Bowen?"

"I am so as to be able to look after the odds and ends; how have you been, Betsy? I haven't set eyes on you this winter."

"As tough as a pine knot, or I couldn't stand what I am obleeged to. Why don't you go out once in a while, and keep up with what's a-going? You might be astonished sometimes at what you'd see and hear."

"See fools, and hear clack."

"It isn't always clack, though I am not sure about the fools."

"What's in the wind now?"

"I do suppose your folks have heard nothing about themselves, have they? I do wish Mr. Ritchings had spoken to Jason before now."

"What is it, for mercy's sake?"

"Charlotte Lang, you know—"

Elsa stooped suddenly, and clutched a clothes-pin, bringing up with it a handful of grass.

"And Parke—they say there's something wrong between them."

"It is a vile lie. Who says so? Where are *they* who say it?"

"Now, Elsa, it is no use; the whole town knows it. *Sam* knows it—he told me last night—and he said, 'God help Philippa.'"

"God help his mother. What is it to Philippa? It can't be so, Betsy."

But Mrs. Rogers convinced her that it was so, by relating all the particulars, and concluded with, "That girl ought to be drummed out of town."

"The hussy!"

"You have got to tell the family; nobody can do it better. There, don't take on so. I knew you would, you faithful, attached creetur; perhaps *all* of it isn't true, after all. I knew I must tell you. Providence sent you out this morning for clothes-pins, and me to buy blue yarn, so that we might meet. I didn't see my way clear at first; I thought of going to Sarah. I'd rather face the cannon's mouth than her. She'll die, or she'll carry it off with the high Parke hand. Didn't my old man know what that was—steel springs covered with satin; though I must say Sarah ain't so smooth. You ain't offended with me, Elsa, for throwing such a burden on you? 'Tis time something happened—you ought to be expecting it; think how long the family have prospered every way. I must be getting along. Do take something when you go in. Think of my Sam's going into icebergs for four year."

"Sam is a credit to you, Betsy," said Elsa, with a strong effort to resume her natural manner.

"But he is a man. You can't trust one, you know. You never can guess the moment he will fail you, and never the one he won't."

Elsa's search in the grass continued a few minutes after Mrs. Rogers had passed on, but she saw nothing there; her thoughts were fixed on the task before her. There was no avoiding it.

Parke's death she could communicate, but to be the bearer of such tidings put her to her trumps. She vowed never to be in such a scrape again; she would keep her eyes open for the future. She must be getting forgetful and stupid, or she would have been on the look-out for his sowing his wild oats. Yes; if ever the shadow of what must be called living trouble fell on the family again, she should cut and run. She was willing, if need be, to bury every one of them; but she could not stand the wear and tear of disgrace and misery.

"Though the day of judgment is at hand," she concluded, "dinner must be seen to, cooked, and eaten." And she went back to the house. Every thing through the morning was finished in her thorough, methodical manner, but she was inwardly debating how she should begin her story, and with whom. Once her heart failed her. It was when Sarah came into the kitchen to show her the new-fashioned plaits in the bosom of some shirts she was making for Parke.

"What if I should not say a word about it?" Elsa asked herself, with her eyes raised above her spectacles, examining the work. "It might blow over in time, and finally come to her ears like a spent storm. But no; some blundering booby would give them all a shock, and they would expose themselves to the public."

"Very handsome, indeed, Sarah," she said, aloud, "but a great deal of trouble."

"I don't mind that for him, you know."

Here was a chance! Elsa wet her lips, caught her breath, and—allowed Sarah to go out without speaking a word.

"That villain, Parke," she exclaimed, "he ought to be sent to State's prison—sentenced to hard labor for his lifetime. It all comes from his having nothing to do. How could he help having riches left to him, though? How could he help taking after one or two of his relations? Poor boy!" And she cried to herself softly, wiping the tears away under her glasses as fast as they came, till Jason's entrance interrupted their flow. He took a seat in the corner of the hearth, and lighted a cigar, which Elsa thought was just the thing to forward her purpose. Taking a basket from the window-shelf, she sat down near him, and began to sort its contents and study his aspect, and the probable effect upon him of what she was about to say. It never struck her till now how stern and upright a look he wore. There was a certain hard, cool air about him, which convinced her that he would go and knock Parke down, as soon as he had heard her story. She instinctively penetrated his view of the case, which would be to side with Charlotte Lang. He would take her wrongs into full consideration. That would be awful. Still, she must trust to his sense, which was the best she knew of.

"Have you been round to the stores this morning?" she asked.

"What upon earth should I go to the stores for, unless sent by you on some small errand?"

"You might hear something, you know."

Her trepidation was painful. She thought he would comprehend instantly something of the truth, and it was a great relief to hear him answer: "Elsa, what do I want to hear the gab of the stores for?"

"I know you don't." And she laughed almost hysterically. It was impossible for her to tell him.

"I have been on board the *Hesper*, though. She hauled down the bay early this morning. I can't imagine why I didn't take to the sea."

"It is too late now. Are you tired of comfort, Jason?"

"Comfort is tedious when it lasts too long."

At that instant Gilbert called Jason away, and Elsa was glad of it. At dinner she lingered with Sarah over a cup of tea, when the rest had left the table and gone.

"Sarah Auster," she exclaimed suddenly, "you are nothing but skin and bone! You must take medicine. The least wind would blow you away."

"It's my business whether I am skin and bone or not," she replied crossly. "I am well enough, and shan't take medicine."

"Oh, very well. I don't recommend any thing at all; but you are sick, you know you are."

The clatter of dishes which Elsa rather resentfully made, drove Sarah from the table, and Elsa remarked to herself that perhaps their sorrows had only just begun. Something certainly ailed Sarah, and none of them had perceived it. She took a desperate resolve, and went to Philippa's room, and found her embroidering a cushion.

"Philippa Luce, you might as well know it as anybody."

"Tell me, then," replied Philippa, calmly sticking her needle in the canvas.

"Mrs. Rogers told me this morning that Sam told her last night that it was all true. It is all over town—everybody knows it."

"I don't know it yet."

Elsa turned her back to Philippa, and began to dust the shelf with her apron.

"Charlotte Lang has made mischief."

"Well," said Philippa, rising like an automaton.

Still dusting the articles on the shelf, Elsa told the tale. Philippa was so still that she turned to look at her. She was chewing a bit of silk floss, and her eyes were fixed on the floor.

"And," continued Elsa, "*you* have got to tell Jason and Sarah."

"Never."

"Oh Lord, Philippa!"

"I never will speak of it to one human being—unless it be to Parke, or," she added, with a frightful hauteur, "to that slave."

"Yes," cried Elsa, "she is Parke's slave, and you know it. But whose slave will be Parke's child, with your blood in its veins?"

"That will do," said Philippa, shuddering with disgust.

"No, it won't do, Philly; don't feel so. Don't you know human nature?"

"No." And she looked away from Elsa, out of the window. The world seemed stretching round her a wide, flat, lonely plain, over which she must plod by herself, for she had no "human nature" like this. An acute vision of Parke's abandonment to a wild, isolated happiness, such as she knew *he* could enjoy, passed before her mind, and for an instant she felt his utter separation from her. But not even this glimpse into the abyss of passion suggested the idea of renouncing him. It created a barrier against her which filled her soul with hatred, but not with despair.

"We are punished for human nature, though," said Elsa; "and what will his punishment be?"

"In what he makes me suffer."

"Oh," exclaimed Elsa, ironically, "it will be no injury to his mother, of course. And the pride of the Parkes won't be taken down in Crest! The last of them has exceeded all the evil-doers of the name."

Philippa had not thought of Sarah. She had thought of no one besides herself. But now she asked what Jason would do.

"He won't have a breach of promise case, I assure you."

With an inward trembling Philippa resumed her embroidery, and, like Imogen,

> "Pricked her fingers every stitch,
> And left in every bud a stain."[59]

"What do you mean?"

"Enough said, at present," she answered, in a loud, cheery voice. "I've got plenty to do, and I'll go and do it. I'll wash my hands, just now, of everybody's business but my own."

Philippa threw down her work, and with locked hands and a rigid face turned the matter over in her mind. She determined to show no emotion before Jason and Sarah, let come what would. Neither for any one, nor in any cause which pertained to that unhappy affair, would she change one habit, intention, or plan. She was somewhat shaken when she went down stairs and met Parke in the hall, and exclaimed involuntarily, "I know it all—you—"

His hand was on her mouth.

"Not a word shall pass between us," he said. "Never, Philippa. Cross the gulf in silence, or let it be impassable."

The nervous pressure of his hand against her mouth subdued her; she stood still and dumb, with her eyes averted. His hand fell, and he bent forward to look at her; the sight gave him a curious sensation of pain and surprise. She was evidently in an inward fury; he noticed her strange eyes—the spots in them seemed alive—her scarlet, burning lips, and her waving, vivid hair; he thought of the "Sphinx" again, and wondered if Theresa would not give her the name of Pythoness, now.

"I am going to Theresa, to-morrow," he said, gently.

A faintness came over her, which she struggled against. She grew so pale that he extended his arm to catch her, but she caught hold of the balusters for a support, and then raised her eyes to his face, so full of mad resolution and defiance that he forgot it was Philippa.

"Say adieu," he said haughtily, "and kiss me."

She struck him so violently in the face that he was blinded, and could not see her as she ran up stairs again.

While he was gone on his visit to Theresa, Sam Rogers sailed on his voyage to the Arctic seas. It was between daylight and dark that he went to Jason's to say farewell, the day before his departure. He hoped no lamps would be lit; he would rather not see their conscious faces, for he supposed that Jason had heard the truth. After a hurried chat, he rose to shake hands.

"I have got to row off in a hurry, after all. Shall I bring you an Esquimaux waiting-maid, Philippa, or a reindeer?"

Their hands were grasped tightly, there was no need of words.

"You'll never see *me* again," said Elsa, half jocosely, half sorrowfully; "I am going to step out."

"Who will step in your shoes, Elsa?"

"Oh, plenty."

"Elsa wants to be coaxed to live," said Sarah.

"Live, I entreat you," he begged, and bending over her, whispered a few words in her ear.

"I promise," she answered.

Sarah took his hands in hers, and looked at him sadly.

"Four years is a long time, Sam; but I do not know that we should doubt them, any more than we doubt to-day. I am truly sorry to lose you."

"God bless you, Mrs. Auster. All hands, good-by. I shall meet Jason outside." And waving his hat, he dashed out. Philippa had already disappeared. As the gate swung to after him, he saw her standing under the firs, in the corner he must pass. There was too much light still for him to escape, or he would have rushed by, feigning not to see her.

"You sent no message to Parke," she said, quietly, when he reached her.

"Oh," he answered, carelessly, "I said my last words to him."

"Will you send your love to him?"

"My love isn't worth sending to man nor woman."

"You lie, Sam; it is worth sending to both."

"Ha! you begin to appreciate my immense goodness."

"May I tell Parke, I ask, that you sent him your love?"

"Tell him what you please. Give me one kiss, Philippa?"

She stood on tiptoe and met his lips; then tapped him on the shoulder, with a nod, which sent him on his way smiling and sighing.

CHAPTER XXIII

||||||||||||||||||||||||||||||||||||||||||||||||||||||

WITHIN SIGHT OF THE *Hesper*'s sails, as she bore down the bay next morning, Philippa started on a walk, in the hope of finding something on the earth, or in the air, to culminate or dissipate her mood. Charlotte Lang also wandered forth aimlessly, and they met in a cross-road, beyond the town, which was bordered on both sides by a thicket, bursting into leaf, and alive with the songs of birds. Charlotte was gathering violets along the edge of the thicket when Philippa saw her.

"She can think of flowers," Philippa observed.

"There comes Philippa Luce," thought Charlotte, bending close to the ground. Philippa stopped in the path, like a soldier ordered to halt.

"What are you doing?" she called.

Charlotte turned, and held up a handful of violets; her hair, blown about her face, her languid, wistful eyes, the faint color rising in her cheeks—she was the picture of a sad, lovely Innocence. "Will you have them?" she asked, in a singularly melodious voice, with a childish treble in its accent, slowly approaching. Philippa's eyes so filled with dazzling beams that crashed down from her brain, that for a moment Charlotte looked a dark, vague shape, whose coming overpowered her with hate and horror; but when she saw more clearly, and saw the composure with which Charlotte stood before her, an irritation like madness possessed her.

"What do you mean?" she asked, harshly.

"You spoke to me, and I answered."

"I would have died first," said Philippa, incoherently, and stamping her foot with a measured thud on the ground. "Do you know the misery you have made?"

Charlotte looked at her earnestly: "*You* would have died. *I* wanted to live."

The maddening vision of a happiness which she had had no part in, and could have no part in with *Parke*, again rose before Philippa's mind.

The violets fell to the ground one by one.

"Could you 'live' no other way than by going out of your place? You are not his equal."

"That is your way of thinking," Charlotte answered with a sullen frown. "He came after me, remember. I never asked any thing of him. I never shall. Why didn't you keep away from me?"

Philippa turned scarlet from the most womanly feeling she ever had.

"But," continued Charlotte, "I act according to his wishes. He governs me."

"Insensible, heartless, beastly African!"

Limpid tears dropped from Charlotte's eyes, as pure as the fresh violets at her feet.

"Oh, where is he?" she moaned.

A sound of wheels made them look round, a chaise was coming down the road, with Sarah in it, who was returning from some business concerning the Dorcas Society[60]: the floor of the chaise was covered with bundles of work, and Gilbert was driving it. His quick eye caught sight of the girls, and he tried to pass before Sarah could discover them.

"Isn't that Mrs. Lang's girl?" she asked. "What can Philippa be speaking to her for?"

"I bleeve so," he answered adroitly, tickling the horse to make it jump, and it went by the girls on the leap. "Peers to me that's Mr. Auster's boat, off the ledge there; do you s'pose he is coming back from the *Hesper*, marm? Do tell me if you see her sails yet, bearing off the light? I see Mrs. Rogers about an hour ago; her eyes were bunged up with crying."

She stretched her head to follow the motion of the boat, and Gilbert said to himself that they had had a pretty close shave of it to ride by *that* danger.

Charlotte exchanged glances with Philippa when she recognized Sarah, and an expression of painful dismay passed over her face.

"I wish," she cried, "that I might never set eyes on any of you again."

"Amen."

"I wish he would take me, and go with me to the everglades."

"Wish to be dead," said Philippa sternly.

"I won't," she answered, with a pretty, petulant shrug; "you needn't think it. I am strong enough to bear every thing. But"—with an assumption of dignity—"I forgive you, Miss Luce, for your wish. Why, what is the chaise coming back for?"

Philippa surmised the fact that Gilbert had been sent to bring her home. He reined the horse beside her with so careless and contemptuous a disregard for Charlotte's place in the path, that the wheels grazed her dress; she was not mindful of his sneering face, for she was observing the horse—an old friend. One more effectual word Philippa longed to say, which, through Charlotte, might pierce Parke like an arrow and cut like a sword; but it was an emergency she had no weapons for. She parted from her without even a last look.

"Dear me," said Gilbert, shaken from his stolidity and respectful reserve; "things have come to such a pretty pass that I think we might as well shut up shop to our house—give up the ghost and call it square. *I* haven't got the leastest mite of ambition or courage left in me. To this day Mrs. Auster hasn't found it out. What's to be done? It must not go on so. Are they going to be allowed to carry on so, Miss Philippa, and the family not know it? God bless me, *you* know it. I presume that gal was making complaint to you."

"Hush, Gilbert," said Philippa, much distressed. "Wait; something will be done. You must not put your mind upon it so."

"Very well," he answered, with dignity. "We are all demeaning ourselves by going on in this way."

It was as bitter a moment as she had endured. Gilbert was right, but his making common cause with her as a matter of principle, was most galling to her pride. She felt that he had made himself the mouth-piece of the sense and the rights of a moral community, and her soul rebelled against it; she would, if possible, so isolate her family from its influence and opinions, that even their vices should not be meddled with.

Parke came home that day with the dash and flavor of travel about him. At the tea-table he gave a lively account of his meeting with a college chum who had just returned from Germany. His recapitulation of the stories of German life was so entertaining, he so thoroughly entered into their spirit, that Philippa felt as if the old atmosphere was obliterated. He was a spectacle to Elsa, who every moment, since her interview with Mrs. Rogers, considered herself as walking over a volcano. "There's something more than human in him," she thought; "nothing will beat him down."

"I wish we could stay in Germany," said Philippa absently.

"By the way," exclaimed Sarah, "what were you saying to Charlotte Lang this morning?"

Philippa made no answer, but fixed her eyes upon Parke, who suddenly felt in his pocket for his handkerchief. Elsa glided from the room without a sound, and stationed herself before the door to prevent ingress.

"The time has come—I saw it in Philippa's eyes, and now Master Parke is going to walk on the edge of the burning plough-share." She spoke, unconsciously tucking up her wristbands, as if she contemplated being called upon to participate in the *mêlée* when it should be at its height.

An ominous silence prevailed at the table. Sarah, astonished at Philippa's not replying to her, looked up, and, following the direction of her gaze, saw that in Parke's face and manner which startled and perplexed her; but Jason, looking from one to the other, divined some evil he would rather not know of; he rose, and opened the door to find Elsa pacing to and fro before it like a sentinel. She waved him back, and pushed the door against him so resolutely that he turned and dropped into a chair beside it. Philippa's eyes were still fixed on Parke with a growing light, which, to him, seemed to spread over all the room; but he bore her gaze like a man, and it clinched the purpose he had brooded over.

"Mother," he said, at last, "what could Philippa have to say to her? Imagine?"

"Tell me, my son, I can't," she entreated, in a stifled voice, for she felt appalled at Philippa's face.

"It is probable that she reproached her; the virtuous woman, you know, is not only so for herself, but for the whole sex."

"Charlotte Lang is—what then?" asked Sarah, her nostrils white and rigid.

"What she is, mother, *I* have made her; and, as her cup of disgrace is full, so is mine, and I shall drink it."

Jason sprang from his chair, with a deep oath, and stood beside him like a tower.

"To the dregs, sir," he said.

"You understand me. Would you like to strike me?"

"It is too late," he answered, regarding Philippa mournfully; but she would not meet his eyes, and turned her head from him.

"What's too late?" snapped Sarah.

Parke put a cigar in his mouth without lighting it, and twisted it apart, and, after a moment, said: "I do not pretend to give an account of myself. I do not know what I expected to do in the beginning of this business; so far, perhaps, I have done just as other men do; but, mother, I am going to marry Charlotte Lang. Not a word against it. You may call it dregs, or honor, or obstinacy, or love. It must be."

Sarah literally obeyed him; her composure was so strange that Parke lost his presence of mind. He walked up and down the room, and sobbed like a woman, and her eyes followed him, rolling in her head, as if that had been turned to stone. He threw himself on his knees before her, and buried his face in the folds of her dress,

"Don't," she said, in the voice of one waking from a dream; "lift up your face, I am your mother—not Philippa, not Jason—I forgive you."

"No, mother, I do not ask that; but I have killed you."

"Philippa," she cried, angrily, "have you no feeling? What passes through your mind?"

"Sarah," said Jason, in a voice of thunder, "let my daughter alone."[61]

"Eh," she uttered, with a smile at Parke, as if there had just been effected a tacit bargain, which divided him and Philippa with Jason and herself—Parke was hers!

Philippa did not heed what was passing. She was trying to analyze her own personality, which seemed to be so worthless a thing to others, and of so much value to herself, that out of it she had built a great, strong edifice, which had just fallen into a ruin. Parke raised his tear-stained face, and again Sarah addressed Philippa.

"Go to Mrs. Rogers for me, will you, and ask her if she will come over to-morrow? She must be lonesome without Sam. Go quick!" she ordered, with rising irritation; "it is late."

Philippa rose slowly, and left the room. Jason went out by another door immediately, and confronted Elsa.

"Well?" she said.

"How long have you known this?"

"A few days. Money will settle it."

"No."

"What will, you foolish man?"

"He is going to marry her."

"Cat's-foot, Jason; you are as mad as a March hare to let him do it. Make him wait a while, and he will give it up; he is remorseful, now, and frightened."

"Not frightened; he is brave, Elsa."

"You can't affirm that you believe he ought to marry her!"

"Don't ask me, I don't know. Keep your eye on Sarah; she has had an awful blow."

"Yes, the hardest one."

Breaking away from her, he wandered far away that night, and the burden of his thoughts was: "It was the deed of my own son; but, of all men, *I* should forgive him."

CHAPTER XXIV

‖‖‖‖‖‖‖‖‖‖‖‖‖‖‖‖‖‖‖‖‖‖‖‖‖‖‖‖‖‖‖‖‖‖‖‖‖‖‖

A COOL NOTE FROM Parke announced to Mr. Ritchings his
wedding-day, and engaged him to perform the ceremony in his
study, on a certain evening. When he received the application,
which from his position he could not refuse, he fell into a revery,
which was ended by his taking his hat, walking over to Jason's,
and asking for Philippa. He half expected to feel some shock, to
see some change, when she entered the room, but her impassive
countenance was the same. She met his conscious manner with
one so imperturbable, that he would have felt disconcerted if he
had not come with a purpose nothing could shake. He carefully
reviewed the period of their past acquaintance, and then made
her an offer of his future, promising to consecrate it to her happiness. She declined it. He made a resolute attempt at reason-
ing with her, but she remained obstinately silent. He set before
her his ideas of the basis of a true marriage, and she merely
smiled in an absent way, as if her thoughts were elsewhere. He
left with a burning heart, and an undesired sense of freedom.
It was certainly all over between them now, and the world was
all before him to teach him how to love anew. When he woke
the next morning he felt the loss of his forlorn hope, and started
upon his duties, cold and spiritless. Even Philippa felt the end
of an episode which connected her with love, in one heart, at
least. For a moment she was mindful of the generosity which
prompted Mr. Ritchings to come to her when under the cloud
of disgrace; but she forgot it, to count the days to Parke's wed-

ding, for Mr. Ritchings had told her of the appointment. She
wondered why he waited a day;—there could be no bridal array
for Charlotte! How would they look side by side, he holding her
hand and she his, in the what-God-hath-joined-together-let-no-
man-put-asunder bond? The bond of perpetuation! What would
her father, Osmond Luce, have said had he been present in the
family conclave when Parke declared his resolve! She blushed
at the thought that he might have laughed at their feeble resistance—their patient yielding to his will. Perhaps had her father
been there he might have influenced him; she recalled the incident of their mutual fondness when she first came to Crest, of
Parke's clinging to him and begging him to return—while she
sat aloof, silent, and neglected. That they were something alike,
she reflected for the first time; she had never dreamed of thwart-
ing or disputing her father's will;—how should she have been so
infatuated as to imagine she could bend and subdue Parke?

After the day was appointed for the marriage, Jason and Parke
were closeted for several days. During that time Parke made his
will, but asked Jason not to read it, who was so troubled at the
fact that he informed Philippa, not daring to tell Sarah.

"If he has made his will he is going away," she said.

"That is it; why did I not think of it?"

She rejoiced in the idea: "He would never think of living with
Charlotte Lang!"

"He will be a wanderer," continued Jason, sadly, "all his life."

"It is far better so, Jason."

"I cannot believe it; why do you think so?"

She hesitated, and he saw into her feelings.

"Shame on your want of generosity, Philippa! Are not your
own feelings deep enough for him for you to have some mercy
on hers?"

"I have no mercy on her miserable weakness."

"I believe," he said simply, "that I shall end in hating your sex."

"Oh no; for I shall stay here always with you. And you cannot shake me off."

His expression changed.

"I have no hope of your happiness here—but you are so young yet. Could you really have been my daughter, the idea of a lifetime in this atmosphere would be a different one to you."

"There's nothing of the Bedouin in my composition. I could not be happy, I think, to go from home under any circumstances. I am like lichen—a thin crust, but a permanent one."

"But you will accompany Parke. Your soul and the soul of his mother will grow round him wherever he is; and if you do not know where he is, you will have an imaginary tabernacle for him, where your brightest, best self will centre."

How strangely he was speaking of *their* following Parke! Had he no interest in him? she thought. But had it not been so always? She could look back now to years of indifference on Jason's part.

"I don't know," she answered thoughtfully, "how much my soul could gather round any thing foreign to Crest. When I say Crest, I mean our own surroundings, you know; lately my vision narrows to these walls, our acres, each rock and tree, the sea before the house, the sky over it. Nothing else can contain me."

Her words seemed a promise to Jason; his thoughts sped down the vista of future years, and he saw her beside him ever, and all the powers she had spoken of harmoniously arranged in his life. An hour afterwards, he found Sarah in her room, holding her head in her hands. He observed her strange, opaque, yellow paleness, and asked her if she was ill.

"Not well," she replied.

"Would she have any assistance?"

"Nothing."

It was so evident to him, however, that she was ill, that he grew anxious and impatient. He moved about softly, in the hope of attracting her attention; then he pushed the chairs, folded up her work on the table, piled the books together, rustled the papers—all to no purpose. She was motionless, and her eyes were fixed on vacancy. At last he went out and returned with Elsa. In his absence Sarah had put her hands over her eyes. Elsa shook her finger at him as she said,

"Sarah, you feel poorly to-day."

"I have no heart to set those things to rights that we spoke of last night."

"Never mind that; what shall I get you?"

No answer came from her.

"Do go to bed."

"To-morrow."

Elsa beckoned Jason out of the room.

"Now, Jason," she said in a lively voice, "you needn't worry because I say so—but Sarah is coming down with a fit of sickness."

A feeling of every thing's falling in upon itself to utter ruin oppressed him. Chaos and night would come, should Sarah go.

"Better get things in order," she continued; "Gilbert has been wanting you this hour."

Hurrying back to Sarah, as he mechanically obeyed her suggestion, she felt her head, hands, and feet, without discomposing her.

"Sarah, you ought to go to bed; Jason is worried."

She refused to move. All day she sat in her chair, but at night she called to Jason in a hurried voice to bring her night-clothes. With a wild haste she undressed, dropped her comb on the floor, and thrust her black curls under her cap, swaying to and fro. Jason was afraid to offer any help, but followed her to the bed. With a sigh she dropped down upon it suddenly, and as suddenly sprang up with a terrible cry which brought every soul in the house to the chamber. Jason threw his arms round her: "Sarah, Sarah, what is it?" he cried.

"I shall die," she screamed; "I shall die."

"Where is the pain, mother?" Parke asked, pale with dread.

"Philippa," she said; "oh, my head."

Philippa made a movement towards her, and stood looking upon her with a cold helplessness.

"Philippa," she reiterated. "What do you there?"

Parke crowded the pillows together, and Jason inclined her gently upon them; she let her head fall back, still keeping her eyes fixed, with an expression of terror, upon Philippa, who now came forward and endeavored to smooth the covers.

"In the name of all that's good and great, Mary, why are you so mum?" said Elsa. "Send for the doctor."

"I'll go," said Parke.

"Stay here," whispered Elsa.

"I can't stand it," he replied. "I must get out."

But the paroxysm subsided; Sarah wiped the sweat from her forehead and closed her eyes, and all stole from the chamber except Jason. Philippa went into one of the dark parlors, for she wanted to be alone, and lament over her cold dislike for Sarah which nothing could overcome. A thick gloom shut her in upon herself, in the face of the apprehension which beset her—of the senseless, fatuous pride of life, which any hour might reduce to the most pitiful straits—and betrayed in black relief how unlovely a thing she was. Sarah's perpetual coldness, irritation, and anger proved that one at least understood her unhappy idiocrasy. She exonerated Sarah from that moment, and made no merit of the perception which led her to consider how impossible it was for her to be considered any thing except an intruder and an encumbrance; but her heart was not softened an atom. The door opened softly.

"Philippa," called Parke, "are you here? I have been looking high and low for you."

"I am on the sofa."

He groped along till he found a place beside her.

"The doctor thinks mother is going to have a nervous fever; she is easy now. Father is going to sit up to-night. What do you think Elsa is doing?" And his head went down on Philippa's shoulder.[62]

"I don't know," she murmured, exquisitely alive to the fact that his hair brushed her cheek.

"She is making cake that will 'keep,' she says."

"She does so, because she has been much disturbed."

"Did you ever think of the strangeness of mother's character, Philippa?"

"I have just been thinking of it."

"Such revelations come so unexpectedly from those who are the nearest to us! There is something appalling behind the screen of every-day life, countenance, custom, clothes. What is it?" he added so abruptly, that she started.

"It is *us*" she answered, scarcely knowing what she said.

"I see now that mother does not love you. What has happened between you?"

"My name, my coming, and myself."

There was no gainsaying her answer; it comprehended her whole history with his mother.

"Poor girl!"

"No, not that;—not because of her; I have had a life apart."

"You have a strength of your own."

He took her hand and held it silently. "Revelations," she thought, "go only just so far." A bar of moonlight slanted in through the shutter, fell across their clasped hands, and made a lattice of light at their feet. As the moonbeam entered the room, but did not encompass it, so did Parke's presence enter the gloom which oppressed her, but did not envelop it. They had never been together as in that moment; it seemed as if he had yielded to her something of himself he was afraid to keep that night. What protection could he feel with her—he had fallen asleep on her shoulder! His fair forehead pressed against her mouth, his soft hair fell on her neck; she wished that he would sleep forever. The moonlight traversed the floor, and died against the opposite wall before he stirred.

"Oh, Philippa, are we here?" he said, drowsily, and stretched out his arms to infold her; "kiss me."

She bent her head, and they kissed each other. For an instant the life-long hunger of her soul was stayed.

"You won't strike me again, Philippa?"

It was all over. How she had been mocked! She started to her feet.

"Why did you let me sleep so long?" He still held her hand, though she was going over the floor, nor would he release her till they reached the door of Sarah's chamber; then he asked her to go in and inquire how his mother was. Her eyes were wide open, but they wore a tranquil look. Jason's head was bent over the bedside, as if he had fallen asleep.

"Is Parke out there?" Sarah asked.

Philippa nodded. "He wishes to know how you are."

"I am here," she answered, in so clear and natural a voice, that he put his head in at the door, and gave her a smile.

"Go to bed, boy," she said.

Jason looked up, and remarked that he believed he could be trusted as a watcher, and Philippa glided out.

CHAPTER XXV

THE NERVOUS FEVER CHANGED to a fatal disease which consumed Sarah slowly. Silent and passive as she lay in her darkened chamber, the pulse of household life was still subordinate to her influence; its ways depended on her condition from hour to hour; for the first time it tacitly owned a common individuality, of which she was the centre. Parke confined himself to the house absolutely; flitted in and out of her chamber twenty times a day, smoked perpetually, changed from chair to chair, sofa to sofa, in all the rooms, where he carried piles of books, which he vainly tried to read. He dwelt upon every favorable symptom which appeared with a vehemence that betrayed a doubt; the unfavorable ones he passed over with a dogged silence. He wrote to Charlotte, in the beginning of Sarah's illness, that she must not expect to see him while his mother's life hung by a thread, but that she would get well. As an occupation, a relief, he wrote to all his friends—he wished no nearer approach from outside life—even including Theresa. She replied, and for several weeks a curious, semi-oblivious correspondence was kept up.

Jason watched by Sarah's bedside night and day; he attended to no calls whatever. Gilbert assumed authority over affairs out of doors, and inside Elsa conducted them with quietness and dispatch. But, as only the ordinary details necessary were dispatched, she was tormented by a waiting leisure which preceded a dreaded crisis; day after day she had nothing to do but recall her experiences in sickness and compare them with the present, or recount to Mary, and the neighbors who came to inquire for Sarah, the cases which had ended in death. In the chambers of her memory death showed so placid and commonplace an aspect that his coming wore no terrors; but his shadow darkened Philippa's soul. All that she looked upon was touched with Decay; nothing had been made to escape the vanishing Hand. A peremptory restlessness prevented her from inhabiting any familiar spot. Her own room now looked like a guest-chamber; she wandered often in the garden, in the orchard, and over the hill. Many times a day she put in order the cups and vials on the table and mantel in Sarah's chamber, but rarely exchanged any words with her. Sometimes she sat near her while Jason was at his meals; then Sarah's eyes followed her movements with an expression which was interpreted in the old way. Once when their eyes met Sarah asked her if Parke was married. She shook her head for a reply, not trusting herself to speak, and hoped that Sarah would say more—they could at least unite on that subject—but she turned her face to the wall. Again she asked if the cinnamon roses had bloomed. Philippa gathered some for her; she turned them over and over in her hand, inhaled their perfume for an instant, and handed them to Jason, with a motion that they should be taken out of her sight.

"Philippa," she called, once more, "what kind of a day is it?"

"The sunshine is level everywhere."

"Level! So shall I be soon. Shall you stay here afterwards?"

"Do you wish me to?"

"Stop. Yes, or no."

"Yes."

"I knew you would."

"And I know that you do not desire it."

"I cannot."

For the most part, Sarah was silent towards Jason. Not a word passed between them concerning Parke or Philippa; he accepted what her will had enforced now, as always. If he had any hope of a nearer, clearer communication, he was disappointed. He vainly watched for an opportunity to give her some fragment of himself that would leave him with the feeling that she had some clue to his spiritual being. Savages have a belief that when they are in the clutches of the lion and the tiger a happy paralysis seizes them—they do not feel the terror of being rent asunder; it may be that there is a magnetism of Death, in which all the powers of life are painlessly wrapped. It seemed so with Sarah.

The morning dawned when Jason saw in her face the bewildered, flitting look of a departing soul. He kneeled by her with a solemn mien, and fixed his eyes upon hers, and a sad intelligence passed between them. She said nothing, but for a moment returned his gaze; then she laid her feeble hand on his, and shut her eyes. He kissed her tenderly, and she gave a sigh which ploughed his heart with anguish, and tempted him to cry aloud. He buried his face in her pillow, and presently he felt her hand moving round his neck, and drawing him close to her. Then she was still. The voice of Elsa broke the silence.

"She is going to heaven, Jason, swiftly, and she does not sense it."

"Call Parke and Philippa."

Her soul passed over the threshold of the world of spirits, just as they reached the room. Parke saw her hands flutter, and darted forward with a cry of "Mother!" caught them in his grasp, but their helpless deadness appalled him so he dropped them and staggered backward. Philippa stood by Jason, self-forgetful, absorbed in the dread spectacle. Her brain whirled with the questions which pressed upon her. "What is that in the place of her identity?" "Where is she?" "Why was she ever alive?" "What does it all mean?"

"It is all over," Elsa announced, in a composed voice, laying Sarah's hands straight beside her, and closing her eyes.

"Oh God!" cried Parke, "this is too horrible. Talk about infinite Goodness before such a sight as this!"

Philippa gave a loud, hysterical cry, at which Jason rose to his feet, looked wildly about him, and struck his hands out as if he could not see.

"Take care of Parke, Jason," said Elsa, and he was obliged to lead him away, reeling.

"I'll put you to bed, miss," said Elsa to Philippa, leading her from the room tenderly, and crying bitterly.

When the doors were opened for the coffin-bearers, the sun streamed its hot, yellow rays through the house, and laid bare its loneliness. Something was gone from every nook and corner. No sweet, gracious, lovely spirit had vanished therefrom, but a dominant, exacting, forcible presence had gone forever. The sun's rays fell from the wide, blue summer sky, and travelled with the funeral procession that still afternoon when Sarah was buried, and rested on the mound of sand heaped beside the grave—on the black pall—on the mourners—with a glory that mocked the shadows of the Valley of Death.

CHAPTER XXVI

||||||||||||||||||||||||||||||||||||||||||||||||||||||||

SEVERAL NEIGHBORS REMAINED in the house after the procession left, to restore the rooms to order, and prepare supper against the return from the grave. One of them, crossing from one parlor to the other, saw a stranger standing on the steps before the open door. She set down the chair she was carrying, and went towards him.

"What is the matter here?" he asked.

"There is a death in the family."

"Whose?"

"Mrs. Auster's. The procession left the house but a few minutes ago."

"Ah!"

"Will you walk in and take a seat, sir?"

"Thank you, no; but I'll lounge about till the family return."

Sauntering down the gravel-walk, as if it were a pleasant thing to do at that moment, he repeated over and over again, "That girl, Sarah," then came back and sat upon the lowest step.

"Whoever stayed away ten years, though," he thought, marking an S in the gravel with his cane, "without somebody's dying? I wonder I did not hear the bell toll! Have they given over the custom of letting the world know the ages of those carried away feet foremost? Three of us left—myself, the boy, and Philippa. I might have asked for Philippa, but I should have been bothered by the curiosity of these people. Will Sarah's ghost object to my staying here? I could divide honors with Jason, never with her.

I wonder if her curls ever came out? How many times have I tried to pull them straight! She should not be buried there—it's not the right kind of clay. She should be put where there is an eternal tramp. Pah! I could hear the worms crawl under the sod up there, it is so still."

Those within were informed that a stranger was on the door-steps, and it was concluded that he must be a relative of Jason's, too late for the funeral. An examination from the upper windows, however, proved the conclusion incorrect. Some one discovered his likeness to Parke, still strong, though Osmond Luce (for it was he) had changed in the last nine years. His once bright hair was gray over his forehead, though round his massive neck a row of brown ringlets still crept. His eyes were still reckless and gay, but deep wrinkles had gathered round them, and the lids looked tight and drawn, like those of birds of prey. There was something loose in his figure, and weak, in spite of his size and vigor. The women called him a handsome, grand-looking man. How easy he was behaving, too, out there on the gravel-walk, breaking the twigs and flowers as if they were his own!

A little girl came through the open gate, and hurried up the walk, stopping when she saw him.

"Mrs. Lang wants to know if the folks have come home from the funeral?" she said.

"They have not," he replied.

"She sends word to Parke that he must come up there right away. Charlotte is sick."

She looked in at the open windows with curiosity, and over the yard. She had heard what had happened, and expected to meet something strange.

"What ails Charlotte?" he asked.

"Oh, I don't know."

"I'll tell him as soon as I see him."

"Right away," she repeated, but made no motion to go, scanning the yard.

"You wish for a flower, don't you?"

"Yes, sir."

"Pick that red one yonder."

"That's London Pride. Do you live here?"

"No; do you?"

"I guess I do."

"How many inhabitants are here?"

"Inhabitants!"

"People—folks."

"I can't tell; mother says that most all the old people are dead, and that the place ain't what it was once."

"What was your mother's name when the old people were alive?"

"Eliza Ames; now it is Smith."

That name carried him back twenty years. He was walking the streets of Crest on a moonlight night beside a handsome, gay girl, who had jilted him, and whom he was beseeching again with love! "To this favor has she come," he thought, "an eleven-year old, sandy-haired Smith."

Leaving the step, he traversed the flower-paths till he found the bitter aromatic southernwood; breaking off a bit, he said, "Take this to your mother, and tell her that Prince Osric[63] sent it to her."

"Its only southernwood," she uttered with contempt; "but I'll take it to her. Good-by, sir."

In a few moments he heard the sound of slowly approaching wheels, and, planting his hat firmly over his brows, rose to meet the persons he expected to see. A number of carriages halted at the gate; the first contained Jason, Parke, and Philippa. Jason came forward like one walking in his sleep, and did not see Osmond till he touched his outstretched hand.

"Cousin Jason, we meet again."

"Oh yes," he answered, looking past him into the house.

"You know me, Osmond Luce?"

"Yes. Sarah is dead, though; you could not come before, I suppose." And he half turned as if to recommend him to the notice of Parke and Philippa, who were behind him, and, pushing by him, he went up the steps.

Philippa knew her father, and put out her hand silently; he took it, and, extending the other to Parke, said: "My poor fellow, my mother was buried on such an afternoon as this; the sunset seems the same. I remember that I counted the red bars in the sky as the company got out of the carriages."

Tears moistened his eyes as they dwelt on Parke, whose tearless gaze roved the sky, showing that he had heard the sense of Osmond's words, but he did not speak.

"Come in," said Philippa; "the rest are coming up the steps."

"You are the same, Philippa," said her father abruptly.

"No change," she answered, as they entered the old familiar, panelled room. "Parke, you had better go after Jason."

"Yes," said Osmond, "it is the best time for friends to keep together. We remember how attached the lost one was to this one or that, and feel charitable; moreover, we pity each other as victims of the same future, and resolve a mutual protection. After a while, though, we separate with a fresh eagerness for our different ways."

"You are the same, father," said Philippa quietly.

"I am glad of it, Osmond," said Parke, who had paid no attention to her request. "I am glad you are here. Open that shutter, Philippa; the people will stay in the other room, will they? Get me some water, will you, then?"

"Do you draw water, Philippa?" Osmond asked with some sharpness.

"When I ask her, she does," Parke said.

"Did you and Sarah love each other, Philippa?" her father asked, under his breath.

"No."

"I thought so. By the way," turning to Parke, "a little girl was here not long ago, with a message for you. Mrs. Lang sent for you because Charlotte was sick."

"Is she sick?" he muttered confusedly, looking from one to the other. Philippa's expression underwent so sudden a change that Osmond comprehended there was a mystery. Parke took his hat, hesitated—"Osmond," he called. Before he could reply, Philippa made so negative and imperious a gesture, that Parke abruptly left the room.

Elsa had recognized Osmond at once, but she thought it best not to bruit his arrival; she therefore marshalled the guests into supper, and then bustled in to see him. They fell into a deep talk, and Philippa escaped from them without notice.

"These are wretched particulars, Elsa," said Osmond; "have I come to see the old ship go down?"

"Sarah *was* at the helm always, you know."

"We must lash the helm down, and let the craft drift into smooth water again; it will, you know, in time."

"No lashing for me. I am going; if I can't die, I can move!"

"Nonsense; because Parke has been foolish, or because Jason is a widower?"

"Put it all together, or sort it out, just as you like. As for Parke's being foolish, he has only been as much as a man can be—that is, not much, you know. As for Jason's being a widower—though he is soft, I don't think he could help it."

"In view of all the facts, I think that Parke had better leave Crest."

CHAPTER XXVII

⁣||||||||||||||||||||||||||||||||||||||||||||||||||||

PARKE SAT BY ANOTHER BED of death, dull and exhausted. He listened to Mrs. Lang's reproaches, Clarice's accusations, and Charlotte's dying sighs, with a stupid composure. Before sunrise he looked upon the face of his dead mistress, with her dead child beside her. The awe of death was ushered in the chamber with the pale dawn. A yellow light crept round the walls, over the figures of Mrs. Lang and Clarice, who sat motionless and heavy, like the mutilated statues in the sand of Thebes[64]—over the defaced, haggard glory in Parke's face; over the dumb, marble Charlotte. Not until Mrs. Lang and Clarice stole out of the room did he move from the position he had maintained for hours; then he stood before the bed. Charlotte's hair had fallen across her arm in a coil; he untwined it, and held it—the talisman of the past—and studied the mystery in her face—that which the dead bear away with them, and never reveal. As dead as this prostrate, powerless creature, were the feelings which she had created in his heart. Their existence had ceased with hers; but his heart was killed too—by depletion. How beautiful she was still! The images of the women he had known rose up before him in their living power, and it seemed to him that of them all Charlotte could only die; that of Theresa Bond glowed with color, and streamed in upon his thoughts like a pane of stained glass in a gloomy cathedral. Pity, though, that so much beauty, so loving a heart as Charlotte's, must be entombed;—he wept pure tears of pity for her, which her spirit must have rejoiced over. No hand

185

but his, he determined, should touch those beautiful tresses, he had so often slept against. He called Mrs. Lang in again, and told her his wish. Some ribbon was found, and with that they were arranged; but Mrs. Lang observed that his face was averted from the child, which lay as if slumbering on the pillow.

"The Lord has not taken off the babe dis time; it was some other body."

"You know," he said, "that I have not seen it. I shall not look at it; that shame may be spared me at least. Hide it in her bosom, if you choose, it is already hidden in mine—the monument to remind me to hate myself; in hers, it may turn to a pitying angel. Now keep everybody away. Send for your minister, if you choose, no one else."

"Yes, my minister wanted to baptize her! Ha! Charlotte baptized! Any of my chil'n baptized—isn't that a joke—oh, Almighty, give me patience." And Mrs. Lang wrung her hands, and screamed like a maniac.

"Hush," said Parke, "one of you is dead at any rate."

"Stay with us," she implored.

"Yes—till I go to the grave with her. After that there will be nothing I can do for you."

The manner which he instinctively assumed she understood at once, and told Clarice that Charlotte would be buried for good with him, and they also on the day of the funeral.

"Of course," she replied, "there are no more Charlottes to seduce; why shouldn't he leave? Mother, can't we go from here?"

"No; we should have to take what we are with us, wherever we went."

"True, we will stay, and rub in our humiliation, and keep the brand bright. Ashes are good where the flesh is raw."

"You are a beast of a child; Charlotte was better. I wanted her to live."

"I say she was bad."

"Bless them that despitefully use you," sang Mrs. Lang, "and I bless you, Clarice."

"Pooh, you are melted just now."

Parke sent a note to Philippa with the particulars, informing her that he should not be at home at present. Philippa, for reply, sent him some money and a change of clothes, by a messenger she picked up outside. She then gave the note to Jason, who read it, and returned it without comment. But it had the effect of sending him out of doors. His pale, stern face appeared everywhere for the three days following. People were made sensible, such was the force of his presence, that he was Parke's protector. As for Osmond, the pressure of circumstances, as he teasingly told Elsa, was such that he thought he had better "sing small."

"When I hear one of your diabolical set 'singing small,' I shall hear a new kind of music," she replied.

Philippa defied the devil, as Elsa commented; it was impossible to guess from her behavior that any calamity was weighing upon her. She repelled every inclination of sympathy that might have strayed in her direction. Somehow Elsa obtained all the particulars concerning Parke, and knew the exact moment when he issued from Mrs. Lang's door to follow the coffin in company with her and a few of the immediate neighbors.

"I'll bet," she said, "that this day he is his mother's own child. I should like to see how he bears comparison, as he stands among his respectable dead relations."

He was well worth the seeing. A number of people, as curious as Elsa, had gathered about the gate of the burying-ground, and there were loungers down the length of the picket-fence—of that class whose tongues are the hot-beds for startling crops of surmises. A group of young men, Parke's acquaintances, were waiting for his arrival with mixed feelings—of admiration at his pluck, and gratification at the strait he was brought to. These persons had taken a common privilege: funerals were not affairs that belonged to friends and relatives merely—they were the right of the public, who liked to feel the pulse of grief.

With all his imperfections on his head, Parke never looked so much a man as then; he walked up the gravel-path with Mrs. Lang on his arm, passed his mother's grave, whose mound rose brown and bare among the grassy hillocks which surrounded it, and stood before the heap of sand which was to cover Charlotte. Then all the followers saw that she was to be buried among the Parkes, with his own family. This proud concession implied more than they could define. His self-possession was astonishing; there was so much cold authority in his mien that not one of them would have been willing to meet his eye. The women retreated, but, with the petty bitterness of women, and hypocrisy, said to each other, "Did you ever see such brass?" and "Isn't it a pretty thing that the wolves in sheep's clothing are having it all their own way?" But the men were silent for a moment; then they burst out with, "By Jove, sirs, there's stuff!" and "Who can blame the girl?"

Though Clarice staggered in her convulsive weeping, she was conscious of a sentiment of gratitude towards Parke for giving Charlotte the place among the dead of his race that he would have given her had she been his wife. That she would be his wife, had she lived, Clarice had never believed, though she was aware of his promise—made on the day of the awful discovery of the nature of the connection between them.

Mrs. Lang muttered so strangely when the coffin slid on its

cords, that he pulled her vail over her face, and held a warning arm round her. When the minister had spoken the earth-con-secrating words, he raised his hat, and, still leading Mrs. Lang, moved down the path; but he did not return home with her and Clarice; after placing them in the carriage, he turned into a soli-tary by-road, and walked by himself.

He entered the room where Osmond sat reading, and Philippa was sewing, and stood before them a moment in silence. A smile, which trailed the whole past over his face, struck Osmond and Philippa with the feeling that they had not seen him for ages.

"Crystallization has taken place," thought Osmond; "he is too young, the boy, for that." Then he said aloud, "Crest won't do for me, my boy, without you. Jason is monotonous, and Philippa is—Philippa."

Parke laid his hand lightly on his shoulder, turned from him, and sat down by her. She was sewing a long seam on white cloth, which he remembered to have seen in her hands, six weeks, or six years, before. She looked up, full of the effort to speak to him, but Jason entered, and she remained silent. Parke instantly rose and faced his father, thus paying his first tribute of respect to him. Jason turned his head to the window, to the doors, towards Parke, and nodded with a nod which contained the old permis-sion of full liberty.

"Upon my soul," Osmond silently commented, "that man is a genius, and an honor to human nature. If he develops, I should like to make a raree show of him."[65]

Philippa rolled up her work, and made some stir over her work-basket, wondering why they did not speak—this was the occasion! Presently, as the silence continued unbroken, with a mixture of courage and simplicity she said, "Silence is sometimes a want of truth."

"Always," said Jason; "but what are you going to do about it?"

"Philippa is simply an idiot," thought Osmond.

"Is it not enough that I have returned?" said Parke; "or will you have a sermon preached?"

"Oh, that has been preached," Jason answered.

"I thought so," said Parke.

CHAPTER XXVIII

LINK BY LINK the family chain was parting. For a few weeks Elsa transacted domestic affairs as if under the supervision of Sarah. Jason resumed his old out-of-doors life, and Parke went hither and thither, driving with Osmond, playing the piano, and skimming books. Philippa's habits appeared the same also. But there was not a day, rain or shine, that she did not pay a visit to the hill—the most solitary spot in Crest, near as it was to the streets. The cedars, brown with age, crooked from wrangling with the sea-wind, hid her as she ascended the path to the top, and the oaks, the rocks, and the bare side of the grassy mound which met the sky, protected her. There her eyes were not tormented by the confining walls and their familiar objects; they rested on the small treasures which Nature offered her—grass, weeds, moss, seeds, and mould—but they rested vacantly. Not even the higher glories of the provident Mother, the trees, the air and clouds, the sea, immense and eternal as was their aspect, appeased the hunger of her heart. Parke's music became to him a new thing; he played the changes of his soul—the accents of his experience sounded through all his compositions; but to her it seemed only an increased attention he was giving the piano from *ennui*. It was the time when they were most together. He asked her once if music was becoming a companion.

"No," she answered, "the companion of a companion."

"This is a pretty life," Osmond thought, when he observed them together. "Arcadian, mild, quiet, but flavorless; the salt of life is confined to the sea here. Of course a ripple is coming in its current, which I shall wait for. *Dolce far niente*[66] is a plant that never reaches maturity in this climate; even imported specimens peak and pine, and resemble celery which is transplanted to the cellar."

The ripple, or a snap in the chain, was caused by Elsa, who again informed Osmond that now she was going in earnest. She should take up her abode in her own house — an ancient dwelling, standing on the bay neck, in a solitary spot, with a few acres of arable land around it, which she had farmed out for years without a dollar's profit. "It was time for her," she said, "to look after her own property." He offered to purchase it, if she would remain with Philippa; but she declined, arguing that it was the best thing to be done for Philippa, who would never do any thing for herself, so long as she had her to lean upon. "I shall tell her," Elsa concluded, "that she will have to be her own cook and bottle-washer, with Mary's help; unless, indeed, she wants to fill up the house with new-fangled servants, which she can never do, on Jason's account."

"For all that," returned Osmond, "you will come back."

"I suppose you think I ought to die in harness; but if there is not a Parke worth living for even, what is the beauty of staying here to die?"

"We shall see," he answered provokingly; but he saw she was determined on the point. A day or two afterwards she told Jason, who begged her to give him lessons in house-work before she went, for he should endure no stranger in her place.

"Philippa must take my place."

"Nonsense, Elsa; what can she do?"

"She must learn; there won't be much to do, the family will be small."

"How small?"

"You don't imagine Osmond Luce is going to settle down in this spot at this late day. And when he begins his rounds again, Parke will begin his also."

Jason appeared struck. "Poor Philippa!" he said absently.

"Did you ever know a young man to remain at home for the sake of a 'poor Philippa,' or anybody else, when the spirit of wandering has seized him? — and it has seized Parke."

"Do you think so? He has every thing to stay for."

"He hasn't."

"His estate, his associations — Philippa."

"And the Langs."

"Oh, I forgot those."

"Jason, you are the strangest man I ever saw."

"I wonder if I hadn't better go."

"Now, where would you go?"

"To where I started from, with my trunk. Where is my trunk, Elsa? Is there an old pincushion in it, do you know? Perhaps I could find the girl who gave it to me, twenty years ago."

"Pincushion and trunk are among the things that were."

"Then I must stay."

"You had better, if you want things to hold together."

Besides some desire for a change from the scene of her cares and sorrows, Elsa was oppressed by a presentiment, which she did not try to account for. To use her own expression, Jason, Parke, and Philippa were at loose ends, and there was no telling what changes might take place; she would not remain, to embarrass them, nor herself. They were also of another day and generation than the one she had lived for, and she felt herself incapable of assuming their responsibilities.

She hurried away with an eagerness that was ominous to Mary, who bewailed the necessity of taking charge of the household. The day she left, accompanied by Parke and Philippa, was one late in September; the autumnal winds had not yet devastated the woods, but the leaves fluttered down, seeking their place of repose in the gay shroud which the summer bequeathed. Vigorous blossoms, red, blue, and yellow, covered the ditches and fields, flaunting above the sear grass, forgetful of the dance of death they were preparing for when the winter winds should blow. The pale amber atmosphere stained the calm sea, and blurred the sky. Parke loved the sadness and sweetness of the day; but Philippa, unforgiving towards Elsa for leaving her, was petulant, nervous, and behaved more oddly than usual. Elsa was occupied with wondering whether Mr. Clapp's folks would be ready to receive her.

"There," she said, as they turned into a lane, at the end of which her house stood, "the bars are down, and the Clapps are looking out; the window blinking in the sun is my best-room window."

"How you will enjoy yourself!—what a lovely spot!" said Philippa satirically. "How agreeable a walk must be in this lane; and the Clapps, I judge, will be ample society for you."

"Not so much but that I shall be glad to see you; you will come and tea with me, won't you?"

"She is never coming to tea," cried Parke; "we are going to break with you entirely."

"But you won't."

He wilfully refused to go inside the door; but, after he had turned the carriage, jumped out, seized her on the threshold, and gave her withered cheek a hearty kiss, and jumped back again. Hurrying in to the house, followed by Philippa, to conceal that she was crying, she threw herself into a chair, and exclaimed, "I have buried myself with a vengeance."

"Go back with us," Philippa urged; "it is not too late. You know that you are making a mistake."

"Go right home; I've got other fish to fry just now than to listen to you."

"May their bones choke you!"

"Spiteful thing, good-by. Clear out."

"How fast that young man drives!" said Mrs. Clapp, watching him down the lane; but Elsa would not leave her seat till she knew the carriage was out of sight; then she started up, and declared she was going into the orchard.

"There hasn't been any windfalls yet to speak of, and I told my old man it wasn't worth while to turn in the hogs; they'd only make a mess on't with rooting," Mrs. Clapp droned, but Elsa was gone.

"Mercy on us," Mrs. Clapp went on, "she will make it as lively as a hornet's nest for us. May be she won't hire us the place another year."

With her cap border flying back, and her arms folded, Elsa skirted the old orchard with fleetness. The sound of wheels rolling over a little wooden bridge half a mile below the house caught her ears. She stopped.

"There they go, rolling over my heart! Lord God!" and she eyed the trunk of a venerable plum-tree with a fierce rigidity, "what is the use of my reading the Bible all my days, if I am not going to bear it better than this?" Something in the look of the tree arrested her,—she darted forward, "Upon my soul, there's borers in this tree, and that's the reason," scanning the branches, "there's not a plum on it."

The tide was checked; she returned to the house composed, and convinced Mrs. Clapp, before bedtime, that she was an uncommonly cheerful woman, for her age. In a week, the Clapps, tenants at will, were under her control, and she began to feel at home.

CHAPTER XXIX

"'A MIGHTY WIND ARISES, roaring seaward, and I go,'"[67] said Osmond, one wild morning.

"Are you 'flying, flying south'?"[68] Parke asked.

"Yes; will you take a pinion with me?"

"Certainly, I am ready when you are. I have said nothing of my purpose; I thought a suggestion of the sort might hurry you away."

"I shall go to General Paez,[69] provided he is in retirement; would you like to be a mighty cattle-hunter on his pampas?"

"I should like nothing better."

"Think well of it;—a life of adventure once begun never ends, except by the casualties incident to it, which are many. You have something—a great deal—to keep you here; you are your own master. I was not when I left Crest; not until I put this ancient town far behind me did I know what it was to belong to myself. You have almost too much money to commence my career picturesquely."

"Can't we spend it?"

Osmond snapped his fingers. "Ossa on Pelions of it."[70]

A glimmering of Osmond's disposition dawned in Parke's mind; he mused.

"You gave up your share of your grandfather's property, didn't you?" he asked.

"If I hadn't I should have made ducks and drakes of it. Owing to your mother, I think, my pride would not allow me, so I made it over to Philippa. I had a trifle then, besides."

"Poor Philippa!"

"Don't be Quixotic; she is not too grateful to me, you see."

"I'll leave the best of mine here."

"Make the offer to your father; give him what you don't want—the income, I mean."

"As much as he'll take, of course; but you must know that he has been as generous with me as you have been with Philippa."

"That is, he absolutely refused to be indebted to his wife."

"It appears to me that we are a lot of proud fools together. I'll go and confer with him now."

"You don't mind leaving Philippa?" Osmond asked, experimentally.

Parke stopped—looked into the recesses of his hat.

"Yes, by Jove, she will miss me. I hate to tell her. What can she do in this cursed spot alone?"

"She can weave a web, like Penelope."[71]

"But no suitors will drop in."

"Mr. Ritchings."

"That's over, some time ago."

"Sam Rogers—her paragon."

"Old Sam is a hero. To him she is an idol, to be worshipped from afar; to her he is something better than her dog, only she hasn't one—a little dearer than *my* horse."

"You put him on a high pedestal."

"He is a noble man, but a blockhead, you know."

Osmond doubted whether he was so much a blockhead, for Elsa had given him a pretty correct impression of the strength of Sam's character; but he did not mention his doubt.

"Philippa is cut out for an old maid," continued Parke. "She is self-absorbed, not selfish—as I have every reason to know, and nobody ever seems to attract her; she is the most impassive creature I ever knew, and the coolest."

"That being the case, I propose to send her a King Charles, from New York."

It was a pleasant thought, Parke said, as he went to look for Jason.

After he had gone, Osmond concluded to look up Philippa, and study her a little. He discovered her in the kitchen with a heated face, in the act of compounding cake.

"Those little tins, those little tins," he said, "remind me of my boyhood's sins."

"I expect," remarked Mary, "you scraped the inside of 'em."

"I did."

"Were you punished?" Philippa asked.

"I was."

"Laws," said Mary, "I heard you were never punished for any thing."

"I was punished regularly with indulgence; every soul in the family was devoted to me—devoted; do you understand devotion, Philippa?"

"I was born a Catholic, you know," she answered, quietly proceeding into the parlor; but he followed her.

"Good heavens! do you remember the day of your birth, and your christening?"

"I remember my black rosary; the one who gave me that was devoted to me, I am sure."

"Who was it?"

"Philip."

"The deuce—your cousin. The life here, though—you like it?"

"Well enough never to leave it."

"To follow no one's fortunes?"

"The *Ignis Fatuus* only chases his brother."[72]

"When I go from Crest what will you give me?"

She hesitated so long, thinking that he meant and wanted money, feeling no willingness to be generous towards him, yet anxious to oblige him, if she could do so without conferring a sense of obligation, that he burst into a laugh.

"Whose child are you? What hour were you begotten? When the sordid New England wind blew?"

The cool insolence of his manner enraged her; she shook her hair back, and knit her brows.

"Not so impassive, after all," he thought, as she flashed upon him.

"You make me feel," she said, with her words coming from tightened lips, "the torment and torture of life. Let me alone. I'll tell you, though, what I shall do with your money, which belongs *here*—return it to Parke. You see that I am 'devoted' to an idea."

"You are not devoted to him, I trust. If so, you are, indeed, devoted to an idea—a hopeless one."

Cooler than himself—cool, indeed, for an icy chill crept over her—she said, in a sharp, appealing tone, "Fathers should be the confidants of their daughters' feelings, where there is no mother; I confess mine to you: I am devoted to him."

A sad groan came to his lips, but he exclaimed harshly: "What stuff have you in your head about woman's constancy and sacrifice? But, no! I know you better; in fact, I understand you all at once. If we are not the besotted instruments of a logical Fate, what are we? I'll test it." A burning blush rose in his face, a wild light rushed into his eyes. "Philippa, will you join *my* fortunes? Will you go to South America with me?"

A spark of nature was elicited in both at last; their faces wore the same eager, passionate, overcoming expression. For an instant she was seized with his nomadic spirit, and set her foot forward as if to enter upon his free, salient, purposeless life. With outstretched hands, he urged her in a voice so altered by tenderness and entreaty that she wondered at the feeling of resistance which compelled her to struggle with the phantoms of Liberty and Pleasure which his words had evoked. He saw a cold shade drop over her face, and divined that he could not shake her resolution. He was bitterly tempted for a moment to tell her that Parke was going with him, and let her feel how narrow had been the chance between her and the happiness she was trying to buy, but he forbore.

"I must remain," she said. "How can I tell," she added, so unaffectedly he could hardly help smiling, "whether I could bear the license of your life? I succumb to tradition and custom because I love them. But if these barriers should be removed, I feel I have that within which could rise, and overtop all excess. When are you going?"

"At an early day; none is yet named. You are fixed, then?" resuming his careless manner; "granite is nothing to you."

"Stay longer."

"Entreat me."

"What will Parke do when you go?"

"Hang Parke, or drown him—a puppy's proper fate. I am sick of the beauty—he is sweet, though, magnetic, and has a wonderfully delicate but strong power of self-assertion. He is dull beyond a certain limit, however, and is profound nowhere. Do you agree with me?"

"Yes."

"And you say you are devoted to him?"

"You left me here a child—a child loves the beautiful. Was there any thing lovely in Sarah or Jason? Parke was lovely, and

I turned to him. He is still the same to me. Though I do not have any proof of his goodness, I am faithless as to his faults. Tell me, if you can, how do certain men make a universal impression, which they do not account for in words or works?"

"I see. Parke, Dante, and Shakespeare must be great, because they have made us believe so."

She nodded.

"You are a kind of witch, I believe; curious looking, too."

"I know I am ugly," she answered, coloring painfully.

"By no means. You have good eyes; witches always have."

"And diabolical, cruel, revengeful yellow hair."

"Why, girl, what ails you? you are no conjurer, at any rate. The truth is, you are half foreign; in your native town I have seen dozens of girls like you—with a difference."

He left her in a melancholy mood, wishing that he had not disturbed her or himself. It was a foolish and hazardous experiment he had been trying; she might have accepted his life, which was not fit for so frail and unique a creature. But his heart had been set in motion; it ploughed through and through him, upturning memories, old desires, and instigating new ones; he was perturbed with the pain and longing of a boy. But somehow his melancholy softened him to thankfulness that one remained with power to convince him that his soul was still alive.

Parke found Jason at the dock, preparing to tar the seams of his boat, which had been hauled on a raft; he seated himself on the cap-log, near the tar-pot.

"You are just in time to keep up the blaze for me," said Jason, jumping down on the raft, and proceeding with the work. Parke collected the sticks within his reach and poked them into the fire, feeling unaccountably nervous; his heart fluttered and his hands felt weak. Suddenly he sprang down on the raft, which tilted into the water, so that he nearly lost his balance. Jason calmly laid down the tar-swab, and motioning Parke towards a box, took a seat beside him; he felt what was coming, but looked phlegmatic. Parke's eyes roved over the bay, whose waters were almost level with his sight, with a consciousness that he had been in the same scene before, and about to say the same thing. The faded woods opposite the rocky points shelving into the sea, the islands lifted over the horizon, the hulls and masts looming above him, the stagnant basin they were floating in, were the marshals of that reality and this dream.

"The tar will cool," said Jason, crossing his legs.

"I'll begin, then, what I have to say."

His voice was so agitated that Jason turned, looked, and pitied. "I can guess what you have to say, Parke."

"Do you object to my leaving home?"

"No.

"I propose to *live* elsewhere."

"Why?"

"Why should I live in Crest?"

"Because you are a son of the soil."

"So you were, but you left home."

"I owned nothing, not even a father's love."

"Do I own the latter?"

"Yes; but I cannot interfere with your plans."

"Then I can go?"

Jason walked up and down the raft, returned to his seat, and said: "Those Generals of Independence will use up your money."[73]

"How do you know anything about them?"

"Do you suppose that I have known nothing of Osmond's career in Venezuela?"

"Will you manage as you always have for me?"

"If you go, I desire you to take every dollar out of my hands; the old uncertainties connected with the wanderings of the family shall not be renewed in my case. I must be as free of you as you are of me. Perhaps for your own sake it is best that you should go; your prestige is gone. I must tell you, however, that Osmond's hands are by no means clean; the men of your race have single vices, and run them hard. I warn you against him. Moreover, I ask you not to go. I ask you to live at home on Philippa's account."

"She is willing, of course," cried Parke, with heat.

"Has she said so?"

"I have not told her."

"Go and tell her, then."

"At all events, I shall go."

"Very well. We will talk business in that case."

CHAPTER XXX

‖‖‖

PARKE WENT TO SEE Elsa next, and for the sake of reflection, perhaps, walked to her house, a distance of three miles. She saw him coming up the lane, threshing the thistles with a cane, and kicking the loose pebbles down the gullies.

"I am barrelling my potatoes to-day," she screamed at the door, when he came within hearing.

"I wish you would include me with them," he replied, taking her hand. She drew him into the house, to her own little sitting-room, and bade him take his ease on her new moreen-covered lounge. A wood fire burned on the hearth, which led to inquiries concerning the merits of her woodland, and then she asked him for news, being as famished as a dog for the article.

"I am going to Venezuela, Elsa."

"Vene—cat's foot."

"Cat's paw, possibly, for I mean that you shall tell Philippa my purpose.[74] An impression seems to have got abroad that my going will have a disagreeable effect upon her, which effect I do not like to face."

"I shan't do any such thing for you, sir. I have withdrawn my finger from all your pies. Since I have eaten humble pie with you, somehow I have lost my relish for any more of your baking. I don't think your going will kill Philippa, however. I suppose Jason is worried about her—there is nobody else to take her part; he is apt to think of other people's feelings."

"I never thought him apt that way; indeed, he is too indifferent. You are a cunning, cruel jade, and I am sorry I came to you."

She was angry with him for telling her that what she had fore-seen and waited for was at hand, but rather enjoyed his calling her names. Disposed to aggravate him, she said: "At any rate, Jason knows when he is in the right place. I must say, that if I admire any thing, I admire a steadfast disposition, and that is his."

"I did not come to discuss his character. However, I will agree with you on that point. He is all that you say, and a great deal more. I find him not only the right kind of a father, but a *friend*."

"Yet he consents to your leaving home, and with *Osmond*?"

"Will you, or will you not, tell Philippa?"

"Why has she been kept in the dark till now?"

"It seems to be considered my business to inform her, and hear her opposition. She is so queer, though, she may not mind it at all."

"Now you are lying."

"You and Sam Rogers have had a quiet way of holding her up to me as a terror of tacit superiority. We are mutually attached, I hope, but my idea of attachment leaves us perfect freedom still. I trust she would dislike this silent interference she has been made, as much as I do."

"Bats, moles, and men are akin," thought Elsa; but she said aloud, "The sooner the better. You talk with her; I refuse flat to open the subject. I am going up to the shore about dark, and I reckon I'll stay all night, to look over your shirts."

"Never mind the shirts."

"Somebody must bear them in mind, or you won't have any on your body—though I don't know as the foreign beasts you are going amongst wear such things. I might have known the day Osmond Luce came back, that you would go off with him. I did look for it pretty soon after."

"His influence was nothing."

"There is some good in him, though, if you'll have patience to look for it."

"Elsa!" and Parke took her chin in his hand, compelling her to meet his eye, "between man and woman now, do you not think that I had better go from Crest?"

"I think that you could not do a wiser thing, and I hope you will stay forever."

"Enough! I am off."

The thistles were unmolested, and the pebbles were suffered to rattle without his aid on the walk home. Instead of going in at the main door, he entered the premises by the barnyard gate. He saw Gilbert milking in a corner, and, on the other side of the fence, Philippa going up the garden with a shawl over her head. A resolve took possession of him. Waiting till she was beyond view, he leaped the fence, and followed her slowly, till he saw her seated among the trees on the top of the hill. A line of crimson light gleamed in the west—the arc of sunset; overhead the purple clouds of November rolled together and drew apart in the tumult of the sea-wind, which tossed them as it tossed the waves whose deep moan rose and fell round him as if baffled by the height he had reached.

"I thought I saw you," Philippa said quickly. "Isn't it cold up here?"

"Too cold to spend the evening, but I like it just now. What are you up here for?"

"I often come."

"I had no idea you indulged in sunset reveries. How far out to sea can you look?"

Climbing the rock against which she rested, he peered through the bare boughs rattling over her head, and continued: "Oh yes, the high bank at the south end of Prince Island is illuminated with the rays of the sun that has left us, and the outlet next it looks like a dark tunnel. Don't it make you think of Sam Rogers when you look out there?" And he carelessly dropped down beside her.

"I never look there."

"What do you look at?"

"Myself."

A conviction that his task might be more difficult than he had supposed fastened upon him, but it steeled his purpose, and somewhat increased his irritation against those who had thrown it upon him.

"Give me a corner of your shawl to keep off the wind — there — this is comfortable." His arm was round her waist, and her head was against his shoulder. "Will you look out seaward for me?"

"Why should I?"

"Figuratively speaking, I shall be behind the outlet; literally, I am going away with your father."

Her fingers twisted in the lapels of his coat; she held him down with a strength that made him catch his breath with the effort to release himself.

"You shall not go."

"Oh yes, Philippa," and, tearing from her, he bounded to his feet, "and you must consent. Do you want me to remain in this wretched spot? I can be little to you — miserable myself. You must make some change, too. You have the right and the means to be free and happy."

The sea roared in her ears, the wind tossed her hair across her eyes; she threw back her head madly, and he caught the knowledge in her face which struck him like lightning, and she rolled over at his feet as if she were stone dead.

"Why, she loves me!" he said, in a loud, stupefied voice, looking down upon her. "My God, what is there in me to love?"

He tried to raise her from the ground, but she lay like lead, heavy and lifeless. He shook her, rubbed her hands, pinched her cheeks, and at last she opened her eyes.

"I want you," she said.

"No, you don't. I am a worthless fellow. Do you desire Charlotte Lang's lover, husband, in your presence always?"

"I am so dizzy," she said, trying to get up.

"I know you are." And he wrapped her shawl round her, kissing her hand, and then trying to kiss her lips.

"Don't kiss me."

"Very well."

"If you do, I must remember it," and she burst into a wild fit of crying, which drove Parke to his wits' end. The tears fell from his own eyes without his knowing it. They descended the hill, but stopped again in the orchard, as if by mutual consent.

"I suppose you think me a dreadful fool, Philippa, but I never dreamed of this."

"It was always so."

Again she looked at him with such an unutterable passion in her face, that he knew he stood by the portals of a world he alone could enter, and, that once shut from his vision, he would never see it again. His own act had shut it out forever, and her innocence could not comprehend it!

"Now, now, by God, I will go. I am not base enough to take you—to give *myself* to you."

She loosed her hold, and they walked on again.

"I am not sorry," she said in a moment, restored to that calmness which the sea shows after a storm, "that I have told you the motive of my life; it may protect you."

"It may, but I shall not return; and, wherever I am, I shall escape from that protection, if possible."

Going on as if he had not spoken, and still calmer, she said: "Telling it, has prevented me from dragging it round as a purpose. Telling it, has put it to death with so much ease! All the care and fostering of this motive is buried in the grave of your knowledge. Its ghost will never rise. Was I not foolish with plans—which even God's judgment did not avert?"

It was not necessary for him to speak; he had dismissed the subject.

"I shall always love you, though," she concluded as he opened the porch-door, "because you are beautiful."

An expression of self-contempt passed over his face; it was impossible for him to appreciate the value of being loved for that.

Elsa was warming her hands by the kitchen fire.

"Ha!" she exclaimed, surveying their pale faces—"hum; I have been looking round this kitchen, and it is just as I expected—a place for nothing, and nothing in its place. I told Parke his going away would not kill you."

"No more than your going did."

"Oh, lud a massy!"

Parke, lighting a cigar, went out by the same door that he had just entered. Who can tell what motive or train of thought led him to Mrs. Lang's? Without knocking, in the old familiar way, he entered her house once more. She, with Clarice, was sitting by a table, singing hymns in rotation from a little hymn-book in her hand. Her eyes fell on Parke, and she stopped in the middle of a line to reply to his "Good-evening." Clarice did not speak.

He threw off his overcoat, took a chair near the fireplace, and sat buried in thought, smoking cigar after cigar. The loud tick of the clock, the wind shaking the windows, and the suppressed yawns of Mrs. Lang only disturbed the silence, for Clarice was as still as Parke. The evening wore on. What fascination held his eyes to the consuming brands? Did he see Mephistopheles in his scarlet coat and cock's feather, with his eternal grin? Did he hear Margaret cry: "Day! yes, it is growing day! The last day is breaking in! My wedding-day it was to be."[75]

A despairing, louder yawn from Mrs. Lang roused him at last; he threw his cigar in the fire, turned from it, and, in a low voice, asked her if there was any last favor he could do for her.

"You have done all the favor you could do," Clarice interposed, before her mother could speak. "Sent one of us to the grave."

"I know it, Clarice," he replied gently. She looked at him for the first time since his entrance. A deep sadness was in his eyes, and his face had grown sharp.

"Do you mourn for her?" she hastily asked.

"I cannot tell you a lie. No."

"Clarice, you stop," ordered Mrs. Lang.

"I have come to say, that *she* has sent me away."

"Oh, pity, pity," cried Mrs. Lang; "it would not be so if we were anywhere else."

"Slave," hissed Clarice, "to take part against yourself."

Parke rose and threw his coat over his arm.

"Stop you, Clarice," Mrs. Lang continued. "I'll call it the ole story then; don't *I* know that men are men, and women are women, and I think it is foolish for him to give up his birthright for a mess of pottage."

"Go, will you?" begged Clarice.

"As I would take Charlotte always under my wings, so, Parke, I will take your part," Mrs. Lang added.

"Well, then, there is no enmity between us. Good-by."

"Farewell," she said, and then in an undertone, "It's all done right now, as the Lord would have it."

Clarice took up the lamp to follow him out, and shut the door upon her mother.

"Forget me, Clarice, in mercy to me."

"It is like going to the grave again, to part with you, for all that I have hatefully said. You were the link that attached me to a world I do not belong to. Pray that I may die. You are lucky, and your prayer may be answered."

"If you desire it, and for my own death too."

They stood in silence a moment, and then parted, never to meet again.

"Much more of this business will kill me," he said to Osmond the next day.

"Let us begone. You will rise elastic in another atmosphere. Has Jason transferred your bank stock?"

"He is about ready with his statistics."

"I named Garcia & Co., who have a branch house in New York, for your bankers. Jason is singular; why does he want to wash his hands of all your filthy lucre?"

"Between you and me, he has no great opinion of managing for the Parkes."

"Right enough. *He* is a brick, though."

"Regular."

"Made himself after the pattern of the Hebrew bricks, for he wasn't worth a straw when he started."

"Here he is now."

"Now," said Jason, entering, "as far as business is concerned, you can go."

"'O'er the glad waters of the dark blue sea,'[76] then," said Osmond.

"Better take Byron along," said Jason.

"No books allowed. Jason, you are an aboriginal; I should think my way of life would suit you."

"Is yours a community of equal rights?"

"If we can take them."

"Am I really going?" asked Parke of Philippa, as she came in.

"It seems so."

"I mind leaving you, girl," said Osmond. "Take care of her, Jason."

"She will take care of herself."

"Keep yourself safe, old fellow, for she is alone."

"Hadn't you better bestow that advice on yourself?"

"Last words don't amount to much," Parke observed.

"It is respectable, though, to say something," answered Osmond.

At the last moment, Parke sought Philippa, and was alone with her till Osmond sent him away.

"Philippa," said her father, "a man does not escape from the environments of ten or twenty years scot-free, many times."

"You mean, that we may not meet again?"

"That is it."

"Take me up in your arms, as you did on board the ship, years ago, and I will kiss you."

He caught her in his embrace, and when he released her his tears were on her face, and she turned away weeping.

CHAPTER XXXI

||||||||||||||||||||||||||||||||||||||||||||||

TASTE AND COLOR were wanting in the details of family life which were now mechanically performed by Philippa and Mary. Excepting these, each day was a disintegration, and every person went apart to enjoy or suffer an existence which appeared to depend upon itself merely.

Mary was hypochondriacal, and the grasshopper was a burden;[77] her mental eyes were fixed upon the progress of an imaginary liver complaint, an impending cancer, or a slow consumption; the falling of the sky would have been connected with her ailments, and noticeable only on that account. She had long had an inclination for chronic complaints, but Elsa's unsparing ridicule had kept it under; when she left, it cropped out. Gilbert, her husband, naturally a silent man, became more so under this tic-douloureux influence; home was finally but a deposit for clean shirts, his Bible, and the temple of his meals. Year by year he had grown a part of the "choring" institution which belongs to all respectable families, for Jason had given him full power to trade, train and work the live stock, and it was more interesting to him than human beings. Any thing transpiring outside of his occupation should be disposed of and forgotten as soon as possible; death, marriage, religion, politics, caused time to be lost, which must be made up by extra diligence in his business. But Gilbert was most respectacle in all his ways, and bore a high reputation as a "hired man."

Mary made various comments on the subject of Parke's leaving home, which he answered promptly, and so completely that it was not renewed.

"Philippa thinks she feels bad about his being away," said Mary, "and she does; but she would feel worse if she was me: besides, she is a young girl."

"I expect she does," Gilbert answered; "and what if she does? Young gals always feel bad about something; they haven't got any thing else to do; it's a pity there is gals."

"Mr. Auster does less than ever; but he is no trouble at all in the house."

"It isn't necessary for him to negotiate round—that's my business. Folks that have learned trades never amount to much. As for trouble, I should like to know if men are ever troublesome? they don't meddle with things of no concern to them."

"Nothing must be meddled with but cattle, according to your way of thinking. Cattle are not of much importance."

"If there was more attention paid to cattle, there wouldn't be so much trouble among folks. If *you* knew something about critturs, perhaps you would be easier; take my advice at present, though, and just attend to your house-work, and your ague, and let the rest go."

So Philippa was allowed to rest under a cloud, without further notice. It was a murky, smothering vapor which enveloped her; her sympathies were exhausted; she found nothing efficacious in herself, or in those about her. She said of herself, that the threads of her being were ravelled, because that which had knit them together into a consistent web had vanished, and could nowhere be found.

Jason took to fancy-carpentering; day after day she heard the whistling of his plane or the turning-lathe, in a little room which he had converted into a workshop. His labor must have been tedious and slow, for no article appeared as its result; but, as

Mary said, he was no trouble. Philippa saw little of him, and the time she passed in his presence belonged merely to the routine with which he was connected. But the cold, dull, spiritless sphere where she moved contained a vivid, palpable core, which the virgin silence of his soul prevented him from laying bare. To his simple mind it appeared as if all nature now had his secret—or why should he feel so strange a joy in those wild winter days! The driving snows, the cold rains which dashed round the walls, the misty sea sobbing under the rim on the shore, or whirling on the tide the jagged ice, or congealing in gray calm the northern gales which bore the prolonged cries of the deep into the naked woods, the wintry sunlight which fell on their delicate black boughs—on the level, brown sodden fields, the moonlight rolling over the ancient town in a tumult of clouds—exhilarated him as with wine.

The winter was an awful one. Storm followed storm; between December and February the roads were scarcely passable, and no vessel put out to sea. The old people talked of the memorial snows and gales in Crest, and said none severer were in their annals. The house was so cold that Philippa closed the parlor where the piano was, and the dining-room connected with it, leaving for occupation the small east parlor, which was attached to the kitchen by a square passage—a bedroom in the Squire's time. She gave no reason for selecting this room, nor did she explain why she brought from the garret a set of old Indian chintz curtains, whose deep yellow ground was covered with long-tailed macaws in brilliant dyes, and hung them before the windows—there were three in the room, two facing the terrace, beyond which, through the leafless shrubs, a line of sea was visible, and one in the end wall, from which the prospect was cut off by the row of Scotch firs which bordered that side of the yard. To this window she brought her work-basket, inkstand, portfolio, and a few books; but she never looked out of the front windows, always keeping the curtains down. Here she set up a methodical system of passing all the hours of daylight, and to Jason the spot grew more and more intelligible. His meals were served there, and in the evening he allowed himself a chair by the fire while he smoked a cigar. Never in the habit of conversing with her, his silence was not remarked, and she made no effort to break it. As neither had discerned the beginning of the drama which united them years ago, and as one was blind, and the other dumb—"what sequel?"[78] Fate, however, was in her house, and as much at home in that insignificant spot, with those insignificant persons, as she was when she sat watching Napoleon on his march to Russia. While Jason sat by the fire in the evening, Philippa remained by the window sewing interminable seams; when he left the room, she folded her work, and, after turning down the lamp, moved to the hearth, and ruminated by the firelight till bedtime. Her thoughts were not confided to the portfolio even, for she never opened it; perhaps their endless repetition required no aid. Though the same ground was canvassed night after night, the embers and ashes made no reply; they listened in obstinate silence to her questioning cries. Why was it ordered that she should have no wishes granted? Had she asked so much? Were the environments of her life so pleasant naturally that they must be beset with crosses? Was it supposed that she could bear these crosses with resignation, or cast them away as the evils of a day? These she asked, with a dogged hate towards the power she questioned. Jason guessed the tenor of her feelings, and, until he heard her foot upon the stairs, the signal that she was going to bed, he lurked in some dark room or passage; and then went back to her place, and looked into the fire, and round the walls, as if he might find some clue by which to lead her from the labyrinth of her misery. His soul at this period, and in such moments, if delineated, would make a picture as affecting and as incomprehensible as those which travellers discover in strange lands, where Nature creates and wastes things of beauty, which thus accidentally fall under human vision for the first and last time.

Happily there is compensation for the soul for the loss of all it can create. Jason's spirit, pure and simple as the elements, was dominated by an absolute and profound sentiment that made the life-long wilderness of his heart blossom like the rose. He was not happy, he was without hope; yet every hour was exquisitely dear and necessary to him. Philippa, for whom he lived—his consciousness now dared to own, for whom he would die—existed in the exclusive atmosphere divided between them only; so surely was she enclosed with him, that it seemed as if the fact had been accomplished by a band of conspirators, who carried out by intuition the wishes he had never expressed. For the present this sentiment sufficed him; its power paralyzed its inevitable growth. But the time approached when it would no longer confine him, when the symbols which now enchanted would mock him to break them like straw.

Week glided after week, leaving the inmates of the old mansion imprisoned in their ways, as fixed, to all appearance, as

> "Those old portraits of old kings
> That watch the sleepers from the wall,"[79]

in the Sleeping Beauty's palace.

The last of February he launched his boat again, and, while he sailed over the bay, he summed up the days which had passed without an object, without intentions, and thought their flight had been rapid as an arrow's, while the flight of other, ordinary days was fluttering and devious, like flocks of birds.

CHAPTER XXXII

‖‖‖

PHILIPPA, WITH HER CHIN on the sill, was looking out of the parlor window one morning at the black stalks protruding from patches of ice, and the brown birds that hopped in the fir-branches, or ran over the snow with alert dipping motions, and thinking that she should be sorry when the winter was over. She had felt it a protection, shielding her mood with its inclement spirit. With the spring, she must resume something of her old life. The twigs yonder, that had kept upright in spite of the winter storms—what were they hoping?—that they might drop at last, when new leaves pushed through the mould? Fresh leaves, blossoms, and fruit! Her faded self was apart from them—yet the breath of spring must have touched her, for she thought of the deserted hill, its rocks, the old cedars, and the oaks. Then the picture of the house, opened, as it used to be in summer, rose before her; she heard the sound of the summer sea again, and felt its cool, moist balm in the darkened rooms; its murmur crept into the parlor where the piano stood, and mingled with the melody of a wild pathetic waltz, whose eternal round involved *Parke* forever and forever!

She rushed to the front window, thrust the curtains apart, and, jumping on a chair, tried to get a glimpse of the outlet of the bay. The tide was out, for the boulders on Gull's Point stood high out of the water; behind them was the outlet—a purple bar of sea and cloud joined together. A boat shot within the range of her vision, whose sail loomed against the rocks; its hull bulged out of the water, and its side ploughed the waves; she longed to be in it, and steering for another world, which might give her Crest as it had been in the past. She made a descent from the chair, and went into the kitchen.

"Mary," she asked, "do you think Mr. Auster is out with his boat?"

"He has been outside the Point every day this week. He calls the weather *mild*. It is blowing great guns outside, I'll warrant; but if he likes it it is all right. Mrs. Rogers has sent you a bit of a billet by Bill Smith's boy; he told me what was in it. She wants to come and spend to-morrow afternoon with you; she has got some news to bring."

"Certainly; where's the boy?"

"He is coming back for the answer when he darn pleases, he said, which will be in the course of an hour. We ought to make cake; do you recollect how long it is since you made any?"

"No."

"'Twas the day when your father came in, and said the little tins reminded him of his sins—the very last of October."

"And he said, '*Come*,'" Philippa murmured. "If I had answered 'Yes,' what should I be with *them*?"

Mary stared at her, and raising her voice, as if addressing a deaf person, asked, "You don't realize, I guess, that you have been eating my doughnuts, and cookies, and gingerbread all this time; plenty of them, such as they were."

Philippa's eyes were fixed on some remote boundary; she did not hear Mary, who peevishly exclaimed: "She's off to South America. I trust she will get back in time to give that boy an answer; he is a sass-box, that boy."

But Philippa was nearer home, and grappling with an irritating conviction, which the recollection of that interview with her father caused. If, at this moment, she was with Parke, she knew there would be a sediment in her satisfaction, because her plans would still be thwarted. Away from Crest, he could not be to her what she had believed he would be everywhere. The conviction was humiliating, for it proved that he was not single in her heart, but surrounded by other ideas, and selfish ones.[80]

The boy returned, and her revery was broken. A message was sent to Mrs. Rogers; and Philippa, roused with the necessity of doing away her ill opinion of herself by exertion in somebody's behalf, not only made cake, but went all over the house, opened closets, drawers, and windows. By night, she was in a different mood. Mary noticed the change. She had heard an unwonted slamming of doors, and mentioned it to Gilbert, who replied that he supposed she was feeling her oats. When Jason came home, wet, cold, and hungry, Philippa had subsided into her old place by the window, and was engaged with a book. While he was drinking his tea with wondering eyes, he noticed that the long-closed curtains before the front windows were drawn apart, and asked her if she had been looking for spring.

"No," she answered, "has it come?"

"I heard a frog last night; don't the verse-makers call the frog 'spring's harbinger'?"

"I don't read verses; but I fancy it was the cowslip and the violet instead."

"What are you reading?"

"'Robinson Crusoe.'"[81]

"'Robinson Crusoe!'"

He finished his tea in silence, and she went on with her book.

Half an hour afterwards, he knocked the ashes from his cigar, and asked her if she intended to plant the terrace.

"I have not thought about it; the geraniums are dead in the cellar, Mary says."

"Shall I send for some new ones?"

"I don't care."

"So I thought."

"I never was very fond of flowers," she answered in an apologetic tone, shutting her book.

"Why don't Ritchings come here any more?" he asked abruptly.

"He was here last week. By the way, Mrs. Rogers has asked for an invitation to pass to-morrow afternoon with me."

"She has heard from Sam, then. What is Mr. Ritchings doing? How is his sore throat?"

"Poor Mr. Ritchings!"

"Why is he poor? Because he is madly in love with you?"

The tone of his voice was savage and she looked at him, coloring with surprise.

"A woman despises a man," he continued, "for loving her, unless she happens to return his love; is it not so? Inform me; I am green about the sentiments."

"Jason!"

"How is it, I ask, between you and the parson? Have you a contempt for him?"

An angry gesture was all her answer.

"Why don't you pity him?"

"Pity a man?"

"Oh, a man needs it, I assure you, more than a woman ever does."

"You may console Mr. Ritchings, since that is your opinion," she answered, leaving the room.

"Every evening," he said to himself, "for three months, she has kept me in this place, and then, by some damnable force or unrelenting magnetism, compelled me to leave it; but to-night *I* have sent her away,—not in a nice manner, perhaps,—but she is gone, and I feel as if the room was in a state of arrest."

He looked over the little table which stood by the window; it was more disordered than usual, and his eye fell on a daguerreotype. He recognized it, and opened the case. It contained a picture of his wife, taken some ten years before. She looked at him from behind the glass, with her cold, hard, glittering eyes; the lines of her mouth, the black crisp curls over her polished forehead, were no more rigid in the picture than he remembered them in life. It was a stern relief to gaze at the face which had always been inscrutable to him. Could there have been any communion between their spirits, he would have said: "Behold me without the imposition laid upon me by you." He would have asked, if she had yet learned the secret of the destiny which had bound them together, without the aim of self-advantage, or of the higher or more exalted feelings. Though her spirit was unseen, and silent as its image in his hand, he closed the case with the feeling of having made her the witness of his past and present conscience; it was washed clean for the future. He sought out the remaining contents of the table, and detected a dilapidated pocket-book, with the name of "Parke Auster," in half-obliterated gilt letters stamped upon it: inserting his long fingers into one of its compartments, he drew out a bill for some sheets of music, and a little bunch of dried flowers.

"The geraniums are all dead in the cellar," quoth Jason.

In another, he found a battered silver sixpence, strung on a faded silk string, and a card, with "Theresa Bond, 49 Graham Place," engraved upon it.

"Philippa has been stirring about the house to-day, and opened her graves," he said, throwing the pocket-book into the fire. "Theresa's call is returned, and the silver sixpence goes back to the furnace. Parke has turned the key on his memories, and I'll lock up Philippa's."

He found nothing more to attract speculation, and after finding her place in Robinson Crusoe, and reading a few pages, folded his arms on the table, and fell asleep.

He was off by daybreak, Mary told Philippa, with his dogs, a chunk of bread, and a surveyor's scale; so she guessed he was up in the wood-lots. Before tea-time he was at home, and, contrary to his custom, went at once to the parlor, where he found Mrs. Rogers, as cheerful, talkative, and friendly as if she had seen him but the day before, when, in fact, they had not met since the day of Sarah's funeral, more than eight months ago. As he had sur-mised, she brought a letter from Sam, and the early part of her visit had been consumed by its perusal, and the development of her feelings concerning him. The letter was graphic, and Philippa laughed over his account of a "bear-grab"—his meeting with a dingy fellow on the ice, in search of the northwest passage, who had, in the warmth of his greeting, clawed him unpleasantly.

"I wish Sam would come home," she remarked.

"Now, do you? he'd be clawed home, as well as abroad, poor fellow."

"What do you mean?"

"You don't know what paws of velvet can do, do you?"

"Cats'?"

"Women's paws, Philippa."

"Who could have the heart to torment the best man I ever knew?"

"That's what I say; but did you never know of anybody that might do it?"

"Never."

Philippa blushed like a blaze of brushwood at the intrusive torch which Mrs. Rogers applied to her.

"Philippa," she said, "this letter has rather stirred me up, and I have made up my mind to give you a piece of it, because I love you, my dear, and because I want to see you differently situated. I never should have opened my mouth if Parke hadn't left you; now you know he has, you needn't fire up—I know what's what. In my opinion, and I tell you candidly, I wouldn't dare mention it if Sam wasn't on the other side of Jordan, as it were, clawed with bears and harpooned by whales,—but as it is, it is my opinion that Sam Rogers adores the ground you tread on."

"He doesn't," said Philippa, indignantly.

"Oh yes, he does; but he has had his reasons for keeping dark; he might have been afraid of interfering, or of looking too high. But things are changed. What you have, you know, is your own now, and you have got to keep it, too; and Sam is a captain, able to hold his own anywhere; and a sensible, better man never walked."

"He would not thank you for this. I am glad he is thousands of miles from me."

"Of course, he wouldn't thank me—children never thank their parents; but *you* ought to thank me, for wanting to give you something worth living for. You know in your heart of hearts that Sam would stop at no sacrifice for your sake. What ails him? You didn't fall in love with him, that's all. Do you suppose the married state is a state of being in love?"

"I believe that he would sacrifice his happiness for me, but I could not accept it from him. I shall not marry Sam, Mrs. Rogers."

"Well, I can't offer anybody else; but what are you going to do—marry Jason?"

The question fell on Philippa like a thunderbolt; Mrs. Rogers was scared at her aspect.

"Do you dare say that?" she cried.

"Others say that he will marry."

"I tell you that I will make no change — he will make none — we shall live on the same terms as now. Oh the cowardly world, that invents what it contemns!"

"You lamb, you are dreadfully earnest; but Jason is a man, my dear; do not believe that he is going to be mewed up this way forever."

"Why not?"

"Every man has in his life a period of breaking out. It has always seemed to me that Jason has never had his turn; there is something smouldering in him, you may be sure. I presume he is not aware of it himself, but it will make no difference, he will have his day, according to his nature. I have noticed, over and over again, that men belie the character the world and circumstances give them. There was Lem Baker, till forty-nine he was a sober man, spoke at all the temperance meetings, and never showed the least mercy for those who tasted ardent spirits; before he was fifty, he was an awful drunkard. And there was Eben Millet, who was so devoted to his wife, and always leading about his children; one scarce ever saw him without a child fastened to his forefinger, and he was always talking about what his wife thought and said and did; but on the fifteenth year of his marriage, he went mad after a young woman, who drove him to his grave."

"These cases do not prove what the race is."

"Race! there isn't but one race all over the world, and Jason belongs to it."

"The grovelling fools talk about him, do they? Why do people marry twice?"

"Although I have been married twice, I don't think I can tell you."

"I did not know it."

"The first time was long before you were born, when Sarah Parke was growing up. My second wedding came off when I was twenty-three. I then married Mr. Rogers, who was forty-three."

"I almost wish myself in the Arctic seas, among the *mute* beasts."

"The *must be's* are there, Philippa, as well as here; but I am dreadful sorry I have upset you so. How the afternoon has slipped away! I do believe it's getting towards five o'clock."

Jason was a welcome sight to her at this moment. She had been no advantage to Philippa, that was certain; but what would become of the wilful, innocent, friendless girl, if Jason should bring a strange woman into the house as his wife? That jade, Elsa, must have been of her way of thinking, or she would not have left her. With all her money, Philippa was no better off than the poorest girl in Crest with a mother. Mrs. Rogers felt little disappointment in her scheme as far as Sam was concerned, for she had the fullest confidence in his ability to weather any thing, from Cape Horn to the stormiest passions which rage in the region of the soul.

They sat down to tea, and her first observation was, "What a change!" The second embodied a joke, and the third contained the exclamation, "Why, Jason, you are getting gray."

"I am old," he replied.

"Philippa is growing old, too; she stays in the house too much. Did you never think the house was damp? It has been built near a hundred years; its beams and foundation must be rotting."

"It may fall on us some day," said Philippa.

"I hope nobody will take the trouble to unroof us if it happens," said Jason.

"Be sure to let us alone, Mrs. Rogers," Philippa added.

"Old Mr. Turner's house came down by the run—you recollect, Jason," Mrs. Rogers remarked.

But he made no reply; he was occupied in observing Philippa, for her last remark was an enigma to him. If Mrs. Rogers had not been there, he would have prayed for the walls to fall, for the sake of solving it. She raised her eyes to his face, and was struck with an uneasy surprise; it contained an information that caused her to look about her, and discover where she was. With a sudden instinct, forgetting the presence of Mrs. Rogers, she asked him where the pocket-book was. He indicated the fire, and asked her, in a gentle voice, whether she had finished Robinson Crusoe.

"You haven't thieves in the neighborhood, have you?" Mrs. Rogers inquired. "Becky Freeman was telling me that her chickens had disappeared lately."

"I should not be surprised if we had," cried Philippa; "how can we punish them?"

"There is a great deal of rubbish, that might as well be stolen as not," said Jason; "why should we punish one for taking what he can't get except by stealing?"

"Why, Jason, where's your religion?" asked Mrs. Rogers.

"Safe enough; whenever I want to use it, it will be at hand."

An argument set in between them, which was closed by her declaring that she must go home, and attend to her cat and parrot. Philippa accompanied her to the gate, and watched her down the street; instead of returning to the parlor, she went to her chamber, and spent the evening in darkness.

CHAPTER XXXIII

"It is most time," said Mary, as she was taking up the ashes in the parlor fireplace, "to be thinking of pine boughs for the jambs, instead of live coals."

"Pine boughs," echoed Jason, with a dreamy stare at the ashes, "we won't have any."

"It is a very warm day, for the time of year; the sooner we go to house-cleaning, the better."

"Don't upset things, Mary."

"This room can remain as it is for a while longer; Philippa takes good care of it. I often find her dusting and setting things to rights at odd times, but she don't seem to care for the rest of the house any longer; she hasn't said a word for or against a thing that has happened since Parke went away."

"Ah! Where is she now?"

"She's up stairs; she said, just before you came in, that she should soon remove her work-basket to her own chamber."

"Ah!"

"It will be cold this evening for the wind has changed, and a good fire will be wanted."

"Yes, I think so. I am going to the Comet Rocks to-day; put off supper till I come back."

Surprised at the unusual request, she asked him if there was more company to-day again; he replied that he might possibly bring home some fish—that was reason enough, was it not?

Afterwards she told Philippa that a word musn't be said against a late supper that night, for there would be a reason for it. With the change of wind a storm came up before sunset, which Gilbert said was the sheep-storm; the air was filled with a cold, rolling mist, rising and falling over the town, as the wind compelled. Philippa, in the restlessness which had lately come upon her, watched its rifts, which disclosed glimpses of gray water passing the shore in dismal haste, and masses of half-opened leaves shedding showers of condensed fog, or the dingy umbrellas which wavered along the street, protecting the few loungers going between houses and shops. But she was quiet by the shaded lamp in the parlor, when she heard Jason's voice in the passage telling Mary that it had taken him a long time to tack across the bay. He entered, inquiring for his supper, and, contrary to his wont, in his boating costume; he threw his battered hat into a corner, and dropped his pilot's jacket on the floor. Philippa could not help being conscious of his proceedings. Would he take off his boots, she wondered, and suspended her sewing to look at them; they were wet and heavy, evidently, and his trowsers were tucked into them, but he made no movement to pull them off. Her eyes were irresistibly drawn up to meet his—he was gazing at her.

"Excuse my boots," he said.

She nodded slightly.

"And allow me to disabuse myself of this neck-tie; the ends blew out like a sail, and they are wet."

He untwisted it as if it had been choking him, and dropped it beside him. She had resumed her sewing, but she knew when it fell, and she knew, too, that he was very pale, and that his blue eyes were shining in strange relief against the circle of his thick, black, curved eyelashes. Mary had set on the supper, and was gone; but he sat down by the fire, unmindful of it, till Philippa called him to the table.

"I didn't expect the fish, Mr. Auster," said Mary, reentering with another dish; "so here is something in the place."

"Fish!" he said, facing round in his chair; "what fish?"

Philippa looked at her so impatiently that she thought it best not to answer him, but to disappear again, and leave them to their supper. Philippa felt there was something dangerous about Jason just then, and preferred that he should display his eccentric mood to herself alone.

"You need your tea, Jason," she said, in a conciliatory voice.

He laughed, stretched out his long arm (for he had not left his chair), and demanded: "Give it to me, then. Come and hold the cup to my lips—I haven't the strength to do it."

"Nor have I."

His manner, in spite of her cool reply, confused her a little. Instead of taking her own seat at the table, she walked round it, with a plate in her hand, and filled it with bread.

"I say I am thirsty, Philippa, and hungry,—bring me something."

"Take it, then." And she gave him a cup of tea, which he swallowed at once.

"More tea," he begged, "and something to eat, or I must famish."

She reflected. It was his determination, she perceived, not to go to the table. She, herself, had suddenly lost her appetite. It would not do for Mary to find the supper untouched, and Mary at that moment represented the whole censorious world, which Philippa felt, for the first time, afraid of. Seizing the last dish which Mary had brought in, she threw its contents into the fire, and then deliberately drank some tea and ate a morsel of bread.

"Right," he said, watching her till she had finished and called Mary in to clear the table. While it was being done, he thought he detected Philippa in the act of retreat, which he cut off by promenading between her and the doors.

"Philippa," he said, suddenly wheeling towards her, when alone, "I am tired of reigning in hell and serving in heaven. I would be master of Paradise."

"Move to another place, then," she curtly answered, thinking how much she could bear, that was painful and disagreeable, from him.

"*Here* is my place—with you. Put down your foolish work, for I am going to teach you something. I, *Jason*—can you imagine it?"

"No. Is it a necessary knowledge you are about to teach?"

"I make it so."

He moved a chair opposite her and sat down. She saw him, but with false eyes. Any other woman there would have seen a man filled with the beauty which passion gives to the plainest, the most simple—she would have seen her lover, ardent, resolute, overpowering. Philippa merely saw him in a position and mood of perplexing inconvenience, which she could not dispose of. Doubtless he felt her obtuseness, for he remained silent some minutes, and then prefaced his subject with the remark: "How the wind howls!"

"Are you listening to that, all this while?" she asked, irritated at his deliberate propinquity.

"Philippa, how do you think I have lived?"

"I know how, without thinking."

"What has been my value?"

"Value?"

"I have been a husband, a father, and your guardian; was I any thing else?"

"No, not to me."

"I was nothing to myself either,—for a long time, a long time."

"Why should you have been more, sir? Your relations implied all the possibilities of life."

"It implied little with me beyond duty. Reflect."

The memory of Sarah's loveless ways, of Parke's indifferent neglect, was too clear for her not to follow his suggestion. But what was all this to her? The result of his life was like that of hers—disappointment; and he must tell of it, perhaps with the hope of convincing her that it was the common lot.

"You found no satisfaction in duty! Who does? Something that we esteem, however, pushes us on towards its aim, as strenuously as if it were our most beautiful ideal. You wish me to understand that you are disappointed."

"I was not disappointed, for I hoped nothing. I never, at any time, in youth or manhood, was in a position that might have accepted hope."

A comprehension of his intention dawned in her mind, which he perceived by a change in her countenance.

"Are you ready to admit," he continued, "that I have done well as a chrysalis? or do you intend to warn me presently that if I break through the traditions built round me by the masons who mortar the mass together by plummet and line, I shall be deprived of every claim of support from my fellows?"

She began to feel the recklessness which always came over her when she was in collision with an antagonist.

"Have you a hope now, Jason?"

"Yes, one that a free man is entitled to."

She started to her feet, but he compelled her back to her chair.

"You are going to tell me that you love me. Well, begin, so that it may end."

"I love you, Philippa—"

Her eyes shot sparkles of anger, and her lips made a mocking motion, but she did not speak.

"And I ask you to be my wife—"

A gesture of contempt did not deter him in his speech.

"The slow years having taught me what manner of man I am, and, with a patience equal to my own, removed all obstacles to my desires, do you believe that I shall not conquer your will—it shall not stand in my way. Accept me, Philippa."

"Parke! Parke! Parke!" she said, between her teeth.

"Will you make *father* and *son* a watchword? Let the world do that; but, Philippa, *you* know that I have been faithful to him till there is no longer need of faith. What! Would you like to say that I am like a whipped hound, slinking back to the place of contention, to hold the rights I could not maintain, except alone!"

He caught her hands, and drew her so near him that she was obliged to meet his burning, pleading, indignant eyes, and to dwell on his quivering lips, which were as white as death. It was more than she could bear; but she must still listen.

"If your love, which is now mere pride with you, had remained where it had its birth, in the depths of your *self*, instead of governing your actions, blazoning itself on your existence, it would be easy to turn its current into that vague, emotional sea which ebbs and flows in every human soul, but which does not sway its destiny, unless, as you have, one commits his emotion to the public. Who may not have felt as you have felt? We are much alike."

"Now, have you finished?"

He passed his handkerchief over his face, to hide a sickening agitation, for the struggle shattered him. Philippa was so pitiless! Hard and bright as a diamond, cold as a glacier, ignorant, obstinate, insensible—and yet he loved her so, that he swore silently that he would never go beyond the spot that contained her.

She drew her watch from her belt, and turned its face towards him.

"Yes, it is late," he said.

Then he folded his arms and walked up and down the floor, stopping before her at each turn, to meet the eyes of a combatant determined to end the subject at once and forever.

The fire went out, the astral lamp waned, the storm died away, the rain ceased to beat against the windows, the wind to roar round the house, but the sea bayed the shore with a monotonous roar, which echoed through the room. He resumed his seat, and fell into deep thought. The years that he had boasted of had cheated him after all—they had not given him the key to Philippa's nature. She herself did not possess it, he was convinced. To open those sealed perceptions, that was his task—how could it be done, where was the key? She thought, at last, so absorbed he seemed, that he must have forgotten her—she rose without attracting his attention, and went to the door, paused, and looked back. Something in his attitude and his profile gave her an impulse to go and shake him by the shoulder, and ask him what his thoughts were; resisting that, she was weak enough to stand by the door, till he carelessly raised his head, and turned to look at her. An expression of pity, speculation, and doubt passed over his face, which was now perfectly composed, and gave her a bitter sense of humiliation; her brain, her heart, her eyelids were burdened with a weight which bore her to the floor. With a faint gasp, and throwing up her arms to drive it away, she fell forward, and he caught her.

CHAPTER XXXIV

||||||||||||||||||||||||||||||||||||||||||||||||||||||||

PHILIPPA WROTE THERESA BOND, and begged her to come to Crest. Though the letter merely outlined the events of the past year, omitting all mention of Jason, Theresa read it with an impression that it had been dictated by stronger feelings than she had given Philippa credit for possessing. She replied that curiosity, and *redivivus*[82] also, tempted her to accept the invitation, but she could not, because she was about to be married to a youth who would not permit her to leave him. She pretended to ascribe his refusal to a base jealousy of the past, which she had made him acquainted with. Philippa could imagine how she wanted to come—what a monumental time they might have! Had Philippa found a confessor yet? Was she prepared to own that the beautiful Parke hadn't proved a joy forever? Justice must be done him, however; she, herself, was obliged to admit that there had never been the shadow of deceit in his conduct towards her. How was Cousin Jason? Was he an exception to the sex, in the character of a bereaved husband? Or, was he already on the point of falling in love? She didn't believe, by the way, that he ever had been in love; she thought him like the aloe—that he wouldn't bloom till towards a hundred. Think of the woman who could gather the blossom! "Stuff," thought Philippa, "I wish she would come and take it; I dare say she would try." The letter concluded with an invitation to her wedding, not yet appointed.

Jason brought Theresa's letter to her, and asked what its contents were.

"I sent for Theresa to visit me," she replied.

An angry cloud spread over his face, and his eyes flashed; it gratified her to see the calmness which had possessed him, since their last interview, broken up.

"You sent for her as a protection against me," he said.

"Yes; I did not know what else to do," she replied, ingenuously.

"She has not accepted the invitation!"

"She cannot come."

"She will not come. Theresa understands me."

Philippa looked at the letter in her hand with astonishment. Could he read it from the outside?

"How do you know she understands you?"

"Because she is a woman who has been taught by her passion."

"It is a pity she is not here."

"It is not a pity; it is enough for me to witness your heart of ice and steel."

"What do you make me out to be? I never was romantic—less so now than ever. *I* see myself, as a young woman, refusing to marry a man much older than herself,[83] with whom she has lived as a relative."

For the life of her she could not name the character of the relation; he never had appeared like a father, and she had never thought of him as a brother.

"That is the arithmetic of the subject," he answered.

"There are other reasons, too."

"Reasons?"

"Why I should not listen to you, even."

"No—no, Philippa, there are none. Give me your conscience, your will; I can keep them from tormenting you. Shelter yourself in the abyss of my love, which is as wide and deep as the air."

He was beside her chair—on the floor at her feet: she could not resist his folding her in his arms, nor move her head from his breast; but she could shut her eyes against him, and she did.

"Little flower," he said, "live with me and be happy, as I shall be happy."

She was like a statue.

"Give me," and he shook her in his embrace, "this Philippa—this solitary, friendless girl, to be the life of this solitary, friendless man."

No answer came from her; but when he sighed like one in pain she opened her eyes, and they looked upon each other from the prison of the soul. They saw that their personality was a sacred essence that could not be tampered with, and then each spirit retreated to its confines. His eyes rested on the beautiful lips, so near his own.

"May I kiss you?" he asked.

"You hold me here by force; why ask for such a trifle, that depends on your will?"

Although her sweet, warm breath made the current of his blood thunder in heart and brain, he released her as if she were a log.

"Does it? Then I shall never kiss you—*never.*"

"One point, at last, is settled between us."

A long period of silence followed this interview, in which neither looked at or spoke to the other. They met at the table, passed each other in the passages, or on the stairs, but made no stay together anywhere. The silence was terminated by Jason's being obliged to consult her respecting the division of some land, through which a street had been cut, into building lots. The land on one side of the new street belonged to Parke, and that on the other side was hers. She refused to look at the diagram of the street.

"You are acting," she said, angrily, "as if Parke were dead; and I won't sell."

"An agent must follow his instructions. Mine are to raise money—to make new streets in the Republic of Venezuela, probably. The land can be sold to advantage, if all parties consent; a company wants both sides of the street. Will you sell?"

She proposed going to the spot; he assented, internally cursing the infatuation, which, strong as it was, had no power to break his own. They had to cross a field on the outskirts of the town, and climb a stone wall before reaching the ground. Jason stepped over the wall with a stride, but Philippa slipped on a mossy stone, and fell over, with her dress hanging to it; he was obliged to extricate her, and laughed as he did so, for which irreverence she gave his cheek a blow with her glove. At the next wall he took her in his arms and carried her past the hedge-row, over a brook bordered with alder bushes and wild roses, and deposited her on the disputed territory. She saw the advantage at once of breaking up the ground into building lots; it would increase the value of the whole tract, especially on that side nearest the town, which belonged to Parke.

"Sell it, if you choose," she said.

"What shall I do with your share of the money?"

"Take care of it, as you always have."

"You choose, then, to continue me as your guardian."

Biting her lips, she turned away without being generous enough to tell him that she would rather trust him than any man in the world. The anomaly of her position was most trying—unheard of, and yet she had no thought of ever separating from him. He did not walk beside her, as she expected, but remained by the brook, gazing into its little brown pools, and peeling a willow wand. When she reached the wall she stopped and looked back, as she had done once before when he seemed to forget her! How tall he looked against the background of the sky! She wondered if that was the way he passed so much of his time when in the woods. Perhaps he was poetical; that might be his musing secret, and he had never found anybody to share it with. He was a strange man. Liking to live apart from human sympathy so many years, why had he at last loved and sought her? Tears surprised her—an involuntary tribute paid to the honor and generosity of his nature, which she could not suppress. He looked up suddenly, and, observing her standing by the wall, hurried up to her, with a gentle apology for keeping her waiting. They returned through the main street, and she was perplexed in trying to recall the time when they walked together last. The street looked pleasant, with its willows, deep yards full of lilacs and rose bushes on one side, and its quaint, miscellaneous shops on the other, and she said so. He pointed to the sea, which appeared to be wedging up between the storehouses on the upper part of the street, and told her how it looked the night before in moonlight. He sauntered along the street, and she was compelled to regulate her gait by his. They met many people, but she noticed that none accosted him; his slight nods were returned by marked respect, and he was closely observed by all who passed him with a certain air of curiosity, which puzzled her.

The walk induced a restlessness which would not permit her to resume her in-door employments; she had suddenly acquired a longing for change, and bethought her of a promise made to Elsa, of a two or three days' visit. She packed a valise on the spur of the recollection, and started for Elsa's with Gilbert. On her arrival, she found that Elsa had been expecting her, and her reception was a warm one. Gilbert was directed to tell Jason not to send for her; she would take her own time in returning.

"If you hadn't come, miss," said Elsa, when they were alone, in two rocking-chairs, "I should have made my way up to your house; there's something in this pleasant weather that drives me wild when I am alone. I look out at the ring of trees round me, and feel as if they were waiting to catch me; the fields of green, shining grass are awful lonesome—it seems as if all human life had passed away forever. The seed is all in the ground, 'tisn't haying yet, and I am put to it to pass away the time. I wish the Old Harry[84] had the place."

"You don't mean to own that you are tired of it?"

"That's it, exactly."

"And that you would like to go back?"

"You've said it."

"What did you ever leave for, you contrary old woman?" And Philippa felt more provoked with her than ever, for having left her.

"Never you mind—I haven't gone back yet. I don't know whether it is safe."

She looked at Philippa, with such cunning, crafty eyes, that she was disposed to turn away from them.

"Dear me, Elsa, what an old gipsey you are."

"A dark-complected man is going the same road that you are. You will meet, if a light-complected man, who is not thinking of you, does not cross the seas in three days, three months, or three years. A piece of bad luck is coming from the Jack of Spades to you all."

"Patience, and shuffle the cards."

"They are talking about Jason. How is it, Philippa? I didn't know why I went away hardly, but you see I found a reason after all. Clouds no bigger than a man's hand sometimes blow over, but this hasn't. I do mistrust that Jason means to marry you. I don't care *much* whether you make up your minds, you two, to be yoked together; but I intend to keep out of the way till it is settled one way or the other. Sarah Auster shall not accuse me at the Judgment of making, or marring; nor shall the tell-tales of Crest accuse me of matchmaking."

"It is all settled."

"Are you sure? I can see by your face which way."

Without any previous intention of doing so, Philippa unburdened her mind to Elsa, who heard the recital of Jason's conduct without a single comment. The representation that Philippa made placed her conduct in a new light before her own mental vision, and changed him also; he was a different man in her description from what he had appeared in reality, and she could not account for it.

"I guess," said Elsa, "that I won't come up till green corn comes."

She would not say another word on the subject, but she was astonished at the insight she had obtained into Jason's character; making an excuse to Philippa, she went into the garden, with the feint of picking green gooseberries to stew.

"Did you ever," she said, under her breath, as if addressing the gooseberry-bush confidentially, "hear the like before? It is certain to my mind, that Sarah had no more comprehension what kind of man she had for a husband, than I have had; live and learn, though. It is well she died. Come to think of it, there was never any love lost between them. Poor Sarah! I wonder I didn't see him better—he is a remarkable man; but his fire was put out by the Parke sun—that's the truth. Who hasn't been put out by them, if in their way? And Philippa's trying to put him out too, but he has got the best of her, I'll bet. But I must stay a while longer in my jail."

She carried in her gooseberries, and told Philippa to pick them over. Then she brought out some ends of muslin and lace, and set her to cap-making. Various other matters were entered upon, which seemed unimportant to Philippa, but they served Elsa's purpose, to keep up a desultory conversation and restore composure.

CHAPTER XXXV

ELSA STIPULATED for a week; it came to a close before Philippa heard from home; then some unexpected news was brought from the shore by Clapp, who had gone thither for some stores. As he heard it, he said, he would tell them, but couldn't say whether the particulars were just so. It was on a Tuesday, the day after Philippa left her house, that Jason Auster went to the woods with his gun, and was found there by Jehu Bates, insensible, and with his right hand blown off at the wrist. He laid right in a pool of blood, that made Jehu Bates sick; but he had sense enough to hold up Jason's arm, and to tie his whip-lash round it, which stopped the blood's running, and brought him to so that he was able to walk to Jehu Bates's ox-cart, that was in the woods after a cord or two of yellow pine; and Jehu Bates brought him home, where he now lay in a raging fever.

"He's been there ever since Tuesday," screamed Elsa, "and now it's Saturday, and we have not been sent for."

"Maybe he is out of his head," was Clapp's consolatory reason for the omission.

With strangely cold, tremulous fingers Philippa began to fold the articles that were to be packed in her valise, and arranged them as leisurely and carefully as though she were not thinking of what she had just heard. Nothing seemed so plain to her, so imperative, as the getting of her hair-brush, her thimble, her shoes into this valise; but every instant a weight was growing heavier and heavier upon her, which impeded her progress, and was forcing time to stand still with her, while it sped with Jason, hurrying him to his last hour. Elsa broke the spell by asking her if she was ready; her own bonnet was on, and the wagon was at the door.

"The corn that I didn't think of may be ripe for the harvest," she thought; "I must go and see it gathered."

Every step of the way she urged Clapp to "gee up," or they wouldn't reach the house time enough to be of the least use to anybody. They soon clattered into the premises by the barnyard gate, and she started for the porch-door like a deer, forgetting Philippa, in her eagerness to get into the house and resume its duties, exactly at the point where she had left them months ago. Philippa looked over the orchard paling, and at the hill, for it might be her last view of their familiar aspect, and then walked towards the house with reluctant feet. On the threshold her heart recoiled against meeting Jason—the man she could not love, but could not endure to lose.

"Just see," said Elsa, when she entered, "this ring of ashes on the hearth; kitchen looks as if it hadn't been inhabited. Mary is up stairs; the doctor is dressing the wound. Gilbert is there, too. Mary says he walks round the chamber outside Jason's door in his stocking feet, day and night, just as his dogs do in the yard. She says he is as rational as she is, which isn't saying much. You'd better ask the doctor for directions. I hear him on the stairs."

She gave Philippa no chance, however, to speak to him, but assailed him with questions, beginning with asking why in the world he hadn't sent post haste for her and Philippa. Jason strictly forbade the sending of any message, he replied, and it wasn't really necessary; he was getting along very well, his fever wasn't so high, and unless mortification set in he would be up in a few days.

"Mortification!" exclaimed Elsa; "do, if you dare let that take place."

Philippa slipped out of the kitchen while they were talking, and went up stairs. She must see Jason, and the sooner the shock of the meeting was over the better for her plan, which was that she should be his nurse. She entered the chamber, and saw that he was sleeping. Mary sat by the bed, fanning away the flies with a bunch of peacock's feathers.

"Elsa wants you down stairs," Philippa whispered; "I'll stay up here now."

Mary relinquished the brush, and crept out, making a series of contortions to describe the effect of the accident upon her own condition, but not daring to speak on account of Jason's slumber.

As soon as Philippa took her seat by the bedside, he began to sigh, appearing to be in a painful dream; his lips quivered like a child's, when it is on the point of weeping grievously for some mysterious reason. He moved his head from side to side, but, even in his restless sleep, how motionless his right arm lay outside the counterpane! Presently he waved his left hand, and opened his eyes.

"I thought we were going down," he said, "water-logged."

His pallid, wandering eyes, and weak, wailing voice, told her how terrible the accident had proved. Every thought fled from her, except the one which made her heart full—that she must watch him, and care for him.

"A little water," he begged, without noticing her.

She held a glass to his lips; the diamond ring caught his attention; he touched it with his finger.

"Philippa, they don't give me half enough water; won't you let me have more?"

"Yes."

He smiled, and tried to wipe his mouth. "It's awkward with the left hand," he said.

She took the handkerchief from him, and gently brushed his bearded face with it, and smoothed his dry, tangled hair. While she was doing this, he looked at her with a happy, childish gravity, and said, "The lamp went out last night."

"It shall not happen again."

"Shall you be here all the time?"

"Day and night till you are well."

For the first time he cast a peculiar glance towards his mutilated arm—a glance of gratitude; he was thanking the gun. He looked back again at Philippa, whose tears were falling in spite of herself.

"You mustn't cry, yellow-bird." But he began to weep, too, and Elsa, opening the door, found them both crying.

"You are a pretty one for a sick-room," she fiercely whispered to Philippa; "clear out, if you can't do better than this."

Philippa was meekly obeying her, for she felt she had been guilty of a dangerous, weak display of feeling, when Jason, his eyebrows knitting with anger, clutched Elsa by the sleeve, and said, "She promised to stay. She shan't go. Why have you come?"

"There, there, Jason; Philippa is only going out to rest half an hour, and I have only come to take care of her clothes, and get her meals while she waits upon you."

"Well, well, that will do." And he closed his eyes with exhaustion.

"Ha, ha!" said Elsa, sarcastically, stepping into Philippa's room, as soon as he slept again; "you could not keep from running over, could you? It's a poor plan to be troubled with feelings at the wrong time; seems to me you haven't calculated right, unless you do want to kill him out and out."

"I'll do what you think best."

"Go back and play cheerful, humor him in every thing; and, when you can't humor him, cheat him."

"Will he recover?"

"If the Lord wills."

"I asked your opinion."

"*I'm* dubious; still, my judgment is not worth much, for I have had no experience in gunpowder accidents—except in the case of Eli Coffin, whose legs were blown a mile into the air, boots and all, when he was blasting rocks: *he* died."

Philippa smiled slightly, and Elsa saw her seated beside Jason again, satisfied that her nerves were strung to the right pitch for the sick-room. Her own spirits rose to the occasion, as they always did before positive calamity; the perils of the imagination she could not face, but the plain facts of misfortune she could endure cheerfully; and she bore their progress with the more equanimity because she herself had been so long exempt from the various distractions of humanity. It was years since she had suffered an acute mental or physical pain; her voyage over the sea of trouble appeared to be ended. This immunity had engendered the grotesque humor which looked unfeeling, even to herself, sometimes. She felt so light-hearted at being able to resume her former sway in the house, that she tried to account for it on the ground of a special intervention to the end of bringing her back to the family, and instinctively threw a sop to Providence by affirming that Jason would get well to carry out a scheme which had long been ripening. But Jason was in no hurry, it seemed, to finish it; his weakness outlasted the fever which supervened his wound, till the wound was healed. He maintained a neutral ground, which neither permitted the invasion of death, nor allowed the forces of life to occupy it. In case a struggle should rise between the two powers, it was evident that he would be quite indifferent to the result. By no word or token did he convey to Philippa one remembrance of his love. After the flash of feeling occasioned by her return, when his mind was so unhinged, he accepted her attentions as a soldier, when taken to the rear, accepts attentions from his passing comrades going to the front. As his illness continued, her feelings changed; their law warred with the law of her will. Their development was sanctioned by his inability to triumph over them, either from abstraction, blindness, or inclination. In spite of her being shut in that darkened room so many hours, her eyes grew bright, and the fine gold of her hair seemed to gain lustre. Elsa's sharp wits discerned the change. She took occasion one day, when Gilbert, who sometimes relieved Philippa, was present, to suggest to Jason the propriety of his recovery, in order to give Philippa a chance to have a fit of sickness.

"Isn't she well?" he asked.

"How can anybody be well who does not undress of nights, has odd naps on sofas, and gets no regular meals?"

"Of course not. Has she been here every night?"

"Certainly; haven't you been aware of it, Jason?"

"I suppose I must have been, but took no thought of it; I have troubled her too much, then?"

"Oh no! A helpless man, six feet without his stockings, with one—with only one person in his family besides himself, is no trouble or anxiety to that person. Oh no!"

He sighed wearily.

"Gilbert must stay up here more. Can't you, old fellow? I am no more stupid than your oxen."

"Yes, I can," said Gilbert; "but 'pears to me you are gaining now, and the cattle ain't; 'cause you see nobody understands 'em but me, and I don't know as anybody understands me but them; and so it 'pears as if somebody might do better for you than I can."

"How do you feel to-day, Jason?" asked Elsa.

"The doctor will tell you."

"If you don't know how you are, it is a sign you are better. You must sit up, Jason—your strength will never come back unless you try for it. Pull him out of bed, Gilbert, but don't gee and haw too much about it. Jason, if you don't get well, every thing will go to rack and ruin."

"Where's my clothes?" asked Jason. "Help me up, Gilbert; I thought I was too weak, but Elsa knows best."

"Mercy on me," said Elsa, leaving the room in search of some clothes for him. "The loss of that hand seems to have changed his sex. He is as spleeny as Mary; but he is coming out of that bed, anyhow."

About nine o'clock that evening Gilbert made his appearance in Jason's room in a pair of list shoes and a woollen night-cap.

"Where is Philippa?" Jason asked, with some energy.

"I am here," she answered, without leaving the sofa, which the bed-curtains intercepted from his view.

"You are too far off for me to speak to you."

Surmising what he had to say, she went to his bedside. "You have been here all this time, Philippa—it has been hard for you; I have not known it always—I thought you were in and out, and time has passed so. I must have confounded night with day. You must let Gilbert relieve you."

"Very well," she answered, with a pain in her heart, because he had not always known she was there—near him. "Good-night."

Gilbert snored so at his post that Jason kept awake half the night, and finally told him to go to the devil.

CHAPTER XXXVI

〜〜〜〜〜〜〜〜〜〜〜〜〜〜〜〜〜〜〜〜

A FEW HOURS OF complete solitude, or this trifling effort of
will, placed Jason on the road to recovery. But convalescence has
its pangs, and it was some days before he left his chamber. In that
period the anniversary of Sarah's death occurred. It was passed
by him in gloomy silence. Elsa celebrated it by an old-fashioned
bake in the oven, such as she and Sarah were wont to enjoy
in cherry-time; and matter-of-fact as her day's work appeared,
Sarah was recalled every moment—her looks, her ways, her
speech—with an affectionate fidelity which would have surprised
her could she have been cognizant of what she had no proof of
in her lifetime. Philippa acknowledged the day by a visit to the
hill—her first since summer opened—and reflections on the vast
difference between that time and the present. Though last year's
leaves were replaced, last year's grass renewed, and the cedar
boughs imprisoned the familiar sea-wind, and the oaks glittered
with the familiar sunshine, her heart was not moved with the
association which belonged there—

> "The touch of a vanished hand,
> And the sound of a voice that is still."[85]

Her eyes sought the gray roof below the orchard, beneath which
all that made her life a hopeful and a sorrowing one had trans-
pired. The stork returning from the palms of Egypt to the roof
in his patriarchal village, with the wise, bitter pain and delight

which all wanderers feel, could not hover over it with more unreasoning fancies than her thoughts hovered over that, which was now her most desired shelter. It stood so near the summit of the hill, so plainly in sight, that she thought the winter storms must have destroyed some of the intervening trees; but the truth was, she had not looked upon it before with the same eyes. She examined the trees—they were all there, in the full glory of summer, a glory that saddened her; it was no longer a place for her to linger in. As she descended the path she remembered a poem which she heard Parke read to Theresa once, and was tormented by it, as one is pursued and tormented by the fragment of some old melody which half repeats itself in the brain. When she saw Jason the words flashed into her mind:

> "But the laden summer will give me
> What it never gave before;
> Or take from me what a thousand
> Summers can give no more."[86]

By degrees she withdrew from his room; but it was still her habit, as he was in bed by sundown, to spend the early part of the evening with him, which was enlivened by the exit and entrance of Elsa, and an occasional call from Mrs. Rogers.

A stormy day came, the evening of which was undisturbed. Jason and Philippa were alone, and had not spoken for an hour; he had asked her to open the window, and was lying with his face towards it, listening to the boom of the sea, which mingled with the moaning wind.

"I am sorry," he said, at last, "that you have never loved the sea."

"Why, Jason?

"That I might have had the shadow of an excuse for fancying that we were kin."

"Do you feel the need of an excuse?" she asked complacently.

"Yes, I would forgive myself for my infatuation, which blood-letting has cured me of."

"Infatuation!"

"What name will you give it, then? How could I have made a greater fool of myself, than when, like a mad Quixote, I rode a tilt at the armor you buckled on years ago — believing that I could hack it off?"

She could not gainsay the good sense of his discourse, but received it in the faith that he would return to his folly.

"You have something to pardon," he continued, his voice taking the tone of an order. "I beg your forgiveness — not for the feeling which prompted my assaults upon you, but for the assault; give it, and let us be at peace."

She left her seat, and went to the bedside, and kneeled down by him.

"Jason, you may kiss me."

He shook his head, with a smile.

"We are not mates, Philippa."

"I know that; but I have found a flaw in that armor."

"I don't believe it."

She rose from her knees, and stood looking at him with eyes that flashed a tumult of shame, anger, and deprecation; but behind all this there shone a new light which smote his senses, and made him thrill from head to foot, in spite of all his resolutions.

"It is only me, Jason Auster — mutilated," he exclaimed, motioning her away, unable to bear her eyes any longer. He pulled beside him the little table at the head of the bed, with a shaded lamp upon it, for a barricade between them. She retreated just beyond the circle of lamp-light, which revealed his face completely: it was luminous—full of shifting expression. She sought among its changes a resemblance to Parke; it was a satisfaction to find nothing that reminded her of his winning, delicious beauty in the haggard, bearded man before her—of whom she was beginning to feel a wholesome dread.

"I have but little more to say," he added presently, with rather a husky voice. "I have made up my mind to leave you—simply, because I have no reason for staying. Your business affairs are so ticketed, that you can manage them, and Parke's also. By the way, did you never think what an advantage your money would have been to me?"

She started up, crying:

"You will go a poor man!"

"Yes; but I shall go to the West, where I expect to acquire fortune and fame as the 'One-handed Backwoodsman,' or 'The Lone Bee-Hunter.' A poor man! Have I been a rich one ever? Ungenerous girl, think a moment of the nonentity, me—who, for twenty years, have managed the Parke property—which, like a beast, has welked and waved its horns before all the family, including yourself—and held you in thrall."[87]

He was reading her to herself! She made a movement towards him, and, with a gasp, said, "Curse it!"

"Oh no, Philippa; you live in Crest, and the family graveyard is here."

His manner was too painful for her to bear; she laid her hand on the door-latch.

"You won't ask me to stay, then?" he said loudly.

"I will tell you no lies. If you leave me, you will take with you every hope that remains in my heart. But I do not ask you to stay; neither will I offer you money."

"I thought so."

"I will go now—if you have finished."

"The token of forgiveness, you offered just now," he said, in a faint voice, "I accept it."

"I said that you might kiss me. Shall I come back, that you may do so?"

"No; go—for I do not believe in your hopes. And I will not comfort your methodical soul, by trussing up the interview with proper feeling and fine words."

She closed the chamber-door.

CHAPTER XXXVII

||||||||||||||||||||||||||||||||||||||||||||||||||

CONSIDERATION FOR PHILIPPA induced Jason to write a note to Mr. Ritchings to inform him that he was going on a tour to the West for his health. He also told Mrs. Rogers, who significantly remarked that his plan was a very good one. In a day or two he was gone, without sounding a note of preparation, with no leave-taking, no instructions—unless giving Philippa his office-key might be considered in the light of an instruction. He had no destination, but stopped by chance, as he had done more than twenty years before, at a town hundreds of miles from Crest, whose name he had never heard—new enough to have a perspective of aboriginal forest, from which the panther and the wild-cat, the inhabitants said, had scarcely retreated. Here he sought repose, but did not find it. He must go farther, he concluded, and resumed his journey. His health and strength came back, but he was restless and miserable; the roots of his existence tugged him backwards, and he retraced his steps slowly, contesting every inch of the way with resolutions, to be put in practice at the stopping-place before him! Within fifty miles of Crest he had reached the spot favorable for reflection concerning the future, giving his resolutions, for the present, the go-by; but his reflections did not get beyond the starting-point, which was, "If I go back to her—"

He bought a fishing-rod, and went up to the trout streams among the hills, where he passed many hours a day in not catching fish. In the evenings he practised writing with his left hand,

and chose for copy letters to Philippa, which he tore up as soon as he saw "Jason Auster" written at the end.

At the time of his departure Philippa made resolutions also, which were better kept; she determined to live as if all she was ever to possess could be contained in the limits of each day. Too much time had been wasted in expectation and preparation for events which had never taken place, and now never would. Her years had glided away in getting ready for happiness; happiness must be left out in her plan. She thought of all the old maids she had known with property—there were several scattered over the area of Crest—and she remembered them as cheerful, hard-headed women, with few amusements and a good deal of business. Then she thought of the widows of her acquaintance—Elsa was one, and she would apply to her for information.

"What is the nature of your feelings from day to day?" she asked her.

"Lord a mercy, Philippa, which way is the cat jumping now?"

"I mean, have you any happiness without a particular object to live for?"

"Object?—You mean Bowen. He was an object. As for happiness, I haven't thought about it; but I will, and let you know my conclusion immediately."

"No matter, don't think: if you do, I know the conclusion you will come to."

Elsa screamed with laughter, and told her she was just cutting her eye-teeth; eye-teeth meant that all was vanity of vanities.

Strong-minded as Philippa thought she must be, she felt a great reluctance to approach any thing like business; but the time came when she was obliged to turn the key of Jason's office. It seemed to her, as she looked over his books and papers, as if he had for a long time expected to be called suddenly away. Instead of pursuing her new calling, she cried, and went home with a headache.

About this time Jason wrote a letter, which he posted. It contained a few words, so strangely and tremulously written, that Philippa's heart felt a pang at the sight of them.

"I am coming back," he wrote, "to ask your forgiveness a second time."

"I have received a letter from Jason," she said to Elsa; "he will be home soon."

"What did he go away for? Just for the sake of turning round and coming back? Where is the letter from?"

Philippa, ashamed to tell the post-mark, held the envelope before her; when she spelt the name of the town so near them, she looked at Philippa and said, "I always knew that Jason Auster was a fool."

But Philippa saw that she was glad.

"Mind you," she continued, discovering that her joy was detected, "I approve of his coming back, because it is respectable to have a man about who goes by the name of the 'head of the family;' Jason never had any thing more than the title—"

"Being a fool," interrupted Philippa.

"And I think it is a pity," she went on, "that somebody shouldn't take care of you—you poor, lone girl that never was befriended in your life."

Tears, rare visitors, dimmed her glasses, but Philippa could not share them; she patted her, walked round the table on tiptoe, and finally put her fingers in the dough Elsa was preparing, and rubbed it in her wrinkles, to smooth her old face.

A sentiment not to be accounted for, led Philippa at dusk to the unfrequented parlor. The air there was tranquil and lifeless, as it is in uninhabited rooms. She paced the soft carpet; the dry odor of its undisturbed dust floated in the air, and strangely reminded her of flowers.

"If Theresa Bond were in my place," she thought, she would have filled the vases here with flowers; the 'rose of expectancy' would be visible everywhere."

She took up the vases on the mantel-shelf and looked into them. One had some dried leaves in it; she shook them out on the carpet, thinking they were green when Parke was there; he might have gathered them, for he had a way of bringing flowers into the house, and placing them in vases, books, on the floor, on the piano. The piano—when had that been opened? She raised the cover, and struck the keys with fingers that brought out a wandering, wailing discord.

A heavy hand was laid on her shoulder, which brought it to an end.

"Jason," she said gently, without turning round.

"Yes, I have just arrived. Why are you in this room? Did I hear the lament of the damned?"

He sighed, and she turned quickly towards him. His arm was still in a sling. Before he comprehended what she was doing, she took the sling from his neck, put it round her own, and slipped his arm through it again.

"My burden," she said, "that I love."

He enclosed her with his other arm.

"And my protection, that I love better."

"It is enough," he answered.[88]

CHAPTER XXXVIII

‖‖

WHEN PHILIPPA'S PROSPECT was limited to the Scotch firs in the yard, and the curtains of Indian chintz before the parlor windows, Parke's extended over the savannas of Apure,[89] where the grasses, verdant through the year, were more beautiful than the flower-beds of the terrace at Crest. The earthly paradise, peopled with birds of the most brilliant colors, and almost every variety of animal, was at present invaded by a party on a cattle-hunt, which party, including Parke and Osmond Luce, was composed of military men, Llaneros, and negroes.[90] The expedition, starting from Maracay weeks before, had traversed an extensive tract of country, stopping at the various cattle-farms on the devious route to the pampas, to hunt among the wild herds of the native proprietors, or the still wilder herds with no proprietor at all.[91]

Parke, dressed in a check flannel shirt, breeches buttoned tightly at the knee, and with a checkered handkerchief bound round his head, was as much at ease, and looked far handsomer than any Llanero the pampas could boast of. Seated on a stool of stretched hide, in a hut thatched with palm-leaves, and plastered with mud and straw, he impressed those around him with the air of having been to the "manor born."

"Our foreign friend," observed a young man, "seems to carry us all in his eye."

"He plays the Llanero well, though," replied another.

"He is not the desperate player our comrade Osmond Luce is."

"At card-breaking, you mean."

"Hist, he is looking at you, and he brought some capital pistols from the States."

"How much past daybreak is it?" inquired Parke. "I want to get a jaguar-skin before night."

"Time enough for that," replied young Castejon. "But I say, sir, I have taken a fancy to that cream-colored horse of yours. Will you part with him?"

"You shall have him," Parke replied, "if you will break for me the black stallion we saw in the corral last night."

"Excuse me."

"Pshaw!" cried Osmond. "Break him yourself, Parke. As for the cream-colored, we'll stake him."

"Play," said Parke. "Oh yes—for '*el ultimo mono siempre se ahoga*.'" (The last monkey is sure to be drowned.)[92]

"What! are you apt at our proverbs already?" asked Castejon. "Let us go and look at the stallion."

"No," said Parke, lazily. "You go, and bring me a lock of his mane."

"Something is going on now in the *majada*,"[93] cried one.

All rushed out except Parke and Osmond. The latter lighted a cigar, and Parke took his knife from his belt and examined its edge. Keeping his eye on it, he said:

"The bats dropped into my hammock so last night that I could not sleep, and with the first light I sauntered out. I swear to you that the atmosphere was so transparent that it seemed to bring within my vision the terrace and the windows of the old house. The casement didn't grow a 'glimmering square,'[94] but the panes glittered in the morning light, as I have sometimes seen them glitter at sunset."

"You've got the mirage—home-sickness."

"No, I am not home-sick. But why do I ask myself questions concerning Philippa, lately?"

"No thought of her belongs in these scenes. Suppose we go and shoot crocodiles this forenoon. We might dissect one on account of its tears."

"Her spirit comes," continued Parke, "when I do not call for it."

"And never comes when *I* do," said Osmond, tearing a cigar to pieces.

"Poor Philippa!" mused Parke.

"You continue to believe in your star—don't you?" Osmond asked, irritably.

"Certainly, in the star of my will."

"And that has brought you to the pampas."

"And it may take me back."

Osmond laughed.

"I'll bet you a herd that when you do go back, you will find Philippa married."

"To whom?"

"Jason Auster."

"Never! It is impossible."

IIIIIIIIIIIIIIIIIII

FINIS

NOTES

1. Wilson Barstow Jr. (1831–1869) was Elizabeth Stoddard's favorite brother. At the time that *Two Men* was written, he was serving in the Union Army.

2. From Ralph Waldo Emerson, "Experience" (1844).

3. Most likely Albert's Brisbane's *Social Destiny of Man; or, Association and Reorganization of Industry* (1840), a condensation of the views of French social theorist Charles Fourier.

4. In the second edition of *Two Men*, published in 1888 and reprinted in 1901, the final sentence of this paragraph reads simply, "He appeared indifferent, shy and cold" (3). See *Two Men* (Philadelphia: Henry T. Coates & Co., 1901).

5. A lath is a thin strip of wood or metal, usually nailed in rows to framing supports as a substructure for plaster, shingles, slates, or tiles.

6. From Washington Irving, "The Voyage," in *The Sketch Book of Geoffrey Crayon* (1819–1820).

7. "[T]enth point of the law" refers to the popular English common-law phrase "possession is nine-tenths of the law." "Nine Holes" is a name for a nine-hole row game, which has a long history going back to ancient Egypt. Stoddard is saying that the appearance of wealth initially blinds Jason to the fact that he owns none of it and renders him unable to function effectively in the Parke family, which is accustomed to money and its benefits.

8. From Isaiah 64:8.

9. From part 22, line 12 of Alfred Tennyson's 1833 poem "In Memoriam A. H. H.," mourning the death of his good friend Arthur Hugh Hallam.

10. Ecclesiastes 1:3.

11. From Esther 5:13.

12. Reference to the parable of the prodigal son in Luke 15:11–32.

13. From Ephesians 4:14.

14. An adaptation of Ezekial 18:2 and Jeremiah 31:29.

15. The Spanish Main encompassed the Caribbean coast of the Spanish Empire in Central and South America. Its ports were the point of departure for the famous Spanish treasure fleets transporting the region's enormous wealth (gold, silver, gems, spices, etc.) back to Spain.

16. From Shakespeare, *The Merchant of Venice*, act 4, scene 1, line 339.

17. Nemesis is the Greek goddess of divine justice and vengeance, portrayed as a stern woman with either a whip, a rein, a sword, or a pair of scales in her left hand. One's "nemesis" is a tormentor who can potentially bring about one's downfall.

18. A reference to the legend of the sword of Damocles. Damocles, a Greek nobleman, commented once too often on the power and happiness of his king. In order to demonstrate the pressures he experienced as king, the king held a banquet and seated Damocles under a sword that was suspended from the ceiling by a single hair.

19. An adaptation of Hosea 8:7.

20. A cockatrice is a legendary creature resembling a giant rooster, with some lizard-like characteristics, born from an egg laid by a cock and incubated by a toad or a serpent. Its reputed magical abilities include turning people to stone by either looking at them, touching them, or sometimes breathing on them.

21. From the Latin Gloria Patri, meaning "Glory be to the Father." The Glory Be prayer is prayed during the rosary on the large beads which separate the five sets of ten smaller beads, called decades, upon each of which a Hail Mary is prayed.

22. Annuals were popular nineteenth-century literary miscellanies intended to be given away as gifts.

23. In the second edition Stoddard deleted "and the curious specks in the brown irises of her eyes."

24. In Greek mythology the sphinx is a hybrid creature with a woman's head and a lion's body; she also has wings and sometimes a serpent's tail. The sphinx was sent by Hera to guard the gates of Thebes, killing anyone

who could not answer her riddle: "Which creature in the morning goes on four feet, at noon on two, and in the evening upon three?" Oedipus correctly identified the "creature" as man, and the sphinx committed suicide. Answering the riddle successfully enabled Oedipus to marry his mother, thereby fulfilling the prophecy made at his birth.

25. From Fredrika Bremer, *Brothers and Sisters* (1848).

26. Charlotte Brontë's *Jane Eyre* was originally published under the male pen name Currer Bell in 1847.

27. In the second edition Stoddard changed this sentence to read, "Genius casts its glamour over ordinary things: we who have none say there is a discrepancy between the real and the ideal" (86). This defense of romantic genius accords better with Stoddard's identification of herself as a romantic, rather than a realistic, writer late in the nineteenth century.

28. From Thomas Haynes Bayly's song, "The Pilot," in which a sailor tells his passenger to have faith in God in the midst of a storm.

29. Lines 3 and 6 Alfred Tennyson's "The Eagle," first published in 1851.

30. Lines 5–6 of William Wordsworth's "Lines Written in Early Spring," first published in 1798.

31. An adaptation of Alexander Pope's *An Essay on Criticism* (1711), part 3, line 66, which states, "For fools rush in where angels fear to tread."

32. Referenced in all four of the Gospels: Matthew 13:57; Mark 6:4; Luke 4:24; and John 4:44.

33. In the second edition of the novel this sentence reads, "One by one his primitive instincts were revealed to him; he knew that he was a natural, free powerful being" (103).

34. Reference to Genesis 2:9.

35. The calla, or lily, is the national flower of Ethiopia.

36. A front is a band of false hair worn by women over the forehead.

37. In the second edition Stoddard added, "Selfish to the core" (122).

38. In the second edition this sentence reads, "Philippa felt towards her a repulsion which acted like a charm; she wished—in a dreary way, however—that the charm would take some shape so she could hurt her" (134).

39. Adaptation of lines 24–25 of Samuel Taylor Coleridge's "The Picture, or the Lover's Resolution" (1802).

40. "Christabel" is an unfinished gothic poem by Samuel Taylor Coleridge in which the title character is seduced or bewitched by a mysterious female figure named Geraldine. "Christabel" was originally intended for the second edition of Coleridge and Wordsworth's *Lyrical Ballads* (1800), but was excluded, probably by Wordsworth's decision. Although the poem was circulated in manuscript, it remained unpublished until 1816.

41. This sentence is deleted in the second edition.

42. From line 36 of Samuel Taylor Coleridge's "The Picture, or the Lover's Resolution" (1802).

43. French for "blue blood," a phrase used to describe a person of aristocratic breeding. In the second edition Stoddard omits the French and simply has Parke say, "blue blood would not cover the floor." Sam responds, "Confound you!" (143).

44. The cabin is used as living quarters by a ship's officer or passengers, while the forecastle is a superstructure at the bow of a merchant ship where the crew is housed.

45. The second edition deletes the last part of this sentence: "and he felt his will rising imperiously."

46. From Genesis 2:23. Mrs. Lang uses the phrase "bone of my bone, flesh of my flesh" to refer to her daughters, while the phrase is usually meant to refer to a man's wife.

47. Here Sam refers to the parable of Lazarus, from Luke 16:19–31, in which Lazarus, a beggar, dies and goes to heaven because he has virtuously accepted poverty, while a rich man goes to hell after his own death because he has neglected to use his wealth wisely or generously.

48. Universalism has its roots in eighteenth-century American Christianity. Universalists believed that all people were worthy of salvation, regardless of their sins. From its beginnings Universalism challenged its members to reach out and embrace people whom society often marginalized.

49. Stoddard replaced the words "without emotion" with "unconsciously" in the second edition (156).

50. In the second edition the final sentence of the paragraph, "That was all he remembered," was deleted.

51. Opening lines from book 1 of John Milton's *Paradise Lost*, first published in 1667.

52. From Daniel 5:5. The phrase "the handwriting on the wall" recalls this Old Testament story in which Daniel is called upon to decipher the mysterious writing on the wall of the king's palace. Daniel interprets it to mean that God intends the king and his kingdom to fall. The king is slain that night. Figuratively, the expression means that some misfortune is impending.

53. From line 58 of William Wordsworth's "Intimations of Immortality from Recollections of an Early Childhood," published in 1807.

54. Switchel is a strongly flavored drink combining apple cider vinegar, molasses, sugar or honey, ground ginger, and sometimes oatmeal and water.

55. From a song called "Lucy Long" or "Miss Lucy Long," frequently performed in blackface minstrel shows, and first published in 1842. The chorus is, "Take your time Miss Lucy / Take your time Miss Lucy Long / Rock de cradle Lucy / Take your time my dear." Stoddard deleted the reference to "Miss Lucy" in the second addition.

56. From Ecclesiastes 12:6.

57. Niggerhead is a strong black chewing tobacco, usually in twisted plug form.

58. Reference to William Shakespeare's *Macbeth*, act 1, scene 3, line 84.

59. Lines 42–43 of Richard Henry Stoddard's poem "Imogen," published in *The Poems of Richard Henry Stoddard* (1880).

60. The Dorcas Society was a charitable group of local people, often church affiliated, that provided clothes for the poor. The first Dorcas Society was founded in 1834 on the Isle of Man after cholera forced the poorer families to destroy their bedding and clothing to prevent a further outbreak of the disease. It is named after the character Tabitha (also known as Dorcas) described in chapter 9 of the Acts of the Apostles. The irony here is that Sarah is doing charity work to help the poor, but is otherwise rather coldhearted, especially to Charlotte and Philippa.

61. In the second edition Jason calls Philippa "our girl" rather than "my daughter" (191).

62. The final sentence was deleted from this paragraph in the second edition.

63. A reference to the Scottish Prince Osric of Bernicia, who died at the battle of Fin Eoin in 629 AD.

64. Possibly a reference to the two statues guarding the outer gates of the mortuary temple of Amenhotep III. The seventy-five-feet-high statues, which are badly damaged from nature and centuries of tourists, depict Amenhotep III with his mother, Mutemwiya, in the north and with his wife, Tiy, and one of his daughters in the south.

65. A "raree show" is a spectacular display.

66. Italian for "sweet doing-nothing" or "sweet to do nothing."

67. Last line of Alfred Tennyson's "Locksley Hall" (1842).

68. From line 1 of Alfred Tennyson's "The Princess: O Swallow," first published in 1847.

69. José Antonio Páez was General in Chief of the army fighting Spain during the Venezuelan War of Independence, and the first president of Venezuela.

70. From Virgil's *The Georgics*, part 1. "Ossa on Pelion's" is used as an expression to mean "a lot" or an excessive amount.

71. In Homer's *The Odyssey*, Penelope's husband, Odysseus, is delayed for ten years on his return from the Trojan War. Beset by suitors, Penelope attempts to put them off by insisting that she cannot remarry until she has finished weaving a shroud for Odysseus's father, Laertes. After working each day at her loom, she secretly unravels the cloth each night.

72. Literally "the foolish fire." The "Ignis fatuus" is a phenomenon of spectral lights whose purpose is allegedly to herald death or to play tricks on travelers at night.

73. The Generals of Independence fought with José Antonio Páez in the nineteenth-century Venezuelan wars of independence from Spain. Many "caudillos" led private armies and used their military might to achieve power in the newly independent states. Often they merely replaced those in power without changing the existing social order.

74. A "cat's paw" is a person used by another person as a dupe or a tool. The expression originates from a fable about a monkey who used the paw of a cat to pull chestnuts out of a fire.

75. From the Faust legend, in which Doctor Faustus sells his soul to Mephistopheles, or the devil, for knowledge and power. Faust is also given a potion to fall in love with the ugly Gretchen (or Margaret). He later impregnates her and is forced to leave her after dueling with her brother Valentine. The Faust legend has been retold countless times, most notably by Christopher Marlowe and Johann Wolfgang Von Goethe.

76. Opening line of Lord Byron's *The Corsair*, published in 1814.

77. From Ecclesiastes 12:5.

78. From line 2 of Alfred Tennyson's "Love and Duty" (1842).

79. From part 3, lines 7–8 of "The Sleeping Palace" in the longer Alfred Tennyson poem "The Day-dream" (1842).

80. In the second edition Stoddard deleted the last part of this sentence: "for it proved that he was not single in her heart, but surrounded by other ideas and selfish ones."

81. *Robinson Crusoe* by Daniel Defoe was published in 1719 and is sometimes regarded as the first English novel.

82. Come back to life.

83. "[M]uch older than herself" is deleted in the second edition.

84. Old Harry is a familiar name for the Devil.

85. Lines 11–12 of Alfred Lord Tennyson's "Break, Break, Break," published in 1842.

86. Lines 8–11 from an unnamed poem (beginning "Many's the time I've sighed for summer") by Richard Stoddard (*The Poems of Richard Henry Stoddard* 67).

87. In the second edition Stoddard changed "welked" to "walked." It isn't clear whether or not "welked" was a typographical error.

88. In the second edition Stoddard replaced the line "'It is enough,' he answered," with the arguably more positive "'My wife,' he answered" (300).

89. Apure is one of Venezuela's twenty-three states (though it was not officially founded until 1901).

90. A llanero is a Venezuelan or Columbian cowboy, usually of mixed race. Llaneros are known for their superior horsemanship and their supposed imperviousness to harsh weather. The name is taken from the Llanos—the vast grasslands or savannah—of Venezuela and Columbia.

91. Maracay is the capital and most important city in the Venezuelan state of Aragua, officially established in 1701. The pampas are an extensive, grass-covered plain in South America extending west from the Atlantic coast to the Andean foothills.

92. In the second edition Stoddard deleted the translation of the Spanish phrase.

93. A "majada" is a sheepfold.

94. From lsine 14 of Alfred Tennyson's "Tears, Idle Tears" (1847).

In the Legacies of Nineteenth-Century American Women Writers series

The Hermaphrodite
By Julia Ward Howe
Edited and with an introduction
by Gary Williams

In the "Stranger People's" Country
By Mary Noailles Murfree
Edited and with an introduction
by Marjorie Pryse

Two Men
By Elizabeth Stoddard
Edited and with an introduction
by Jennifer Putzi

*Emily Hamilton and Other
Writings*
By Sukey Vickery
Edited and with an introduction
by Scott Slawinski

*Nature's Aristocracy: A Plea for
the Oppressed*
By Jennie Collins
Edited and with an introduction
by Judith A. Ranta

*Selected Writings of Victoria
Woodhull: Suffrage, Free Love,
and Eugenics*
By Victoria C. Woodhull
Edited and with an introduction
by Cari Carpenter

*Christine: Or Woman's Trials
and Triumphs*
By Laura Curtis Bullard
Edited and with an introduction
by Denise M. Kohn

*Observations on the Real Rights
of Women and Other Writings*
By Hannah Mather Crocker
Edited and with an introduction
by Constance J. Post

Selections from Eliza Leslie
Eliza Leslie
Edited and with an introduction
by Etta M. Madden

To order or obtain more
information on these or other
University of Nebraska Press
titles, visit www.nebraskapress
.unl.edu.